John Timbs

Things Not Generally Known Curiosities of History, with New Lights by John Timbs

John Timbs

Things Not Generally Known Curiosities of History, with New Lights by John Timbs

ISBN/EAN: 9783742808752

Manufactured in Europe, USA, Canada, Australia, Japa

Cover: Foto ©Andreas Hilbeck / pixelio.de

Manufactured and distributed by brebook publishing software (www.brebook.com)

John Timbs

Things Not Generally Known Curiosities of History, with New

Lights by John Timbs

GENTLE READER,

The success of my little volume of "THINGS NOT GENERALLY KNOWN" has proved, like Seneca's "good turn, a shoeing-horn to another,"—in the present volume.

The book now submitted to you is, indeed, an extension of the design of its predecessor to "THINGS NOT GENERALLY KNOWN IN HISTORY;" or, where known, but imperfectly understood.

First, I have endeavoured to seize upon a great number of the salient points of History; and, wherever practicable, to throw New Lights upon Old Readings.

Next, I have attempted to supply in this volume what has long appeared to me to be a want. Every reader of a newspaper is aware how often historic incidents and classical quotations are employed by public writers, by way of illustrating their subject. The plan is doubtless a good one; although it takes for granted a much wider acquaintance with history and classic lore than it generally falls to the lot of some to receive, or, having received, to remember. Now, to inform the one class, and to assist the memory of the other, it is hoped that each section of this little book may contribute.

For this object I have sought, by condensation and re-writing, to present to you the main points of the subject ; and, by acknowledgment of authorities, to refer such as desire further detail to the most accredited sources.

Another aim of this book is to examine a few of the *Popular Errors of History*, of which there exists a plentiful crop. This has been specially attended to in the section of "Historic Doubts ;" and has not been lost sight of throughout the volume.

History is a world-wide field ; but, by taking Donne's advice, and getting

"Up into the watch-tower,"

I hope to have succeeded in separating the fallacies from the facts, and in presenting in the most picturesque forms many hundred Events and Incidents, Sayings and Origins, and noteworthy instances of Human Action, which may be read with pleasure and permanent advantage. For this purpose,

A world of things must curiously be sought,
A world of things must be together brought ;

and by these means I have endeavoured to render the "CURIOSITIES OF HISTORY" worthy of public favour.

June 1859.   L. T.

CONTENTS.

	PAGE
THE SACRED STORY	1-11
GREECE AND ROME, BABYLON AND CARTHAGE, &c.	12-55
LEGENDARY AND FABULOUS	56-70
VOYAGES, TRAVELS, AND ADVENTURES	71-78
MODERN HISTORY	79-109
BRITISH HISTORY	110-149
THE SEVEN WONDERS OF THE WORLD	150-157
HISTORIC SAYINGS AND ORIGINS	158-187
ENSIGNS, LAWS, AND GOVERNMENT	188-213
HISTORIC DOUBTS	214-234
MISCELLANEA	235-240

SIR WALTER RALEIGH WRITING HIS "HISTORY OF THE WORLD."

RALEIGH was first imprisoned in the Tower of London in 1592 (eight weeks) for winning the heart of Elizabeth Throgmorton, one of Queen Elizabeth's maids of honour, "not only a moral sin, but in those days a heinous political offence."

Mr. Payne Collier, F.S.A., thus circumstantially details Raleigh's next imprisonment: "In 1603, in the course of a few months, Raleigh was first confined in his own house, then conveyed to the Tower, next sent to Winchester gaol, returned from thence to the Tower, imprisoned for between two and three months in the Fleet, and again removed to the Tower, where he remained until released thirteen years afterwards to undertake his new expedition to Guiana." (Archæologia, vol. xxv, p. 218.) Mr. Collier possesses a copy of that rare tract, A Good Speed to Virginia, 4to, 1609, with the autograph on the title-page, "W. Raleigh, Turr. Lond.," showing that at the time this tract was published, and read by Raleigh, he recorded himself as a prisoner in the Tower of London.

In the frenzy of despair, in 1604, Raleigh attempted to stab himself, as proved by his letter to his wife, "after he had hurt himself in the Tower;" the said letter being in Sergeant Yelverton's Collection, in All Souls College, Oxford. During part of the time Lady Raleigh resided with her husband; and here, 1605, was born Carew, their second son. Sir Walter's prison-lodging is considered to have been the second and third stories of the Beauchamp Tower. He devoted much time to chemistry and pharmaceutical preparations: here he prepared his "Rare Cordial," wrote his political discourses, and commenced his famous History of the World, which he published in 1614. Of this stupendous production Fuller has observed, that "its only defect (or default rather) is, that it wanteth the half thereof:" It has been thought by a far better judge, Hume, "to afford the best model of the ancient style" of composition. The portion completed comprehends the period from the Creation to the downfall of the Macedonian Empire, about 170 years B.C. Mr. Tytler, with justice, commends the style of this work as "vigorous, purely English, and possessing an antique richness of ornament, similar to what pleases us when we see some ancient priory or stately manor-house, and compare it with our more modern mansions." A disingenuous attempt has been made by Mr. Disraeli to show that Raleigh was materially aided in his History by the contributions of his learned friends; but Mr. Tytler, in his excellent Life of Raleigh, has shown that Raleigh was not more indebted to his friends than are literary men in general when similarly circumstanced; and this was known long before Mr. Disraeli's fancied discovery.

Raleigh wrote his History avowedly for his patron, Prince Henry of Wales, the heir-apparent to the throne; upon whose death Raleigh is stated to have burnt the continuation of the work, which he had written. Another account relates that Raleigh was so mortified at the coolness with which the published portion of the history had been received, that he burnt the manuscript continuation, saying to his printer, "the second volume shall undo no more; this ungrateful world is unworthy of it." This anecdote may have been fabricated upon the well-known impetuosity of Raleigh's temper, for it has not sufficient authority to entitle it to credit.

There is related another motive for the burning, but upon no better authority. Still, the alleged incident well illustrates "the worth of history," more especially the difficulty of recording with truth occurrences in the historian's own time. The following version is from the Journal de Paris, May 1787.

"Raleigh, being confined in the Tower of London, there employed himself in the composition of the second volume of his immortal History of the World. Being at the window of his apartment, and thinking gravely of the duty of the historian, and the respect due to truth, suddenly his attention was attracted by a great noise and tumult in the court under his eyes. He saw a man strike another, who, from his costume, he supposed to be an officer, and who, drawing his sword, passed it through the body of the person who struck him; but the wounded man did not fall till he had knocked down his adversary with a stick. The guard coming up at this moment seized the officer, and led him away; while at the same time the body of the man who was killed by the sword-thrust was borne by some persons, who had great difficulty in penetrating the crowd which surrounded them.

Next day Raleigh received a visit from an intimate friend, to whom he related the scene which he had witnessed the preceding day, and which had made a strong impression on his mind. What was his surprise, however, when his friend said that there was scarcely a word of truth in any of the circumstances he had narrated; that the supposed officer was no officer at all, but a domestic of a foreign ambassador; that it was he who gave the first blow; that he did not draw his sword, but that the other had seized it and passed it through the body of the domestic before any one had time to prevent him; that at this moment a spectator among the crowd knocked down the murderer with a stick; and that some strangers bore away the body of the dead! He added, that the court had sent an order to try the murderer immediately, and to show him no mercy, because the dead man was one of the principal servants of the Spanish ambassador.

'Allow me to tell you,' replied Raleigh to his friend, 'that I may be mistaken about the station of the murderer; but all the other circumstances are of the greatest exactitude, because I saw every incident with my own eyes, and they all happened under my window in that very place opposite us, where you may see one of the flag-stones higher than the rest.' 'My dear Raleigh,' replied his friend, 'it was on that very stone that I was sitting when the whole occurred, and I received this little scratch that you see on my cheek in wrenching the sword out of the hands of the murderer; and, upon my honour, you have deceived yourself on all points.'

Sir Walter, when alone, took the manuscript of the second volume of his *History*, and, reflecting upon what had passed, said, 'How many falsehoods must there be in this work! If I cannot assure myself of an event which happened under my own eyes, how can I venture to describe those which occurred thousands of years before I was born, or those even which have passed at a distance since my birth? Truth! truth! this is the sacrifice that I owe thee.' Upon which he threw his manuscript, the work of years, into the fire, and watched it tranquilly consumed to the last leaf."

The Vignette.

THE DOG OF ALCIBIADES.

This celebrated work is stated to have been executed by Miron, the famous Greek sculptor; and is in the collection of Lord Feversham, at Duncombe Park, Yorkshire. The ancient sculptors excelled in dogs; and this exquisite work is one of the finest dogs of antiquity. It illustrates the state-craft of Alcibiades, the distinguished man who exercised so great an influence over the counsels and the fortunes of Athens. Plutarch thus relates the incident: "Alcibiades had a dog of an uncommon size and beauty, which cost him seventy *minæ*; and yet his tail, which was his principal ornament, he caused to be cut off. Some of his acquaintance found great fault with his acting so strangely, and told him that all Athens rung with the story of his foolish treatment of the dog: at which he laughed, and said, 'This is the very thing I wanted; for I would have the Athenians talk of this, lest they should find something worse to say of me.'"

In Boswell's *Life of Johnson* this beautiful work of sculpture is thus referred to:

F. I have been looking at this famous antique marble dog of Mr. Jennings', valued at a thousand guineas, said to be Alcibiades' dog.

Johnson. His tail most, then, be docked. That was the mark of Alcibiades' dog.

E. A thousand guineas! The representation of no animal whatever is worth so much. At this rate a dead dog would indeed be better than a living lion.

J. Sir, it is not the worth of the thing, but of the skill in forming it, which is so highly estimated.

CURIOSITIES OF HISTORY.

The Sacred Story.

WHERE DID CAIN SLAY ABEL?

" DAMASCUS is as much as to say, shedding of blood; for there Chayn slew Abel, and hid him in the sand."—*Itiecon's Polychronicon*. Mandeville also says: " In that place where Damascus was founded, Kayn sloughe Abel his brother." Julian calls Damascus "the eye of the whole east:" it is one of the oldest cities in the world.

ENOCH AND EARLY DEATH.

The history of the prophet to whom the book of Enoch is attributed, or rather whose visions it relates, is recounted as follows in Gen. v. 18-24 : " Jared, at the age of 162, begat Enoch; who, at the age of 65, begat Methuselah, and afterwards walked with God 300 years, and begat sons and daughters. All the days of Enoch were 365 years. He walked with God, and was not, for God took him." (Compare Ecclesiasticus xliv. 16; Hab. xii. 5.) The translation of Enoch has been compared with the ancient mysterious burial at sunrise of noble and comely youths who prematurely died. They are said to have been not really dead, but carried up alive to the region of light, in consequence of their being loved by the Supreme Being. The story of Ganymede is an instance. (See the learned disquisition on the subject in Montfaucon's *Religion des Gaulois*, tom. ii. p. 305, &c.; and in his *Explication des Textes difficiles*, tom. i. p. 132.) Hence the well-known axiom, "He whom the gods love dies young." Plutarch, *De Consolatione Philosoph.*

ENOCH'S PILLARS.

Enoch, or his forefather Seth, being informed by Adam that the world was to perish, once by water, and a second time fire, did cause two pillars to be erected—the one of stone against the water, and the other of brick against the fire; and that upon these pillars was engraved all such learning as had been delivered to, or invented by, mankind: and from thence it came that all knowledge and learning was not lost by means of the flood, by reason that one of the pillars (though the other perished) did remain after the flood; and Josephus witnesseth till his time.—*Antiq. Judaic.*

Methuselah was the oldest of the antediluvian patriarchs, whose great ages are recorded in Genesis v. 21, 22. At the age of 187 years he begat Lamech, the father of Noah; after which he lived 782 years, making altogether 969 years.

TRADITIONS OF ARARAT.

This celebrated mountain of Armenia, when seen from afar and in certain positions, has, in its summit, *a striking resemblance to a ship.* The whole country round is full of traditionary stories about Noah's Ark and the Flood. The Armenians call Ararat, Mountain of the Ark; the Persians, Mountain of Noah. The remains of the Ark, converted into stone, are still believed to rest on the summit; and in a church at Nova Schamachia, they show a cross made from a plank of the Ark. At Erivan, they point out the spot where Noah first planted the vine; and the name of another town, Nachichevan, means, according to Chardin, "the place of descent," being the place where Noah first settled when he came out of the Ark. Tournefort states, that in the middle region, and even the borders of the snow-limit of Ararat, he saw tigers; and that the young ones are caught in traps by the people round the mountain, to be exhibited in shows of wild beasts throughout Persia.

AARON'S BREASTPLATE.

Josephus and others maintain that the precious stones of Aaron's breastplate were the *Urim* and *Thummim;* and that they discovered the will of God by their extraordinary lustre, thereby predicting the issue of events to those who consulted them.

THE JEWISH TABERNACLE.

In 1848 the Rev. Mr. Hartshorne exhibited in London his "Models of the Tabernacle and Encampment of Israel." The first represents the encampment of the Jews in the Plain of Moab; that of the Levites being complete, with the Tabernacle in the centre; and in the distance are the tents of Ephraim, with a view of the Dead Sea, and mountain scenery. The second model gives the court of the Tabernacle in detail, with its sixty pillars, embroidered curtain, altar of burnt offering, and the other costly accessories of the Jewish ceremonies. The miniature candlestick, sacred vessels, &c., are of gold or silver; the curtain of the holy place is exquisitely embroidered;

the water-vessels have been carefully copied from specimens in the British Museum. A miniature high priest presides at the altar, surrounded by a group such as one might imagine to be present on some high festival.

THE WAR-HORSE OF JOB.

The stirring description of the War-horse in the book of Job commences, "Hast thou given the horse strength? hast thou clothed his neck with thunder?" Dr. Larduor, in his admirable *Museum of Science and Art*, says it always appeared to him that the second member of the verse here quoted was, as translated, destitute of meaning. He consulted two eminent Hebraists,—Dr. M'Caul, of King's College, and Professor Marks, of University College,—and their conclusion (after citing various authorities and "primitives") was, that the translation was incorrect. "Hast thou clothed his neck with thunder?" is not the sense of the original Hebrew, which would be correctly rendered thus: "Hast thou clothed his neck with a shaking (or flowing) mane." It appears, however, that the Hebrew word which has been translated *thunder* never means lightning, and the rapid quivering of the mane may be poetically rendered thunder. The old English translator had a sense of the picturesque and sublime.

THE SEVEN HOLY ANGELS.

The book of Tobias speaks of Seven Angels superior to all the rest; and this has been constantly believed, according to the letter, by the ancient Jews and Christians. So, the seven that have the greatest power, the first-born angels (Tob. xii. 15): "I am Raphael, one of the *seven holy angels*, which present the prayers of the saints, and go in and out before the glory of the Holy One." And this Daniel may very well be thought to mean when he says, chap. x. 13, &c.: "Michael, one of the chief princes, came to help me." That some angels were under the command of others may be collected out of Zechariah ii. and iii., where one angel commands another, "Run, speak to this young man," &c.; and out of Rev. xii. 7, where Michael and his angels fought with the dragon and his angels. The number of just seven supreme angels Grotius conceived to be drawn from the seven chief princes of the Persian empire; but it may be doubted whether the seven there were so ancient as this tradition. Three names of these seven the Scripture affords—Michael, Gabriel, and Raphael; but for the other four —Oriphiel, Zachariel, Samael, and Anael, let the authors of them answer, as likewise for their presiding over the seven planets.—*Cowley's Notes to his Davideis.*

THE HOLY ROSE OF JERICHO.

This curious plant (*Anastatica hieropuntica*) grows among the sands of Egypt, Palestine, and Syria, and is found in Barbary. It is cruciform; and when its flowers and leaves have withered and fallen off, the branches, as they dry, curl inwards, and form a round mass, thence called a rose. The roots die; the winds tear the plant up, and blow it about the sands till it lodges in a moist spot, or is wetted with the rain; then the curled-up globe expands, and suffers the seeds to escape from the seed-vessel in which they were enclosed; and becoming embedded in the sands, they germinate anew; hence its name, *Anastatica*. It is venerated in Palestine from the tradition that it blossomed at the moment when our Lord was born, and was endowed with qualities propitious to nativity. Wherefore the eastern women, when occasion requires, are anxious to have one of these dried plants expanding in a vase of water beside them, firmly believing that it has a salutary influence. It is an article of commerce, and bears a high price in the East. There is a madrigal by an old Italian poet, Benedetto dell' Uva, very applicable to this "Rose," to whose existence and expansion moisture is so necessary.

THE PERSON OF CHRIST.

In the church of Santa Croce at Florence is the Crucifix of Donatello, one of his early carvings. Being proud of it, he showed it to Brunelleschi, who told him that he had placed on the cross a figure of a peasant rather than a representation of Christ, whose person was of the greatest possible beauty, and who was in all respects the most perfect man that ever was born.

In the church of Santa Maria Novella at Florence is a crucifix of wood, which Brunelleschi executed in rivalry, after he had rallied Donatello upon the inelegance of his in Santa Croce. It is said by Vasari, that when Donatello saw this production of his rival, he was so surprised with its excellence, that, lifting up his hands in astonishment, he let go his apron filled with eggs and cheese for his dinner, all of which fell upon the ground, saying, "To you belongs the power of carving the figure of Christ; to me that of representing day-labourers." Yet the work of Brunelleschi is somewhat open to the criticism which Sir Joshua Reynolds made upon the early paintings of the Crucifixion—that they represent our Saviour as if He had been starved to death.

"I. H. S."

In a circle above the principal door of Santa Croce, the "Westminster Abbey" of Florence, are the letters "I. H. S.," remarkable as having been placed there by St. Bernardine of

Sienna, after the plague in 1347. Having remonstrated with a maker of playing-cards, which were then illuminated, upon the sinfulness of his calling, the man pleaded poverty and the needs of his family. "O," replied the saint, "I will help you;" and writing the letters I. II. S., he advised the card-maker to gild and paint these upon cards, and sell them; and they succeeded greatly. The letters are usually thought to signify *Jesus Hominum Salvator;* they are, however, of Greek origin, and denote the holy name IHΣOYΣ.

HISTORY OF THE HOLY CROSS.

In 1831, Lord Mahon read to the Society of Antiquaries the history of this sacred relic, of which the following is an abstract:

In the reign of the Emperor Constantine the Great, his mother Helena, when almost an octogenarian, undertook a pilgrimage to Jerusalem, in search of the Holy Sepulchre, and the Cross on which Jesus Christ had suffered. A vision, or perhaps dream, disclosed the place of the Holy Sepulchre; the three crosses were found buried near it, and that of the Saviour is said to have been distinguished from the others by its healing powers on the sick, and even restoring a corpse to life.[*] The spot was immediately consecrated by a church, called the New Jerusalem; and of such magnificence, that the celebrated Eusebius regarded it as the fulfilment of the prophecies in the Scriptures for a city of that name. A verse of the sibyl was also remembered or composed, which, like all predictions after the event, tallied in a surprising manner with the object they so happily revealed.

The greater share of the Cross was left at Jerusalem, set in a case of silver; and the remainder was sent to Constantine, who, in hopes of securing the prosperity and duration of his empire, enclosed it within his own statue on the Byzantine Forum. The pilgrims also, who thronged to Jerusalem during a long course of years, often obtained a small fragment of the Cross for themselves; so that at length, according to the strong expression of St. Cyril, the whole earth was filled with this sacred wood. Even at present there is scarcely a Roman Catholic cathedral which does not display some pretended pieces of this relic; and it has been computed, with some exaggeration, that were they all collected together they might prove sufficient for building a ship of the line. To account for this extraordinary diffusion of so limited a quantity, St. Cyril has asserted its preternatural growth and vegetation, which he ingeniously compares to the miracle of the loaves and fishes.

From this period the history of the holy Cross may be clearly traced through the twelve succeeding centuries. In spite of its frequent partitions, say the monkish writers, the Cross remained undiminished at Jerusalem until the year 614, when that city was besieged and taken by the Persians, who removed the relic to Persia, where it continued fourteen years, until the victories of the Emperor Heraclius, who restored it to its former station on Mount Calvary; the emperor laying aside his diadem and purple, and bearing the Cross on his own shoulders towards the Holy Sepulchre. An officer was then appointed to its po-

* For the discovery of the Cross, compare *Theodoret,* lib. 1. c. 18; *Socrates,* lib. 1. c. 17; and *Sozomen,* lib. III. c. 83.

culiar care, with the title of *Staurophulax;* and the anniversary of this event, the 14th of September, is still celebrated in the Greek Church as a festival, under the name of the Exaltation of the Cross.

Only eight years afterwards (A.D. 636), an army of Arabs, proselytes of Mahomet, invaded Palestine; the imperial forces were routed at Termuck, and Heraclius, downcast and dismayed, returned to Constantinople, bearing with him the invaluable fragment, whose alleged miraculous powers were never exerted for its own protection. It was, however, preserved at Constantinople with the utmost veneration in the church of St. Sophia, and the honours paid to it are attested by the father of English historians, Bede. Never but on the three solemn festivals of the year was its costly case unclosed; when a grateful odour pervaded the whole church, and a fluid resembling oil distilled from the knots in the wood, of which the least drop was thought sufficient to cure the most inveterate disease.

In the year 1078 the holy Cross recommenced its travels. During the tumultuous deposition of Michael VII., a wealthy citizen of Amalfi secured the Cross in its golden case set with jewels, and offered the relic at the shrine of St. Benedict, at Casinum. We next trace the Cross to Palestine, where the Crusaders bore it in the van of their armies when marching against the Mussulmans; during one of their battles with Saladin, the sacred relic was broken, and one-half of it was captured by the enemy, and most probably destroyed.* The remaining fragment, early in the thirteenth century, took the field with the King of Hungary and the Duke of Austria; from whom it passed into the hands of their brother-crusaders, the Latin sovereigns of Constantinople; but it was not received with its ancient share of veneration—a new Crown of Thorns, alleged to be that of the Passion, held at this period a far higher rank with the public.

In the year 1238, the pressure of poverty and impending ruin compelled the Emperor Baldwin II. to sell what the piety of Louis, king of France, induced him as eagerly to purchase. A very considerable sum was given in exchange for the holy wood; and on its arrival in Paris, it was deposited by King Louis in a chapel which he built on this occasion.† There the Cross remained for above three hundred years, until May 20, 1575, it disappeared from its station: the robber could not be traced, nor the spoil recovered, when it was reported that Henry II. had secretly sold it to the Venetians; and to appease the angry murmurs of his subjects, Henry, the next year, on Easter-day, announced that a new Cross had been prepared for their consolation, of the same shape, size, and appearance as the stolen relic, and asserted that in Divine powers, or claim to religious worship, it was but little inferior to its model; and "the people of Paris," say Estoile, an eyewitness of this transaction, "being very devout, and easy of faith on such subjects, gratefully hailed the restoration of some tangible and immediate object for their prayers." Of the original fragment no further trace has been found.

It should be added, that Constantine the Great obtained, at the same time with the Cross, the pretended nails of the Passion. He melted part of them into a helmet for himself: and the other part was converted into a bridle for his horse, in supposed obedience to a prophetic text of Zechariah: "In that day shall there be upon the bells (bridles) of the horses, holiness unto the Lord" (Zech. xiv. 20). Yet, though the

---

* There is some account of its recovery by a Genoese, but it is clouded with miracles: he walked over the sea as over dry land, &c. See *Muratori.*

† The restoration of this beautiful edifice (Saint Chapelle) was completed in 1836.

helmet alone might appear to have required all the nails which could possibly be employed in a crucifixion, it is not unusual in southern Europe to meet with fragments of old iron for which the same sacred origin is claimed. Thus Lord Mahon saw at Catania, in Sicily, one of these nails, which is believed to possess miraculous powers. There is another in a private oratory of the Escurial. All the nails from the time of Constantine are rejected as spurious by Cardinal Baronius; yet Pope Innocent VI. expressed his belief in their authenticity. One of the nails is stated to have been used in the Iron Crown of Lombardy.

THE GARDEN OF GETHSEMANE.

This venerated scene of our Lord's Passion is about a third of an acre in extent, and is surrounded by a low wall. When Mr. Catherwood was there, in 1834, taking the drawings for his beautiful Panorama of Jerusalem, the garden was planted with olive, almond, and fig trees. Eight of the olive-trees are so large that they are said to have been in existence ever since the time of Jesus Christ; although we learn from Josephus that Titus cut down all the trees within 100 furlongs of the city. These trees are highly venerated by the members of the Roman communion here, who consider any attempt to cut or injure them an act of profanation. Should any one of them be known to pluck any of the leaves, he would incur a sentence of excommunication.

"THE POTTER'S FIELD."

On this site, also known as Aceldamus, Dr. Wild discovered, in 1839, a cave containing a great number of skulls, which, according to his statements, were not those of Jews, but of foreigners. By this circumstance the fact was established beyond doubt that this is the very field which was bought for the thirty pieces of silver paid to Judas as the reward of his treason. Since then, other travellers have visited the cave; and new chambers have been discovered, where the bones of thousands lie mouldering. In fact, the vicinity of Jerusalem abounds in caves and subterraneous passages, where the bones of the millions who once worshipped on Mount Moriah, are whitening. It has been often a matter of surprise to travellers that so many skulls should be heaped together in one cave. It is explained in the Talmud, which informs us that it was the custom of the Jews to bury their dead in a particular place, and, after the flesh was destroyed, to gather the bones together, and place them in some vault. Many families had their own vaults.

BEELZEBUB.

The name of the Prince of Devils, or Beelzebub (Matt. xii. 24), or the Lord of Flies, some think to be a name of scorn given by the Jews to this great Jupiter of the Syrians, whom they named from the sacrifices in his temple being infested with multitudes of flies, which, by a peculiar privilege, notwithstanding the daily great number of sacrifices, never came (for such is the tradition) into the temple at Jerusalem. Others believe it was no mock name, but a surname of Baal, as he was worshipped at Ekron, either from bringing or driving away swarms of flies, with which the eastern countries were often molested; and their reason is, because Ahaziah, in the time of his sickness (when it is likely he would not rally with the god from whom he hoped for relief), sends to him under the name of Beelzebub.—*Cowley's Notes to his Davideis.*

EGYPTIAN WORSHIP OF CATS, CROCODILES, AND BEETLES.

These animals, it is thought, were at first worshipped in Egypt as representative symbols only of the deities to whom they were respectively sacred; but, in the progress of idolatry, became adored as manifestations upon earth of these divinities themselves.

The Cat, many embalmed specimens of which animal have been found in the Egyptian sepulchres, appears to have been sacred either to Isis, or to her half-sister Nephthys.

Strabo, relating his own observations, states that "in the city of Arsinoe, which was formerly called Crocodilopolis (in Upper Egypt, now called Medinet-el-Fay-um), *the Crocodile* is worshipped; and a sacred crocodile is kept in a pond, who is perfectly tame, and familiar with the priests. He is called Suchus; they feed him with corn and meat and wine, which are continually brought him by strangers." One of the Egyptian divinities, apparently that to whom the crocodile was consecrated, was pictured a crocodile's head; and is denoted in the hieroglyphic inscriptions by a representation of that animal with the tail turned under it.

The Beetle was regarded by the Egyptians as a particular personification of Phthah, the father of the gods: that insect is used in the hieroglyphics for the name of this deity, whose head in the pictured representations of him either bears a beetle, or is itself in the form of a beetle: in other instances the beetle, in hieroglyphics, has clearly a reference to generation or reproduction; which is a sense attributed to this symbol by all antiquity, and from which Dr. Young, in his hieroglyphical researches, inferred its relation to Phthah,—an inference since confirmed by the inquiries of Champollion. The Egyptians embalmed and preserved all the animals they adored; and in the Royal Egyptian Museum at Berlin are some mummies of the sacred beetle.

Mrs. Hamilton Gray, in her work on the *Sepulchres of Etruria*, observes:

"As scarabæl existed long before we had any account of idols, I do not doubt that they were originally the invention of some really devout mind; and they speak to us in strong language as to the danger of making material symbols of immaterial things. First, the symbol came to be trusted in, instead of the being of whom it was the sign; then came the bodily conception and manifestation of that being, or his attributes, in the form of idols; then, the representation of all that belongs to spirits, good and bad; then the deification of every imagination of the heart of man, a written and accredited system of polytheism, and a monstrous and hydra-headed idolatry."

This was the history of the scarabæus; an insect which so early attracted the notice of man by its wonderful and industrious habits, that it was selected by him as the image of the Creator; and, cutting stones to imitate it, he first wore them in acknowledgment of the Divine presence, probably having no idea of attaching any further importance to them. This symbol, there is reason to believe, existed anterior to Abraham.

THE SEVEN-EARED WHEAT.

This is the kind of Wheat formerly raised in Egypt and Syria, and often mentioned in the Bible under the name of *orn*, which meant then any sort of grain of which bread was made. What the Americans call corn, that is, Indian corn, was not known except to American Indians till about two hundred years ago. Pharaoh dreamed about the seven-eared corn; and we do not know that the one-eared corn was raised in Egypt. The wisdom of God is strikingly shown in the stalk of Egyptian wheat: if it was hollow and weak, like common corn, it would break with the weight; but it is *solidly filled* with a sort of pith, and thus rendered sufficiently firm.

APIS, THE SACRED BULL OF EGYPT.

Apis was a black calf, with a square white spot on its forehead, the figure of an eagle on its back, a double tuft of hair in its tail, and the figure of the cantharus (the sacred beetle) under its tongue. When an animal bearing these marks was found, or manufactured, the birth of Apis was announced to the people; a temple was built on the spot, where he was fed for four months; and after various ceremonies, he was finally conveyed to Memphis, where he spent the rest of his life in a splendid palace, receiving divine honours.

"MUMMY-WHEAT."

Sir Gardner Wilkinson, during his late travels in the Thebaid, opened an ancient tomb, which probably had remained unvisited by man for nearly three thousand years; and from some alabaster vases therein Sir Gardner took a quantity of wheat and barley that had been there preserved. In 1840, a few of these grains were planted in an open garden at Albury, near Guildford, and there flourished. The increase of the wheat was very great, the ears averaging seven inches long, and from fifteen to twenty ears on each root, springing from one grain: it was "bearded," and resembled that which is sometimes called by farmers "Egyptian wheat." Other instances are related of this resuscitated wheat: thus, in 1842, a specimen of Egyptian wheat, from a mummy imported in 1839, was in luxuriant growth in the Botanic Society's Garden at Bath; and, in 1841, a sample of wheat grown from seed taken from a mummy was shown to the British Association by Mr. Long, of Hurts Hall, Suffolk.

Mr. Tupper, of Albury, who first sowed this antique wheat, believed his plant of wheat to be the product of a grain preserved since the time of the Pharaohs; and that we moderns may thus eat bread made of corn which Joseph might have reasonably thought to store in his granaries.

EGYPTIAN EMBALMING.

All that has been written by modern authors upon this interesting subject seems to have been gathered from the account first given to us by Herodotus. Those writers — Diodorus Siculus, Pliny, Dioscorides, Galen, &c.—who followed soon after, appear to have stated nothing that was not originally advanced by Herodotus. He tells us that there were three different ways of embalming. The most magnificent was bestowed only upon persons of distinguished rank, and the expense amounted to a talent of silver, about 137*l.* 10*s.* (Calmet says, about 300*l.*) sterling; but twenty minæ, or sixty pounds, was considered moderate; and the lowest price was very small.

When a person of distinction died, the body was put into a coffin; the upper exterior of which represented the deceased, with suitable embellishment. The coffin itself was usually made of sycamore wood, which, according to Dumont, is almost incorruptible: sometimes deal was used, in which case it was brought from abroad.

The embalming of the body occupied from forty to seventy days. It consisted mainly of the introduction of astringent drugs and spices into the body, anointing it with oils of cedar, myrrh, and cinnamon, and saturating it with nitre. It was then washed, and wrapped in linen bands dipped in myrrh and gum,—these bands in some instances being one thousand yards long,—commencing at the head, and terminating at the feet, avoiding the face. The body was then restored by the embalmers to the relations, who placed it in the coffin. A less expensive process of embalming was simply to inject into the bowels a liquid extract of cedar, and wrapping up the body in salt or nitre; others were soaked, or, as some think, boiled in

ı kind of bitumen made of mixed resinous substances. They
were then placed, without any other covering than the band-
ıges-saturated with this substance, in sepulchres, and there
ieposited in rows by thousands.

USE OF MUMMIES.

That mummy is medicinal (says Sir Thomas Browne), the
Arabian doctor Haly delivereth, and divers confirm; but of
;he particular use thereof there is much discrepancy of opi-
1ion. While Hofmannus prescribes the same to epileptics,
Johan de Muralto commends the use thereof to gouty persons;
Bacon likewise extols it as a styptic; and Junkenius consi-
lers it of efficacy to resolve coagulated blood. Meanwhile
we hardly applaud Francis I. of France, who always carried
nummies with him as a panacea against all disorders; and
vere the efficacy thereof more clearly made out, scarce con-
:eive the use thereof applicable to physic, exceeding the bar-
ıarities of Cambyses, and turning old heroes into unworthy
ıotions. Shall Egypt lend out her ancients unto chirurgeons
ınd apothecaries, and Cheops and Psammitticus be weighed
ınto us for drugs? Shall we eat of Chamnes and Amosis in
ilectuaries and pills, and be cured by cannibal mixtures?
'urely such diet is dismal vampirism; and exceeds in horror
he black banquet of Domitian, not to be paralleled except in
hose Arabian feasts, wherein Ghoules feed horribly.—*Frag-
nent on Mummies, unpublished.*

THE LATEST MUMMIES.

One circumstance connected with the history of mummies
ıas much puzzled the learned, viz. what period was the latest
.t which mummies were prepared in Egypt? Count Caylus
Egypt. Antiq.) thought that no mummies were made after
he conquest of Egypt by the Romans, which was about the
ime of Diodorus; but in this he was quite mistaken, for Blu-
nenbach has shown, and St. Augustine (*Opera*, tom. v. p. 981)
nforms us, that so low down as his own times, in the early
ıart of the fifth century, mummies were certainly made in
ögypt. This being the case, there is no reason why these
nore recent ones may not have reached us, and the difference
n their composition seems thus reasonably accounted for by
he great discrepancy in the ages in which they were prepared.
'hus, some mummies have been found with long beards, and
ıair reaching down below their knees; some have very long
ınils; some have tutelary idols and figures of jasper put in their
ıodies; some have a piece of gold placed under the tongue.
Vilkinson states that he found the mummies of the poorer
lasses wrapped round with a number of palm-sticks, and fastened
ogether with string, like a mat.—*Topography, &c. of Egypt.*

Greece and Rome, Babylon and Carthage, &c.

GREECE AND EGYPT.

CHAMPOLLION says : " It is evident to me, as it must be to all who have thoroughly examined Egypt, or have an accurate knowledge of the Egyptian monuments existing in Europe, that the arts commenced in Greece by a servile imitation of the arts of Egypt, much more advanced than is vulgarly believed at the period at which the first Egyptian colonies came in contact with the savage inhabitants of Attica, or the New Peloponnesus. Without Egypt, Greece would probably never have become the classical land of the fine arts. Such is my entire belief on this great problem."

Coleridge has left this strange oracular opinion : " I cannot say that I expect much from mere Egyptian antiquities. Every thing that is really intellectually great in that country seems to me to be of Grecian origin."

LOCALITIES OF GREECE.

Colonel Mure, in his *Tour in Greece*, remarks, that one of the most interesting features of the history of the country is the contrast between its narrow limits and its boundless influence on the destinies of mankind. The Colonel says :

This reflection is forcibly brought home to the mind when one actually sees clustered, within the ordinary distance of English market-towns from each other, the ruins of cities far better known to fame than many a mighty empire, with its countless myriads of square miles or of population. A ride of less than twelve hours, at a foot-pace, enabled us to visit at least four places of distinction in Homer's age, with an ease and rapidity which cannot be better represented than by the flowing lines in which he has recorded their names :

Πλάτά τι στυχόωσαν,
Κρῖσαν τι ζαθίην, καὶ Δαυλίδα, καὶ Πανοπέα.

'The rocky Delphi, Crissa the divine,
Daulis, and Panopea.'

The three succeeding days would have sufficed a traveller more favoured by the elements than myself, to traverse, with the same equipage, at the same pace,—besides numerous other small states of less distinction,—the territories of Thebes, Platæa, Eleusis, and Athens. Argos, Mycenæ, and Tiryns,—the cities of Danaus, Hercules, Perseus, Agamemnon, with their colossal walls, bearing living testimony to the gigantic energies by which those heroes so well deserved the renown that still attends their names,—are all within the compass of a pleasant day's walk to a tolerable pedestrian. The whole population of the

tato of Athens, in its best ages, is computed to have been about one-
hird of that of London ; while the whole of that of Greece proper at
he present day, which during eight years resisted the concentrated
nergies of the Mahometan empire, is considerably less than that of
:onstantinople.

THE ANCIENT AND MODERN GREEKS.

Next to the pleasure enjoyed by the traveller in contem-
lating the ruins of Greece must be ranked that of comparing
he singularity of the manners of the present inhabitants with
hose of the ancients. In many of the ordinary practices of
.fe this resemblance is striking. The hottest hours of the day
re still devoted to sleep, as they were in the times recorded by
:enophon, when Conon attempted to escape from the Lacedæ-
ionians at Lesbos, and when Phœbidas surprised the citadel
f Thebes. The Greeks still feed chiefly upon vegetables, and
alted or pickled provisions. The eyebrows of the Greek women
re still blackened by art, and their cheeks painted occasionally
'ith red and white, as described by Xenophon. This latter
ustom in particular is universal in Zante among the upper
lasses. The laver, from which water is poured by the hand
revious to eating, appears by many passages in the *Odyssey*
) have been a common utensil in the time of Homer; and
)mething like the small movable table, universally used in
le Levant, seems to have been common amongst the ancient
reeks. According to Herodotus, in his description of the
auquet given by the Theban Antigonus to Mardonius and
le chiefs of the Persian army, there were two men, a Persian
ud a Theban, placed at each table; which circumstance, being
) particularly remarked, was probably a deviation from the
ustom of each person having a table to himself.—*Turner's.
'our in the Levant.*

DID HOMER COMPOSE THE ILIAD AND ODYSSEY?

Seneca reckons among the idle questions which were un-
orthy of wise men the dispute whether Homer wrote both
le *Iliad* and the *Odyssey*, and in what countries Ulysses wan-
ered. It is said that the art of writing, and the use of manage-
ble writing materials, were entirely, or all but entirely, un-
nown in Greece and its islands at the supposed date of the
)mposition of the *Iliad ;* and that if so, this poem could not
ave been committed to writing during the time of its com-
osition ; that in a question of comparative probability like
lis, it is a much grosser improbability that even the single
'iad—amounting, after all curtailments and expungings, to
pwards of 15,000 lines—should have been actually conceived
id perfected in the brain of one man with no other help
ut his own or other's memory, than that it should, in fact,

be the result of the labours of several distinct authors; that if
the *Odyssey* be counted, the improbability is doubled; that if
we add, upon the authority of Thucydides and Aristotle, the
Hymns and *Margites*, not to say the *Batrachomyomachia*,
that which was improbable becomes impossible; that all that
has been so often said as to the fact of as many lines, or more,
having been committed to memory, is beside the point in
question, which is not whether 15,000 or 30,000 lines may be
learned by heart from a book or manuscript, but whether one
man can *compose* a poem of that length, which, rightly or not,
shall be thought to be a perfect model of symmetry, or con-
sistency of parts, without the aid of writing materials; that,
admitting the superior probability of such a thing in a primitive age, we know nothing analogous to such a case; and that
it so transcends the common limits of intellectual power as at
the least to merit, with as much justice as the opposite opinion,
the character of improbability.—*H. N. Coleridge.*

THE SEVEN WISE MEN OF GREECE.

Neither the number nor the names of this constellation of
wise men are given by all authors alike. Dikæarchus numbered ten, Hermippus seventeen: the names of Solon the Athenian, Thales the Milesian, Pittakus the Mityleneau, and Bias
the Prienean, were comprised in all the lists; and the remaining names, as given by Plato, were, Kleobulus of Lindus in
Rhodes, Myson of Chênæ, and Cheilon of Sparta. Among
their sayings or mottoes, inscribed in the Delphian temple,
were, 'Know thyself,' 'Nothing too much,' 'Know thy opportunity,' 'Suretyship is the precursor of ruin.' Bias is praised as
an excellent judge, and Myson was declared by the Delphian
oracle to be the most discreet man among the Greeks, according to the testimony of the satirical poet Hipponax. This
is the oldest testimony (540 B.C.) which can be produced in
favour of any of the seven; but Kleobulus of Lindus, far from
being universally extolled, is pronounced by the poet Simonides to be a fool. Dikæarchus, however, justly observed that
these seven or ten persons were not wise men or philosophers
in the sense which those words bore in his day, but persons of
practical discernment in reference to man and society—of the
same turn of mind as their contemporary the fabulist Æsop,
though not employing the same mode of illustration. Solon,
Pittakus, Bias, and Thales, were all men of influence in their
respective cities. Kleobulus was despot of Lindus, and Peri-
ander (by some numbered among the seven) of Corinth. Thales
stands distinguished as the earliest name in physical philosophy,
with which the other contemporary wise men are said not to
have meddled. Most of them, if not all, were poets, or com-

posers in verse; and there is ascribed to them an abundance of pithy repartees, together with one short saying or maxim peculiar to each, serving as a sort of distinctive motto; indeed, one test of an accomplished man about this time was, his talent for singing or reciting poetry, and for making smart and ready answers.—Abridged from *Grote's Hist. Greece*, vol. iv.

EXPLOITS OF NESTOR.

Nestor, the last of the twelve sons of Neleus, not only defended and avenged Dylos against the insolence and rapacity of his Epeian neighbours in Elis, but also aided the Lapithæ in their terrible combat against the Centaurs, and as companion of Theseus, Peirithöus, and the other great legendary heroes who preceded the Trojan war. In extreme old age he lost his once marvellous power of handling weapons; but his activity remained unimpaired, and his sagacity and influence in council were greater than ever. He not only assembled the Grecian chiefs for the armament against Troy, but took a vigorous part in the siege itself, and was of pre-eminent service to Agamemnon. After the conclusion of the siege he returned to his dominions, and was there found in a strenuous and honoured old age, in the midst of his children and subjects,—sitting with the sceptre of authority on the stone bench before his house at Dylos,—offering sacrifice to Poseidon, as his father Neleus had done before him,—and mourning only over the death of his favourite son Antilochus, who had fallen in the Trojan war.—Abridged from *Grote's Hist. Greece*, vol. i.

THE WOODEN HORSE AT THE SIEGE OF TROY.

The Conquest of Troy has been well designated a Cadmeian victory (according to the proverbial phrase of the Greeks), wherein the sufferings of the victor were little inferior to those of the vanquished.

The Palladium having been conveyed away by stealth from the citadel, one final stratagem was planned for the capture of the town. At the suggestion of Athene, Epeius of Panopeus constructed a hollow wooden horse, capable of containing one hundred men. The *élite* of the Grecian heroes, Neoptolemus, Odysseus, Menelaus, and others, concealed themselves inside the horse; and the entire Grecian army sailed away to Tenedos, pretending to have abandoned the siege. The Trojans, issuing from the city, were astonished at the fabric which their enemies had left behind, and the more cautious spirits distrusted the enemy's legacy; but Laocoon, a priest, striking the side of the horse with a spear, the sound revealed that it was hollow. He, with two of his sons, was soon after destroyed by two serpents sent by the gods out of the sea; and by this terrific spectacle, together with the perfidious counsels of Sinon, a traitor whom the Greeks had left behind, the Trojans were induced to make a breach in their own walls, and drag the horse with triumph into the city. A night of riotous festivity ensued, during which Sinon kindled the fire-signal to the Greeks, and loosened the bolts of the wooden horse, from out of which the enclosed heroes descended. The city, attacked from within and without, was sacked and destroyed, and the larger portion of its heroes and people slaughtered or made captive.*

Epeius, the constructor of the Trojan horse, subsequently settled at Lagaria, near Sybaris, on the coast of Italy; and the very tools which he had employed in that remarkable fabric were, according to Strabo and others, shown down to a late date in the temple of Athene at Metapontum.

THE PLAINS OF TROY.

The Plains of Troy, so famed and flourishing in ancient days, are now barren and desolate. The classic Scamander is but a muddy stream, winding through an uncultivated plain, covered with stunted oaks, underwood, and rushes. At the opposite extremity of the plain stood the tombs of Hector and Achilles; that of the latter near the Hellespont, where the Greek fleet was moored. Near is the grave of his friend Patroclus. Athenian glories are now reduced to a few tumuli about thirty feet high.—*Webster's Travels.*

THE OLYMPIC GAMES.

This great festival was held on the banks of the Alpheius, in Peloponnesus, near the old oracular temple of the Olympian Zeus (Jupiter), and attracted its crowds of visitors and maintained its celebrity for many centuries after the extinction of Greek freedom; and only received its final abolition, after more than eleven hundred years' continuance, from the decree of the Christian emperor Theodosius, in 394 A.D. The games were originally a match of runners in the stadium, or measured course; and a series of the victorious runners, formally inscribed and preserved by the Eleians, beginning with Korœbus in 776 B.C., was made to serve by chronological inquirers from the third century B.C. downwards as a means of measuring the chronological sequence of Grecian events, hence called Olympiads. The competitors contended not for money, but for glory; and the prize was a wreath from the sacred olive-tree near Olympia, and the honour of being proclaimed victor. In the 18th Olympiad were added the wrestling-match, and the complicated Pantathlon, including jumping, running, the

* The second book of the *Æneid*, containing the exploit of Sinon and the Trojan horse (as Macrobius observeth) Virgil hath verbatim from Nicander.— *Sir Thomas Brown's Vulgar Errors.*

quoit, the javelin, and wrestling. In the 23d Olympiad (688 B.C.) was added the boxing-match ; and in the 25th (660 B.C.) the chariot, with four full-grown horses. In the 33d Olympiad (648 B.C.) were added the single racehorse, and the Pankration, or boxing and wrestling conjoined, with the hand unarmed or divested of the hard leather cestus worn by the pugilist, which not only rendered the blow of the latter more terrible, but at the same time prevented him from grasping his adversary. Among other novelties added were the race between men clothed in full panoply and each bearing his shield ; matches between boys, colts, &c. At the maximum of its attraction, the Olympic solemnity occupied five days; but until the 77th Olympiad, all the various matches had been compressed into one—beginning at daybreak, and not always closing before dark. Thus, during two centuries succeeding 776 B.C., the festival gradually passed from a local to a national character, bringing together in temporary union the dispersed fragments of Hellas, from Marseilles to Trebizond. During the sixth century B.C., three other festivals, at first local, became successively nationalised—the Pythia near Delphi, the Isthenia near Corinth, the Nemea near Kleonæ, between Sikyon and Argos.—Abridged from *Grote's History of Greece*, vol. iv.

•

PRODIGIOUS STRENGTH OF MILO OF CROTONA.

Milo was six times victorious in wrestling at the Olympic games. He is said to have carried his own statue to Altis ; and it is further reported of him that he held a pomegranate so firmly in his hand, that it could neither be forced from him by any other person, nor could he himself dismiss it from his grasp. And as he once stood anointing his quoit, he made those appear ridiculous who, by rushing against him, endeavoured to push him from the quoit. The following circumstance, too, evinces the greatness of his strength : he would bind his forehead with a cord, in the same manner as with a fillet or crown, and compressing his lips and holding in his breath, he would so fill the veins of his head with blood, that he would burst the cord through the strength of the veins. It is also said, that having let fall against his side that part of the arm which reaches from the shoulder to the elbow, he would extend the other part, which reaches from the elbow to the fingers, with his thumb turned upwards, and his fingers pressed close together ; and that when his hand was in this position no one by the greatest exertions could separate his little finger from the rest. They say that he died through wild beasts ; for happening, on the borders of Crotona, to meet with a withered oak, into which wedges were driven in order to separate the wood, he endeavoured, through confidence in

c

his strength, to tear the oak asunder. In consequence of this, the wedges giving way, Milo was caught by the closing parts, and was torn in pieces by the wolves with which that country is much infested. And such was the end of Milo.—From the *Posterior Eliacs* in the description of Greece by Pausanias, vol. ii. ch. 14 : Taylor's translation.

THE "WOODEN WALL" OF ATHENS.

When the Athenian envoys consulted the Delphian oracle as to their hopes at Salamis, the priestess assured them that "'the wooden wall' alone should remain unconquered," The people inquired what was meant by 'the wooden wall.' Some supposed that the acropolis itself, which had been originally surrounded with a wooden palisade, was the refuge pointed out; but the greater number, and among them most of those who were by profession expositors of prophecy, maintained that the wooden wall indicated the fleet, as it does at this day in our national boast of "the wooden walls of Old England."

AMPHION AND HIS LYRE.

When Amphion became king of Thebes, availing himself of his tuition by Hermes, and possessing exquisite skill on the lyre, he employed it in fortifying the city, the stones of the walls arranging themselves spontaneously in obedience to the rhythm of his song. Pausanias states that the wild beasts as well as stones were obedient to Amphion's strains ; and the tablet of inscription at Sicyon recognises him as the first composer of poetry and harp-music.

IS THE MOON INHABITED ?

Anaxagoras of Clazomene was the first of the Ionic philosophers who did not allow the sun and moon to be gods. On this account he was accused of impiety, and thrown into prison; but released by Pericles. "Are they not dreams of human vanity," says Montaigne, "to make the moon a celestial earth, there to fancy mountains and vales, as Anaxagoras did ?" Bishop Wilkins, one of the early fellows of the Royal Society, maintained that the moon was a habitable world, and proposed schemes for flying thither !

HOW AGESILAUS WAS DISABLED FROM THE FIGHT.

Agesilaus was going up into the counsel-house of his castle, when he was seized with cramp in his left leg, and put to great pain. A physician being there, opened a vein under the ancle of Agesilaus' foot; which made the pain cease, but

:t forth so much blood that they could not stanch it, so that
c swooned often, and was in danger of death. At length
ic bleeding was stopped, and they carried him to Lacedæmon;
here he lay sick a long time, so that he was *past going to the
ars any more.*

XENOPHON AND THE TEN THOUSAND GREEKS—THEIR MARCH AND RETREAT.

One of the most memorable events in Persian and Grecian
story is the March of the Ten Thousand Greeks into the
art of the Persian empire, and their still more celebrated
treat. The march from Sardis up to the neighbourhood
Babylon, conducted by Cyrus the younger, and under-
ken for the purpose of placing him on the Persian throne
the room of his elder brother Artaxerxes Mnemon, was
mmenced in March or April 401 B.C. In six months after-
rds, at the battle of Kunaxa, Cyrus lost his life. The Greeks
re then obliged to commence their retreat; which occupied
out one year, and ultimately brought them across the Bos-
orus of Thrace to Byzantium in October or November 400 B.C.
e body of the Greeks, immortalised as the Ten Thousand,
re for the most part persons of established position; half of
m were Arcadians, or Achæans.

The reaching of the sea, on the fifth day of the march, was
ceno of excitement which has few parallels in history. From
: summit of a mountain called Theches the Euxine Sea
me visible. An animated shout burst from the soldiers
o formed the van-guard: to Xenophon and the rear-guard
; cry was unintelligible; but every moment the shout
me louder, as fresh men came to the summit and gave
it to their feelings; so that Xenophon grew anxious, and
loped up to the van with his handful of cavalry to see what
l happened. "As he approached," says Mr. Grote, "the
ce of the overjoyed crowd was heard distinctly crying out,
alatta, Thalatta (the sea, the sea), and congratulating each
er in ecstasy. The main body, the rear-guard, the baggage-
liers driving up their horses and cattle before them, became
excited by the sound, and hurried up breathless to the
nnit. The whole army, officers and soldiers, were thus
mbled, manifesting their joyous emotions by tears, em-
ces, and outpourings of enthusiastic sympathy. With spon-
:ous impulse, they heaped up stones to decorate the spot by
onument and commemorative trophy; putting on the stones
1 homely offerings as their means afforded,—sticks, hides,
n few of the wicker-shields just taken from the natives.
the guide, who had performed his engagement of bringing
n in five days within sight of the sea, their gratitude was

unbounded. They presented him with a horse, a silver bowl, a Persian costume, and ten darics in money; besides several of the soldiers' rings, which he especially asked for. Thus loaded with presents, he left them."

CROSSING RIVERS ON INFLATED SKINS.

Among the Nimroud sculptures in the British Museum are three slabs, bearing representations of the King of Assyria crossing the Euphrates, in whose suite are soldiers inflating skins, and others swimming on inflated skins; which corresponds with a method thus described by Xenophon, in his *Anabasis:*

"And while they were at a loss what to do, a certain Rhodian came up, and said: 'I am ready to ferry you over, O men! by 4000 heavy armed men at a time, if you furnish me with what I want, and will give me a talent as a reward.' And being asked of what he stood in need: 'I shall want,' said he, '2000 leathern bags; and I see here many sheep, and goats, and oxen, and asses; which being flayed, and (their skins) inflated, would readily furnish a means of transport. And I shall require also the girths which you use for the beasts of burden. And on these,' said he, 'having bound the leathern bags, and fastened them one to another, and affixing stones, and letting them down like anchors, and binding them on either side, I will lay on wood, and put earth over them. And that you will not then sink, you shall presently very clearly perceive; for each leathern bag will support two men from sinking, and the wood and earth will keep them from slipping.'"

GREEK FIRE.

In the east of Europe the Greek fire was known as early as the year 673; when, according to the historians of the lower empire, Callinicus, the philosopher, taught the use of it to the Greeks. He himself had, probably, derived the knowledge of this composition from the Arabians; for, though powder acting by *detonation* (and consequently cannon) appears to have been first produced in Europe, and that not earlier than the beginning of the fourteenth century, the Asiatics had the use of powder that would *fuse* at a very early date. The Greek fire was discharged from tubes, which could be turned in any direction. The Princess Anna Comnena, in the *Alexiad,* describes its use as it was employed by the Emperor Alexis against the Pisans, from tubes fixed at the prow of his vessels: "They (the Pisans) were astonished to see fire, which by its nature ascends, directed against them, at the will of their enemy, downwards, and on each side." The receipt for the composition of the Greek fire may be found in the treatise of Marcus Græcus. The terrors of these early fire-mixtures were enhanced by the belief that not only they, but the flames kindled by them, were inextinguishable by water. The Greek fire did not, however, reach the west of Europe till a much later period. —*Hewitt on Ancient Armour.*

MEMORIALS OF MARATHON.

Upon this scene of splendid victory the Athenians did not
.il to discharge the last duties to the dead. A tumulus was
·ected on the spot (such distinction was never conferred by
thens except in this case only) to the one hundred and ninety-
vo Athenian citizens who had been slain. Their names were
scribed on the pillars erected at the spot, one for each tribe;
ere was also a second tumulus for the slain Platæans, a third
r the slaves, and a separate funeral monument (afterwards
lded) to Miltiades himself. Six hundred years after the
ttle Pausanias saw the tumulus, and could still read on the
llars the names of the immortalised warriors; and even now
conspicuous tumulus exists about half a mile from the sea-
ore, which Colonel Leake believes to be the same: it is
·out 30 feet high, and 200 yards in circumference.

In the time of Pausanias, this memorable battle-field was
·ard to resound every night with the noise of combatants and
·e snorting of horses. The battle was painted on one of the
·mpartments of the Pœcile portico at Athens; and the 6th
· the month Boëdromion, the anniversary of the battle, was
·mmemorated by an annual ceremony, even down to the time
· Plutarch.—Abridged from *Grote's History of Greece*, vol. iv.

.EONIDAS AND HIS BAND.   MEMORIALS OF THERMOPYLÆ.*

When Leonidas himself was slain, the little band of defend·
·s retired with the body of their chief, and sat all together
·a hillock; and thus surrounded by the enemy, they were
·erwhelmed with missiles, and *slain to a man;* "not losing
·urage even to the last, but defending themselves with their
·maining daggers, with their unarmed hands, and even with
·eir mouths."—*Grote.*

Thus perished Leonidas and his heroic comrades. The
·ply ascribed to the Spartan Dienekes became renowned:
The Persian host (he was informed) is so prodigious that
·cir arrows conceal the sun." "So much the better (he an-
·ered); we shall then fight them in the shade." Herodotus
·rnt the name of every individual among this memorable
·ree hundred; and even six hundred years afterwards, Pau-
·ias could still read the names engraved on a column at
·arta. On the hillock within the pass, where this devoted
·nd received their death-wounds, a monument was erected,
·th a marble lion in honour of Leonidas, decorated appar-
·tly with an epigram by the poet Simonides.

* Thermopylæ, or Hot-Gates, was named from its consisting of two narrow
·nings, with an intermediate road and hot-springs between them: sometimes
·as called more briefly, *Pylæ*, the Gates.

An inscription on the spot transmitted to posterity the formal boast that 4000 warriors "from Peloponnesus had here fought with 300 myriads, or 3,000,000 of enemies." Near it was another inscription, destined for the Spartan dead separately : "Stranger, tell the Lacedæmonians that we lie here in obedience to their orders."

XERXES SCOURGETH THE HELLESPONT.

When Xerxes had bridged the Hellespont (an English mile in breadth) with boats, for his march against the Greeks, a storm arose and destroyed the bridge. The wrath of the monarch knew no bounds. He first caused the heads of the engineers to be struck off. The strait was then scourged with three hundred lashes, and a set of fetters was let down, with, it is said, even irons, for branding the rebellious Hellespont. "Thou bitter water, (exclaimed the scourgers while inflicting the punishments) this is the penalty which our master inflicts upon thee because thou hast wronged him, though he hath never wronged thee. King Xerxes *will* cross thee, whether thou wilt or not ; but thou deservest not sacrifice from any man, because thou art a treacherous river of (useless) salt water." Herodotus may well call these insulting terms "non-Hellenic and blasphemous."

THE RETREAT OF XERXES.

Throughout history there is not, perhaps, a more memorable instance of defeated ambition and lost hope than is presented by the Retreat of the Persian invader. After forty-five days' march from Attica, he at length found himself at the Hellespont, where his fleet, retreating from Salamis, had arrived long before him. But the short-lived bridge had already been knocked to pieces, so that the army was transported on shipboard across to Asia. Justin tells us that Xerxes himself was obliged to cross the strait in a fishing-boat ; but this is disbelieved. In the time of Herodotus the citizens of Abdara still showed the gilt cimeter and tiara which Xerxes had presented them, in token of satisfaction, when he halted there in his retreat. At length the repulsed invader re-entered Sardis, with a broken army and humbled spirit, only eight months after he had left it as the presumed conqueror of the western world.—*Grote's Hist. Greece,* vol. v.

HOW SARDIS WAS TAKEN BY THE PERSIANS.

When Cyrus had arrived in the plain before the town of Sardis, he devised a stratagem whereby Crœsus's Lydian cavalry was rendered unavailable—placing in front of his line the baggage camels, which the Lydian horses could not endure either

ɔ see or smell ; so that the horsemen of Crœsus were obliged
ɔ dismount, and were driven into the town. Here Crœsus
ɯas shut up, waiting the arrival of his allies. Sardis was con-
idered impregnable, and the Persians would have been reduced
ɔ the slow process of blockade. The town was well fortified
ɯ every side except towards the mountain Tmolus, which
ɯas so steep that fortification was thought unnecessary. How-
vor, a Persian soldier having seen one of the garrison descend
his precipitous rock to pick up his helmet, which had rolled
own, watched his opportunity, tried to climb up, and suc-
ceded. Others followed his example ; the stronghold was thus
rst seized, and the whole city was speedily taken by storm.

" AS RICH AS CRŒSUS."

The wealth of Crœsus, which has passed into a proverb,
ɯas been variously accounted for. The possessors of Sardis,
he capital of the Lydian kings, were enriched by the neigh-
ɯourhood of the river Pactolus, which flowed down from Mount
'molus towards the Hermes, and brought with it considerable
ɯantities of gold in its sands. To this cause historians often
ɯscribe the abundant treasures belonging to Crœsus and his
redecessors ; but Crœsus possessed besides other mines near
'ergamus, and another cause of wealth is also to be found in
he general industry of the Lydian people. They were the
irst (according to Herodotus) who ever carried on retail trade,
ɯd the first to coin money of gold and silver.

When Cyrus had captured Sardis, he destined Crœsus to
ɯe burnt in chains, together with fourteen Lydian youths, on
ɯ vast pile of wood ; and we are even told that the pile was
ɯready kindled, and the victim beyond the reach of human
ɯid, when Apollo sent a miraculous rain to preserve him.

OMEN OF THE COCK.

In Lloyd's *Stratagems of Jerusalem* we are told, " Themis-
ɯocles was assured of victory over king Xerxes and his huge
ɯrmy by crowing of a cocke, going to the battle at Artemi-
jium, the day before the battell began. Having obtained so
ɯreat victory, he gave a cocke in his ensigne ever after."

HOW ŒDIPUS WON A KINGDOM.

On the death of Laius, when Creon succeeded to the kingdom of Thebes, the country was under the displeasure of the
gods, and was vexed by a terrible monster, with the face of a
woman, the wings of a bird, and the tail of a lion, called the
Sphinx.* She had learned from the Muses a riddle, which she

* The Sphinx (or *Phix*, from the Bœotian Mount, *Phikium*) is as old as the
Hesiodic theogony.

proposed to the Thebans for solution; on every occasion of failure, she took away one of the citizens, and ate him up. Still no person could solve the riddle; and so great was the suffering of the people, that Creon was compelled to offer both the crown, and his sister Jocasta in marriage, to any one who could save the city. At this juncture Œdipus arrived, and solved the riddle; when the Sphinx threw herself from the acropolis and disappeared, and Œdipus was made king of Thebes, and married Jocasta.

HONEY OF THE HYMETTUS.

Hymettus was anciently supplied with flowers so strongly scented, that hounds, on that account, frequently lost traces of the game when hunting in these regions. But the Hymettus has now no better vegetation than the other mountains of Attica.

Throughout Greece honey is more agreeable and aromatic than in other lands, owing to the heat being moderate; for which reason the juices of the plants are in a more concentrated state. The honey of the Laurian mountains was much prized; and *Erica Mediterranea* grows there in abundance. But the honey of the Hymettus, anciently esteemed the best in Greece, may have been overrated from its being obtained in the neighbourhood of the capital, and its fame being thus identified with the sweetness of ruling Athens. Now, at least, the honey of the Hymettus is eclipsed by that of other localities: in the Cyclades it is finer and more aromatic. The shepherds of the Hymettus keep bee-hives; and the honey from Pentelicon is reckoned among the hymettic. The number of hives on these mountains yielding honey averages 5000. The principal food of the bees is *Satircia capitata, Lentiscus, Cistus, Salvia, Lavandula,* and other herbs; otherwise the Hymettus is very bare.—*Dr. Fiedler's Journey through Greece.*

HOW GLAUCUS WAS SAVED FROM DROWNING IN HONEY.

Glaucus, the youngest son of Minos, pursuing a mouse, fell into a reservoir of honey, and was drowned: no one knew what had become of him, and his father was inconsolable. At length, the Argeian Polyeidus, a prophet wonderfully endowed by the gods, both discovered the boy and restored him to life, to the exceeding joy of Minos.

HOW DARIUS WON THE CROWN OF PERSIA.

Herodotus tells a story of the seven princes, who, having destroyed the usurper of the crown of Persia, were all of them in competition for it. At last they agreed to meet on horseback at an appointed place, and that he should be acknow-

ɣed sovereign whose horse first neighed. Darius's groom,
a subtle trick, contrived that his master should succeed.

PORUS ON HIS ELEPHANT.

We first read of elephants in a field of battle in the accounts
ʃhe battle of Arbela, 331 B.C., when Darius had among his
ːes fifteen of these animals. When Alexander forced the
sage of the Hydaspes (Jelum), the Indian Porus stood pre-
ed to dispute the passage with a formidable force of Indians,
l many trained elephants, which were skilfully managed.
·us, a prince of gigantic stature, mounted on his elephant,
ght with the utmost gallantry ; but at length, wounded and
ishing with thirst, he was only preserved by the special di-
tions of Alexander. When Porus was brought before him,
·xander asked what he wished to be done for him. "That
ɩ should treat me as a king," was the reply of Porus ; which
delighted Alexander, that he not only insured to him his
ual kingdom, but enlarged it ; and the conqueror found in
ɩ a faithful and efficient ally.

REASONABLE APPEAL.

Philip, Alexander's father, gave sentence against a prisoner
a time when he was drowsy, and seemed to give small
ention. The prisoner, after sentence was pronounced, said,
appeal." The king, somewhat stirred, said, "To whom do
ɩ appeal ?" The prisoner answered, "From Philip when he
·c *no ear*, to Philip when he shall give *ear*."—*Bacon.*

PHILIP AND ALEXANDER.

Amidst the intoxication of a marriage-banquet, Macedon
l well-nigh lost its mighty monarch. It appears that, one
ʃhe guests having proposed a toast and prayer offensive to
·xander, he hurled a goblet at him. Incensed at this pro-
ding, Philip started up, drew his sword, and made furiously
ɩis son Alexander ; but fell to the ground from passion and
oxication. This accident alone preserved the life of Alex-
ler, who retorted : "Here is a man preparing to cross from
rope into Asia, who yet cannot step surely from one couch
ɩnother."

HOW PHILIP WAS ASSASSINATED.

"How shall I become famous ?" once asked a desperado at
ɩ oracle of Delphos. "Go and slay some one already famous,
l your name shall be handed down to posterity along with·
ʹʹ was the reply. And so Philip of Macedon fell by the·
ːger of an assassin.

HOW ALEXANDER CUT THE GORDIAN KNOT, AND THUS WON AN EMPIRE.

When Alexander halted with his troops at Gordium, 333 B.C., there was preserved in the citadel a rude waggon, said by the legend to have once belonged to the peasant Gordius and his son Midas, the primitive rustic kings of Phrygia. The cord (composed of fibres of the bark of the cornel-tree) attaching the yoke of this waggon to the pole was twisted and entangled in a knot which no one had ever been able to untie. An oracle had pronounced, that to the person who should untie it, the empire of Asia was destined. When Alexander went to see this ancient puzzle, on inspecting it, he was as much perplexed as others had been before him ; until, in a fit of impatience, he drew his sword and severed the cord in two. By every one this was accepted as a solution of the problem, thus making good his title to the empire of Asia ; a belief which the gods ratified by a storm of thunder and lightning during the ensuing night.

PERILS OF ALEXANDER AT THE GRANICUS.

When Alexander had crossed the river, he spurred his horse forward against Mithridates (son-in-law of Darius), into whose face he thrust his pike, and laid him prostrate on the ground ; he then turned to another of the Persian leaders, Phœsukes, who struck him a blow on the head with his cimeter, knocked off a portion of his helmet, but did not penetrate beyond. Alexander avenged this blow by thrusting Phœsukes through the body with his pike. Meanwhile a third Persian leader, Spithridates, was actually close behind Alexander, with hand and cimeter uplifted to cut him down ; when Kleitus, one of the ancient Macedonian officers, struck with full force at the uplifted arm of Spithridates, and severed it from the body, thus preserving Alexander's life. Other leading Persians, kinsmen of Spithridates, rushed desperately on Alexander, who received many blows on his armour, and was in much danger. But the efforts of his companions near were redoubled, both to defend his person and second his adventurous daring.[*]

ALEXANDER AND DIOGENES.

When Alexander was at Corinth, B.C. 335, to the universal

---

[*] *Grote's Hist. Greece*, vol. xii. Within a few years, B.C. 328, at the banquet of Marakanda, Kleitus, indignant at Alexander's hatred of Philip's old soldiers, reproached him with these words: " Recollect that you owe your life to me: this hand preserved you at the Granicus;" when, in wrath and intoxication, Alexander rushed upon Kleitus, and thrust him through on the spot. This tragic incident has furnished one of the most effective situations in Nat. Lee's play of *Alexander the Great*

eference and submission which greeted him one exception
as found,—the cynic philosopher Diogenes, who was satis-
ed with a tub for shelter, and the coarsest and most self-
nying existence. Alexander approached him with a nu-
erous suite, and asked him if he wished for any thing; upon
hich Diogenes is said to have replied: "Nothing, except
at you would stand a little out of my sunshine." Both the
ilosopher and his reply provoked laughter from the by-
anders; but Alexander himself was so impressed with the
ndependent and self-sufficing character manifested; that he
claimed, "If I were not Alexander, I would be Diogenes."

Seneca says: "That tumour of a man, the vain-glorious Alexander,
is used to make his boast that never any man went beyond him in
nefits; and yet he lived to see a poor fellow in a tub, to whom there
is nothing that he could give, and from whom there was nothing that
could take away."

THE SIEGE OF GAZA.

Around this town Alexander caused a mound to be carried,
as to render it approachable from every point; this Her-
lean work being 250 feet high all round, and two stadia
240 feet) broad. After the siege, Alexander reserved one
isoner for special treatment—the prince, or governor, himself,
e eunuch Bactis, whose feet were bored, and brazen rings
ere passed through them; after which the naked body of
is brave man, yet surviving, was tied with cords to the tail
a chariot driven by Alexander himself, and dragged at full
eed amidst the triumphant jeers and shouts of the army; an
t of cruelty copied from the ignominious treatment described
the *Iliad* as inflicted on the dead body of Hector.

PAYING THE DEBTS OF AN ARMY.

When the Macedonian soldiers pressed their discontent
ith the Asiatising intermarriages promoted by Alexander, he
ftened their aversion by proclaiming that he would himself
scharge their debts, if they would give in their names and
ate the sums due. Now it was known that the debtors were
imerous; yet few came to enter their names, the soldiers
specting the proclamation to be a stratagem to detect spend-
rifts, and obtain a pretext for punishment. Alexander was
irt at their mistrust, and proclaimed that paymasters and
bles should be planted openly in the camp, and that any
ldier might receive money enough to pay his debts without
ing bound to give in his name; when application was made
such numbers, that the total distributed reached, according
some, 10,000 talents; according to Arrian, 20,000 talents,
4,600,000*l.* sterling.—*Grote's Hist. Greece*, vol. xii.

THE STORY OF NINEVEH.

Nineveh, or the dwelling of Ninus, was the metropolis of the great Assyrian empire, the residence of a long line of illustrious princes, and once the largest and most populous city in the world. We learn from the book of Genesis that Asshur, one of the sons of Shem, "went forth" from the land of Shinar, and built Nineveh ; but we hear nothing more of it in the sacred writings till Jonah, its inspired missionary, describes it as "an exceeding great city," and its population must have been 600,000. The prophet Nahum describes it as a city with many strongholds and many gates with bars, her merchants as multiplied above the stars of heaven, her inhabitants and princes numerous as the locusts. Nahum's prediction was literally fulfilled by the destruction of the city in the year 606 B.C., by the combined armies of Cyaxares, king of Persia and Media, and Nabopolassar, who was either king of Babylon or, as Mr. Layard thinks, the Assyrian governor of the city. The walls of Nineveh are described by profane writers as 100 feet high, 60 miles in circumference, and defended by 1500 towers, each 200 feet ʼin height. Diodorus Siculus informs us that the city was destroyed partly by water and partly by fire ; and Lucian, a native of Samosata, near the Euphrates, in the second century (between A.D. 90 and A.D. 180), states that Nineveh had utterly perished, and its site could not be pointed out. During the eighteen centuries which have elapsed since the time of Lucian, Nineveh was known only by name. Enormous mounds on the left bank of the Tigris, opposite the modern city of Mosul on the right bank, had been noticed by several travellers, and the traditional tomb of Jonah was pointed out on the top of one of the mounds : in 1820 the site was explored by Mr. Rich, who, however, did not attempt to excavate the mound ; and, until 1840, "a case scarcely three feet square enclosed all that remained, not only of the great city Nineveh, but of Babylon itself." In 1843 M. Botta commenced his excavations, the result of which has been the splendid collection of Assyrian Antiquities in the Louvre, at Paris ; and in 1845 Mr. Layard commenced his works on the mounds of Nimroud, which have been rewarded by even finer discoveries than those which M. Botta had exhumed. The whole of Mr. Layard's discoveries are preserved in the British Museum, and form a national collection unsurpassed even by that of Paris.

It is a remarkable proof of the complete destruction of Nineveh, that none of the historians of Alexander's campaigns allude to it, though he must have passed within a few miles of it, on his way to fight the battles of Arbela and Gugamela. Xenophon, in the Retreat of the Ten Thousand, probably did see its ruins ; though we cannot speak with

tainty from his description. But Lucian of Samosata confirms the
sy of Nineveh, which he had probably good means of knowing.—
S. W. Vaux.

PELASGIC, CYCLOPEAN, AND ETRUSCAN ARCHITECTURE.

These three terms have been strangely misapplied to speci-
ns of ancient architecture in middle Italy, merely because
style is colossal compared with the later works of Roman
struction; whereas, to apply the term Cyclopean to the
:uscan style is not less absurd than to identify the Druidical
iples of Stonehenge and Abury with the massive style of
early Saxon architecture.

The *Pelasgic* construction was almost invariably polygonal,
isisting of enormous blocks of stone; the angles of one ex-
ly corresponding with those of the adjoining masses; and
; together without cement, so accurately as to leave no in-
stices whatever. The Pelasgi built, eighteen centuries be-
o Christ, the walls of Lycosura, which Pausanias calls "the
st ancient, and the model from which all other cities were
lt." The *Cyclopean* wall is composed of large irregular
ygonal masses, with smaller stones filling up the interstices
ween them. The finest specimens are the walls of Tiryns
l Mycenæ, upwards of 3000 years old. The *Etruscan* walls
generally built of parallelograms of soft calcareous stone or
:ufa, laid with more or less regularity in horizontal courses,
hout cement.

AN ARMY TERRIFIED BY AN ECLIPSE.

After Alexander was on his march to Babylon, during the
ht an eclipse of the moon occurred, nearly total, which spread
sternation among the army, combined with complaints of
:xander's overweening insolence, and mistrust as to the
known regions on which they were entering. Alexander,
ile offering sacrifices to sun, moon, and earth, combated the
vailing depression by declarations from his own prophet
stander, and from Egyptian astrologers, who proclaimed
t Helios favoured the Greeks, and Selene the Persians:
ice the eclipse of the moon portended victory to the Mace-
iians,—and victory too (so Aristander promised) before the
:t new moon.

HOW BABYLON FELL.

The history of this great event may be found at large in
·odotus and Josephus, in Strabo, Xenophon, and Diodorus
ilus. The manner of the capture of the city was singular.
)ut 540 B.C. Cyrus had invaded Babylon: his armies had
u every where victorious; yet, trusting in the prodigious

strength of the city, and the wise counsels of Nitocris the queen-mother, the Babylonians derided the efforts of the Persians. They had provisions sufficient for twenty years' consumption ; the walls of their city were of prodigious strength, being 350 feet high and 87 thick, and built of bricks cemented together with a glutinous earth, so as to be harder than granite. For the reduction of this apparently impregnable capital, Cyrus constructed a number of wooden towers higher than the walls, and attempted to carry the place by storm, but was foiled. After two years' unavailing blockade he succeeded by stratagem. The king, Belshazzar, had a great feast, when Cyrus, expecting it to be a scene of the grossest riot, posted part of his army close to the spot where the river Euphrates entered the city, and another at the opposite side where it passed out, with orders to enter the channel wherever it was fordable. He then detached a third party to open the head of a canal connected with the Euphrates, and thus admit the river into the trenches which he had opened round the city. By this means the river was so completely drained by midnight, that the troops easily made their way along its bed ; and the gates upon the banks having been left unclosed during the confusion of the festival, the besiegers uninterruptedly entered the city, and met, according to agreement, at the palace-gates. Here they overpowered the guards, cut to pieces all who opposed them, slew the king, and within a few hours received the submission of Babylon the mighty.

John Martin, in his celebrated picture and print, has represented the Chaldean capital in its glory. In the distance is seen the Tower of Babel, which he supposes to have been still standing upon the plains of Shinar. Upon the banks of the river is the temple of Belus, with its tower 600 feet square at the base, and 600 feet high. Next, on the right, is the temple of Semiramis, four miles in circumference. The river is spanned by the bridge built by Nitocris; in the right-hand corner is the palace of Nebuchadnezzar, eight miles in circumference, and surmounted by the celebrated hanging-gardens, occupying a square of 400 feet, and consisting of spacious terraces, raised one above the other to the height of the city-walls; the whole pile being supported upon immense arches built upon other arches, and borne by a wall 22 feet thick. In the bed of the river is the enemy setting fire to the Babylonian navy ; on the right is the Persian horse, headed by Cyrus ; and in the foreground is the enemy slaughtering the king in sight of several of his concubines, who had escaped with him from the palace.

Babylon was a second time reduced, when Darius caused the walls and gates to be demolished, and 3000 of the principal citizens to be crucified.

WHO WERE THE ETRUSCANS?

The Etruscans, long before the period in which the foundation of Rome is placed, flourished—a rich, commercial, and highly-cultivated people. The earliest institutions of Rome were Etruscan. Etruria was the parent of her religion; thence were derived the principles of her primitive constitution and government. The Tarquins were an Etruscan family, and we are almost tempted to believe Rome herself an Etruscan city. After the utter downfall of Etruscan independence, the religious rites and ceremonies of Etruria, her emblems of power—the lictors, the fasces, and the curule chair—remained witnesses of her former influence; the reputation of her augurs and diviners subsisted until the first ages of the empire; and the noble youth of Rome received the first lessons of science and learning in Etruscan seminaries, until the philosophy of Greece prevailed, and the colleges of Etruria were deserted for the groves of Academe.

Etruria has left but few materials from which to trace her history. There are architectural fragments, but the name and memory of their builders are gone. There is a language in which we find inscriptions. They are legible, for the character is like the ancient Greek or Phœnician. We can trace the letters and form of words, but their meaning is hidden. They are more unintelligible than the hieroglyphics of Egypt. Two words alone have as yet been interpreted: RIL AVRIL, " years lived." The sentence seems an epitome of our Etruscan history. But one class of remains is rich in information. The funeral monuments of Etruria show us their mode of life. They perpetuated it in their graves. There we can read largely of their customs, and habits, and manners. The contents of these tombs tell us of their widely-extended trade and commerce. They enclose the products of Greece and Egypt, and even of Persia and India.—*North British Review*, No. 6.

THE STORY OF ROMULUS AND REMUS.

Rome was founded by Romulus, whose early history appears to have been a national lay. He is said to have been found, with his twin-brother Remus, by Faustulus, a shepherd, in a rude cradle, or trough, which had been carried by the current of the Tiber to the foot of a wild fig-tree, and there left by the retreating waters. The shepherd preserved the foundlings, and carried them home to his wife, who, from her former dissolute life, had obtained the name of Lupa, which gave rise to the fable that Romulus and Remus, her foster-children, had been *suckled by a wolf*. The more probable part of the tradition is, that for some services performed for Numitor, king of

Alba, by Romulus and Remus, that sovereign bestowed upon the brothers some waste lands lying about the Tiber for the site of a city and colony.*

Sculpture has transmitted to posterity this poetic legend in a bronze group of the She-wolf suckling Romulus and Remus, which was found in an excavation at the foot of the Palatine Hill, close to where stood, in the times of the Republic and the Empire, a small temple appropriated to its reception, adjoining the ruminal fig-tree, under which, according to the legend, the infants were found by the shepherd Faustulus. The group was an object of great veneration with the Romans, and is mentioned by several of the classic writers. It has been decided that the infants belong to a more recent period of art than the wolf. The group is now placed in the Palace of the Conservators, on the Capitol.

The finding of Romulus and Remus by the shepherd, and his bringing them to his wife, has also been nobly painted by Pietro da Cortona.

ROME FOUNDED ON THE SITE OF A VOLCANO.

The nucleus of the city destined to become the future mistress of the world occupied the hollow of an extinct volcano,—a conclusion at which Sir Charles Lyell has arrived by a survey of the ground; the appearance of the hills, and the immense deposit of pozzolana still underlying the foundations of ancient Rome, sufficiently establishing a fact which throws some light upon one of the most picturesque traditions of the old Republic,—the leap of the young Roman warrior Curtius upon horseback into "the gulf," an immense opening in the Forum, to which the soothsayers had declared the principal strength of the Romans must be sacrificed.

One of the hills at least, the Aventine, still bears some lingering traces of its fiery origin: blasts of smoke and flame are imagined at times to issue from it; and long after these have become traditionally extinguished, the memory of them survives among the tribes of the vicinity, who believe that the spot is still the fastness of a monstrous giant, who robs them of their cattle, and defies the challenge of their champion by vomiting fire from his throat.

THE SEVEN HILLS OF ROME

form a river-bank of moderate elevation. From the *Capitoline* on the north, which comes within three hundred yards of the Tiber, to the *Aventine* on the south, which falls almost directly

---

* Niebuhr disbelieves this story, and converts the foundling brothers into the rival towns Roma and Remuria, and has actually discovered a place which seems to be called by the latter name. A great linguist conjectures that Italy was colonised by Greeks and Celts, and that Latium, lying between these colonies, spoke a mixed language, and that language was Latin.

nto it, these hills form a segment of considerably more than
alf a circle. The *Quirinal*, the *Viminal*, the *Esquiline*, and
he *Cælian*, which lie more inland, are all tongues of land
projecting from the common ridge which bounds the valley,
nd which slopes away·on the farther side insensibly into
he Campagna. Arnold compares these projecting tongues of
ill to the fingers of an open hand, the knuckles representing
he ridge from which they spring, and the back of the hand
he gentle slope outwards. The Capitoline and Aventine
stand apart as sentinels to guard the stream; and between
hem, in the centre of the whole group, lies the sequestered
Palatine, closely embraced by three connected valleys. The
heights of these hills, level or nearly so at their summits,
hardly any where exceed 150 feet from the level of the Tiber.
The Palatine is a trapezium, two sides of which are about 300,
and the other two about 400 yards in length. It may be compared in size and shape with the block of buildings enclosing
Hanover-square, between Oxford-street and Conduit-street,
in London. The Aventine, less regularly shaped, is about
equal in dimensions; the Capitoline, with its two summits
and saddle between them, is the smallest of the Seven Hills,
and does not much exceed 350 yards in length by 100 in
breadth. Of the other eminences, which have few distinct
features, and are in fact merely undulations of a simple hill,
the Viminal is the smallest and best defended; the Esquiline
and the Cælian extend over considerable spaces. These two
latter, and the Quirinal, have each more than one knoll, to
which at an early period distinct names were assigned, but
which were lost to view and recollection when covered with
the buildings of the city.

The Palatine was traditionally the cradle of the Roman
state: the founders of Rome were a band of brigands and outlaws; and none of the Seven Hills was so well calculated for
the retreat of those "wolves of Italy" as the scarped summit
of the Palatine encompassed by marsh and jungle. But the
Roman hills form an isolated cluster in the centre of a wide
extended plain; and it is probable that more than one of them
was seized from an early period for the fastness of the tribes
which roamed over the Campagna.

A bird's-eye view of Rome may be thus obtained. The
Janiculan hill rises nearly 100 feet above the highest elevation
on the left bank; and from its arx, on the site of the gate
of San Pancrazio, the Seven Hills lie expanded to the view in
their full dimensions. "From this point," says Martial, many
centuries later, "you might behold the seven lordly mounts,
and measure the entire size of Rome."—Abridged from the
Quarterly Review, No. 198.

CURTIUS AND THE GULF.

In 301 A.U.C. an earthquake opened a great chasm in the Forum at Rome, which continued to increase in depth and width, terrifying the people, who in vain laboured to fill it up by casting in earth and stones. The augurs, when consulted, declared that the danger could not be averted until that in which the power and strength of the Roman people consisted was cast into the chasm, when the offering would procure from the gods the eternal duration of the Roman state. Each individual threw in the most valuable of his worldly possessions; but the chasm remained unclosed, till Marcus Curtius, a Roman noble youth, declared that " Rome had nothing more precious to offer than arms and valour ;" then, mounting his charger, he entered the Forum at full speed, and turning towards the Capitol, invoked at the chasm the infernal and celestial deities, declaring that he offered himself as a sacrifice for the welfare of his country. Then, spurring his horse, he plunged headlong into the flaming gulf; the people flung down upon him many precious movables, and then, it was said, the chasm was speedily filled up—most likely by another shock of earthquake.

CORIOLANUS.

Near Frascati, at a short distance from the tumulus in which the celebrated Portland Vase was found, is the site of the famous temple of Fortuna Muliebris, erected in honour of the wife and mother of Coriolanus, who here dissuaded him from his threatened attack on Rome, and where he found that he was not " of stronger earth than others :"

> " Ladies, you deserve
> To have a temple built you : all the swords
> In Italy, and her confederate arms,
> Could not have made this peace."

Antiquaries fix at Monte Giove the site of the celebrated city of Corioli :

> " If you have writ your annals true, 'tis there
> That, like an eagle in a dovecote, I
> Flatter'd your Volsces in Corioli."

Its site could not be traced in Pliny's day.

THE EAGLE A BIRD OF OMEN.

In Lloyd's *Stratagems of Jerusalem* we read: " Aristander the soothsayer, in the battell at Arbela, being the last against Darius, was then on horsebacke hard by Alexander, apparelled all in white, and a crowne of gold upon his head, encouraging Alexander, by the flight of an eagle, the victory should be his over Darius." . . . . " So Tarquinius Priscus, an eagle tooke

his cappe from his head and fled up high to the skies, and
after descended and let his cappe fall on his head againe, signifying thereby that he should be king of Rome."

PECUNIA—MONEY.

The Roman coinage issued by Servius Tullius bore the image
of a sheep (*pecus*), and was thence called *pecunia*, the term
subsequently applied to money in general; but this is by no
means certain.—*Niebuhr.*

The first silver money was coined at Rome A.U.C. 482; the
mint was in the Temple of Juno Moneta, and this circumstance occasioned the origin of our word 'money.'—*Hooke's
Rome.*

PRICES OF PROVISIONS AT ROME IN THE FOURTH CENTURY.

In 1827, there was found by Mr. William Bankes at Stra-
tonicea (now Eskihissar), in Asia Minor, part of a table of stone,
inscribed with an edict of Diocletian, published A.D. 303, fixing
the price of labour and food in the Roman empire ; the second
part of which table was brought from Rome to London by M. de
Vescovali.

Of this precious archæological document M. Moreau de Jonnes has
formed a table, whence we quote a few of the mean prices in English
money. *Price of labour:* a day-labourer, 4*s.* 8*d.* ; for interior works, a
mason, or maker of mortar, 9*s.* 4*d.* ; a marble-cutter, or mosaic cutter,
11*s.* 4*d.* ; a tailor, 9*s.* 4*d.* ; for making shoes for the patricians, 1*l.* 8*s.* 1*d.* ;
for the military, or senators, 18*s.* 8*d.* ; for curry-combing and cleaning
a horse, 3*s.* 9*d.* To an advocate, for a petition, 2*l.* 6*s.* 9*d.* ; for the
bearing of a cause, 9*l.* 7*s.* 6*d.* *Wines*, the English pint : Sabine, Sur-
rentine, and Falernian, 5*s.* 4*d.* ; old wines, first quality, 4*s.* 2½*d.* ; spiced
wine of Asia, 6*s.* 4*d.* ; beer of Egypt, 2*d.* *Meat*, per lb. : beef or
mutton, 2*s.* ; lamb, kid, or pork, 3*s.* ; lard, 4*s.* ; belly of tripe, 4*s.* ;
Westphalia ham, 6*s.* ; pig's liver, fattened on figs, 4*s.* ; pork-sausages,
two weighing 1 oz., 4½*d.* *Poultry and game:* fat peacock, 2*l.* 6*s.* 9*d.* ;
fat peahen, 1*l.* 17*s.* 9*d.* ; a fat goose, 2*l.* 16*s.* 9*d.* ; lean goose, 18*s.* 8*d.* ;
a hen, 11*s.* 4*d.* ; a duck, 7*s.* 4*d.* ; a partridge, 6*s.* 8*d.* ; a hare, 1*l.* 6*s.* 1*d.* ;
a rabbit, 7*s.* 4*d.* *Fish* : sea, 4*s.* 6*d.* each ; river, half price. *Vegetables* :
cabbages and cauliflowers, 9*d.* each ; beet-roots, 5*s.* 9*d.* Honey, best,
was 15*s.* per lb. ; vinegar, 2*s.* 8*d.* per pint ; and dried cheese, 3*s.* 4*d.*
per lb. From this document we gather that two-thirds, or even three-
fourths of the Roman people, were reduced to live on fish and cheese,
and drink piquetto, when the expense of the table of Vitellius amounted
in a single year to 475 millions of francs (19 millions sterling).

SLAVERY IN ROME.

Slavery appears to have been in ancient ages the lot of men
of much higher cast of character than any who have been its
victims in modern times. Virgil made a slave of his a poet,
and Horace himself was the son of an emancipated slave. The
physician and the surgeon were often slaves. So, too, the

preceptor and the pedagogue, the reader and the stage-player, the clerk and the amanuensis, the buffoon and the mummer, the architect and the smith, the weaver and the shoemaker, the undertaker and the bearer of the bier, the pantomime and the singer, the rope-dancer and the wrestler,—all were bond-men. Even the *armiger*, or squire, was a slave. You cannot name an occupation connected with agriculture, manufactur-ing industry, or public amusement, but it was the patrimony of slaves. Slaves engaged in commerce; slaves were wholesale merchants; slaves were retailers; and the managers of banks were slaves. Educated slaves exercised their professions for the emolument of their masters. Of course, the value of slaves varied with their health, their beauty, or their accomplish-ments. The common labourer was worth from 15*l.* to 20*l.*, the usual price of a negro in the West Indies when the slave-trade was in vogue. A good cook was worth almost any price. An accomplished actor could not be valued at less than 1000*l.* A good fool was cheap at less than 160*l.* Beauty was a fancy article, and its price varied. Mark Antony gave 1600*l.* for a pair of beautiful youths, and much higher prices were paid. About as much was paid for an illustrious grammarian. A handsome actress was worth far more; her annual salary might sometimes be 2000*l.* The law valued a physician at 48*l.* Lu-cullus, having once obtained an immense number of prisoners of war, sold them for 3*s.* a head,—probably the lowest price for which a lot of able-bodied men was ever offered.

FORTUNATE DREAMS.

We owe unto dreams that Galen was a physician, Dion an historian, and that the world hath seen some notable pieces of Cardan; yet he that should order his affairs by dreams, or make the night a rule unto the day, might be ridiculously de-luded; wherein Cicero is much to be pitied, who, having ex-cellently discoursed of the vanity of dreams, was yet undone by the flattery of his own, which urged him to apply himself unto Augustus.—*Sir Thomas Browne.*

"THE BELLY AND THE MEMBERS."

When, A.U.C. 259, the Roman people were in open revolt, Menenius Agrippa replied to the plebeian orator, L. Junius Brutus, in the following apologue:

"The members of the body once mutinied," said he, "against the belly, and accused it of lying idle and useless while they were all labour-ing and toiling to satisfy its appetites; but the belly only laughed at their simplicity, who knew not that though it received all the nourish-ment into itself, it prepared and distributed it again to all parts of the body. Just so, my fellow-citizens, stands the case between the senate and you. For necessary councils and acts of government are productive of advantage to you all, and distribute their salutary influence upon the whole people."

'The wisdom of Menenius Agrippa made a deeper impression upon the mutinous soldiery than the fiery oration of Brutus. It has since had the honour of being quoted by St. Paul, in the 12th chapter of the 1st of Corinthians, who has enlarged upon it for the benefit of his early converts to Christianity.—*Strickland's Rome, Regal and Republican.*

There is little in oratory, ancient or modern, that will bear comparison with the address of Volero upon his new law respecting tribunitial election : " Romans," he said, " I am not so ready at speaking as doing ; come to-morrow, and I will get the law passed, or die upon the spot before you." And the law was passed.

THE SATURNALIA.

The three days' festival of the Saturnalia was founded by Servius Tullius as a holiday for the servile class, to which he himself once belonged ; for though the Latin authorities assure us that the captive of Corniculum was of a noble family, that circumstance did not render slavery less bitter. Juvenal alone speaks of him as the son of a poor maid-servant.

THE EARLIEST RECORD OF ROME.

To Cato the Censor Rome was indebted for its earliest records, known as the Pontifical Annals, which, though styled by Niebuhr "a dry and meagre skeleton of history," are valuable in giving some stability to facts adorned by poetry and commemorated in the songs of an ancient people. These brief chronicles were written by the pontiff upon a whited table, and set up in his house : they bore the events of the year, such as prodigies, pestilences, famines, campaigns, triumphs, and the obituaries of illustrious men.

THE FIRST BAIL IN ROME.

The first instance in which Bail was offered and accepted in the annals of the Republic was in the case of Cæso, the son of Cincinnatus, accused of having murdered the brother of Volicius in a drunken frolic ; when Cæso, considering himself prejudged, fled into Etruria, and thus *forfeited his recognisances.*

HOW THE CAPITOL WAS SAVED BY THE CACKLING OF GEESE.

In A.U.C. 345, the Gauls, under Brennus, had scaled the Capitol, without even arousing the sentinels or the watch-dogs, when the sacred geese kept in the court of the temple in honour of Juno heard the approach of the enemy, and commenced a noisy cackling. The patrician Manlius, struck with the clamour, roused his fellow-soldiers, when the Gauls were slain or driven back, and the besieged delivered from their perilous position. Thenceforth Roman geese were fattened, but never eaten; a privilege not extended to those of other countries. In Italy, even at this remote period, a goose is never brought to table. In Rome, a golden image of a goose was made to commemorate their vigilance; and upon a certain day in every year one was placed in a sumptuous litter, and carried in state about the city; while a dog was impaled upon an elder-stake to denote the national contempt for that animal.*

THE HORATII AND CURATII.

In the war between Rome and Alba, it was agreed by the two states that the question of national superiority should be decided by a contest between three Roman and three Alban champions—the three Horatii and the three Curatii, the offspring of two single births. Before the commencement of the combat, the champions affectionately embraced each other. They fought valiantly, and two of the Horatii fell beneath the swords of the Curatii; the surviving Horatius then fled; but when pursued by the Curatii, he successively killed them all. Although Livy relates this legend upon the authority of an attested document, which was extant in his time, Niebuhr supposes these three champions really represent the three tribes into which the people of Rome and Alba were divided; a far more probable conclusion than that the rival cities each possessed three individuals so distinguished.

SPORTS OF THE ROMAN CIRCUS.

The earliest exhibition of wild beasts was U.C. 502, when one hundred and forty elephants, taken in Sicily, were produced; and Pliny relates, that these animals had been seen in Rome twenty-three years before, in the triumph of M. D. Den-

* Professor Owen relates the following interesting confirmation of this tradition: "Opposite the cottage where I live is a pond, which is frequented during the summer by two brood-flocks of geese belonging to the keepers. These geese take up their quarters for the night along the margin of the pond, into which they are ready to plunge at a moment's notice. Several times, when I have been up late, or wakeful, I have heard the old gander sound the alarm, which is immediately taken up, and has been sometimes followed by a simultaneous plunge of the flocks into the pool. On mentioning this to the keeper, he, quite aware of the characteristic readiness of the geese to sound an alarm in the night, attributed it to the visit of a foumart, or other predatory vermin. On other occasions, the cackling has seemed to be caused by a deer stalking near the flock. But often has the old Roman anecdote occurred to me when I have been awoke by the midnight alarm-notes of my anserine neighbours, and more than once I have noticed, when the cause of alarm has been such as to excite the dogs of the next-door keeper, that the geese were beforehand in giving loud warning of the strange steps. I have never had the smallest sympathy with the sceptics as to Livy's statement; it is not a likely one to be feigned; it is in exact accordance with the characteristic acuteness of sight and hearing, watchfulness and power, and instinct to utter alarm-cries, of the goose."—*Notes and Queries.*

tatus over Pyrrhus. Pliny also states, that lions first appeared in any number v.o. 652; but these, probably, were not turned loose. In 661, Sylla, the prætor, brought 100 lions. In 696, besides lions, elephants, bears, &c., 150 panthers were shown for the first time. When Pompey dedicated his theatre, v.c. 704, 17 elephants and 600 lions were killed in the course of five days, besides 400 panthers, &c. A rhinoceros also appeared for the first time; and a strange animal called *chaus* or *cepos*, and a *lupus cervarius* from Gaul. Marc Antony had some of these beasts yoked to his carriage. Cæsar, in his third dictatorship, v.c. 708, showed, among a vast number of animals, 400 lions and a camelopard, which, Pliny tells us, the Ethiopians call *nabis*: in the neck it resembles a horse, in the feet and legs an ox, a camel in the head, and in colour it is red with white spots. A tiger was exhibited for the first time at the dedication of the theatre of Marcellus, v.c. 743: it was kept in a cage. Claudius afterwards showed four together.

Titus exhibited 5000 beasts in one day; Adrian had 1000 slaughtered on his birthday; and Commodus killed several thousands with his own hand. The emperor Gordian, besides showing 100 African beasts and 1000 bears in one day, had a temporary wood planted in the circus, and turned into it 200 stags, 30 wild horses, 100 wild sheep, 10 elks, 100 Cyprian bulls, 300 ostriches, 30 wild asses, 150 wild boars, 200 ibises, and 200 deer; when the people were allowed to enter the wood and take what they pleased. Probus imitated this wood, and turned into it 1000 ostriches, 1000 stags, 1000 bears, 1000 deer, 1000 ibises, besides wild sheep, &c. Pliny mentions a boa-constrictor; and tells us that Claudius had one killed in the Vatican Circus, in the inside of which a child was found entire! Suetonius mentions a boa 50 cubits in length, which was exhibited in the Forum. In these displays the beasts were made to fight, either with one another or with men, who occasionally fought without any weapons. The animals were excited by applying fire, or by lashing them with whips. The elephants were intoxicated with incense and wine, the latter not the juice of the grape, but a liquor made from rice and reeds. Cloths were used to irritate the lions and bears; and wild boars had a strong aversion to white cloths.

There were other sanguinary spectacles, in which gladiators either contended in single combat or large bodies of horse and foot. Cassiodorus chronicles that the athletic games were first exhibited in the year of Rome 567; and Livy tells the same thing. The emperor Gordian had sometimes 500 pairs of gladiators exhibited in one day. In Cæsar's games we find 500 foot and 300 horse engaged together, with 20 elephants. Nero was not satisfied with having slaves as gladiators,—he

made 30 knights destroy each other in that capacity; another
of his battles was between 400 senators and 600 knights.

Naval engagements (*naumachiæ*) were sometimes exhibited
in the Circus Maximus, which could easily be filled with water.
Cæsar had a lake dug, in which biremes, triremes, and quad-
riremes, represented the Tyrian and Egyptian fleets, engaged
with a vast number of men on board. Elagabalus upon one
occasion filled the Euripus with wine, and had naval exhibi-
tions performed in it.

These descriptions would be applicable to the Roman people
at any period, from the age of Julius Cæsar to the time in
which they were written. When the amusements of the circus
ceased it would not be easy exactly to define. The combats
of men and beasts seem to have lasted till Justinian's days. It
is certain that such sanguinary spectacles existed to the time
of Theodoric, about A.D. 500; for we have in Cassiodorus a
letter to the above king, in which he reprobates the custom
extremely.

CÆSAR PASSING THE RUBICON.

On the ever-memorable night when Julius Cæsar resolved
to take the first step (and in such a case the first step, as regarded
the power of retreating, was also the final step), which placed
him in arms against the state, it happened that his head-quar-
ters were at some distance from the little river Rubicon, the
boundary between Italia and Gallia Cisalpina, and consequently
the limit of Cæsar's military command. With his usual caution, that no news of his motion might run before himself, on
this night Cæsar gave to his friends an entertainment, in the
middle of which he slipped away unobserved, and with a small
retinue proceeded through the woods to the point of the river
at which he designed to cross. The night was stormy, the
torches of his escort were blown out by the wind; so that the
whole party lost their way, and wandered about until early
dawn enabled them to recover their true course. The light
was still gray and uncertain, as Cæsar and his retinue rode
down upon the banks of the fatal river—to cross which, with
arms in his hands, since the further bank lay within the territory of the Republic, *ipso facto* proclaimed any Roman a rebel
and a traitor. We may suppose Cæsar to have been deeply
agitated when looking down upon this little brook; for the
whole course of future history, and the fate of every nation,
would necessarily be determined by the irretrievable act of the
next half-hour. Cæsar was yet lingering on the hither bank,
when, says the story, suddenly, at a point not far distant from
himself, an apparition was descried in a sitting posture, and
holding in its hand what seemed a flute. What is singular in

the story, on any hypothesis which could explain it out of
Cæsar's individual condition of exhaustion and intense anxiety,
is, that others saw the phantom as well as he, both pastoral
labourers and some of the sentinels stationed at the passage of
the river. These men fancied even that a strain of music issued from the aerial flute. A few Roman trumpeters advanced ;
and from one of them the phantom suddenly caught a trumpet,
and blowing through it a blast of superhuman strength, plunged
into the Rubicon, passed to the other bank, and disappeared
in the dusky twilight of the dawn. Upon which Cæsar exclaimed : "It is finished : the die is cast ; let us follow whither
the guiding portents from heaven and the malice of our enemy
alike summon us to go." So saying, he crossed the river with
impetuosity ; and in a sudden rapture of passion and vindictive
ambition, placed himself and his retinue upon the Italian soil ;
and, as if by inspiration from heaven, in one moment involved
himself and his followers in treason, raised the standard of revolt, put his foot upon the neck of the invincible Republic
which had humbled all the kings of the earth, and founded an
empire which was to last a thousand and half a thousand years.
In what manner this spectral appearance was managed, whether Cæsar were its author or its dupe, will remain unknown
for ever.—Abridged from a paper in *Blackwood's Edinburgh
Magazine*, 1832.

The Rubicon is considered by Cluverius and D'Anville to
be the Fiumecino of Italy, and their opinion is supported by
the inhabitants of Rimini, in whose territory it is ; the point
being a ford on the road from Ravenna. The celebrity of the
event has passed into a proverb : hence, to *pass the Rubicon* is
to take a desperate step in an enterprise, or to adopt a measure from which one cannot recede, or from which he is determined not to recede.

CÆSAR'S TRIUMPHS.

Julius Cæsar is said to have fought fifty battles, and to
have killed of the Gauls alone, 1,192,000 men, and as many
more in his civil wars. In the inscription which Pompey
placed in the Temple of Minerva, he professed that he had
slain, or vanquished and taken, 2,183,000 men.

POMPEY'S MISTAKES.

Sir Thomas Browne oddly asks whether Pompey committed
not two great oversights in the war against Julius Cæsar : the
one in not returning out of Greece with his army into Italy,
while Cæsar was gone into Spain ; the other in deferring battle,
and not setting upon Cæsar when he was so distressed for
victuals.

CÆSAR AND THE BIRD OF OMEN.

On the night before Cæsar was assassinated, he dreamt at intervals that he was soaring above the clouds on wings, and that he placed his hand within the right hand of Jove. It would seem that, perhaps, some obscure and half-formed image floated in his mind, of the eagle as the king of birds; secondly, as the tutelary emblem, under which his conquering legions had so often obeyed his voice; and thirdly, as the bird of Jove. To this triple relation of the bird, his dream covertly appears to point. And a singular coincidence is traced between this dream and an anecdote brought down to us, as having actually occurred in Rome about twenty-four hours before Cæsar's death. A little bird, which by some is represented as a very small kind of sparrow, but which, both to the Greeks and the Romans, was known by a name implying a regal station (probably from the ambitious courage which at times prompted it to attack the eagle), was observed to direct its flight towards the senate-house, consecrated by Pompey, whilst a crowd of other birds were seen to hang upon its flight in close pursuit. What might be the object of the chase, whether the little king himself, or a sprig of laurel which he bore in his mouth, could not be determined. The whole train, pursuers and pursued, continued their flight towards Pompey's hall. Flight and pursuit were there alike arrested; the little king was overtaken by his enemies, who fell upon him as so many conspirators, and tore him limb from limb.—From a paper in *Blackwood's Edinburgh Magazine*, 1832.

DRUTUS AND HIS MOTHER.

When the Tarquinii consulted the Delphian oracle, the reply was: "Young men, whichever of you shall first kiss your mother, he shall possess the sovereign power at Rome." Brutus, who was present, fell to the ground, as if accidentally, and touched with his lips his mother *earth*.

CALIGULA AND HIS HORSE.

Caius Cæsar, the fourth of the Roman emperors, was named *Caligula* from *caliga*, a kind of shoe, which was worn by the common soldiers, and which he frequently wore himself, in order to gain their affections. He had a favourite horse, *Irritatus*, whom he had fed upon gilt oats from an ivory manger in a marble stable, and his drink was delicious wines; he is even said to have appointed the horse consul, and to have assigned him a house and establishment that he might entertain company.

THE ROMAN FORUM.

Of all the localities of Rome, the most celebrated in history, as well as the most superb in architectural decoration, was the district called the *Roman Forum*. It bore that name from its comprising within its precincts the far-famed Forum Romanum, now a desolate field of ruins called by the undignified name of Campo Vaccino, *Anglicè* Bullock Field. Here stood the Temple of Concord, which so often resounded with the eloquence of Cicero, Cæsar, and others of the great " conscript fathers," during the deliberations of the senate. In this region also the great Temple of Jupiter reared its lofty marble elevation upon the Capitol ; and around, or adjoining the Forum, were the Temple of Saturn, the Temple of Castor and Pollux, the Temple of Janus, the Temple of Fortune, the Temple of Jupiter Tonans, the Tabularium (in which were deposited the bronze tablets on which were engraved the decrees of the senate and other public acts), the Arch of Tiberius, the Temple of Vespasian, the Arch of Septimus Severus, the Curia Julia (where the senate usually assembled), the Arch of Titus, the Græcostasis, the Temple of Vesta, the Julian Basilica, the Temple of Antoninus and Faustina, &c.

NERO'S GOLDEN HOUSE.

On that part of the site of the ruined city of Rome lying between the Palatine and the Esquiline Hills—a space more than a mile in breadth—Nero erected his celebrated " Golden House," the vastness and varied magnificence of which, and its ornamental grounds, are too well authenticated to admit of doubt. Within its enclosure were spacious fields, groves, orchards, and vineyards, artificial lakes, hills, and dense woods, after the manner of a solitude or wilderness. The palace itself was raised on the shores of the lake : the various wings were united by galleries, each a mile in length. The " house" or dwelling of the emperor was gorgeously decorated. It was tiled with gold (whence its name) ; with which precious metal also the marble sheathing of the walls was profusely decked, being at the same time embellished with ornaments of mother-of-pearl (which was in those times valued even more highly than gold), and with a profusion of precious stones. The ceilings and wood-work were inlaid with ivory and gold, and the roof of the grand banqueting-hall was made to resemble the firmament. It was contrived to have a rotatory motion, so as to imitate the supposed motion of the heavenly bodies ; and from it were showered perfumed waters. The vastness of the plan prevented the Golden House being finished during Nero's life ; it was completed by Otho, but was in part destroyed by Vespasian, who commenced on the site the celebrated Coliseum ; and a fire in Trajan's reign proved fatal to many of its majestic piles of building.—From a *Description of Rome*, by W. J. O'Llea.

FINAL OVERTHROW OF ROME.

Belisarius entered Rome in 536. During the following sixteen years, Rome was captured no less than four times successively : viz. by Totila the Goth, in 546 ; by Belisarius, in 547 ; by Totila again in 549 ; and finally by the Greek general the eunuch Narses, in the year 552. The various assaults, sieges, and efforts at defence, which mark this fatal era, filled up the measure of destruction, and completed the deformity of the wide-spread ruins which now occupied the site of the Imperial City. During those fearful sixteen years, upwards of 15,000,000 of human beings perished by the sword, famine, and pestilence ; the most fertile provinces were made desert ; the most flourishing cities laid in ruins ; and the entire order of things, which had grown up into a matured system under the power of old Rome and the civilisation of Paganism, was literally blotted out of existence, and the very memory of its grandeur became almost effaced from the minds of men ; whilst Christianity, unimpeded in its growth and progress amid the wreck of empires, expanded into fuller and more perfect development.—From a *Description of Rome*, by W. J. O'Hea.

THE ARCH OF TITUS, AT ROME,

erected by the senate and people, in honour of the emperor Titus, to commemorate the conquest of Jerusalem, as a record of Scripture history, is the most interesting ruin in Rome. To the Jews it is so deeply affecting, as a record of humiliating calamity, that it is said, no Jew will ever willingly pass under it. It is a single arch of Greek marble, with fluted composite columns, and sculptures of the triumph of Titus, the most important of which is a procession bearing the spoils taken from the temple of Jerusalem ; as the golden table, the silver trumpets, and the seven-branched massive gold candlestick, which fell into the Tiber from the Milvian bridge during the flight of Maxentius from the onslaught of Constantine ; the size of this candlestick appears to be nearly a man's height, corresponding in size and form with the description given by Josephus, who was an eyewitness of the triumph. The sculptures were executed from the objects themselves, which, although they were not the same sacred vessels made under the direction of Moses, had been made by persons well acquainted with their form, the general outlines of which may be traced in Exodus xxv. 3-36. These holy instruments and vessels having been formed 3346 years ago, bear undeniable evidence to the truth of the Mosaic history. On one of the keystones, also, is the figure of a Roman warrior, nearly entire.

THE COLUMN OF TRAJAN, AT ROME.

This, the most beautiful historic column in the world, was built by Apollodorus, A.D. 114. It consists of thirty-four pieces of white marble; the base and capital are Tuscan, the shaft is Doric, and the mouldings of the pedestal are Corinthian. The pedestal is covered with bas-reliefs of warlike instruments, helmets, and shields, and the inscription. A series of reliefs forms a spiral round the shaft, presents a continuous history of the military achievements of the Emperor Trajan, and is unrivalled as a record of costume. The bas-reliefs are two feet high in the lower part, and nearly four feet high at the top. They represent the successive events of the Dacian wars, including the passage of the Danube by a bridge of boats, the construction of fortresses, attacks on the enemy, the emperor addressing his troops, the reception of ambassadors who sue for peace, and other incidents of the campaign, as described in Rossi's *Colonna Trajana disequata.* The sculptures contain 2500 figures, besides horses, fortresses, &c. Within the column is a spiral staircase of 184 steps, leading to the summit, on which stood a colossal statue of Trajan, holding the gilded globe supposed to have contained his ashes. A bronze-gilt statue of St. Peter, eleven feet high, was placed upon the column by Sixtus V., about the end of the seventeenth century, when the feet of Trajan's statue are said to have been visible. The height of the column, exclusive of the statue, is 132 feet: it represents the height of that part of the Quirinal Hill which was cut away to make room for the Forum, as expressed in the inscription, which also states this monument to have been dedicated by the senate and Roman people, while Trajan held the tribunitian power for the seventeenth time; thus fixing the date about the period of the Parthian wars, from which the emperor did not live to return, so that he never saw the column.

THE WALLS OF ROME,

Including those of the Trastevere and the Vatican, are from fourteen to fifteen miles in extent. The line on the left bank of the Tiber, about fifteen miles, is substantially the same as that traced by Aurelian, A.D. 271;* but, after the lapse of fourteen centuries, not much of the original structure can be recognised in the present walls. We know that they were repaired by Honorius, Theodric, Belisarius, Narses, and by several popes. The left walls present an irregular polygonal outline; they are of brick, with occasional patches of stonework.

* The Latin settlement attributed to Romulus was situated on the Palatine Hill, the scene of the earlier settlement of Evander and his Arcadians, and was probably not more than a mile in circumference.

They have no ditch, but are erected with nearly three hundred towers; on the outside they are about fifty feet high, inside scarcely thirty; and they have sixteen gates, four walled up.

The Freuch, in 1849, directed the brunt of their attack upon the bastions to the left of the *Porta San Pancrazio*, on the Janiculum. In the struggle, the existence of a considerable portion of the Aurelian wall within the circuit of the bastioned line of the popes, gave the besieged great advantage in this struggle ; for as that ancient wall, built chiefly of tiles, is more than four yards in thickness, and from ten to twelve yards in height, and moreover is flanked with towers, it formed a real fortress within the outer wall, upon which the French had first to direct their fire.

THE CLOACA MAXIMA OF ROME.

This great common-sewer of ancient Rome,—a lasting memorial of the solidity of Etruscan architecture,—was built by Tarquinius Priscus, the fifth king of Rome, one hundred and fifty years before the foundation of the city, for draining the marshy ground between the Palatine and the Capitoline. Strabo says that a wagon laden with hay might have passed through the cloaca in some places ; and Dionysius describes it as one of the most striking evidences of the greatness of the Roman empire. Pliny was surprised that it had lasted eight hundred years, unaffected by earthquakes and the inundations of the Tiber. The exterior archway is composed of three concentric courses of immense blocks of peperiuo, put together, like all Etruscan works, without cement. The archway is twelve feet high where it enters the Tiber ; but the surface of the river rarely sinks more than four feet below the keystone. The interior of the channel is constructed of red volcanic tufa ; the length of the cloaca is three hundred paces. According to Abcken, the architect has provided for the cleansing of the channel, first, by a considerable fall ; secondly, by the oblique angle of 60°, at which it enters the Tiber ; and thirdly, by the gradual contraction of the diameter from 13·12 to 10·3 feet.

THE DROWNING OF TURNUS.

Between the hill of Marino and the ridge of Alba Longa, near Rome, is the deep and beautifully-wooded glen, in which Tarquinius Superbus compassed the death of Turnus Herdonius, the chieftain of Aricia. Livy relates that Tarquin had convened an assembly of chiefs at daybreak, but did not arrive himself till evening, when Turnus, having openly expressed his anger, quitted the meeting. Tarquin, to revenge himself, hired a slave to conceal arms in the tent of Turnus, and then accused him of a conspiracy to assassinate his colleagues. The arms were of course discovered; Turnus was thrown into the fountain "caput Aquæ Ferentiæ," where he was kept down by a grating and by large stones, until he was drowned. The description of Livy, if written to record an event of our own time, could not apply more accurately to the ground; even the depth of the pool of the fountain seems to have undergone no change; and it would be impossible to execute a sentence similar to that on Turnus without such a contrivance as his destroyers adopted.

"THE FEARLESS BATTLE."

This early and important victory was gained, B.C. 368, by the Spartan Archidamus over the Arcadians and Argeians, near Midea, when the latter fled with scarcely any resistance. The pursuit was vehement, and the slaughter frightful. Ten thousand men (if we are to believe Diodorus) were slain, without the loss of a single Lacedæmonian. On the news being transmitted to Sparta, so powerful was the emotion produced, that all the Spartans who heard it burst into tears; Agesilaus, the senators, and the Ephors setting the example. "A striking proof," says Mr. Grote, "how humbled, and disaccustomed to the idea of victory, their minds had recently become!—a striking proof, also, when we compare it with the inflexible self-control which marked their reception of the disastrous tidings from Leuktra, how much more irresistible is unexpected joy than unexpected grief, in working on these minds of iron temper!"—*Hist. Greece*, vol. x. p. 364.

TUSCULUM.

There are few spots upon the earth which have attained such historic celebrity as Tusculum, the city of ancient Latium, founded by Telegonus, the son of Ulysses and Circe. Its ruins may be traced upon the lip of the ancient crater of Monte Albano. Fortified by Pelasgic walls, Tusculum was so strong as to resist the attacks of Hannibal. It afterwards became more memorable as the scene of Cicero's "Tusculan Disputations," and as the birthplace of Cato. The city was entire at the close of the twelfth century, when it for some years gallantly struggled with Rome. In 1167 the Romans attacked Tusculum in the name of the Pope, when the Romans left two thousand dead upon the field. Next year the inhabitants surrendered to Pope Alexander III., and Tusculum became for many years his favourite residence. Here, in 1178, he received the ambassadors sent by Henry II. of England to assert his innocence of the death of Thomas à Becket. In 1191 the Romans put the inhabitants of Tusculum to the sword, and desolated the city; and upon its ruins arose Frascati. Among the

excavated Tusculan remains may be traced the granaries of
Cicero's villa, the theatre, and city walls and gates, the citadel,
and some fine examples of Pelasgic walls.   Between Frascati
and Rome is the Camaldoli monastery, where Cardinal Passionei
collected in his pleasant garden eight hundred inscriptions
found among the ruins of Tusculum : one of his frequent guests
in this retreat was the Pretender, James III. of England.

VIRGIL'S RURAL ECONOMY.

Few persons would think now-a-days of resorting to Virgil's *Georgics* for a practical system of rural economy.   Yet the
traveller in Italy finds pursued to this day the very methods of
agriculture, the very management of bees, the very culture of
the vine, the very arboriculture of Virgil, throughout the sunny
vales and vine-clad steeps of lovely Italy, irresistibly recall-
ing, at every step, the time-honoured phrases of the Mantuan
swan.

CAMILLUS AND WELLINGTON.

In their military renown and political career, Camillus, the
greatest commander of Rome, and Wellington, presented many
points of resemblance.   Both these illustrious men delivered
their country from impending danger, and both experienced
the ingratitude of their countrymen in the insults of lawless
mobs ; both were distinguished by great attachment to their
own order ; both lived over eighty years, of which sixty were
passed in the service of their country ; both lived to recover
their popularity, and were lamented by every order in the state,
receiving public funeral honours, and descending to the tomb
mourned by the tears of their countrymen.—See *Strickland's
Rome, Regal and Republican.*

EVERLASTING LAMPS OF THE ANCIENTS.

St. Augustine describes a lamp placed by the seashore,
which neither wind nor rain extinguished. In the sepulchre of
Tullia, the daughter of Cicero, was found a lamp, supposed by
Pancirollus and others to have burnt above 1550 years ! Now,
the flames in such cases are thought to have been caused by
the inflammable air so frequently generated in pits and caverns;
which is confirmed by a discovery in 1753, on the opening of
an ancient sepulchre at Naples.

THE CHANCES OF NAVAL FIGHTS.

In most naval fights, some notable advantage, error, or
unexpected occurrence, hath determined the victory.   The
great fleet of Xerxes was overthrown by the disadvantage of
a narrow place for battle. In the encounter of Duillius the
Roman with the Carthaginian fleet, a new invention of the

iron *corvi* (beaks) made a decision of the battle on the Roman
side. The unexpected falling off of the galleys of Cleopatra
lost the battle of Actium. In the fight between King Philip
and Attalus, the great excursion which Attalus made from his
squadron unto the loss of his galley, made the victory disput-
able ; though Philip suffered so great a loss and destruction of
his men, that he had but two arguments left to pretend unto
the victory,—that he had kept his station, and taken the
galley of Attalus. Even in the battle of Lepanto, if Caracoza
had given unto the Turks orders not to narrow on account of
the number of the Christian galleys, they had, in all probability, declined the adventure of a battle; and, even when
they came to fight the unknown force, an advantage of the
eight Venetian gallenses gave the main stroke unto the victory.[*]

Upon the latter battle, Sir Thomas Browne demands:

How the patience of Don John is to be justified, who, having hidden
four hundred valiant men under the hatches for a reserve in extremity,
would be thrice repulsed after he had boarded the Turkish admiral,
before he called up the reserve !

And though it succeeded well upon a tired enemy, yet, whether it
was handsomely done, to cut off Ali Bapa, the admiral's head, and
fastening it on the top of a pole, to erect it in his own galley ?

ARTIFICE OF THE THONG IN FOUNDING CITIES.

Most ancient writers agree in following an old tradition,
that Carthage was founded about a hundred years before Rome,
by Dido or Eliasa, upon her arrival in Africa, after her flight
from Tyre; when the wily queen purchased as much land of
the natives of the former place as she could cover, or rather
enclose, with an ox's hide; and thereupon cut the hide into
thongs, and thus included a much larger space than the sellers
expected. Now, the place which afterwards became the citadel of Carthage was called Betzura, or Bosra, *i.e.* the castle;
a name which the Greeks altered into Byrsa, a hide, from the
shape of the peninsula resembling an ox-hide. This tale,
which is either related or alluded to by Appian and Dionysius
the geographer amongst the Greeks, and by Justin, Virgil,
Silius Italicus, and others of the Latins, has been applied by
later writers. Thus, Sigebert, monk of Gemblours, in 1100,
relates that Hengist, the first Saxon king of Kent, purchased
of the British king, and enclosed, a site called *Castellum Cor-
rigiæ*, or the *Castle of the Thong ;* but there being several
more edifices named *Thong*, or *Tong*, in England, as in
Kent, Lincolnshire, Shropshire, and Yorkshire (Doncaster being
written in Saxon *Thongceaster*), the story has been applied to

[*] Sir Thomas Browne : Ms. Sloan. 1827.

E

most, if not all of them. It is true that Sigebert knew nothing
of the Greek authors, but he was well acquainted with Justin
and Virgil, and Geoffrey of Monmouth, 1159, who has the
same story. Again, Saxo Grammaticus, in 1170, applied the
tale to Ivarus, who, by the thong artifice in respect of Hella,
got a footing in Britain. The like story has travelled to the
East Indies. " There is a tradition," says Hamilton, " that
the Portuguese circumvented the King of Guzerat, as Dido
did the Africans, when they gave her leave to build Carthage, by describing no more ground than could be circumscribed in an ox's hide, which having obtained, they cut a fine
thong of a great length," &c. Now, the Indians knew nothing
of the Greek or Latin authors, nor probably did the Portuguese,
who first made the settlement at Dio ; though it may have
been carried there as a tradition by missionaries from Europe.
—*Gentleman's Magazine,* 1771.

This legend seems to have gone round the world. Hassun Subah,
the chief of the Assassins, is said to have acquired in the same manner
the bill-fort of Allahamowt. The Persians maintain that the British
got Calcutta in the same way. An English tradition avers that it was
by a similar trick Hengist and Horsa got a settlement in the Isle of
Thanet ; and it is somewhere stated, that this was the mode by which
one of our colonies in America obtained their land of the Indians.—
Foreign Quarterly Review, No. 27.

THE STORY OF DIDO.

When the citadel Byrsa had grown up into the great city
of Carthage, Dido was soon solicited in marriage by several
princes of the native tribes, seconded by the clamours of her
own people ; but, determined to remain faithful to her first
husband, she escaped the conflict by putting an end to her
life. She pretended to acquiesce in the proposition of a second
marriage, requiring only delay sufficient to offer an expiatory
sacrifice to the manes of her first husband : a vast funeral
pile was erected, and many victims slain upon it, in the midst
of which Dido pierced her own bosom with a sword, and
perished in the flames. Such is the legend to which Virgil
has given a new colour by interweaving the adventures of
Æneas, and thus connecting the foundation legends of Carthage
and Rome, careless of his deviation from the received mythical
chronology. Dido was worshipped as a goddess at Carthage
until the destruction of the city ; and it has been imagined,
with some probability, that she is identical with Astarte, the
divine patroness under whose auspices the colony was originally
established, as Gades and Tarsus were founded under those of
Herakles,—the tale of the funeral pile and self-burning appearing in the religious ceremonies of other Cilician and Syrian
towns.—*Grote's History of Greece,* vol. iii.

" What relates historically to Carthage," says the eloquent Lamartine, " is more poetical than its poetry. The heavenly death and obsequies of St. Louis; blind Belisarius; Marius expiating amongst wild-beasts on the ruins of Carthage — a wild-beast himself — the crimes of Rome; the lamentable day in which, like a scorpion surrounded by flames, which pierces itself with its poisoned sting, Carthage, surrounded by Scipio and Massinissa, set fire itself to its edifice and its riches; the wife of Asdrubal shut up with her children in the temple of Jupiter, reproaching her husband with not having been able to die, and lighting herself the torch destined to consume her and her children, with all that remained of her country, leaving nothing to the Romans but its ashes! Cato of Utica, the two Scipios, Hannibal — all these great names still rise on the abandoned cape, like the columns yet standing of a fallen temple; and I prefer the naked promontory of Carthage, the melancholy cape of Sunium, the barren and infested shore of Pæstum, to place in them the scenes of time past, to the temples, the triumphal arches, the Coliseum, of expired Rome, trodden under foot in living Rome, with the indifference of habit and the profanation of oblivion."

CARTHAGE AND GREAT BRITAIN COMPARED.

Napoleon I. was wont to compare our countrymen to the Carthaginians; both being distinguished by their success in commerce, their command of the sea, and their numerous colonies. And for reasons which appeared satisfactory to his penetrating mind, he predicted that a similar fate, originating in similar causes, would at no distant period overtake his great rival.—*Dr. Russell's History of the Barbary States.*

The comparison is, however, imperfect; for, as Dr. Russell elsewhere remarks: " The reputation of the Carthaginians was not equal to that of their country, and the reproach of Punic faith (*Punica fides*) still adhered to their inconstant and subtle character."

HOW HANNIBAL EAT THROUGH THE ALPS WITH VINEGAR.

Hannibal not being able to march with his army over some rocks in his passage on the Alps made fires upon them; and when the stone was very hot poured a great quantity of vinegar upon it, by which it being softened and purified, the soldiers by that means were enabled to cut a way through it. See *Livy,* 1st book of the 3d decade; *Juvenal :*

> " Et montem rupit aceto."
>> *Cowley's Notes to Pindarique Odes.*

" That Hannibal ate or brake through the Alps with vinegar (says Sir Thomas Browne) may be too grossly taken, and the author of his life annexed unto Plutarch affirmeth only he used this artifice upon the tops of some of the highest mountains. For as it is vulgarly understood, that he cut a passage for his army through these mighty mountains, it may seem incredible not only in the greatness of the effect, but the quantity of the efficient, and such as behold them may think an ocean of vinegar too little for that effect."—*Vulgar Errors.*

Upon this Dr. Wren notes: "There needed not more than some few hogsheads of vinegar; for, having hewed down the woods of fir growing there, and with the huge piles thereof calcined the tops of some cliffs which stood in his ways, a small quantity of vinegar poured on the fired glowing rocks would make them cleave in sunder, as is manifest in calcined flints, which being often burned, and as often quencht in vinegar, will in fine turn into an impalpable powder, as is truly experimented, and is dayly manifest in the lime-kilns."

Dr. M'Keevor (*Annals of Philosophy*, N. S., vol. v.) discusses this question, and considers the expansive operation of the fire on the water, percolating through the fissures of the rocks, may have led to the detachment of large portions by explosions, just as masses are detached from cliffs by a similar physical cause; and icebergs, with summer-heat, break away. Or perhaps the only vinegar employed might be the pyroligneous acid produced by the combustion of the wood. But Mr. Brayley supposes Hannibal might have used vinegar to dissolve a particular mass of impeding limestone. Hannibal crossed the Alps by the Little or Great St. Bernard: it is much disputed which.

MARIUS ON THE RUINS OF CARTHAGE.

After Sulla had compelled Marius to quit Rome, he wandered through many parts of Italy, and escaped with the greatest difficulty to Africa; but he had no sooner landed at Carthage than Sextilius, the governor of the province, sent word to him, that unless he quitted Africa he should treat him as a public enemy. "Go and tell him," was the reply, "that you have seen the exile Marius sitting on the ruins of Carthage."

Marius received great marks of honour from Scipio: one evening when supping with him, Scipio was asked where they should find so great a general when he was gone, he is said to have replied, placing his hand upon the shoulder of Marius, "Here, perhaps."

CONFLICT OF REGULUS WITH THE GREAT SERPENT.

On the banks of the river Bagrada, not far from Carthage, Regulus, in his career of conquest, had the passage of his army opposed by an enormous serpent. Not a man dared cross the guarded stream, and the legions regarded their opponent with superstitious dread, considering it as an omen fatal to the success of the African expedition. Regulus, however, commanded his war-engines to be brought out against the monster, at which the ballistæ threw great stones, and crushed the creature, whose hard scales had been proof against the showers of darts hurled against them; thus leaving the passage of the Bagrada free to the Roman soldiers. Regulus sent the skin of this serpent to Rome, where it was preserved in a temple.

Pliny assures us that it measured one hundred and fifty feet, and was very bulky.*

SILVER SHIELD OF SCIPIO AFRICANUS.

In 1656, a fisherman found on the banks of the Rhone, in the neighbourhood of Avignon, a large plate or dish, thickly encrusted with hardened mud, which he at first thought to be iron, but which subsequently proved to be of pure silver, perfectly round, more than two feet in diameter, and weighing twenty pounds. This relic, which had been buried in the Rhone for more than two thousand years, was the votive shield presented to Scipio by the inhabitants of Carthago Nova, now the city of Carthagena, for his generosity and self-denial in delivering one of his captives—a beautiful virgin, betrothed to Allucius, a Spanish prince—to her lover. This act, so honourable to the Roman general, who was then in the prime vigour of manhood, is represented on the shield, which is engraved in the curious and valuable work of M. Spon.

THE BRAZEN BULL OF PHALARIS.

Phalaris, the despot of Agrigentum, was notorious for his exactions and cruelties towards his own subjects, and his Brazen Bull has passed into imperishable memory. This piece of mechanism was hollow, and sufficiently capacious to contain one or more victims enclosed in it, to perish in tortures when the metal was heated: the cries of these suffering prisoners passing for the roarings of the animal. The artist was named Perillus, and is said to have been the first person burnt in the bull by order of the despot.

The reality of this ingenious torture appears to be better authenticated than the nature of the story would lead us to presume; for it is not only noticed by Pindar, but even the actual instrument—the brazen bull itself—which had been taken away from Agrigentum as a trophy by the Carthaginians, was returned by the Romans, on the subjugation of Carthage, to its original domicile.

DAMON AND PYTHIAS.

The most celebrated instance of the friendship of these two Pythagoreans occurred in the reign of Dionysius the Younger, the tyrant of Sicily; whose courtiers contended that the boasted virtues of the Pythagoreans, their determined spirit, and firm-

* Dr. Shaw, the naturalist, conjectured this "serpent" to have been a crocodile, although the length is treble or four times the extent of any crocodile ever seen or heard of; while it has never been known in that river of Africa. Mr. Harrington calls "the affair of this enormous adder, and Regulus's proceedings in relation to it, *an absurd and incredible fact.*"—*Gent. Mag.* Sept. 1773.

ness in friendship, were mere illusions, which would vanish on the first appearance of danger or distress. To prove this assertion, they agreed to accuse Pythias (properly Phintias) of a conspiracy against the sovereign. He was summoned before the tyrant, accused, and condemned to die. Pythias replied, if it were so, he would only beg the favour of a few hours, that he might go home and settle the common concerns of his friend Damon and himself; in the mean time, Damon would be security for his appearance. Dionysius assented to this proposal; and when Damon surrendered himself, the courtiers all sneered, concluding that he was duped; but on the return of Pythias in the evening to release his bail, and submit to his sentence, they were quite astonished; and none more than the tyrant himself, who embraced the illustrious pair. and requested they would admit him to a share of their friendship.

THE SWORD OF DAMOCLES.

Damocles was a flatterer of the tyrant Dionysius, who, to show him how little was the value of grandeur in the midst of terror, caused a sword to be suspended by a horsehair over the parasite's head, as he sat amidst the enjoyments of the banquet. Hence, "the sword of Damocles" denotes imminent danger in fancied security. Sir Thomas Browne says: "There is no Damocles like unto self-opinion."

"THE EAR OF DIONYSIUS."

This traditional wonder is a remarkable excavation in a rock in the neighbourhood of Syracuse, which is said to have been employed in ministering to the tyranny of Dionysius. It is thus described by Capt. Smyth in his *Memoir descriptive of Sicily:*

"It is in the shape of a parabolic curve, ending in an elliptical arch, with sides parallel to its axis, perfectly smooth, and covered with a slight stalactitic incrustation that renders its repercussions amazingly sonorous. Although a considerable portion of it has been filled up, which I ascertained by excavation, it is still 64 foot high, from 17 to 35 in breadth, and 187 deep. It has an awful and gloomy appearance, which, with its singular shape, perhaps gave rise to the popular and amusing paradox, that *Dionysius had it constructed for the confinement of those whom he deemed inimical to his authority; and that from the little apartment above he could hear all the conversation among the captives.* . . . . He could not, however, have listened with satisfaction or advantage; for if two or more people are speaking together, it occasions only a confused clamour."

THE GREAT SIEGE OF SYRACUSE.

This memorable siege (212 B.C.) by the Carthaginian and Roman land and naval armaments lasted three years, principally through the successful resistance by means of the ma-

chince constructed by Archimedes; and the city was finally
taken by surprise, owing to the carelessness of the besieged
during the festival of Diana. Among the Syracusan defences
were catapults and ballistæ; arrows shot from the top of the
walls and through loop-holes; machines which threw masses
of stone or lead upon the Roman engines previously caught by
ropes; iron hands or hooks attached to chains, and thrown to
catch the prows of the vessels, which were then overturned by
the besieged; and to catch the assailants on the land side and
throw them to the ground. Archimedes is also said to have
set the enemy's ships on fire by burning-mirrors, by Diodorus;
but Galen, in the second century, states this to have been
done by some machine for throwing lighted materials: and
Montucla thinks the statement arose from the joining together
of two others, namely, that Archimedes wrote a treatise on
burning-mirrors, and that he did burn the Roman ships. Ri-
vault, in 1615, was informed by a very learned Greek, who
had translated from that language the lives of the Sicilian
martyrs, and that one of them, a lady named Lucia, was a descendant of Archimedes, and an ancestress of the Bourbons!

WHO WERE THE SYBARITES?

Of the Sybarites, a prosperous and powerful nation in the
Gulf of Tarentum, few statements have reached us, save of
their luxury, fantastic self-indulgence, and extravagant indol-
ence, for which they have become proverbial. Among gay
companies "Sybaritic tales" were the sayings and doings of
ancient Sybarites. Herodotus tells of one Smyndrides of Sybaris, "the most delicate and luxurious man ever known,"
who was said to have taken with him to Greece, on his marriage, 1000 domestic servants, fishermen, bird-catchers, and
cooks. Alkimenes, the Sybarite, dedicated, as a votive offering, in the temple of the Lakinian Hêrê, a splendid figured
garment, fifteen cubits in length; Dionysius of Syracuse plundered that temple, got possession of the garment, and is said
to have sold it to the Carthaginians for 120 talents. Five thousand horsemen, we are told, showily caparisoned, formed the
processional march in certain Sybaritic festivals. Aristotle
relates that the Sybaritic horses were taught to move to the
sound of the flute: and the garments of these wealthy citizens
were composed of the finest wool from Miletus in Ionia, with
which Sybaris carried on great traffic. The town was named
from the river on which it was built, and this from Sybaris, a
fountain in Achaia, which intoxicated the people who drank
of it.

Legendary and Fabulous.

ORIGIN OF THE CENTAURS.

"THUS," says Sir Thomas Browne, " began the conceit and opinion of the Centaurs; that is, in the mistake of the first beholders, as is declared by Servius. When some young Thessalians on horseback were beheld afar off, while their horses watered—that is, while their heads were depressed—they were conceived by the first spectators to be but one animal; and answerable hereunto have their pictures been drawn ever since."

A similar mistake is recorded by Herrera, the Spanish historian of America, to have been committed by the people of New Spain, when they first beheld the Spanish cavalry. They imagined the horse and his rider to be some monstrous animal of a terrible form; and supposing that their food was the same as that of men, brought flesh and bread to nourish them.

Ross, who in 1645 attacked both Sir Thomas Browne and Sir Kenelm Digby, strangely believed certain of the vulgar superstitions of his day. Thus, he says: " There is no doubt but Centaurs, as well as other monsters, are produced, partly by the influence of the stars, and partly by other causes," &c.

"CIMMERIAN GLOOM."

The name Cimmerian appears in the *Odyssey*—the fable describes them as dwelling beyond the ocean-stream, immersed in darkness, and unblest by the rays of Helios, or the sun. They belong partly to legend, partly to history; but they seem to have been the chief occupants of the Tauric Chersonesus (Crimea), and of the territory between that peninsula and the river Tyras (Dniester), at the time when the Greeks first commenced their permanent settlement on these coasts in the seventh century B.C.

THE AUGEAN STABLE.

Augeas, king of the Elians, is designated by Theocritus as the son of the god Helios. He was rich in all sorts of rural wealth, and through the god's favour his cattle prospered and multiplied with astonishing success. His herds were so numerous, that the dung of the animals accumulated in the stable or cattle-enclosures beyond all power of endurance. Eurystheus, as an insult to Hercules, imposed upon him the obligation of cleansing this stable; the hero, disdaining to carry off the dung upon his shoulders, turned the course of the river Alpheios through the building, and swept the encumbrance away. Hence the phrase, to cleanse the Augean stable—to clear away any monstrous abuse.

ARGUS AND HIS HUNDRED EYES.

Argus was one of the mythological heroes of Ovid, and was fabled to have a hundred eyes, of which two only slept in succession. On this account, Juno sent him to watch Io; when Mercury, by command of Jupiter, lulled Argus to sleep with the music of his flute, and then killed him. Juno then transferred Argus's eyes to the tail of the peacock.

PHILOMELA, THE NIGHTINGALE.

The beautiful Philomela, going to visit her sister Procne, the wife of Tereus, king of Thrace, Philomela fell a victim to his barbarous passion; when, the two sisters seeking to be revenged on Tereus, he snatched up a hatchet to put Procne to death: she fled along with Philomela, and all three were changed into birds—Procne became a swallow, Philomela a nightingale, and Tereus a hoopoe. This tale, so characteristic of legend, is alluded to by the Greek historian as an historical fact; and the hoopoe still chases the nightingale.

SINGING SWANS.

From the fabulous but universally received tradition of Swans singing most sweetly before their death (though the truth is, geese and they are alike melodious), the poets have assumed to themselves the title of swans. Horace was believed to be metamorphosed into one. Theocritus terms the poets the Birds of the Muses. Sweet-tongued Pindar was called the Heliconian Swan of Thebes; Virgil the Swan of Mantua; and Shakspeare the Swan of the Avon.

GYGES AND HIS RING.

Plato has preserved a legend of Gyges, according to which he was a mere herdman of the king of Lydia: after a terrible storm and earthquake, he saw near him a chasm in the earth, into which he descended, and found a vast horse of brass, hollow and partly open, wherein there lay a gigantic corpse with a golden ring. This ring he carried away, and discovered unexpectedly that it possessed the miraculous property of ren-

dering him invisible at pleasure.   Being sent on a message to
the king, he made the magic ring available to his ambition :
he first possessed himself of the person of the queen, then
with her aid assassinated the king, and finally seized the
sceptre.   Plato compares very suitably the Ring of Gyges to
the Helmet of Hades.—*Grote's History of Greece*, vol. iii.

RIGHT-HANDED AND LEFT-HANDED.

The Greeks had their superstitions, as directed by right
and left ; and the epithets right-handed man and left-handed
man grew necessarily out of these ominous opinions as common terms of eulogy and reproach.   Thus Aristophanes, in
The Wasps :

> " After much and deep reflection
>   I this last conclusion draw,
>   That for smart right-handed wisdom
>   None my equal ever saw ;
>   But your branded and left-handed
>   Folly I beg leave to pass,
>   That, and more, sirs, at the door, sirs,
>   Drop I of Amyni-Ass !"

CLASSIC CHARMS.

The word *abracadabra*, for fevers, is as old as Sammonicus.
Haut haut hista pista vista were recommended for a sprain by
Cato.   Homer relates, that the sons of Autolycus stopped the
bleeding of Ulysses' wound by a charm.

THE OWL A BIRD OF OMEN.

When Agathocles, the Syracusan, attacked the Carthaginians
with inferior numbers, he sought to encourage his troops by
letting fly in various parts of the camp a number of owls, which
perched upon the shields and helmets of the soldiers.   These
birds, the favourites of Athene, were supposed, and generally
asserted, to promise victory ; and the minds of the soldiers are
reported to have been much reassured by the sight.   The whole
of the Carthaginian army was defeated ; and among their baggage Agathocles found twenty thousand pairs of handcuffs,
which they had brought for fettering their expected captives.

PYTHAGORAS AND BEANS.

" Many errors crept in and perverted the doctrine of Pythagoras (says Sir Thomas Browne), whilst men received his pre-
cepts in a different sense from his intention, converting metaphors into proprieties, and receiving as literal expressions
obscure and involved truths.   Thus, when he enjoined his dis-
ciples an abstinence from beans, many conceived they were with

severity debarred the use of that pulse, which notwithstanding could not be his meaning; for, as Aristoxenus, who wrote his life, averreth, he delighted much in that kind of food himself. But herein, as Plutarch observeth, he had no other intention than to dissuade men from magistracy, or undertaking the public offices of state : for by beans was the magistrate elected in some parts of Greece; and after his days, we read in Thucydides of the Council of the Bean in Athens."—*Vulgar Errors.*

TRANSMIGRATION OF SOULS, AND SACREDNESS OF ANIMALS.

The Egyptians maintained that after death the soul, being immortal, transmigrated into bodies of all kinds of animals, whether birds, beasts, or fishes; and that after the space of three thousand years it again returned to the body which it left, provided that body was preserved from destruction during the long period of its absence. The Egyptians also held that the gods took refuge in the bodies of animals from the wickedness and violence of men; they therefore regarded such animals as sacred, and accordingly worshipped them as containing the divinities whom they revered. This led to the bestowing on them the honour of embalming, while it explains the reason why the mummies of so many animals are found to this day preserved in their catacombs. They placed particular gods in particular animals : thus, Apollo was in the hawk, Mercury in the ibis, Mars in the fish, Diana in the cat, Bacchus in the goat, Hercules in the colt, Vulcan in the ox, &c. These animals, with many others, or parts of them, are accordingly found embalmed with the bodies of the human race in the Egyptian tombs. The animals were not all worshiped during the early history of this people; but one by one was added from time to time, as they became more corrupt.

THE PYTHAGOREAN METEMPSYCHOSIS.

That Pythagoras believed in the metempsychosis, or transmigration of the souls of deceased men into other men, as well as into animals, we know, not only by other evidence, but also by the testimony of his contemporary, the philosopher Xenophanes of Elea. Pythagoras, seeing a dog beaten, and hearing him howl, desired the striker to desist, saying : " It is the soul of a friend of mine, whom I recognised by his voice." Mr. Grote well remarks of this instance : " The particular animal selected is that one between whom and man the sympathy is most marked and reciprocal; while the doctrine is made to enforce a practical lesson against cruelty." The originality of this doctrine is questioned by Herodotus, who intimates that both Orpheus and Pythagoras had derived the doctrine of the metempsychosis from Egypt, but had pretended to it as their own, without acknowledgment.

Pythagoras, according to Heraclides, used to say of himself, that he remembered not only what men, but what plants and what animals, his soul had passed through. And Empedokles declared of himself, that he had been first a boy, then a girl, then a plant, then a bird, then a fish.

PYTHAGOREAN ABSTINENCE.

Pythagoras is also said to have inculcated abstinence from animal food; and this feeling is so naturally connected with the doctrine of the metempsychosis, that we may well believe him to have entertained it, as Empedokles also did after him, as well as the prohibition of eating animal food. Empedokles supposed that plants had souls, and that the souls of human beings passed after death into plants as well as animals. " I have been myself heretofore (said he) a boy, a girl, a shrub, a bird, and a fish of the sea." Pythagoras is said to have affirmed that he had been not only Euphorbus in the Grecian army before Troy, but also a tradesman, and various other human characters, before his actual existence. He did not, however, extend the same intercommunion to plants.

THE TEMPLE OF APOLLO AT DELPHI.

This temple, even if we calculate value as of the present time, was enormously rich. King Crœsus presented one hundred and seventeen blocks of gold, in thickness the breadth of a hand, six times as long, and thrice as broad, each of which weighed two talents; a golden lion of ten talents; a large golden tripod upon which the Pythia sat, with the golden statue of Apollo. Beyond this were cups of gold, each eight talents in weight; and a cup of silver, containing six hundred amphoræ, in which the wine was mixed at the feast of the Theophaniæ. In spite of the various plunderings, in the time of Pliny more than three thousand statues remained. But all is now destroyed; it has disappeared; and on the holy territory of Apollo is a small village of frail tenements.—*Dr. Fiedler.*

THE PYTHON.

The *Pethen* occurs at Ps. lviii. 4, xci. 13; Deut. xxxii. 33; Job xx. 14, 16; and Is. xi. 8. This is supposed to be the asp of ancient writers; and there is considerable authority for believing that the *coluber haje* of Linnæus is the animal here intended. It is extremely poisonous, and was the animal with which the jugglers of Egypt had so much to do. It was from the arts practised upon this animal that those who were sup-

posed to be possessed with a spirit of divination were styled
πυθῶνες (pythones). All the great serpents of Africa and India
belong to this tribe, called the " pythons ;" and it is the opinion of Cuvier that there is not any large boa, properly so
styled, belonging to the eastern world.

Again, the Python was, in mythology, the huge serpent
which is said to have sprung from the mud and stagnant
waters after the Deluge. It was killed by Apollo, who appointed the Pythian games to commemorate his victory. Pythia, the priestess of Apollo at Delphi, was sometimes killed by
the mephitic vapours to which she was subjected when receiving the influence of the god,—probably carbonic acid gas.
Again, the ship belonging to the Carthaginians or Sicilians,
which the Romans burnt in an engagement near the coast of
Sicily, was named the Python, probably from its vast size ; just
as we apply the term " leviathan" to our vast steam-ships.

Harris says, in the Egyptian language the serpent was
called " oub," and was the same in the Chaldee dialect : hence
the word ὄφις. Thus we read, Lev. xx. 27, a man or a woman
that hath a familiar spirit, " oboth," &c. See also xx. 6 ; 2
Kings xxi. 6, xxiii. 24 ; and 2 Chron. xxxiii. 6. The woman
of Endor, who had a familiar spirit, is called a mistress of Ob,
and it is interpreted "Pythonissa." Kircher says that " obion"
is still, among the people of Egypt, the name of a serpent.

THE LABYRINTH OF CRETE

was formed by Dœdalus to secure the Minotaur, about 1210 B.C.
Captain Rochfort Scott, who examined this reputed marvel of
antiquity in 1837, thought it to be one of the natural caverns
common in the island, and which may have served in early
ages as a place of refuge. It is, however, doubted whether
this is the famed labyrinth from which Theseus was delivered
by the contrivance of the love-stricken Ariadne ; the locality
ill agrees with the ancient account of the Minotaur's abode ;
for veracious Greek authors state that it opened on the sea-
shore, whereas the above cavern is six miles from the coast.

"THE CAVE OF TROPHONIUS."

Trophonius, believed by Pausanias and others to have been
the son of Apollo, was worshipped as a god at various places ;
in his temple at Lebadeia the prophetic manifestations out-
lasted those of the Delphi itself. The mention of the honeyed
cakes, both in Aristophanes and Pausanias, indicates that the
ceremonies for those who consulted the oracle of Trophonius
remained the same after a lapse of five hundred and fifty years.
Pausanias consulted it himself.

Trophonius and Agamedes were the architects of the temple

of Delphi ; they built also the thalamus of Amphitryon at Thebes, as well as the inaccessible vault of Ilyricus at Ilyria, in which they are said to have left one stone removable at pleasure, so as to reserve for themselves a secret entrance. They entered so frequently, and stole so much gold and silver, that Ilyricus, astonished at his losses, spread a fine net, in which Agamedes was inextricably caught ; Trophonius cut off his brother's head and carried it away, so that the body, which alone remained, was insufficient to identify the thief. Trophonius was swallowed up by the earth near Lebadeia.— Abridged from *Grote's Hist. Greece*, vol. i.

THE TOWER OF OBLIVION.

Procopius mentions with this name a tower of imprisonment among the Persians : whoever was put therein was as it were buried alive, and it was death for any but to name him. Sir Thomas Browne says beautifully : "Draw the curtain of night upon injuries, shut them up in *the tower of oblivion*, and let them be as though they had not been."

"CABALA WITH THE STARS."

In the jargon of astrologers the above term means "possessed of the key to their secrets ;" *cabala*, a Hebrew word, signifying tradition ; applied originally to the secret science of the rabbinical doctors, and thence to designate any secret science.

A PREDICTION FATALLY VERIFIED.

A curious tale is told in the *Chronicon Nonantulanum*, by Michael Scot, "Astrologus Friderici Imperialis familiaris." Having foreseen that he should meet his death from the fall of a stone of two ounces weight upon his head, he contrived a cap of plate-iron. Being at mass one day, at the exaltation of the host he reverently lifted his cap, when a little stone fell upon his head and inflicted a slight wound. On weighing the stone, he found it to be exactly two ounces ; and then, knowing his doom to be sealed, he arranged his worldly affairs, and died.

THE STORY OF ADONIS.

The inhabitants of Aleppo are said to retain some traces of the solemnities observed in honour of Adonis. Many have conjectured that the name of Adonis, and the rites practised, first in lamenting the loss, and then in rejoicing for the recovery of him, are merely symbolical emblems, either of the sun's course or of the manner in which the fruits of the earth are first buried, and then shoot forth again. But it is more probable that this object of worship among the Assyrians, Egyptians, and Phœnicians, whether he be called Adonis, Osiris, or Bacchus, was some real personage, whose introduction of luxurious improvements among uncivilised people procured him a superstitious regard when living, and an annual commemoration after his decease, though the real cause of his death be veiled in fable:

> " Thammuz next came behind,
> Whose annual wound in Lebanon allur'd
> The Syrian damsels to lament his fate
> In amorous ditties all a summer's day ;
> While smooth Adonis from his native rock
> Ran purple to the sea, suppos'd with blood
> Of Thammus yearly wounded," &c.
>
> *Paradise.Lost,* b. i. 446.

Newton has illustrated this passage by the account which Maundrel gives of the bloody colour that appears annually in the river anciently named Adonis, now called Ibraham Basar.

" ADONIS'S GARDENS."

The *Adonis horti* were portable earthen-pots, with lettuce or fennel growing in them. On his yearly festival, every woman carried one of them in honour of Adonis, because Venus had once laid him on a lettuce-bed. The next day they were thrown away. The term seems to have been mostly used in a bad sense,— for things which make a fair show for a few days, and then wither away; but in *King Henry VI.*, part i., it is applied as an encomium :

> " Thy promises are like Adonis' gardens,
> That one day bloom'd, and fruitful were the next."

There is an account of it in Erasmus's *Adagia ;* but Shakspeare may have taken it from the *Faerie Queene,* book iii.

THE FATE OF NIOBE.

Niobe, the intimate friend of Leto, the mother of Apollo and Artemis, was presumptuous enough to place herself on a footing of higher dignity on account of the superior number of her children, seven sons and seven daughters, all of whom, except one daughter, were killed by Apollo and Artemis in avenging the insult. Niobe, thus left disconsolate, wept herself to death, and was ' turned into a rock ; which the later Greeks continued always to identify with Mount Sipylus.

In the Uffizi Gallery at Florence is the Hall of Niobe, containing the fine figures of Niobe and her children, discovered at Rome before 1583, and shown to have been originally arranged in the tympanum of a temple. They are supposed to be the identical statues by Scopas, which Pliny describes.

THE SLEEP OF ENDYMION.

Of Endymion, who led a colony from Thessaly to Elis, several wonderful things are related. Zeus granted him the privilege of determining the hour of his own death, and even translated him into heaven, which he forfeited by paying court to Here, and was then cast out into the under-world. According to other stories, his great beauty caused the goddess Selene (Luna) to become enamoured of him, and to visit him by night during his sleep on Mount Latmos : hence " the sleep of Endymion" became a proverbial expression for enviable, undisturbed, and deathless repose. This has been a favourite subject with the poets :

> "And while there is a people, or a sun,
> Endymion's story with the moon shall run."—*H. Vaughan.*

It is also the earliest and most considerable of the poems of John Keats.

Pliny accounts for the fiction from Endymion being the first who explained the phases of the moon, and by his studying astronomy on Latmos. From Selene the study of the moon is named *Selenography.*

ÆSCULAPIUS.

This memorable god, or hero, the son of Coronis by Apollo, was brought up by the centaur Cheiron, the leech, from whom and from his own inborn and superhuman aptitude, he became acquainted with the virtues of herbs, and gained a mastery of medicine and surgery such as had never before been witnessed. He not only cured the sick, the wounded, and the dying, but even restored the dead to life ; Hippolytus, Tyndareus, Glaucus, and others, were all affirmed by poets and logographers to have been endued by him with a new life. Pindar says that Æsculapius, or Asklepius, was " tempted by gold" to raise a man from the dead ; and Plato copies him. But Zeus, lest mankind, thus protected against sickness and death, should no longer stand in need of the immortal gods, smote Æsculapius with thunder, and killed him. He was worshipped with great solemnity at Trikka, at Cos, at Cnidus, and at Epidaurus. He left two sons, who were the leeches of the Grecian army at the siege of Troy. Among the many practitioners of medicine, called Asklepiads, were the great Hippocrates and the historian Ctesias. To the temple of Æsculapius came sick persons to be healed, to sacrifice and pray, and to sleep therein, to be favoured with healing suggestions in their dreams ; and in the temple and grounds were hung up tablets to record the maladies of the sick visitors, the remedies, and the cures by the god.

EXPLOITS OF PERSEUS.

These deeds are among the most marvellous and imagina

tive in all Grecian legend : "they bear," says Grote, "a stamp
almost Oriental." Perseus's conquest of the three Gorgons
ended in his bringing back from Libya the terrific head of
Medusa, the only one of the Gorgons who was not immortal.
By the aid of Pluto's invisible helmet, Minerva's buckler, and
Mercury's wings and talaria, and a short dagger made of diamonds, called harpe, he deprived Medusa of life, and carried
off her head in triumph. It was endued with the property of
turning every one who looked upon it into stone. In his return,
he rescued Andromeda, daughter of Cepheus, who had been exposed to be devoured by a sea-monster; but he made her his
wife. At a gymnastic contest, where his grandfather, Acrision,
was among the spectators, by an incautious swing of his quoit,
Perseus struck him, and caused his death, as the oracle had
predicted. Perseus subsequently founded the far-famed city
of Mycenæ, the massive walls of which, like those of Tiryns, of
which Pausanias saw the remains, were built for him by the
Lycian Cyclopes.

THE SIBYLLINE BOOKS.

The Sibylline Prophecies were originally of Teukrian or
early Trojan descent; and the most celebrated of the Sibyls,
or priestesses, plays an important part in the tale of Æneas;
thence she passed to Cumæ in Italy. Her prophecies were
supposed to be heard in dark caverns and apertures in rocks.*
They are thought by Varro to have been written in Greek
hexameters upon palm-leaves, partly in verses, partly in hiero-
glyphs (*Niebuhr*). They were in full circulation in the reign
of Crœsus; and the promises of future empire which they made
to Æneas escaping from the flames of Troy into Italy, were remarkably realised by Rome. Lactantius derives its name Si-
bylla from the Æolic, *sios*, god, and *bule*, counsel. Of the
nine books offered by a Sibyl for sale to Tarquinius Superbus,
six were burnt; when Tarquinius purchased the remaining three
for the price originally demanded for the nine. They were kept
in a stone-chest underground in the temple of Jupiter Capi-
tolinus, in the custody of certain officers, who only consulted
the books at the special command of the senate; and this not
to learn future events, but what worship was required by the
gods when they had manifested their wrath by national calami-
ties or prodigies. When the temple was burnt in B.C. 82, the
Sibylline Books were also destroyed; but they were restored.

The Sibyl, from being believed to have foretold the Saviour's com-

* At Cumæ, in the hill of the Acropolis, in a cave with various apertures
and subterranean passages, in which local antiquaries recognise "the hundred
mouths" of Virgil's sixth Æneid; and within the cave the tunnel mentioned by
Strabo as leading from Cumæ to Avernus, thus shewing the lateness of the
tradition. Antiquaries are said to have identified in this locality two other caves
of the Sibyl mentioned by Virgil.

ing, was not rejected by several Christians. This superstition continued later than is commonly supposed. Bede records some of her prophetic verses; and some Sibylline books appear to have been consulted till the tenth century.—Note in Lord Mahon's *Life of Belisarius.*

THE ELEUSINIAN MYSTERIES.

These Mysteries were originally celebrated at Eleusis, in Attica, with solemn shows and great pomp of machinery, which drew a mighty concourse to them from all countries. The shows are supposed to have exhibited a representation of heaven, hell, elysium, purgatory, and all that related to the future state of the dead; and they are frequently alluded to by the ancient poets. Chillius, in his comments on the sixth book of the *Æneid*, observes, that Virgil, in describing the descent into hell, is but tracing out in their genuine order the several scenes of the Eleusinian shows.—See *Warburton's Divine Legation of Moses*, p. 182.

ORIGIN OF THE GOD HYMEN.

Danchet, the French poet, in his *Dissertation sur Cérémonies Nuptiales*, tells us that Hymen was a young man of Athens, obscurely born, but extremely handsome. Falling in love with a lady of rank, he disguised himself in female attire, the better to carry on his amour; and, as he was one day on the seashore celebrating the Eleusinian rites with his mistress and her female companions, a gang of pirates came upon them by surprise, and carried them off to a distant island, where the pirates got drunk for joy, and fell asleep. Hymen then armed the virgins, and despatched the sleeping pirates; when, leaving the two women upon the island, he sped to Athens, told his adventure, and demanded his beloved in marriage as her ransom. His request was granted; and so fortunate was the marriage, that the name of Hymen was ever after invoked on all future nuptials; and in progress of time the Greeks enrolled him among their gods.

"INCREDIBILIA" OF THE ANCIENTS.

Sir Thomas Browne shows from Palæphatus's book "concerning Incredible Tales"—

That the fable of Orpheus by his music making woods and trees to follow him, is founded upon a crew of mad women retired unto a mountain being pacified by his music, and caused to descend with boughs in their hands: whence the magic of Orpheus's harp, and its power to attract the senseless trees about it.

That Medea, the famous sorceress, could renew youth, and make old men young again; being nothing else but that from the knowledge of simples she had a receipt to make white hair black, and reduce old heads into the tincture of youth again.

The fable of Geryon and Cerberus with three heads was this: Geryon was of the city Tricarinia (Trinacria), that is, of three heads ; and Cerberus, of the same place, was one of his dogs, which, running into a cave in pursuit of his master's oxen, Hercules perforce drew him out of that place : from whence the conceits of those days affirmed no less than that Hercules descended into hell, and brought up Cerberus into the habitation of the living.

Upon the like grounds was raised the figment of Briareus, who, dwelling in a city called Hekatoncheira, the fancies of those times assigned him a hundred hands.

That Niobe weeping over her children was turned into a stone, was nothing else but that during her life she erected over their sepulchres a marble tomb of her own.

When Actæon had undone himself with dogs and the prodigal attendants of hunting, they made a solemn story of how he was devoured by his hounds. And upon the like grounds was raised the anthropophagie of Diomedes his horses.

Diodorus plainly delivereth that the famous fable of Charon had this nativity : who, being no other but the common ferryman of Egypt that wafted over the dead bodies from Memphis, was made by the Greeks to be the ferryman of hell, and solemn stories raised after of him.

The Centaurs were a body of young men from Thessaly, who first trained and mounted horses for repelling a herd of wild bulls belonging to Ixion, king of the Lapithæ. They pursued these wild bulls on horseback, and pierced them with their spears, thus acquiring both the name of prickers, and the imputed attribute of joint body with the horse. (See p. 56.)

The Dragon whom Cadmus killed at Thebes was in reality Draco, king of Thebes ; and the dragon's teeth which he is said to have sown, and from whence sprung a crop of armed men, were in point of fact elephants' teeth which Cadmus as a rich Phœnician had brought over with him. The sons of Draco sold these elephants' teeth, and employed the proceeds to levy troops against Cadmus.

Dædalus, instead of flying across the sea on wings, had escaped from Crete in a sailing-boat, under a violent storm. Kottus, Briareus, and Gyges, were not persons with one hundred hands, but inhabitants of the village of Hekatoncheira in Upper Macedonia, who warred with the inhabitants of Mount Olympus against the Titans. Scylla, whom Odysseus so narrowly escaped, was a fast-sailing piratical vessel ; as was also Pegasus, the alleged winged horse of Bellerophon.

Again, Gal and Westermann, like Palæphatus, interpret Scylla as a beautiful woman surrounded with abominable parasites. She ensnared and ruined the companions of Odysseus, though he himself was prudent enough to escape her. Atlas was a great astronomer. Pasiphae fell in love with a youth named Taurus. The monster called the Chimæra was in reality a ferocious queen, who had two brothers named Leo and Draco. The ram which carried Phryxus and Holle across the Ægean was a boatman named Krius.

Plutarch, however, in one of his treatises, accepts minotaurs, sphinxes, centaurs, &c. as realities ; and Dr. Delaney, in his *Life of David*, produces some ingenious arguments to prove that Orpheus was in reality the same person with David.

GIGANTOLOGY DISPROVED BY SCIENCE.

For many years, the bones of elephants, rhinoceroses, mastodons, whales, &c. were exhibited as those of prehistoric giants.

Very well known to fame is the Sicilian giant, whose skeleton was found at Trapani, in the fourteenth century, which was at once pronounced to be the skeleton of Polyphemus, the Cyclop, and his height was calculated to be three hundred feet ! But the believers forgot that only thirty feet was the height of the cave in which he was said to have been found seated, with the "mast of some high ammiral" for a walking-stick.

Still more celebrated was King Teutobochus, whose remains were discovered in Dauphiny, not far from the Rhone, in 1613. A surgeon named Mazurier conveyed them to Paris, declaring them to have been found in a tomb thirty feet long, inscribed "Teutobochus Rex." He was the Cimbrian warrior slain by Marius; and to prove their identity, fifty coins, bearing the effigy of Marius, were said to have been found inside the tomb; but no one ever saw these coins, and the imposture was exposed. The bones were those of a mastodon.

In a word, all the fossils hitherto discovered, and supposed to belong to giants, have on inspection been proved to belong to brutes. But men of seven and eight feet high are not so rare.

PROMETHEUS AND PROMETHEAN FIRE.

In the primitive legend, Prometheus is not the creator or moulder of man. The race is supposed as existing, and Prometheus, a member of the dispossessed body of Titan gods, bargains with Zeus on their behalf for the partition of the sacrificial animals. Zeus is outwitted; and in his wrath he withholds from mankind the inestimable comfort of fire; and the race would have perished had not Prometheus stolen fire, in defiance of the command of the supreme ruler, and brought it to man in the hollow of a ferule. But Zeus ultimately avenged himself by the creation of Pandora. As a punishment for daring "to compete in sagacity" with Zeus, Prometheus was bound by heavy chains to a pillar, where he remained fast imprisoned for several generations. Every day did an eagle prey upon his liver, and every night did the liver grow afresh for the next day's suffering; until Zeus permitted his favourite son to kill the eagle, and rescue the captive.

Upon this myth Æschylus founded his sublime tragedy of *The Enchained Prometheus*, and another tragedy now lost. The Greeks supposed the place where Prometheus was chained to be Mount Caucasus, and Pompey made a special visit to the spot. Pausanias was shown at Panopæus in Phocis some hardened lumps of clay, described as the remains of that which Prometheus had employed in moulding man.

THE DEUCALIONAL DELUGE.

The Grecian legend runs, that Deucalion having been fore-

warned of the general deluge by his father, Prometheus, saved
himself in a chest, or ark, in which he floated nine days, and
then landed on the summit of Mount Parnassus. He prayed
to Zeus for companions in his solitude: by direction of the
deity, Deucalion and his wife Pyrrha cast stones over their
heads; and those cast by Pyrrha became women, and those by
Deucalion, men. The Greek chronologers believed in this
deluge, and assigned to it the same date as the conflagration of
the world by the rashness of Phaeton. Aristotle places this
flood west of Mount Pindus, near Dodona and the river
Achelous; and he treats it as a physical phenomenon, the result
of periodical cycles in the atmosphere. The deluge was believed at a very late date. In the temple of the Olympian
Zeus at Athens (founded by Deucalion) was shown a cavity in
the earth, through which the waters had retired; and in the
time of Pausanias, at this cavity were periodically made holy
offerings of meal and honey.

ATLAS SUPPORTING THE HEAVENS.

This fable most probably arose from Atlas, the celebrated
king of Mauritania, being the inventor of the sphere, from his
knowledge of astronomy, and from often observing the mysteries of the heavenly bodies on the top of that mountain. Or
it may be a literal impersonation of Atlas being changed into
the mountain of the same name, which runs across the desert
of Africa from east to west, and is so high that the ancients
thought the heavens rested on its summit. (Ovid, *Met.* iv. 656.)
Again, Atlas is described as one of the sons of the rebellious
Titan, Iapetus, for whose sin he was compelled to stand for
ever at the extreme west, and to bear upon his shoulders the
solid vault of heaven.

In the Museo Borbonico at Naples is a kneeling statue of Atlas sustaining the celestial globe, from the Farnese collection ; a very interesting monument of Roman art, and one of great value to the student of
ancient astronomy. Of the forty-seven constellations known to the
ancients, forty-two may be distinctly recognised. The date of this
curious sculpture is fixed as anterior to the time of Hadrian by the
absence of the likeness of Antinous, which was inserted in the constellation Aquila by the astronomers of that period.

STRATAGEMS OF SISYPHUS.

Sisyphus, son of Æolus, was a matchless master of craft
and stratagem. He blocked up the road along the isthmus of
Corinth, and killed the strangers who came along it by rolling
down upon them great stones from the mountains above. He
outwitted even the arch thief Autolycus, who changed the
colour and shape of stolen goods, so that they could no longer
.be recognised. Sisyphus, by marking his sheep under the foot,

detected Autolycus when he stole them, and compelled him
to restore the plunder.   But his greatest offence was his dis-
closure of Jupiter's concealment of the nymph Ægina ; for
which was inflicted upon him in Hades the punishment of
perpetually heaving up a hill a great and heavy stone, which,
so soon as it attained the summit, rolled back with accelerated
rapidity to the plain, thus rendering his punishment eternal ;
and to roll the stone of Sisyphus is figurative of any insuper-
able or endless labour.   But Sisyphus overreached Pluto, and
escaped from the under-world.

> " With many a weary step, and many a groan,
>   Up the high hill he heaves a huge round stone ;
>   The huge round stone, resulting with a bound,
>   Thunders impetuous down, and smokes along the ground.
>   Along the restless orb his toil renews,
>   Dust mounts in clouds, and sweat descends in dews."
>
> *Odyssey : Pope.*

TANTALUS.

This wealthy Lydian, who resided near Mount Sipylus, was
a man of pre-eminent happiness, above the lot of humanity.
The gods received him at their banquets, and accepted his
hospitality in return.   Intoxicated with such prosperity, Tantalus became grossly wicked : he stole nectar and ambrosia
from the table of the gods, and divulged their secrets to mankind.   Tantalus expiated his guilt by exemplary punishment :
he was placed in the under-world with fruit and water seem-
ingly close to him, yet eluding his touch as often as he tried
to grasp them, and leaving his hunger and thirst incessant
and unappeased : (hence, to tantalise).   Pindar, however, describes his punishment to have been a vast stone perpetually
impending over his head, and threatening to fall.—*Grote's Hist.
Greece*, vol. i.

Uopages, Trabels, and Adventures.

THE ARGONAUTS.

THE first sea-voyage of which we read in profane history was that of the Argonauts, who, setting out from the port of Iolchos, or Pagasæ, in Thessaly, sailed to Colchis, at the eastern extremity of the Euxine sea. This voyage is remarkable for its length, as well as its antiquity, comprehending in extent the length of 14½ degrees upon the equator, or more than 1000 English miles. The history of the Expedition has usually been treated as an allegorical tale, invented by the poets; but the numerous traditions and local evidences which Arrian discovered on the coast, and which other writers record as having existed in the neighbouring countries, are strong presumptive proofs that such a voyage was once undertaken, and that its history is a narrative of a real event. It is certainly complicated with poetical imagery and mythological machinery; but that such a hero as Jason commanded such an Expedition seems unquestionable. The proofs of it are not derived from Greece, the region of fabulous invention, but have been found in countries which such a forgery could never have penetrated. Strabo and Diodorus observe, that Armenia, Media, Colchis, Iberia, the whole coast of the Euxine Sea, the Propontis, and the Hellespont, were full of heroic monuments of this Expedition. Tacitus observes, that the Iberians and Albanians, nations almost barbarous, retained notwithstanding, even in his time, the traditions respecting Jason and the Argonautic Expedition. The history of the Crusades,—an expedition almost as unaccountable as that of Jason, undertaken by a set of military adventurers, in an age nearly as rude and as warlike as that of the Argonauts,—is disguised in the prose accounts we have of it with as much imagery* as the poems of Apollonius Rhodius, and scarcely less incredible. Yet we do not, therefore, question the existence of Peter the Hermit, of Godfrey of Bouillon, or

* See the account of the vision that led to the discovery of the head of the spear which pierced the side of our Lord when on the cross, which was to insure victory to those who were in possession of this holy relic (*Robert. Monach.* lib. xii.; *Baldrichi Archi-pisc. Hist. Hierosol.* lib. iii.; *Raymond de Agiles,* p. 155). "Vision of the Crucifixion. and of St. Mark the Evangelist" (*Raymond de Agiles,* pp. 106, 107). "Vision of Peter the Hermit" (*Alberto Aquens,* § v.). "Effects of Pieces of the Cross in defeating the Turks," recorded in the same writer, with much more in the same strain (*Gesta Dei per Francos*).

of Raymond of Toulouse; or deny that such persons conducted armies into Palestine, and actually founded there a kingdom which subsisted for more than two centuries.—Abridged from *Dr. Falconer's Dissertation on Arrian's Voyage round the Euxine Sea.* 4to. Oxford, 1805.

Bryant considers this Expedition of the Argonauts as one of those corrupt traditions in which the recollection of the Deluge, and the preservation of mankind in the Ark, was long maintained. Jason, therefore, he believes to be the arkite deity; and the name of Argo to be connected with and derived from the Ark itself.—See *Bryant's Ancient Mythology.*

THE GOLDEN FLEECE.

The professed object of the Argonautic Expedition was the pursuit of gold; and perhaps the accounts given by Strabo and Appian may be the most probable of any, which state it to be a practice of the Colchians to extend fleeces of wool across the beds of the torrents that fall from Mount Caurasus, and by means of these to entangle the particles of gold which were washed down by the stream. This mode of collecting gold, which is much the same with the one practised new on the coast of Guinea, and other rivers of Africa, made Colchis be regarded as the gold-coast of that early period.

THE ISLE ATLANTIS.

Solon, during his visit in Egypt, was informed by a priest with whom he discoursed concerning the most ancient events, that a vast tract of land, greater than Libya or Asia, situate beyond the bounds of Africa and Europe, had been swallowed up by the ocean. The following was his account: "There was formerly an island at the entrance of the ocean where the Pillars of Hercules stand. This island was larger than all Libya and Asia; from it was an easy passage to many other islands, and from these islands to all that continent which was opposite and next to the true sea; yet within the mouth was a gulf with a narrow entry. In after-times there happened a dreadful earthquake and inundation of water, which continued for the space of a whole day and night, and this island Atlantis being covered and overwhelmed by the waves, sank beneath the ocean, and so disappeared; wherefore that sea is now impassable on account of the slime and mud which has been left by the immersed island."—*Plato's Timæus.*

A MEMORABLE VOYAGE.

In the seventh century B.C., the Samian merchant Kolæus, while bound for Egypt, had been driven out of his course by contrary winds, and had found shelter on an uninhabited island called Platæa, off the coast of Libya. From thence he again started to proceed to Egypt, but again without success; violent and continuous east winds drove him continually to the westward, until he at length passed the Pillars of Hercules, and found himself, under the providential guidance of the gods, an unexpected visitor among the Phœnicians and Iberians of Tartessus. What the cargo was which he was transporting to Egypt we are not told; but it sold in this yet virgin market for the most exorbitant prices: "He and his crew (says Herodotus) realised a profit larger than ever fell to the lot of any known Greek except Sostratus, the Æginetan, with whom no one else can compete." The magnitude of their profits may be gathered from the votive offering which they erected in the sacred precinct of Here at Samos, in gratitude for the protection of that sacred goddess during their voyage,— a large bronze vase, ornamented with projecting griffins' heads, and supported by three colossal bronze kneeling figures: it cost six talents (about 16,000*l.*), and represented the tithe of their gains. The voyage of Kolæus opened to the Greeks of that day a new world, hardly less important than the discovery of America to the Europeans of the last half of the fifteenth century.—Abridged from *Grote's History of Greece*, vol. iii.

"THE PILLARS OF HERCULES."

This was among early navigators the name given to the Straits of Gibraltar. That the waters surrounding their islands and the Peloponnesus formed part of a sea circumscribed by assignable boundaries, intelligent Greeks learnt for the first time from the continuous navigation of the Phokæans round the coasts, first of the Adriatic, and next of the Gulf of Lyons to the Pillars of Hercules and Tartessus. The Pillars of Hercules, especially, long remained deeply fixed in the Greek mind as a terminus of human adventure and aspiration: of the ocean beyond, men were for the most part content to remain ignorant.[*]

THE ADVENTURES OF TELEMACHUS.

In the Lansdowne library was a very ancient Greek romance printed at Florence, in 1645, called *Athene Skeleate*, interpreted by the learned editor, Pietro Proso, to mean *Minerva Cabzonito*, or *Minerva in breeches*. This curious work was purchased by the first Marquis of Lansdowne, at the sale of the

---

[*] The "Pillars of Hercules" has often been adopted in England as a sign for an inn at the remote part of a town. Thus the site of Apsley House, Hyde-Park Corner, was previously occupied by a "Pillar of Hercules" inn, the ground being at that period the western verge of London.

Pinelli library, and is supposed to be the only copy in existence ; though Fenelon had doubtless seen the work, as the fable of his *Telemachus* is evidently founded upon it.　It was embellished with several engravings, of which only one remained.　It represents Mentor leaping after Telemachus, whom he has thrown into the sea from the rocks of the island of Calypso.　This the learned commentator supposes to have been one of the western islands of Scotland ; in which he is certainly warranted by the text, which states it to have been far to the west, beyond the Pillars of Hercules.　And though to some this may seem to apply better to the Canary Islands, yet the further statement, that our travellers there found the days three times as long as the nights, can only apply to the summer of a high northern latitude.　This, too, accounts satisfactorily for the narrations handed down to us of the wanderings of Ulysses.　It is absurd to suppose that he could for ten years wander about the narrow seas, as in a labyrinth ; but if we can imagine him to have been driven through the Straits into the wide Atlantic, there—indeed, being at best but an indifferent seaman, and unacquainted with the compass—his wanderings might have been long enough.

It is probable that the first land Ulysses made was one of the western islands of Scotland ; whence, not daring again to lose the sight of land, he would have had a most tedious voyage back to the Mediterranean.　What still further corroborates this opinion is a fact unknown in the age of the editor of the *Athene Skeleate.*　The island of Calypso is described as having several grottoes, formed of natural pillars of stone, so regularly ranged as to resemble a work of art, "unless," says the romance, "they were fashioned by the hands of the giants."　Now, there is nothing at all resembling this description in any of the islands of the Mediterranean, nor, perhaps, in any part of the world, the Hebrides excepted.

FABULOUS LOCALITIES OF CLASSIC HISTORY.

Mr. Grote, at the opening of his valuable *History of Greece,* gives this very interesting *précis* of certain classic localities, the existence of which has been disproved by the extension of geographical discovery.

"Many of these fabulous localities are to be found in Homer and Hesiod, and the other Greek poets and topographers,—Erythein, the garden of the Hesperides, the garden of Phœbus, to which Boreas transported the Attic maiden Orithya, the delicious country of the Hyperboreans, the Elysian plain, the floating island of Æolus Thrinakia, the country of the Æthiopians, the Lestrygones, the Cyclopes, the Lotophagi, the Sirens, the Cimmerians, and the Gorgons, &c.　These are places which (to use the expression of Pindar respecting the Hyperboreans) you cannot approach either by sea or by land : the wings of the poet alone can bring you there.　*　*　*

In the present advanced state of geographical knowledge, the story of that man who after reading *Gulliver's Travels* went to look in his map for Lilliput appears an absurdity; but those who fixed the exact locality of the floating island of Æolus on the rocks of the Sirens did much the same; and with their ignorance of geography and imperfect appreciation of historical evidence, the error was hardly to be avoided. The ancient belief which fixed the Sirens on the island of Sireneuse off the coast of Naples; the Cyclopes,* Erytheia, and the Læstrygones in Sicily; the Lotophagi on the island of Meninx, near the Lesser Syrtis; the Phæasians at Corcyra, and the goddess Circe at the promontory of Circeium; took its rise at a time when these regions were first Hellenised, and comparatively little visited."†

VERACITY OF MARCO POLÓ.

That the narratives of this celebrated Venetian traveller of the thirteenth century have been too often discredited, is proved by his story of " the Old Man of the Mountain," the whole of which, bating the extravagance of the diction and high colouring of the picture (which, as Marco derived it from Persia, furnishes an additional proof of his fidelity in repeating what he heard), is a well-authenticated historical fact. Divested of the marvellous, it is simply this: the term *mulihet*, or "impious," was applied by the orthodox Mussulmans to an odious or fanatic sect, who began to flourish about the year 1090, and dwelt in the mountainous district of Kohistan. Hassan (the hero of the beautiful tale of Abu Hassan, in the *Thousand and One Nights*) was the name of the founder; but in the time of Marco Polo the reigning "Old Man" was, as he says, Alo-eddin, against whom and his son an expedition was undertaken by the Moghuls, on account of their numerous massacres and other cruelties; and though this intelligent traveller may be mistaken in a few years in the date of Alo-eddin's castle being dismantled, and his paradise destroyed, yet it is quite certain that Hulagu Khan, the grandson of Ghengis, put this chief and, according to Mirkhoud, twelve thousand of his infatuated followers to death about the time of Marco Polo. Such is the origin and history of the " Old Man of the Mountain and his Assassins," a branch of whom, having established themselves in the mountains of Arctic Libanus, rendered these names famous and formidable in the histories of the Crusades.—*Quarterly Review*, No. 48.

EDWARD WEBBE THE TRAVELLER.

In the very rare little volume of *Edward Webbe, an English-*

---

* The Liparean islands, near Italy, being volcanoes, were fabled to contain the forges of the Cyclopes.
† There was no such thing as a map before the days of Anaximander, the disciple of Thales.

man borne,⁕ we find some whimsical and not unimportant details of the countries through which the author passed. Webbe was undoubtedly a great traveller, having first gone into Russia with Jenkinson, and afterwards with Burroughs; he was carried as a slave to Kaffa by the Tartars, and to Persia by the Turks; and he visited Jerusalem, Constantinople, and Grand Cairo. Near the latter city he saw seven large mountains, pointed like a diamond, and built in Pharaoh's time to keep his corn; and it was out of these that Joseph's brethren loaded their asses: this, we believe, is an appropriation of the Pyramids peculiar to Webbe. He also, like Baumgarten, saw the place of the Red Sea where the children of Israel passed over; but the strangest of all the strange sights which he beheld was in Ethiopia. "I have seene," he says, "in a place like à parke adjoyning unto Prester John's court, threescore and seaventeene unicornes and oliphants, all alive at one time, and they were so tame that I have played with them as one would playe with young lambes." The woodcut of the "oliphant" is remarkably well executed; that of the unicorn represents a fierce horse-like animal, with cloven hoofs, and a straight horn in the forehead. Purchas, who has no doubts of the existence of the unicorn, seems to be staggered only by the number; and calls Webbe, rather unceremoniously, a "mere fabler," which he was not.

COLOSSAL ANTS PRODUCING GOLD.

This extravagant fable is related by the Greeks, and repeated by travellers of the middle ages, of ants as big as foxes producing gold. The passage states that the tribes who dwell between the Meru and Mandarn mountains brought lumps of the paipilika, or ant-gold,—so named because it was dug out by the common large ant, or paipilika. Professor Wilson explains this absurdity, by observing that it was believed that the native gold found on the surface of some of the auriferous deserts of northern India had been laid bare by the action of these insects,—an idea by no means irrational, although erroneous, but which grew up, in its progress westward, into a monstrous fable. The native country of these tribes is that described by the Greeks—the mountains between Hindostan and

⁕ It is entitled "The Rare and Most Wonderful Things which Edward Webbe, an Englishman borne, hath seene and passed in his troublesome travailes. In the cities of Jerusalem, Damasko, Bethlem and Galely; and in the lands of Jewrie, Egypt, Grecia, Russia and Prester John. Wherein is set forth his extreame slaverie sustained many years together in the gallies and warres of the great Turk, against the lands of Persia, Tartaria, Spain and Portugale, with the manner of his releasement and coming into England in May last." The "Epistle to the Reader" is dated "from my lodging at Blackwall, this nineteenth of May 1590, Your loving countrey-man Edward Webbe." There is also an epistle dedicatory to Queen Elizabeth. Fronting the title-page is a woodcut representing the traveller armed with a matchlock, rapier, and staff.

Thibet ; and the names given are those of barbarous races still found in those localities.

ARGOSIE.

This term is applied by old writers to a ship of great burden, whether for merchandise or war :

> "Your mind is tossing on the ocean ;
> There, where your argosies with portly sail,—
> Like signiors and rich burghers on the flood,
> Or, as it were, the pageants of the sea,—
> Do over-peer the petty traffickers."
>
> *Shakspeare's Merchant of Venice*, act 1. sc. 1.

It is mentioned in the same sense by Chapman, Drayton, Beaumont and Fletcher, and other writers. In Rycaut's *Maxims of Turkish Policy*, "those vast carracks called *argosies*," are said to be corruptly so denominated "from *Ragosies*, *i. e.* ships of Ragusa," on the Gulf of Venice ; but it is more probable that the argosie derived its name from the classical ship Argo, as hinted by Shakspeare in the play just quoted, when he makes Gratiano, in allusion to Antonio's argosie, say :

> "We are the Jasons ; we have won the fleece."

Sandys, in his *Travels*, applies the term to a ship of force in describing the boldness of the pirates in the Adriatic, observing, that from the timorousness of others they "gather such courage that a little frigot will often not fear to venture on an argosie."

ULTIMA THULE

is the name given in early history to the northernmost part of the habitable world ; hence the Latin phrase, *Ultima Thule*, the utmost stretch or boundary.

Mr. Hogg, in a paper read to the Royal Society of Literature, in 1853, stated that it had been a common opinion that the *Ultima Thule* of the Romans was Iceland, but that he considered this rested upon no good authority. On the contrary, he believed that the Feroe Islands represent their *Ultima Thule*, it not being probable that, if the Romans had reached Iceland, they would have omitted discovering Greenland and America. Nothing certain is known of Iceland till the ninth century, though it has been imagined that the English and Irish were acquainted with its existence, as the Venerable Bede is said to have described the island pretty accurately. The Icelandic chronicles commence with the landing of the Norwegians, and state that a pirate of the name of Naddodr was driven by a storm upon Iceland in A.D. 861.

THE WANDERING JEW.

"The story of the Wandering Jew (says Sir Thomas Browne) is very strange, and will hardly obtain belief ; yet there is a formal account thereof set down by Matthew Paris, from the report of an Armenian bishop who came into this kingdom about four hundred years ago, and had often entertained this wanderer at his table. That he was then alive; was first called Cartaphilus; was keeper at the judgment-hall, whence thrusting out our Saviour with expostulation for His stay, was condemned to stay until His return; was afterwards baptised by Ananias, and by the name of Joseph; was thirty years old in the days of our Saviour; remembered the saints that arose with Him, the making of the Apostles' Creed, and their several peregrinations." Sir Thomas astutely adds: "Surely were this true, he might be an happy arbitrator in many Christian controversies."—*Vulgar Errors.*

WHO WERE THE BUCCANEERS?

An association of sea-robbers or pirates, called also "the Brethren of the Coast," who, for nearly two centuries, constantly waged war against the Spaniards in the West Indies; when the Caribbee Indians having taught the colonists to cure the flesh of cattle, which they called *boucan*, the French made therefrom *boucaner*, which the *Dictionnaire de Trevoux* explains to be, "to dry red without salt;" hence comes the noun *boucanier* and our "buccaneer." The Buccaneers were Europeans, but chiefly natives of Great Britain and France, who first associated about 1524. Several narratives of their ex ploits have been written; that of Dampier, who was engaged in the Expedition of 1684, is strikingly interesting. Montauban, Grammont, Montbars, Vand-Horn, Laurent de Graff, and Sir H. Morgan, were also celebrated traders. Morgan, who found his way across the Isthmus of Darien from the Atlantic to the Pacific Ocean, and took and plundered the rich city of Panama, then 7000 houses, was knighted by Charles II.[*]

BRUCE'S TRAVELS.

Few men have had so much obloquy and discredit thrown upon them by error and prejudice as Bruce, the traveller in Africa; it was even doubted whether he had ever been in Abyssinia, where he resided two years. He was virulently accused of exaggeration and falsehood, from Dr. Johnson to Peter Pindar; yet, says Major F. B. Head, "Bruce's *Travels* do not contain one single statement which, according to our present knowledge of the world, can even be termed improbable." His statements have been corroborated by Jerome, Lobo, Paez, Salt, Coffin, Pearce, Burckhardt, Browne, Clarke, Wittman, Belzoni, Raffles, Denham, and many others; among the latest of whom is Mansfield Parkyns. Yet Bruce's case is a remarkable instance of the axiom, that to be treated with respect when dead is but a poor recompense for being neglected and abused while living.

[*] Certain adventures of these "sea-robbers" have been ingeniously wrought into an historical novel of striking character by Mrs. S. C. Hall.

Modern History.

YOUNG GENIUS.

Mr. Disraeli has, in his *Coningsby*, this striking page:

"Genius, when young, is divine. Why, the greatest captains of ancient and modern times both conquered Italy at twenty-five! Youth, extreme youth, overthrew the Persian empire. Don John of Austria won Lepanto at twenty-five—the greatest battle of modern time; had it not been for the jealousy of Philip, the next year he would have been Emperor of Mauritania. Gaston de Foix was only twenty-two when he stood a victor on the plain of Ravenna. Every one remembers Condé and Rocroy at the same age. Gustavus Adolphus died at thirty-eight. Look at his captains—that wonderful Duke of Weimar, only thirty-six when he died. Banèr himself, after all his miracles, died at forty-five. Cortes was little more than thirty when he gazed upon the golden cupolas of Mexico. When Maurice of Saxony died at thirty-two all Europe acknowledged the loss of the greatest captain and the profoundest statesman of the age. Then there is Nelson, Clive; but these are warriors, and perhaps you may think there are greater things than war. I do not. I worship the Lord of Hosts. But take the most illustrious achievements of civil prudence. Innocent III., the greatest of the popes, was the despot of Christendom at thirty-seven. John de Medici was a cardinal at fifteen, and, Guicciardini tells us, baffled with his craft Ferdinand of Aragon himself. He was Pope as Leo X. at thirty-seven. Luther robbed even him of his richest province at thirty-five. Take Ignatius Loyola and John Wesley—they worked with young brains. Ignatius was only thirty when he made his pilgrimage and wrote the *Spiritual Exercises*. Pascal wrote a great work at sixteen (the greatest of Frenchmen), and died at thirty-seven. Ah, that fatal thirty-seven! which reminds me of Byron—greater even as a man than a writer. Was it experience that guided the pencil of Raphael when he painted the palaces of Rome? He died at thirty-seven. Richelieu was secretary of state at thirty-one. Well, then, there are Bolingbroke and Pitt, both ministers before other men leave off cricket. Grotius was in practice at seventeen, and attorney-general at twenty-four. And Acquaviva—Acquaviva was General of the Jesuits, ruled every cabinet in Europe, and colonised America, before he was thirty-seven. What a career! the secret sway of Europe! That was indeed a position! But it is needless to multiply instances. The history of heroes is the history of youth."

HOW THE EMPERORS OF THE EAST KEPT STATE.

St. Chrysostom tells us "the emperor wears on his head a diadem or a crown of gold, decorated with precious stones of inestimable value. These ornaments and his purple garments are reserved for his sacred person alone; and his robes of silk

are embroidered with figures of golden dragons. Wherever he
appears in public, he is surrounded by his courtiers, guards,
and attendants. Their spears, shields, cuirasses, the bridles
and trappings of their horses, have either the substance or
the appearance of gold. The two mules that draw the chariot
of the monarch are perfectly white, and shining all over with
gold. The chariot itself, of pure and solid gold, attracts the
admiration of the spectators, who contemplate the purple curtains, the snowy carpets, the size of the precious stones, and
the resplendent plates of gold that glitter as they are agitated
by the motion of the carriage."

WHO WAS PRESTER JOHN?

The king of Tenduc, in Asia, who, like the Abyssine or
Ethiopian emperor, preserved great state, and did not conde-
scend to be seen by his subjects above twice or three times a
year. Mandeville, who pretends to have travelled over Prester
John's country, makes him sovereign of an archipelago of isles
in India, beyond Bactria; and says, that

"A former emperor travelled into Egypt, where, being present at divine
service, he asked who those persons were that stood before the bishop.
And being told they should be priests, he said he would no more be
called king, nor emperor, but priest; and would have the name of him
that came first out of the priests, and was called John, and so have all
the emperors since been called Prester John."

HORRORS OF FAMINE.

In 539, the year of the invasion of Italy by Theodebert, was
a season of dreadful famine. In the March of Ancona alone
more than 50,000 persons are stated to have perished from
hunger; and the Tuscans were driven to feed on acorns. Procopius was a personal witness of its horrors. He saw starving
wretches fling themselves down upon herbs and grasses, and
make a faint attempt to tear them from the ground; but
their enfeebled strength often failed them, and they expired
in the effort. He saw their bodies left, as they fell, to
blacken in the sun, and displaying corruption in its most
hideous forms. Yet the ghastly aspect of the dead was exceeded by that of the survivors. Their livid hue is compared
to the colour of an extinguished torch, and their skin seemed
closely adhering to the bones. Their haggard features were
distorted with a wild and fearful expression, and a gleam of
maniac fury shone forth from their hollow eyes. Sometimes
their lips were seen to drip with blood from devouring the
severed limbs of their lifeless companions; yet even the birds
of prey turned from their carcasses, after seeking in vain for
some nourishment in these dry and wasted remains.—Lord
Mahon's *Life of Belisarius.*

OMEN OF STUMBLING.

When, A.D. 540, Nushirvan, king of Persia, invaded the Roman empire, and found himself near Sura, he would in all probability have neglected the siege of that city, had not his stumbling horse conveyed to the Magian priests a promise of success. It is remarkable, that such accidents were likewise looked upon by the ancient Romans, but interpreted in a manner directly opposite.—Lord Mahon's *Life of Belisarius.*

THE END OF TOTILA.

When Totila was driven from Tagina by Belisarius and his troops, he was followed by only five of his train. He was overtaken by some Roman soldiers, headed by Asbad ! but they were ignorant of the importance of their prize. The dangerous secret was revealed by the inconsiderate exclamation of a Goth : "Do you dare to strike the king !" when Asbad, instructed by these words, raised his lance, and pierced Totila with a mortal wound.

EXAGGERATED VICTORY.

The accounts of some ancient victories must awaken incredulity. Thus at the second battle fought on Mount Burgaon, between the Moors under the governor Solomon, and the Romans under Belisarius, it is gravely recorded by Procopius that 50,000 of the barbarians perished, and that not a single Roman soldier was either killed or wounded. So considerable was the number of prisoners, that a Moorish boy or an African sheep might be purchased for equal prices at Carthage. The African sheep are praised by Homer. In his time, we find a young female-slave sold for the price of twenty oxen.

ESCAPES OF BELISARIUS.

When, A.D. 537, Belisarius sallied forth with a thousand of his guards from Rome, to encamp on the shore of the Tiber and observe the movements of the Goths, suddenly he found himself encompassed by the Gothic vanguard of cavalry. On this emergency he displayed, not merely the judgment of a general, but the personal intrepidity of a soldier. Distinguished by the charger whom he had often rode in battle—a bay with a white face—he was seen in the foremost ranks. "That is Belisarius," exclaimed some Roman deserters. "Aim at the bay !" was forthwith the cry through all the Gothic squadrons; and a thousand darts and arrows were directed against this conspicuous mark. "It seemed," says Procopius, "to be clearly felt both by the Romans and their enemies that the fate of

Italy depended on this single life." The boldest Goths rushed forward, and in close combat Belisarius displayed great prowess : many of his assailants fell by his single arm, and his exploits are said to have outdone those of any other Roman on that day, whilst he remained without a wound.

Again, at the siege of Orsino, during a skirmish, the life of Belisarius had nearly been lost by the deliberate aim of a Gothic archer. One of his guards alone perceived the coming danger, and rushed forward to shield the body of his general by the interposition of his own. In this act of devoted fidelity, his hand was transpierced and disabled ; and Unigatus, the name of the brave soldier, is not unworthy of historical record.— Abridged from Lord Mahon's *Life of Belisarius.*

DEGENERATE ROMANS.

" Of all those illustrious men," says Lord Mahon, " who have formed the literature, or revived the arts, of modern Italy, not one has been a native of Rome ; and nearly all have sprung from barbarian ancestry in the ancient Cisalpine Gaul. The soil, once so fertile in heroes, seems weary and exhausted with the number."—*Life of Belisarius.*

Guido was of Bologna, Davila of Padua, Tiraboschi of Bergamo, Correggio and Ariosto of Reggio, Bentivoglio of Ferrara, Maffei of Verona, Alfieri of Piedmont, Muratori of Modena, Raphael of Urbino. Fra Paolo, Goldoni, Titian, and Canova, were Venetians ; Petrarch, Guicciardini, Machiavel, Dante, Michael Angelo, and Boccacio, Florentines. Tasso was born at Sorrento, but his family was from the Milanese. Deduct these, and what remains for southern Italy ?

CHARLES MARTEL.

The great battle of Tours, which was to decide whether Europe should remain Christian or the Cross sink under the Crescent, was fought in October 732, between the Saracens under Abderahman, and the Franks under Charles Martel ; when the triumph of the latter terminated the course of Arab conquest. " Then was Charles first called by the name of Martel (*a sort of battle-axe*) ; for as the martel crushes iron, steel, and all other metals, even so he broke and pounded his enemies and all other nations."—*Chroniques de St. Denys,* lib. xv. 26.

POPE JOAN.

The scandalous story of Pope Joan is as follows. In the ninth century, a woman named Joan conceived a violent passion for a young monk named Folda, and in order to be admitted into his monastery assumed the male habit. On the death of her lover, she entered on the duties of professor ; and being very learned, was elected Pope when Adrian II. died, in 872. Other scandalous particulars follow : " yet until the Reformation the tale was repeated and believed without offence." (*Gibbon.*) Pope Joan is a very old game, and was called Pope Julio *temp.* Elizabeth.—Harrington's *Nug. Antiq.* ii. 195.

BIRTH-PLACE AND BURIAL-PLACE OF CHARLEMAGNE.

The actual birth-place of Charlemagne has been much contested. The most probable account, however, gives the honour to Aacheu (Aix-la-Chapelle). This was unquestionably his favourite residence for many years; and he died and was buried there in the year 814. When his tomb was opened by Otto III., one hundred and eighty years after the interment, the body of Charlemagne was found in an erect position, seated on a marble stool, in full imperial costume, and all undecayed except the point of the nose. His nails had grown so long as to pierce and project through the gloves with which his hands were covered. Otto removed all the adjuncts, to be preserved as imperial relics, extracted a tooth to increase their number, pared the overgrown nails, renewed the lost nose by one of gold, and having placed on him a clean shirt, once more consigned Charles to repose.

ORIGIN OF SFORZA, DUKE OF MILAN.

One day, in the middle ages, as a troop of condottieri crossed the Roman country, marching to inspiriting music and with standards unfurled, a young peasant, James Attendolo, stood under an oak to admire their noble bearing, their richly caparisoned horses, and their brilliant armour. Some of the soldiers, in passing, invited him to follow them. " Often," said they, " are we largely paid for doing nothing, and live at the expense of the people in cities and villages." The peasant listened, and was much tempted to join the adventurers ; but the thought of quitting his old parents, and the cottage where he was born, withheld him; and, according to the custom of the time, he resolved to decide himself by some presage or omen. " Now for it," cried he; " I will throw the axe I hold in my hand against this oak, and if it enters deep enough into the bark to remain fixed, I will be a soldier." So saying, James threw the axe with so much violence, that it penetrated into the heart of the oak and stuck fast. From that moment all hesitation was over : tearing himself from the tears and the arms of his family, he followed his new comrades ; who gave him the name of Sforza, because it was with all his force he threw the axe that was to decide his vocation. He fought in more than one hundred battles with great courage and skill ; and after having successively served in Rome and Milan, at an advanced age perished while endeavouring to save one of his own pages from drowning in a torrent. He left a son, who very soon gained, like his father, renown for talent and bravery : he became of so much consideration in Italy as to be deemed a fit match for Bianca Visconti, the heiress of Milan. Their son, Galeazzo Sforza, Duke of Milan, used to look forth on the fair city, and say, "See what I owe to my grandfather's axe !"

A COMBAT IN THE ICE.

Matthew Paris describes the Frieslanders as a rude and untamable people, skilled in naval warfare, and fighting with great vigour and courage on the ice. It is of the cold regions of this people, and their neighbours the Sarmatians, that Juvenal says, "One had better fly hence beyond the Sarmatians and the icy ocean," &c. "The Frieslanders, therefore, having laid ambuscades among the rush-beds along the sea-coast (in their war with William of Holland), as well as along the country, which is marshy—and the winter season was coming on—went in pursuit of the said William, armed with javelins, which they call *gaveloches*, in the use of which they are very expert, and with Danish axes and pikes, and clad in linen dresses covered with light armour. On reaching a certain marsh, they met with William, helmeted and wearing armour, and mounted on a large war-horse covered with mail. But as he rode along, the ice broke, although it was more than half a foot thick ; and the horse sank up to his flank, becoming fixed in the mud of the marsh. The trammeled rider dug his sharp spurs into the animal's sides to a great depth, and the noble fiery beast struggled to rise and free himself, but without success. Crushed and bruised, he only sank to rise no more."

A CRUSADE OF CHILDREN.

This strange incident of the Middle Ages began in France, where Robert de Courçon, an Englishman, formerly the school or college friend of Innocent III. at Paris, and now his legate there, was preaching a crusade for the recovery of Jerusalem, and after the manner of Peter the Hermit, giving the cross to all descriptions of persons, fit and unfit, indiscriminately. His passionate exhortations, in 1213, had actually enfrenzied a shepherd-boy named Stephen. This lad asserted that the Saviour himself had, in a letter addressed to the king of France, authorised him, Stephen, to preach and lead a crusade. Children of all ranks and of both sexes, in spite of their parents, flocked to this juvenile leader, until he was at the head of 30,000 French boys and girls. From France the mania spread into Germany, where another boy collected an army of 7000 children. The German division crossed the Alps, and reached Genoa ; where the discovery that hence the

way to Palestine was by sea, for which money was indispensable, put a final stop to the progress of the strange army.
Here some hired themselves as servants to the Italians; others
begged, or tried to steal a passage; others in retracing their
steps to return home, were plundered and ill-used; and numbers died of heat, hunger, thirst, or fatigue, by the roadside. A
few only eventually found their way back to Germany. The
lot of the French host of juvenile crusaders was even more
disastrous. Headed by Stephen, borne in state in a tapestried
waggon, they arrived at Marseilles, where they embarked in
seven ships, of which two were wrecked off Sardinia, when
every soul on board perished; and the survivors in the other
five ships were carried to Africa, and sold into Moslem slavery.
—*Mediæval Popes, Emperors, Kings, and Crusaders.*

THE FOUNDER OF PADUA.

The foundation of Padua, perhaps the oldest city in the
north of Italy, was attributed to Antenor by the Romans:

" Antenor, from the midst of Grecian hosts
  Could pass secure, and pierce th' Illyrian coasts;
  Where, rolling down the steep, Timavus raves,
  And through nine channels disembogues his waves.
  At length he founded Padua's happy seat,
  And gave his Trojans a secure retreat:
  There fix'd their arms, and there renew'd their name,
  And there in quiet rules, and crown'd with fame."
                        Virgil, *Æneid*, lib. L: Dryden.

In the year 1274, when the workmen were laying the foundation of the Foundling Hospital, there was discovered a large
marble sarcophagus, containing a second of lead, and a third of
cypress-wood. In the third was a skeleton, larger than the
ordinary stature of men, grasping a sword in the bony hand;
and an inscription upon the inner coffin was interpreted to
indicate that the tomb belonged to Antenor. Though he was
a pagan, these remains were deposited in the church of San
Lorenzo, whither also the sarcophagus was removed, and an
inscription was cut upon it. The church has been demolished,
but the sarcophagus, unquestionably antique, stands at the
corner of a street, beneath a canopy of brick. When Alberto
della Scala visited Padua in 1334, the sarcophagus was opened,
and he obtained as a gift the reputed sword of the Trojan hero.

TAMERLANE'S IRON CAGE.

The indignities of imprisonment have assumed fantastic
forms, as in the treatment which the Sultan Bajazet is said to
have experienced from Tamerlane after his defeat and capture:

" Closed in a cage, like some destructive beast,
  I'll have thee borne about in public view;

A great example of the righteous vengeance
That waits on cruelty and pride like thine."
                        Rowe's *Tragedy of Tamerlane.*

Voltaire and other modern writers have discredited this story,
chiefly on the authority of D'Herbelot; but his objection has
been disproved by Sir William Jones. Again, Leunclavius, in
his History of the Turks, professes to have heard from an old
man who was in Bajazet's service at the time of his defeat,
"that an iron cage was made by Timour's command, composed
on every side of iron gratings, through which he could be seen
in any direction. He travelled in this den, slung between two
horses. Whenever Timour and his retinue, on moving his
camp, made ready for a journey, he was generally carried before; and after the march, when they dismounted, he was
placed upon the ground in his cage before Timour's tent."
Poggio also, who was a contemporary, mentions this strange
imprisonment as an undoubted fact.* (See also p. 89.)

THE IRON CROWN OF LOMBARDY.

When the Emperor Napoleon I. was crowned King of Italy
(at Milan on May 23, 1805), he placed the iron crown of the
kings of Lombardy upon his head with his own hands, exclaim-
ing, *Dieu me l'a donné, gare à qui la touche* ("God has given
it to me, beware who touches"); which Sir Walter Scott desig-
nates as the haughty motto attached to it by its ancient owners.

The crown takes its name from the narrow iron band within
it, which is about three-eighths of an inch broad and one-tenth
of an inch in thickness. It is traditionally said to have been
made out of one of the nails used at the Crucifixion, and given
to Constantine by his mother, the Empress Helena, the dis-
coverer of the Cross, to protect him in battle.† The iron crown
was used at the coronations of the Lombard kings; primarily
at that of Agilulfus, at Milan, in the year 591.

The crown is kept in the Cathedral of Monza. The outer
circlet is composed of six equal pieces of beaten gold, joined
together by hinges, and set with large rubies, emeralds, and
sapphires, on a ground of blue gold enamel. Within the circlet
is "the iron band," without a speck of rust, although it has
been exposed more than 1500 years. After his coronation at

* The Countess of Buchan, for having placed the crown of Scotland on the
Bruce's head, was by Edward I. confined in a cage built upon one of the towers
of Berwick Castle, exposed to the rigour of the weather, and to the gaze of the
passers-by; and one of Bruce's sisters was similarly dealt with.
† In the Benedictine Church in Catania, in Sicily, there is said to be one
of these nails, which, by its miraculous virtue, preserved the monastery from
destruction during the memorable eruption of Mount Etna in the year 1669,
when its walls were surrounded by liquid fire. Another nail is reported to be
in the Treasury of St. Mark at Venice.

Milan, Buonaparte instituted for Italy a new order of knighthood, called " Of the Iron Crown."

"LUKE'S IRON CROWN AND DAMIEN'S BED OF STEEL."

The ancient mode of punishing a regicide, or other criminal, in Hungary, was by placing a crown of iron heated red-hot upon his head: (see *Respublica et Status Hungariæ*, Elzev. 1634). In the tragedy of *Hoffman*, 1631, this punishment is introduced :

> "Fix on thy master's head my burning crown."

Again :

> " Was adjudg'd
> To have his head *sear'd* with a *burning crown.*"

In some of the monkish accounts of a place of future torment, a *burning crown* is likewise appropriated to those who deprived any lawful monarch of his kingdom. Goldsmith alludes to the punishment of the peasant engaged in the Hungarian rebellion above referred to :

> "Luke's *iron crown* and Damien's bed of steel."

In Boswell's *Life of Johnson* (vol. ii. p. 6), it is observed, that though *George* and *Luke* Zeck were both engaged in the rebellion, it was the former who was thus punished ; but George would not suit the poet's verse. The Earl of Athol, who was executed for the murder of James I. King of Scots, was previous to his death crowned with a hot iron. We quote the above from Singer's note to the following passage in Shakspeare's *King Richard III.*, act iv. sc. 1:

> " O, would to God that the inclusive verge
> Of golden metal that must round my brow
> Were red-hot steel, to sear me to the brain !"

CURIOUS FACTIONS.

Nearly through the fourteenth and fifteenth centuries two factions divided and agitated the whole population of Holland and Zealand. One bore the title of *Hoeks* (fishing-hooks), the other was called *Kaabeljauws* (cod-fish). These burlesque denominations originated between two parties at a feast, as to whether the cod-fish took the hook, or the hook the cod-fish. This apparently frivolous dispute was made the pretext for a serious quarrel ; and the partisans of the nobles, and those of the towns, ranged themselves on either side, and assumed different badges of distinction. The *Hoeks*, partisans of the towns, wore red caps ; the *Kaabeljauws* wore gray ones. In Jacqueline's quarrel with Philip of Burgundy, she was supported by the former ; and it was not till the year 1492, that the extinction of that popular and turbulent faction struck a final blow to the dissensions of both.

THE STORY OF RIENZI.

In the year 1437, an obscure man, Nicola di Rienzi, conceived the project of restoring Rome, then in degradation and wretchedness, not only to good order, but even to her ancient greatness. He had received an education beyond his birth, and nourished his mind with the study of the best writers. After many harangues to the people, which the self-confident nobility did not attempt to repress, Rienzi excited an insurrection, and obtained complete success. He was placed at the head of a new government, with the title of Tribune, and with almost unlimited power. The first effects of this revolution were wonderful. All the nobles submitted, though with great reluctance; the roads were cleared of robbers; tranquillity was restored at home; some severe examples of justice intimidated offenders; and the tribune was regarded by the people as the destined restorer of Rome and Italy. Most of the Italian republics, and some of the princes, sent ambassadors to the new power. But with this sudden exaltation Rienzi became intoxicated; he fell as rapidly as he had risen, and was compelled to abdicate, and retire into exile. After several years, some of which he passed in the prison of Avignon, Rienzi was brought back to Rome, with the title of Senator, and under the command of the legate. The Romans at first gladly submitted to their favourite tribune; but in a few months they ceased altogether to respect a man who so little respected himself in accepting a station where he could be no longer free; and Rienzi was killed in a sedition. "The doors of the Capitol," says Gibbon, "were destroyed with axes and with fire; and while the senator attempted to escape in a plebian garb, he was dragged to the platform of his palace, the fatal scene of his judgments and executions;" and after enduring the protracted tortures of suspense and insult, he was pierced with countless daggers, amidst the execrations of the people.

At Rome is still shown an old brick dwelling, distinguished as the house of Pilate, but known to be the abode of Rienzi. It is exactly such as would please the known taste of the Roman tribune, . being composed of heterogeneous scraps of ancient marble, patched up with barbarous brick pilasters of Rienzi's age, exemplifying his own character, in which piecemeal fragments of Roman virtue and attachment to feudal state, abstract love of liberty and practice of tyranny, formed as incongruous a compound.

AN ENGLISH SAILOR'S STRATAGEM.

At the siege of Rhodes, in 1480, the Turkish leader, as a last resource, renewed his attempts upon the Tower of St. Nicholas, which was the key to the fortifications of the island. But a narrow channel intervened between the mole and the Turkish position, to convey the troops across which, the Turks had constructed a sort of movable bridge; and, in order to bring one end of it up to the mole, a Turkish engineer, under cover of the night, conveyed an anchor across, and fixed it to a rock beneath the water. He carried with him also a stout cable, which had one of its ends fixed to the bridge, and passing the other end through the ring of the anchor, he brought it back to be fastened to a capstan on the Turkish side of the channel, by the aid of which the Turks expected to haul their machine up to the point where the anchor was fixed.

It happened, however, that an English sailor, Gervase Roger,—for "history," says the Abbé de Vertot, "has not disdained to preserve his name,"—was by chance upon the spot at the time, and, unseen himself, observed the operations of the ingenious Turk. Having allowed him to depart, the seaman plunged at once into the water, detached the cable, and laid it quietly upon the bank; then took up the anchor, and carried it quietly to the grand master of the Knights of St. John, who rewarded him for his trouble. The unconscious Turks, having got their bridge ready, began hauling with their capstans; but to their great surprise, hauled nothing but their own rope back to themselves, and perceived, of course, that their scheme had been discovered and frustrated. The Turks then ceased their efforts against the tower, and soon after gave up the siege.

JOHN OF LEYDEN AND THE NEW JERUSALEM.

John Buckhold, or Bokehon, a tailor of Leyden, was ringleader of a furious tribe of Anabaptists, who made themselves masters of the city of Munster, where they proclaimed a community both of goods and women. This New Jerusalem, as they had named it, was retaken after a long siege; and John, with two of his associates, was suspended in an iron cage on the highest tower in the city. This happened about the year 1536.

HUGONOT OR HUGUENOT.

Some etymologists suppose this term derived from *huguon*, a word used in Touraine to signify persons who walk at night; and as the first Protestants, like the first Christians, may have chosen that season for their religious assemblies, the nickname of Huguenot may naturally enough have been applied to them by their enemies. Others are of opinion that it was derived from a French and faulty pronunciation of the German word *Eidgenossen*, which signifies confederates, and had been originally the name of that valiant part of the city of Geneva which entered into an alliance with the Swiss cantons, in order to maintain their liberties' against the tyrannical attempts of Charles III. Duke of Savoy. These confederates were called *Egnotes;* and thence, very probably, was derived the word Hugenot, now under consideration. The Count Villars, in a letter written to the King of France from the province of Languedoc, where he was lieutenant-general, and dated 11th November 1560, calls the riotous Calvinists of the Cevennes, Huguenots; and this is the first time that the term is found in the registers of that province applied to the Protestants. (Mosheim's *Ecclesiastical History,* vol. iv. p. 368 in notis.)

Davila, in his *Hist. des Guerres Civiles de la France,* p. 20, folio ed., says : "These people were called Huguenots, because the first conventicles they held in the city of Tours (where that belief first took strength and increased) were in certain cellars underground, near Hugo's gate, from whence they were by the vulgar called Hugonots; and in Flanders, because they went about in the garb of mendicants, they were called Geux."

FLAYING ALIVE.

At the conquest of Cyprus by the Turks, in 1570, the town of Famagosta, after a most gallant defence, was allowed to capitulate ; but the seraskier treated the brave Venetian governor, Bragadino, with frightful cruelty, cutting off his nose and ears, and causing him to be flayed alive, and his skin to be conveyed to Constantinople as a trophy. Again, the Persian king Cambyses caused one of the royal judges, who had taken a bribe to render an iniquitous judgment, to be flayed alive, and his skin to be stretched upon the seat, on which his son was placed to succeed him. A similar story is told of the Persian king Artaxerxes Mnemon ; and in Turkish history, as an act of Mahomet II.—Notes to *Grote's Hist. Greece,* vol. iv.

"THE GREAT SHIP OF NEMI."

In the sixteenth century, the Lake of Nemi acquired considerable notoriety from the discovery in it of a quantity of timber, which Alberti, the celebrated architect, and Marchi, the engineer, described as *the remains of an ancient ship,* said to be five hundred feet in length (the length of the *Great Britain* steam-ship), and attributed either to Tiberius or to Trajan. The existence of a vessel of this size on the Lake of Nemi was, however, questioned ; when Professor Nibby, having carefully inspected the locality, found that the beams recovered from the lake were parts of the framework of an ancient building, of larch and pine, from which numerous metal nails, and other fragments, were obtained. The pavement, consisting of large tiles, was laid upon an iron grating, marked in many places with the name Cæsar, in ancient characters. The tiles, grating, nails, and some of the beams, are now preserved in the Vatican library. Suetonius says, that Cæsar began a villa at a great cost upon this lake, and in a fit of caprice ordered it to be pulled down before it was completed ; whence Nibby infers these fragments to have been the foundations of the villa, which had escaped destruction by being under water.—*Handbook for Central Italy.*

THE ORPHAN OF BRESCIA.

Among the victims of the horrible massacre by the French captors of Brescia in 1512, was a poor boy about ten years of age, who had received a deep wound in his forehead, and lay awaiting his own death on the threshold of a house where all his relations had been killed. A kind-hearted person passing by, and perceiving that the little fellow still breathed, carried him to his house, where, by his unwearied attentions, he healed him of his wounds. But a cut that he received across his lips prevented his speaking with the same ease as before, and on that account he received the name of Tartaglia, or the stammerer. He became, as he grew up, a studious and learned man. He was the first in Italy who applied himself to geometry and mathematics, and revived again in Europe those useful sciences, which had been forgotten for so many long years, and might have been entirely lost but for the orphan of Brescia, who gave to them a new lustre by his laborious studies.

A REAL TRAGEDY.

The history of Sweden records a very extraordinary incident, which took place at the representation of the mystery of the Passion, under King John II., in 1513. The actor who performed the part of *Longinus*, the soldier who was to pierce the Christ on the cross in the side, was so transported with the spirit of his action, that he really killed the man who personated our Lord ; who, falling suddenly, and with great violence, overthrew the actress who represented the holy Mother. King John, who was present at this spectacle, was so enraged against *Longinus*, that he leaped on the stage and struck off his head. The spectators, who had been delighted with the too violent actor, became infuriated against their king, fell upon him in a throng, and killed him.

THE EMPEROR AND THE MERCHANT.

Among the sights of Augsburg is part of the house which once belonged to Anthony Fugger, in the Maximilianstrasse. The present front is entirely new, and the building is now the hotel of the Three Moors. Many of the old rooms remain, and amongst them, the chamber in which its proprietor entertained the Emperor Charles V., and consumed in his presence, in a fire of cinnamon-wood, a bond which he had received for a large sum of money advanced to the emperor as a public loan. This act is commemorated by an inscription in German on one of the walls of the room, as follows: "In the year 1490, Antonius Fugger built this house. In the year 1532, the Emperor Charles V. occupied it; and Antonius Fugger, in the chimney of this his knightly hall, consumed, in a fire of cinnamon, the emperor's bond."—*Sir John Forbes.*

THE PRÉ-AUX-CLERCS AT PARIS.

In 1559, the most frequented public walk in Paris was the *Pré-aux-Clercs*, now a portion of the Faubourg St. Germain. Here the students of the University, who were generally in favour of the reformed religion, had met for many years, when the monks of the Abbey St. Victor refused to allow them to assemble any longer; when several affrays took place, and much blood was shed. The students, being most numerous, carried their point; the monks resigned the field to them, and the Pré-aux-Clercs was more than ever frequented. It became the grand rendezvous of the Protestants, who here sang with devout enthusiasm the psalms of Marot, on fine summer evenings; and such numbers giving confidence, many persons declared themselves Protestants whose rank had hitherto deterred them from such a step.—Browning's *History of the Huguenots.*

THE ESCAPE OF GROTIUS.

During the quarrels between the Calvinists and Arminians, in the United Provinces of Holland, in 1618, Grotius was arrested on suspicion of favouring the Arminian interests, and was condemned to perpetual imprisonment. He was closely confined in the castle of Louvestein, near Gorcum, where his wife obtained permission to share his fate. In this fortress Grotius remained nearly two years; and here he wrote his treatise in Dutch verse, *On the Truth of the Christian Religion,* which formed the groundwork of his celebrated Latin work on the same subject. From this captivity he was at length liberated through the ingenious fidelity of his wife. He had been permitted to borrow of his friends books, which he was accustomed to return to Gorcum in a chest, which also served to convey him a supply of linen from his laundress. The chest was at first regularly searched; but his wife having remarked that the guards neglected the search, advised Grotius to conceal himself in the chest, after having made holes in part of the lid, so as to allow him to breathe. He entered into the scheme, having previously informed the commandant's lady, whose husband was absent, that his, Grotius's wife, was about to send away a large load of books, to prevent him injuring his health by study. At the time appointed, Grotius got into the chest, and was thus conveyed down a ladder by two soldiers. One of them, observing the weight of the chest, jocularly remarked, "There must be an Arminian in it." "There are Arminian books in it," replied the cunning wife. This did not quite satisfy the soldiers, who informed the governor's lady of the circumstance; but she, misled by the information she had previously received from Grotius, directed the removal of the chest unexamined.

Grotius was thus carried to the house of a friend at Gorcum, where he passed through the market-place disguised as a mason with a rule in his hand, and thence went to Antwerp by the ordinary conveyance. Meanwhile his wife pretended that her husband was much indisposed, and thus she afforded him time for his escape; but when she supposed him to be in a place of safety, she told the guards that the bird had flown. She was then threatened with prosecution, and imprisonment in her husband's stead; but she was liberated by a majority of votes of the states-general, and universally commended for having restored her husband to freedom. He secretly left Antwerp for France, where he was protected by Louis XIII., who granted him a pension of three thousand livres. While in France, he wrote his treatise *De Jure Belli et Pacis*, published in 1625, and adopted as a general text-book for lecturers on international policy.

AURUNGZEBE.

Aurungzebe, who, in the same month in which Oliver Cromwell died, assumed the magnificent title of Conqueror of the World, continued to reign until Anne had been long on the English throne. He was the sovereign of a larger territory than had obeyed any of his predecessors. His name was great in the farthest regions of the west. Here he had been made by Dryden the hero of a tragedy, once rapturously applauded by crowded theatres, and known by heart to fine gentlemen and fine ladies, but now forgotten. But one noble passage still lives, and is repeated by thousands who know not whence it comes:

> " Trust on, and think to-morrow will repay:
> To-morrow's falser than the former day;
> Lies worse; and while it says, We shall be blest
> With some new joys, cuts off what we possess'd.
> Strange cozenage! None would live past years again,
> Yet all hope pleasure in what yet remain;

And from the drugs of life think to receive
What the first sprightly running could not give."

Aurungzebe, act iv. sc. 1.

Mr. Macaulay says of this noble passage, "there are not eight finer lines in *Lucretius*."

THE CLOSE OF THE BATTLE OF VIENNA, 1683.

This great battle, fought September 12, 1683, determined whether Vienna under Mahomet IV. should experience the fate of Constantinople under Mahomet II., and whether the empire of the West should be re-united to the empire of the East; perhaps, even, whether Europe should continue Christian or not. The Turks fought under Kara Mustapha, the Christians under John Sobieski, king of Poland; who, on viewing the enemy's dispositions the day before, observed to his German generals, "This man is ill encamped; we shall beat him." The close of the battle, from Salvandy's *Histoire de Pologne*, is thus vividly related in the *Foreign Quarterly Review*, No. 14:

Five o'clock, p.m., had sounded, and Sobieski had given up for the day all hope of the grand struggle; when the provoking composure of Kara Mustapha, whom he espied in a splendid tent, tranquilly taking coffee with his two sons, roused him to such a pitch, that he instantly gave orders for a general assault. It was made simultaneously on the wings and centre. He made towards the pasha's tent, bearing down all opposition, and repeating with a loud voice, *Non nobis, non nobis, Domine exercituum, sed nomini tuo da gloriam!* (Not unto us, Lord God of hosts, not unto us, but unto thy name give the praise!) He was soon recognised by Tartar and Cossack; they drew back, while his name rapidly passed from one extremity to the other of the Ottoman lines, to the dismay of those who had refused to believe him present. "Allah!" said the Tartar Khan, "but the wizard[*] is with them sure enough!" At that moment the hussars raised their national cry of "God for Poland!" cleared a ditch which would have arrested the infantry, and dashed into the deep ranks of the enemy. They were a gallant band; their appearance almost justified the saying of one of their kings, "that if the sky itself were to fall, they would bear it up on the points of their lances." The shock was rude, and for some minutes dreadful; but the valour of the Poles, still more the reputation of their leader, and more than all, the finger of God, routed the immense hosts; they gave way on every side, the khan was borne along with the stream to the tent of the now despairing vizier. "Canst thou not help me?" said Kara Mustapha to the brave Tartar; "then I am lost indeed!" "The Polish king is there," replied the other; "I know him well. Did I not tell thee that all we had to do was to get away as quick as possible?"

ESCAPE OF CHARLES XII.

During the siege of the town of Thorn, Charles perceived that a general in his company named Lieven, dressed in a blue

---

[*] The name given him by the Tartars, after a series of extraordinary victories had fully impressed them with a belief in his supernatural powers.

coat embroidered with gold, was singled out by the besieged as
an aim for their fire. With a feeling of generosity that was quite
natural to him, he desired that officer to change places with
himself; but Lieven had scarcely obeyed than a cannon-ball
struck the spot Charles had quitted, and threw Lieven on the
ground a lifeless corpse. This was regarded by all present as
a sign that the king was specially protected of heaven; and
Charles believed that God had preserved him to accomplish
great things. From this moment, nothing arrested his victorious march.

CHARLES XII. AND THE PEASANT.

When Saxony was invaded by the Swedes, Charles, who
affected to spare the country, commanded his army to observe
the most severe discipline. While riding on horseback in the
environs of Leipsic, he was met by a poor peasant, who, throwing himself at his feet, complained that a Swedish soldier had
carried off all the food of his family. The king immediately
called the soldier into his presence, and demanded angrily if
it was true that he had robbed this man. "Sire," replied the
soldier, "my crime is not so great as your majesty's; for I have
but stolen a turkey, and you have taken a kingdom." Charles
smiled at this bold reply; he gave the Saxon some gold pieces
to pay for his bird, and sent the soldier away without punishment, only saying to him, "Remember, if I have taken Poland from the king of Saxony, I have kept no part of it for
myself."

A PREDICTION FULFILLED.

Among the prisoners brought before Charles XII. after the
battle of Narva was a young Tartar prince from the mountains
of the Caucasus, who had followed the Czar to the siege. The
singular destiny of this Asiatic, born under a burning sun at
one end of the world, and carried a prisoner to the cold country
of Stockholm, appeared a striking contrast to Charles, who
said, "It is much the same thing as if I should one day find
myself a prisoner among the Turks.". These words of prediction, to which little attention was paid at the time, the vicissi-
tudes of fortune soon fulfilled in his disastrous campaign of
the Pruth.

A FAIR OFFER.

Charles XII. having taken a town from the duke of Saxony,
then king of Poland, the duke intimated that there must
have been some treachery in the case. On which Charles
offered to restore the town, replace the garrison, and then
take it by storm.

LOUIS XIV. AND HIS WIG.

The chief majesty of Louis XIV. lay in his wig. He knew this, and every night he allowed his valets to undress his body, but not his head. When the disrobing was completed, save the head, he retired behind the curtains, which were carefully closed. He then removed his wig with his own royal hand, and thrusting it between the curtains, gave it up to a valet, who received it, turning his head modestly away. Before the curtains were opened in the morning the wig was passed back to the monarch, and he placed it upon his own head. Louis XIV. was never seen without his wig, nor tragedy neither.— *Profiles and Grimaces*, by Augustus Vacquerie.

BAVARIAN BRAVERY.

Unter Sendling (Greber's Inn), a village near Munich, is memorable for the bravery displayed by a band of 5000 Bavarian peasants, who, during the war of the Spanish Succession, in 1705, descended from their native mountains, and attacked the Austrian army, which at that time occupied Bavaria. They were literally cut to pieces, and vanquished, after a stout resistance, with a loss of 3000 slain. A fresco painting outside the church commemorates the event. The principal figure represents Balthasar Meyr, the gigantic blacksmith of Kochel, who had on the day previous slain nineteen of the enemy with his own hand ; and now, seeing that all was lost, collected thirty-seven mountaineers, and, followed by them, and attended by his two sons, devoted himself to certain death. He wields in his hand a spiked club, or morning star, with which he long kept his foes at bay, until overpowered by two Hungarian horsemen.

MEMORIALS OF PETER THE GREAT.

A modern French writer enumerates ninety-five authors who have treated of Peter's life and actions, and concludes the list with *et cætera* threefold. Peter was one of the most extraordinary characters that ever appeared on the great theatre of the world in any age or country : a being full of contradictions, yet consistent in all that he did ; a promoter of literature, arts, and sciences, yet without education himself ; the civiliser of his people,—" he gave a polish," says Voltaire, "to his nation, and was himself a savage ; he taught his people the art of war, of which he was himself ignorant ; from the first glance of a cockboat, at the distance of 500 miles of the nearest sea, he became an expert shipbuilder, created a powerful fleet, partly constructed with his own hands ; made himself an active and expert sailor, a skilful pilot, a great captain ;—in short, he changed the manners, the habits, the laws of the people, and the very face of the country."

Peter's visit to England was made with the object of acquiring information on matters connected with naval architecture; but we have scarcely evidence that he worked while here as a shipwright.* His fondness for sailing and managing boats he indulged almost daily on the Thames, where his great delight was, with Menzikoff and three or four others of his suite, to work a small decked-boat, Peter being the helmsman; so that he should be able to teach his people how to command ships when they got home. Having finished their day's work, they used to resort to a public-house in Great Tower Street, close to Tower Hill, to smoke their pipes and drink beer and brandy. The landlord had the Tzar of Muscovy's head painted and put up for a sign, which remained there until the year 1808, when the old sign-board was taken away by a person named Waxel, who painted the landlord a new sign, which retains its station to this day.

Peter was a great favourite with King William, for whom the Tzar sat for his portrait to Sir Godfrey Kneller; and the picture is now in Windsor Castle. The king made him a present of the "Royal Transport" ship; and Peter gave his majesty in return a rough ruby, which he carried to the palace in his waistcoat-pocket, and presented it wrapped up in a piece of brown paper. The ruby was valued at ten thousand pounds sterling, and is now in the imperial crown of England.

In after-life, Peter visited Zaardam, where, some nineteen years before, when learning the art of shipbuilding, he had dwelt in a small cottage. This humble dwelling is surrounded with a sort of screen, which was erected in 1823, by order of the princess of Orange, sister to Alexander, emperor of Russia. In the first room are the small oak table and three chairs; the furniture when Peter occupied the cottage. Over the chimney-piece is inscribed,

PETRO MAGNO
ALEXANDER;

and in Russian and Dutch,

" *To a great man nothing is little.*"

The ladder to the loft still remains; and in the second small room below are some models, and several of Peter's working

---

* Peter's object in remaining at Deptford was chiefly to gain instruction how to lay off the lines of ships, and cut out the moulds; though, it is said, on the testimony of James Sibbon, who was a journeyman shipwright in Deptford yard when the Tzar was there, that he worked with his own hands as hard as any man there. If so, it must have been for a very short time, and probably was only to show the builders that he could handle the adze. Sibbon died in 1769, aged 105 years.

H

tools. Thousands of names are scribbled over every part of this humble residence of Peter the Great.

On entering this cottage, Peter was visibly affected; and, on recovering himself, retired to a small closet in the loft, where he had been accustomed to pray. He remained half an hour; he was then shown a boat of his own making, which he desired to be put on board a ship bound for St. Petersburg; but she was unfortunately captured by the Swedes, and the boat is to this day kept in the arsenal at Stockholm.

Peter's memory is held in the highest veneration by his countrymen. The magnificent equestrian statue, erected by Catherine II.; the waxen figure of Peter in the museum of the Academy founded by himself; the dress, the sword, and the hat, which he wore at the battle of Pultowa, the hat pierced by a ball; the horse which he rode in that battle; the trousers, worsted stockings, shoes, and cap, which he wore at Zaardam, all in the same apartment; his two favourite dogs, his turning-lathe and tools, with specimens of his workmanship; the iron bar which he forged with his own hands at Olonitz; the Little Grandsire, so carefully preserved as the first germ of the Russian navy; and the wooden hut in which he lived while superintending the first foundation of Petersburg;—these, and a thousand other tangible memorials, all preserved with the utmost care, speak in the most intelligible language the opinion which the Russians hold of the *father of his country*.

EFFECT OF A PRESAGE.

When Gustavus Vasa sought to rouse the hardy people of Dalecarlia against the Danish tyrant, he addressed them in few words, relating the woes which the Danes had brought upon Sweden, and the horrible massacre at Stockholm, where so many noble fellow-countrymen had perished. The remarkable features of Gustavus, his words and firmness of purpose, had their weight with his hearers; but no voice was raised in the assembly in favour of the outlaw; every one seemed uncertain of the part he ought to take, when suddenly, a cold wind rising up, and blowing from the north, an old countryman cried out, "God approves of the designs of Vasa, for a north wind is always a happy presage." These words of the old man had the most powerful effect upon the simple people, who shouted aloud, and running to arms, desired Gustavus to conduct them instantly against the Danes. Thus, by the courage of one man, an army was brought together, large and valiant enough to tempt the fate of battle with the valiant and formidable troops of the king of Denmark, and prepared to free their native country, of which all other Swedes had given up the hope.

THE THIRTY YEARS' WAR.

The War of the Thirty Years was the last struggle sustained for the cause of the reformed religion, which, for a hundred years, had served as a pretext for all the trouble that had overwhelmed Europe, from the revolt of the peasants of Swabia under Charles V. to the peace of Westphalia. It is usually divided into four periods : 1. The Palatinate, from the defenestration of Prague to the ruin of the Elector Frederick ; 2. the Danish period, from the attempts made to penetrate into Germany by Christiern IV. of Denmark to the embarcation of Gustavus Adolphus ; 3. that prince's exploits up to the fatal battle of Lutzen ; 4. the French period, from the French armies by Cardinal Richelieu appearing on the borders of the Rhine to the conclusion of peace at Munster.

THE DEFENESTRATION OF PRAGUE.

During the early troubles of the Reformation in Germany, the Emperor Matthias sent to Prague four Austrian noblemen, as governors, to listen to the complaints of the Bohemians, and if possible re-establish peace. One day, when the four governors, with their secretary, were sitting in a room of the Castle of Prague, which was surrounded by a deep moat, an armed multitude entered, with the audacious Count de Thurn at their head. The governors became pale with alarm; the rebel-chief demanded whether they had ordered the churches to be demolished, when they threatened Thurn with the anger of the emperor, and commanded the crowd to disperse. Thereupon the rebels, seizing two of the governors and their secretary, opened the window of the room where they were sitting, and precipitated them into the moat of the castle amid the shouts of the furious multitude. This hasty execution, called in history the Defenestration of Prague, was not, however, fatal to the three victims; for, although they fell, it is said, from a height of forty feet, neither of the three was killed by the fall; and some of their friends having pulled them out of the mud in which they had sunk, preserved them from the fury of the populace.

WALLENSTEIN AND HIS ASTROLOGER.

The Count de Wallenstein, one of the heroes of the Thirty Years' War, was accustomed to pass with an Italian astrologer, named Seni, every moment he could steal from graver affairs, that he might consult him in all he undertook. It was by the predictions of this charlatan, who pretended that he passed his nights in observing the stars, that Wallenstein was persuaded that he would one day wear a crown.

One evening, after Wallenstein had been disgraced by the Emperor Ferdinand, he was sitting with his astrologer, and listening to his predictions, when Seni, fixing his eyes on the starry heavens, declared to his master, that by the stars he read that his fated hour was not yet passed. "Thou art an impostor," cried Wallenstein, in a voice like thunder,—for this imperious man would have the heavens subject to his will,—"or at any rate, thou readest the stars falsely." "Ah, well," replied the astrologer in a prophetic tone, "thou wilt certainly be thrown into a dungeon in a few days, from which thou wilt never come out." "Friend Seni," replied Wallenstein, "if it is there that I am to learn the truth of thy science, I cease to believe it, and will never listen to thee more." Wallenstein then, with strange forebodings, withdrew to his own apartment, giving orders to his servants carefully to fasten all the doors. He had scarcely retired to rest, when an Irish officer, named Devereux, who had always appeared sincerely attached to him, followed by six soldiers, fully armed, presented himself at the entrance of the palace, and was allowed by the guards to pass freely; the seven men soon arrived at the door of Wallenstein's apartment, which they found fastened. On the stairs they stabbed two servants who were about to give the alarm; and the murderers then breaking open the door of Wallenstein's chamber, found him already out of bed, but so surprised, that he had not thought of seizing his sword. "Thou art the scoundrel," cried the Irishman fiercely, "who would deliver the soldiers of the emperor to his enemies, and seize his majesty's crown for thyself." Wallenstein still appeared formidable to his assassins, who stood before him for a few moments as though waiting his reply; and there is little doubt, accustomed as they were to obey him, that one word would have disarmed these men; but the haughty general, whether from surprise or indignation, kept silence, and Devereux, plunging his poniard into his breast, threw him dead upon the floor, without any other movement than that of extending his arms. Thus perished, at the age of fifty-four, the man who had filled Europe with his brilliant renown, and whose name alone was worth all the army of Ferdinand.

GUSTAVUS ADOLPHUS AND WALLENSTEIN.

Few of those who love to loiter in the picture-gallery of history, "amid the painted forms of other times," but have felt their march arrested and their attention charmed by two great figures in the compartment of the seventeenth century—Gustavus Adolphus and Wallenstein. There is in the former a simple sublimity, a diffused and holy lustre, which sets criticism at defiance; and the glory of the saint is distinguishable

around the casque of the Protestant warrior. There is a gloom
in the grandeur of the other,—a shadow of pride, and passion,
and evil destiny, which pains while it fascinates; yet, turning
from both or either, we may wander with quickened step and
an observant eye "through rows of warriors and through ranks
of kings," a host of crowned, and helmeted, and peruked non-
entities, before we look on the like of either again.—*Quarterly
Review*, 1838.

THE SWEDE STONE.

This is one of the simplest memorials ever raised to greatness. In the first battle of Lutzen, fought in the Thirty Years'
War, in 1632, fell Gustavus Adolphus the Great, king of Sweden.
After the battle his body was found under a heap of dead, on
the roadside between Lutzen and Leipsic. It lay near a large
stone, which, in commemoration, is called the *Schwedenstein*
(Swede stone), and which still indicates the spot where the
great vindicator of the religious liberties of Germany terminated his victorious career. The king's buff-coat was carried to
Vienna, where it is still kept; but the body was conveyed to
Weissenfels. The Swede stone is simply inscribed, "G. A.,
1633:" around it are four seats, and in sorrowing beauty over-
hangs a willow.

It is related, that a knight wearing a green scarf was always
seen near Gustavus, on the field of Lutzen, even to the moment of his mortal wound, as though to point him out to the
aim of the imperialists; and that immediately after his fall
this same personage appeared near the Duke of Friedland (Wallenstein), informing him that his royal foe no longer existed.

The joy that the duke experienced on learning the death of
Gustavus was not that which a common mind would have felt
for the loss of so remarkable a rival. "Heaven has ordered it,"
said he; "Germany was not vast enough to contain us both."

PARALLEL OF THE BATTLES OF LUTZEN AND SALAMANCA.

There are some features of the great action of Lutzen which seem
analogous to those of one of the most remarkable feats of arms in our
own times—the battle of Salamanca. The previous objects of the Swede
and the Englishman were indeed not precisely similar. Gustavus was
bent on joining the Saxon, Wellington on retiring into Portugal. Marmont, on the other hand, was pressing his opponent; Wallenstein, as it
appears, had made up his mind to retire into winter-quarters without an
action. It was, however, equally the policy of Gustavus and Wellington
to refrain from a general onset, unless such a contingency presented
itself as great men alone know how to seize. Wallenstein's detachment
of Pappenheim, as affording such occasion, may be compared with that
extension of Marmont to his left which enabled Wellington to turn on
his former pursuers, and in the emphatic phrase which we have heard
attributed to him, to beat 40,000 French in forty minutes. The cir-

cumstances, however, of Salamanca were more striking, and the result more complete, than those of Lutzen. The operations of the Swede, rapid as they were, were spread over a large surface of space and time. He read his letters and marched. Wellington saw, shut his telescope, and charged. An intervening night and day made Wallenstein aware of his danger, and enabled him to bring up Pappenheim's detachment to the conflict. Moulbres was slain, and his division rolled up, before Marmont was well aware of his error. Both were certainly instances of that rapid *coup-d'œil* which appears to be the distinguishing feature and the test of the highest order of military talent.—*Quarterly Review*, 1838.

FREDERICK THE GREAT AND THE MILLER.

While Frederick's palace of Sans Souci was building at Berlin, the architect pointed out to him a mill which destroyed the view from one of the palace-apartments. Frederick ordered the proprietor of the mill into his presence, and proposed to purchase it at the price he should demand. But the miller refused to sell it to the king, whatever price he would give him. The monarch was not prepared for this obstinate resistance. "You know well enough," said he to the man, "I could take it away from you without paying." "That might be," said the miller boldly, "if we had no magistrates at Berlin." This daring reply brought Frederick to himself; he smiled to find his subjects confided in his justice, and he sent the miller away loaded with presents.

MARIA THERESA AND THE FIRST DIVISION OF POLAND.

That the only reproach on one who was "an honour to her sex, and the glory of her throne," should have arisen from what was not her own act, is a hard case; yet such was the lot of the Empress Maria Theresa. The only act of her political life for which she can be blamed is her participation in the first partition of Poland. The plan, however, did not originate with her; and she for some time refused to accede to the treaty drawn up by Russia and Prussia in 1772; she did not consent to the measure until her energy was enfeebled by disease, under the pressing influence of Kaunitz, and, as it should seem, under the fear of a northern league against her. But she wrote under Kaunitz's minute these memorable words: "*Placet*, since so many great and learned men will have it so; but when I have long been dead, men will learn the consequences of this violation of all that has hitherto been regarded as just and holy". . . "I observe well," she added, in another scrap of paper, still preserved, "that I am left alone, and no longer *en vigueur;* therefore I let things take their course, though to my deep sorrow."—*Vehse's History of the Austrian Court, &c.* 1852.

THE SAVING OF SAN MARINO.

The Republic of San Marino, in the Papal States, would long since have ceased to exist, except in history, had it not been saved by the magnanimous conduct of Antonio Onofri, who deserved the title of "father of his country," inscribed by his fellow-citizens upon his tomb. This remarkable man spent his life in its service, and by his bold and decided patriotism induced Napoleon to rescind his decree for the suppression of the republic. When summoned before the emperor, he said, "Sire, the only thing you can do for us is, to leave us just where we are." In spite of all subsequent overtures, Onofri maintained so perfect a neutrality, that he was enabled to vindicate his country before the Congress of Vienna, and obtained the recognition of its independence.

THE SMALLEST MONARCHY IN THE WORLD.

This is reputed to be the territory of the Prince of Monaco, on the Mediterranean, in the Western Riviera of Genoa. It extends about five miles along the coast, and inland about three miles. The present Prince of Monaco is supposed also to be a descendant of Louis XIV. He is a peer of France, and generally resides in Paris; his principality being garrisoned by the king of Sardinia. The prince draws from his little state a revenue of about 12,000*l.* per annum, half of which supplies the charges of administration, the other being spent by the prince in Paris. The number of subjects is about 6000.

MARAT, THE FRENCH REVOLUTIONIST.

Marat, in recommending the massacre of all aristocrats, scrupled not to proclaim, through his paper, the *Ami du Peuple*, that 270,000 heads must fall by the guillotine; and he published lists of persons whom he consigned to popular vengeance and destruction, by their names, descriptions, and places of residence. He was remarkable for the hideous features of a countenance at once horrible and ridiculous, and for the figure of a dwarf, not above five feet high. He was, on his first appearance in the mob meetings of his district, the constant butt of the company, and maltreated by all, even to gross personal rudeness. The mob, however, always took his part, because of the violence of his horrid language. Thus, long before he preached wholesale massacre in his journal, he had denounced 800 deputies as fit for execution, and demanded that they should be hanged on as many trees. His constant topic was assassination, not only in his journal, but in private society. Barbaroux describes him, in his *Mémoires*, as recommending

that all aristocrats should be obliged to wear a badge, in order
that they might be recognised and killed. "But," he used to
add, "you have only to wait at the playhouse door, and mark
those who come out, and to observe who have servants, car-
riages, and silk clothes; and if you kill them all, you are pretty
sure you have killed so many aristocrats. Or if ten in a hundred should be patriots, it don't signify—you have killed ninety
aristocrats."

PET ANIMALS.

One often sees persons of rough natures and unfeeling hearts
bestow extraordinary attention upon favourite animals. The
French Revolutionists presented some remarkable instances
of this anomalous affection. Citizen Couthon, a Hercules in
crime, fondled and invariably carried in his bosom, even to the
Convention, a little spaniel, as a vent for the exuberant sensi-
bilities which overflowed his affectionate heart. This tender-
ness for some pet animal was by no means peculiar to Couthon:
it seemed rather a common fashion with the gentle butchers of
the Revolution. M. George Duval informs us that Chaumette
had an aviary, to which he devoted his harmless leisure; the
murderous Fournier carried on his shoulders a pretty little
spaniel, attached by a silver chain; Panis bestowed the simplicity of his affections upon two gold pheasants; and Marat,
who would not abate one of the 300,000 heads he demanded,
reared doves! *Apropos* of the spaniel of Couthon, Duval gives
us an amusing anecdote of Serjent, not one of the least relent-
less agents of the massacre of September. A lady came to
implore his protection for one of her relations confined in the
abbey. He scarcely deigned to speak to her. As she retired
in despair, she trod by accident upon the paw of his favourite
spaniel. Serjent, turning round, enraged and furious, exclaimed, "*Madame, have you no humanity!*" (See Bulwer's
Zanoni.)

NAPOLEON'S THREATENED INVASION OF ENGLAND.

Doubts have frequently been expressed whether Napoleon
really intended to invade England in 1804. A curious incident
tends to confirm the impression that he did. He had a die engraved by Denon in anticipation of the event; and from this die
a number of medals were struck, with the obvious intention of
being issued from London, should the invasion prove successful.
On the obverse of the medal is a finely-cut bust of Napoleon
(the head bound with a laurel-wreath) encircled by the legend
"*Napoléon Emp. et Roi.*" On the reverse is a spirited design
of Hercules conquering Antæus—the features of the Hercules
being modelled after the Napoleonic type. The principal inscription on the reverse is "*Descente en Angleterre.*" These

words are cut in large capitals. In smaller characters, beneath the feet of the group, are the words "*Frappé à Londres, en* 1804." This inscription settles the question that the invasion was really contemplated, and establishes the curious fact that Napoleon felt so certain of victory as to have a commemorative medal prepared, with a boastful inscription declaring it to have been struck in the conquered English capital. Of course when the invasion was abandoned these medals were carefully put aside ; but some of them were discovered in one of the government offices after the battle of Waterloo, and a number were presented as curiosities to the English ministry. One of them, an excellent impression in bronze, is in the possession of a collector at Birmingham.

WOMEN AT THE SIEGE OF SARAGOZA.

In this memorable siege, in the first year of the Peninsular War (1808), when the carnage was at its most dreadful height, Augustina Saragoza, a handsome young woman of the humbler class, arriving at the battery with refreshments at a moment when not a man was left alive to serve the guns, snatched a match from the hand of a dead artilleryman, and fired off a six-and-twenty pounder, vowing never to quit the gun alive. The Saragozans at this sight rushed forward to the battery, and renewed their fire with greater vigour than ever, and the French were repulsed at all points with terrible slaughter.

During the siege, women of all ranks assisted, forming themselves into companies, some to relieve the wounded, some to carry water, arms, and provisions, to those who defended the gates. "The Countess Burita instituted a corps for this service: she was young, delicate, and beautiful. In the midst of the most tremendous fire of shot and shells, she was seen coolly attending to those occupations which had become her duty ; nor, throughout the whole of a two months' siege, did the imminent danger to which she incessantly exposed herself produce the slightest apparent effect upon her, or in the slightest degree bend her from her heroic purpose. Some of the monks bore arms ; others exercised their spiritual offices to the dying ; others, with the nuns, were busied in making cartridges, which the children distributed."—*Southey.*

SURRENDER OF NAPOLEON I.

An autograph collector possesses the rough draught of Bonaparte's celebrated letter to the Prince Regent on his surrender to the English in 1815. In this manuscript there are two or three verbal alterations : in the sentence, "*M'asseoir sur la cendre Britannique,*" the words "*la cendre*" are erased, and "*le foyer*" substituted ; and in the last sentence, "the most power-

ful, the most constant, and the most generous of my enemies,"
the words "the most constant" are interlined, being probably
an after-thought of the emperor's. In a note appended to it,
General Gourgaud states that it is the "rough draught of the
letter which the Emperor sent me to carry from the Isle of Aix
to the Prince Regent of England on the 14th of July 1815."

PORTRAIT OF NAPOLEON I.

The following description of the person of Napoleon is
given by Captain Maitland in his *Narrative of the Surrender
of Bonaparte*, in 1815: "He was then a remarkably strong,
well-built man, about 5 feet 7 inches high, his limbs particularly well formed, with a fine ancle and a very small foot, of
which he seemed very vain, as he always wore, while on board
the ship, silk stockings and shoes. His hands were also small;
and had the plumpness of a woman's rather than the robust-
ness of a man's. His eyes were light gray, his teeth good;
and when he smiled, the expression of his countenance was
highly pleasing: when under the influence of disappointment,
however, it assumed a dark and gloomy cast. His hair was a
very dark brown, nearly approaching to black; and, though a
little thin on the top and front, had not a gray hair amongst
it. His complexion was a very uncommon one, being of a
light sallow colour, different from any other I ever met with.
From his being corpulent, he had lost much of his activity."

CHARACTER OF NAPOLEON I.

In the *Edinburgh Review* we find the following able estimate of Napoleon:

Sound philosophy and a sound morality equally forbid his being
placed amongst the most illustrious characters "whose names adorn
the age in which they flourished, and exalt the dignity of human
nature." His principal characteristic was an insatiable and selfish ambition, to the gratification of which he sacrificed, without scruple or
remorse, the interests and the happiness of all mankind. The good
which he did bears no proportion to the misery of which he was, directly or indirectly, the cause: havoc, desolation, and death marked
his terrible career, and in the prosecution of his designs and objects he
trampled upon every principle of justice and humanity. He had no
sympathy with his fellow-creatures, and regarded them with such profound contempt that he was indifferent to human suffering, and reckless
of human life. It was not from any pleasure in shedding blood, but in
order to strike terror into the Royalists, that he caused the Duc d'En-
ghien to be kidnapped and put to death. When the deed was done,
he recoiled from the odium to which he saw that it would expose him,
endeavoured to shift it on his instruments, and to cast the blame upon
his precipitate zeal, imitating the behaviour of Queen Elizabeth in respect
to the execution of the Scottish queen. Although he became a mighty
monarch, he never was actuated by the feelings and sentiments of a *gentleman*, and he had a total and habitual disregard for truth. His testa-

mentary approval of the attempt to assassinate the Duke of Wellington is alone sufficient to deprive him of all claim to the praise of magnanimity. Really great men who have been enemies have always esteemed and honoured each other, and it was reserved for Napoleon to reveal to the world the vindictive spite which rankled in his mind to the last against his great conqueror, by the bequest of a sum of money to his assassin. To a character tarnished with such defects, stained by so many crimes, and not elevated by any moral dignity, a career crowned by complete and enduring success must be considered an indispensable condition of the highest order of greatness, and not only was this wanting to Napoleon, but his decline was even more rapid than his rise.

OPENING OF THE SECRET CHESTS OF GUSTAVUS III.

On March 18, 1792, the assassination of Gustavus III. was perpetrated at a masked fête at the opera-house at Stockholm, by the leader of a conspiracy, Ankastrom, a nobleman whom Gustavus had personally offended. The king was warned by some anonymous friend of the plot; but he went to the fête, and being pointed out to Ankastrom, he shot the king through the body from behind, and then mingled with the crowd of masks. The ball was extracted, and the king was borne on a litter on the shoulders of grenadiers from the theatre to the palace. Gustavus died on March 29. His assassin, Ankastrom, was discovered and executed: in his character, and in his conduct in his last moments, a striking similarity may be traced to the wretched Bellingham, who assassinated Mr. Perceval in 1812; the same fanatical satisfaction at the perpetration of the crime, the same presumptuous confidence of pardon from the Almighty.

Gustavus, in his parting moments, strictly forbade, *for fifty years*, the opening of the chests at Upsal, in which his papers were deposited; and the injunction was strictly obeyed. On March 29, 1842, a commission met at the university of Upsala, when the two chests were opened in the presence of a large assemblage of spectators; but in neither was found, as expected, any clue to the secret springs of the conspiracy by which Gustavus lost his life. The result, however, strengthened the suspicion that his brother, the duke of Sudermania, when regent, had abstracted every thing criminatory to himself from among the papers. But the king's autograph instructions, found in the chests, do not refer to any papers later than 1788, when the bequest was made; and there is no positive proof of any papers being subsequently added. Still, certain "Freemason papers" were only to be opened by the reigning king of Gustavus's family, who had fallen from the throne; accordingly the documents remained sealed. The Swedish instructions in Gustavus's handwriting, and the French words with which they are relieved, prove that the king enjoyed the reputation of being a great author without even knowing how to spell.

THE RESULT OF THE AMERICAN WAR WITH GREAT BRITAIN FORETOLD.

"I prophesied," said Colonel Barré, "on passing the Stamp Act, in 1765, what would happen thereon; and I now, in March 1769, I now fear I can prophesy further troubles; that if the whole people are made desperate, finding no remedy from parliament, the whole continent will be in arms immediately, and perhaps *these provinces lost to England for ever.*" This was in March 1769, and certainly a very remarkable prediction.—Professor Smyth's *Lectures on Modern History.*

SUCCESSION TO THE THRONE OF FRANCE.

Not a little remarkable is it to observe, that from the accession of Louis XIV. to the present time not a single king or governor of France,—though none of them, with the exception of Louis XVIII., have been childless,—has been succeeded at his demise by his son. Louis XIV. survived his son, his grandson, and several of his great-grandchildren, and was succeeded at last by one of the younger children of his grandson, the Duke of Burgundy. Louis XV. survived his son, and was succeeded by his grandson. Louis XVI. left a son behind him; but that son perished in the filthy dungeon to which the cruelties of the terrorists had confined him. The King of Rome, to whom Napoleon fondly hoped to bequeath the boundless empire he had won, died a colonel in the Austrian service. Louis XVIII. was, as we have said, childless. The Duke de Berri fell by the hand of an assassin in the lifetime of Charles X.; and his son, the Duke de Bordeaux, is in exile from the land which his ancestors regarded as their own estate. The eldest son of Louis Philippe perished by an untimely accident; and his grandson and heir does not sit upon the throne of his grandfather. Thus, then, it appears that for upwards of two hundred years in no one of the dynasties to which France has been subjected has the son succeeded to the throne of the father. —*The Times Journal*, 1856.

GENEROSITY OF WELLINGTON.

Lord Brougham relates of the Duke of Wellington, that, "while Napoleon passed within range of an English battery at Waterloo, and the officers were about to fire at the group, he at once and peremptorily forbade it. This passage in his illustrious and unstained life is worth a thousand superfluous panegyrics, and puts to flight all imputations upon him as wanting in those feelings which, in the company of more rare and stern qualities, are ever found to adorn the character of the greatest men."

IS FRIDAY AN UNLUCKY DAY?

This question has received the following replies in the *Norfolk* (United States) *Beacon;* which show how little the Americans have to dread "the fatal day :"

"On Friday, August 21, 1492, Christopher Columbus sailed on his great voyage of discovery. On Friday, October 12, 1492 he first discovered land. On Friday, January 4, 1493, he sailed on his return to Spain, which, if he had not reached in safety, the happy result would never have been known which led to the settlement on this vast continent. On Friday, March 15, 1493, he arrived at Palos in safety. On Friday, November 22, 1493, he arrived at Hispaniola, in his second voyage to America. On Friday, June 13, 1494, he, though unknown to himself, discovered the continent of America. On Friday, March 5, 1496, Henry VIII. of England gave to John Cabot his commission, which led to the discovery of North America. This is the first American state-paper in England. On Friday, September 7, 1565, Melendez founded St. Augustine, the oldest town in the United States by more than forty years. On Friday, November 10, 1620, the May-Flower, with the Pilgrims, made the harbour of Province Town; and on the same day they signed that august compact, the forerunner of our present glorious constitution. On Friday, December 22, 1620, the Pilgrims made their final landing at Plymouth Rock. On Friday, February 22, George Washington, the father of American freedom, was born. On Friday, June 10, Bunker Hill was seized and fortified. On Friday, October 7, 1777, the surrender of Saratoga was made, which had such power and influence in inducing France to declare for our cause. On Friday, Sept. 22, 1780, the treason of Arnold was laid bare, which saved us from destruction. On Friday, October 19, 1781, the surrender at Yorktown, the crowning glory of the American arms, occurred. On Friday, July 7, 1776, the motion in Congress was made by John Adams, seconded by Richard Henry Lee, that the United States Colonies were, and of right ought to be, free and independent. Thus, by numerous examples, we see that, however it may be with foreign nations, Americans need never dread to begin on Friday any undertaking, however momentous it may be."

In a pamphlet entitled *Day Fatality,* printed in 1679, several evidences of "days lucky and unlucky" are brought together. "On the 6th of April," says the writer, "Alexander the Great was born; upon the same day he conquered Darius, won a great victory at sea, and died the same day. Neither was this day less fortunate to his father Philip: for on the same day he took Potidea; Parmenio, his general, gave a great overthrow to the Illyrians; and his horse was victor at the Olympic games. Upon the 30th of September, Pompey the Great was born; upon that day he triumphed for his Asian conquest, and on that day died."

British History.

GOG AND MAGOG.

Many learned commentators have asserted that the country occupied in the fourth century by the Huns (a Scythian nation, on the eastern shores of the Sea of Azof) was the same as is mentioned in Ezekiel by the description of Gog, the land of Magog. Magog was the second son of Japhet, and, it is said, gave his name to that part of the world ; the Mogul Tartars, who are unquestionably Scythians, being still known by the name of Gog. Michaelis assimilates the word Gog to that of Kak, or Chak, the general name of kings amongst the ancient Turks, Moguls, and Tartars ; and Dr. Hyde asserts, that the Arabs distinguish the celebrated Chinese wall, which was built nearly three hundred years before the Christian era, as the wall of Gog and Magog ; and it seems probable that Magog was the name given to those vast tracts of land called Scythia by the Greeks, and Tartary by the moderns.—*Chatfield on the Darker Ages*, 1824.

ALFRED AND THE NEATHERD'S WIFE.

Of this interesting adventure we find the following narrative in an ancient "Homily" upon the life and miracles of St. Neot, written in Anglo-Saxon, contained in a Ms. in the Cottonian Library, Vesp. D. xiv.

In the winter of 878, when king Alfred was defeated by the Danes, he fled to Athelney, a secluded spot at the confluence of the Thone and the Parrett. "Here," says the Homily, "he entreated a certain rustic for refuge in his dwelling, where he diligently served him and his 'evil' wife. It happened one day that the wife of this countryman heated her oven, and Alfred sat near it, warming himself by the fire, his protector being all the while ignorant that he was the king. Then that 'evil' woman became suddenly enraged, and said in anger to the king, 'Turn thou these loaves, lest they become too much burnt ; for I notice daily that thou art a great glutton.' He speedily obeyed that 'evil' woman, because need compelled him to do so." "We know," says Sir F. Palgrave, "that Alfred was wont, when happier times arrived, to recount his adventures to his listening friends ; and this anecdote may have been among those which originally rested upon his own testimony.

"One very curious fact remains to be added. The king wore an ornament, probably fastened to a necklace, made of gold and enamel ; which, being lost by him at Athelney, was found there, entire and undefaced, in the seventeenth century. It is now preserved at Oxford (in the Ashmolean Museum) ; and the inscription in Gallic-Saxon which surrounds it, *Alfred het meh gewircan—Alfred caused me to be* (worked) *made*, affords the most authentic testimony of its origin."—*Sir F. Palgrave.*

THE ELEPHANT FIRST SEEN IN ENGLAND.

Polyœnus, who wrote about A.D. 180, has left us this singular picture of Roman strategy, in his *Strategematum :*

" Cæsar attempting to cross a large river in Britain, Cassolaulus, king of the Britons, obstructed him with many horsemen and chariots. Cæsar had in his train a very large elephant, an animal hitherto unseen by the Britons. Having armed him with scales of iron, and put a large tower upon him, and placed therein archers and slingers, he ordered them to enter the stream. The Britons were amazed on beholding a beast till then unseen, and of an extraordinary nature. As to the horses, what need we write about them, since even among the Greeks horses fly at seeing an elephant, though without harness ; but thus towered and armed, and casting darts and slinging, they could not endure even to look upon the sight. The Britons, therefore, fled with their horses and chariots. Thus the Romans passed the river without molestation, having terrified the enemy by a single animal."

Yet, Matthew Paris relates, that in 1255 an elephant was sent by the king of France to Henry III. ; and that, it being the first animal of that species that had been seen in England, the people flocked in great numbers to behold it. Upon the Close Rolls is entered a writ, tested at Westminster the 3d of February, 39 Hen. III. (1255), directing the sheriff of Kent to " go in person to Dover, together with John Gouch, the king's servant, to arrange in what manner the king's elephant, which was at Whitsand,* may best and most conveniently be brought over to these parts ; and to find for the same John a ship, and other necessary things to convey it; and if, by the advice of the mariners and others, it could be brought to London by water:" directing it to be so brought. That the stranger arrived safely, is evident from a similar writ, dating the 23d of the same month, commanding the sheriffs of London to " cause to be built at the Tower of London a house 40 feet in length and 20 feet in breadth, for the king's elephant."

* The shortest and most convenient passage from France to England appears to have been from Whitsand to Dover. The tenure of certain lands in Coperland, near Dover, was the service of holding the king's head between Dover and Whitsand whenever he crossed there.

" THE ELEPHANT AND CASTLE."

The choice of this inn-sign would appear to have been taken from an early traveller's account of the use of the elephant in battle.

Cæsar Frederick, a merchant of Venice, who spent eighteen years in travelling in the East, about the middle of the six-teenth century, states that the king of Pegu had 4000 war-elephants, with wooden castles on their backs.

Milton has the phrase of " elephants indorsed with towers of archers," in his description of the retreat of Antony from Parthia.

We gather also from Florus, that elephants with their war-accoutrements and towers were the rarest parts of the spoils of Dentatus from the Epirot camp.

THE FIRST CHRISTIAN CHURCH IN BRITAIN.

Glastonbury, Somerset, claims to have furnished a site for the first Christian church in Britain ; whence ancient chroni-clers delighted to dignify her as the fountain and origin of all religion in the realm of Britain—" the second Rome"—the "Ealdecherche ;" upon which Southey observes :

" It cannot now be ascertained by whom the glad tidings of the Gospel were first brought into Britain. It is said that the first church was erected in Glastonbury ; and this tradition may seem to deserve credit, because it was not contradicted in those ages when other churches would have found it profitable to advance a similar pretension. The building is described as a rude structure of wicker-work, like the dwell-ings of the people in those days, and differing from them only in its dimensions, which were three score feet in length, and twenty-six in breadth. An abbey was afterwards erected there ; and the destruction of this beautiful and venerable fabric is one of the crimes by which our Reformation was disgraced."—*Book of the Church.*

Here the ancient British kings, Arviragus, St. Lucius, and the renowned Arthur, were reported to be interred. Here also the Anglo-Saxon kings, Ethelred, Edgar, Edmund Iron-side, and St. Edward the Martyr, who was assassinated at Corfe Castle, sleep their last sleep ; besides "many other kings and queens, not only of the West Saxons, but of other kingdoms of the Heptarchy. Several archbishops and bishops, many dukes, and the nobility of both sexes, thought themselves happy in increasing the revenue of this venerable house, and to obtain them a place of sepulture. In the churchyard lay buried St. Joseph of Arimathea and his eleven companions, St. Patrick, and many other saints."—*Eyston's Little Monument.*

KING ARTHUR.

Arthur is said to have lived about the year 530.   Geoffrey

of Monmouth calls him the son of Uther Pendragon, others
think he was himself called Uther Pendragon : Uther signifying
in the Danish tongue a club, because as with a club he beat
down the Saxons; Pendragon, dragon's head, because he wore
a dragon on the crest of his helmet.*

COALS AND WINDOW-GLASS USED BY THE ROMANS IN DRITAIN.

It is now well ascertained that the Romans, in Britain at
least, made use of mineral coal.   The cinders have been found
in some cases in the fireplaces of Roman villas; and in several
places in Northumberland, where the coal-beds came to or near
the surface, the Roman workings have been traced to a very
considerable extent.   On the northern coast of Wales, where
the coal-beds also cropped out, there can be little doubt from
appearances that the Romans worked coal-mines extensively.

In Britain, and in the colder climates generally, the Romans appear always to have warmed their houses with hot air,
and never with fireplaces in the rooms, as at present.   The
floors of the rooms were formed of strong cement, resting on
numerous short pillars; and from the narrow subterranean ap-
partment thus formed, termed the hypocaust, numerous flue-
tiles were run up the internal surfaces of the walls of the
house.   Fireplaces were made at the side of the hypocaust
externally, for the purpose of heating the air within, which
rose up the pipes of the flue-tiles.

Window-glass was no doubt used in the Roman villas in
this country, for in excavating the remains of these buildings
numerous pieces of glass are often found on the original floor
at the foot of the wall, where there had evidently been windows
above.   This glass resembles in quality our common window-
glass, and is of about the same thickness.—*Tho. Wright, F.S.A.*

VENERABLE DEDE.

Beda, or Bede, an English monk, was one of the brightest
ornaments of the eighth century, and one of the most eminent
fathers of the English Church, whose talents and virtues procured him the name of *Venerable Bede.*   He was born about
A.D. 672, at Monkton, Durham (only a few years after the introduction of Christianity into England) ; at seven years of age
was sent to the monastery of St. Peter, where he was carefully educated for twelve years.   He was ordained deacon at nineteen, and priest at thirty, and never quitted his monastery.

His most valuable work is a Latin *History of the English Church,* in
five books, from the time of Julius Cæsar to A.D. 731 ; with a continuation of the Acts of the English before the Saxon Invasion, by an anony-

* See also King Arthur's Round Table, *Things not generally Known,* p. viii.

1

mous author. An epitome of his work, down to A.D. 766, is said to have been made by Richard Lavington, a Carmelite monk of Bristol, and a great writer of divinity, about the end of the fourteenth century. Few works have either so long supported their credit, or have been so universally known and consulted; and it may be considered as an entirely novel subject in England, since the civil histories which existed before it contained but few particulars on ecclesiastical affairs. It was principally compiled from the information of his contemporaries, and the records of religious houses; which may probably account for its favouring the Saxons against the Britons, and its too great credulity as to legends and miracles. The last and best of Bede's works was his Epistle to Egbert, Bishop of York, illustrating the state of the Church in his time, and representing several evils in it, of which he foresaw the increase, and which were afterwards removed by the Reformation.—Thomson's *Illustrations of the History of Great Britain*, vol. i. p. xxxv.

Malmesbury says of Bede: "He was a man, that, although born in the extreme corner of the world, yet the light of his learning spread over all parts of the earth." "With this man was buried almost all knowledge of history down to our times; inasmuch as there has been no Englishman, either emulous of his pursuits or a follower of his graces, who could continue the thread of his discourses now broken short." To him we owe all our knowledge of English history, from the landing of the Saxons in Kent to his time (nearly three centuries), and all our certain information respecting the various tribes who then inhabited this island; from him it is apparent that the Saxon chronicler copied long passages.

BRIAN BOROIHME'S HARP.

It is well known that the great monarch Brian Boroime was killed at the battle of Clontarf, A.D. 1014. He left his son Donah his harp; but Donah having murdered his brother Teige, and being deposed by his nephew, retired to Rome, and carried with him the crown, harp, and other regalia of his father. These regalia were kept in the Vatican till Pope Clement sent the harp to Henry VIII., but kept the crown, which was massive gold. Henry gave the harp to the first earl of Clanricarde, in whose family it remained until the beginning of the eighteenth century; when it came by a lady of the De Burgh family into that of M'Mahon of Glenagh, in the county of Clare, after whose death it passed into the possession of Councillor Macnamara of Limerick. In 1782 it was presented to the Right Hon. William Conyngham, who deposited it in Trinity College Museum, where it now is. It is 32 inches high, and of good workmanship; the sounding-board is of oak, the arms of red sally; the extremity of the uppermost arm in part is capped with silver, well wrought and chiselled. It contains a large crystal set in silver, and under it was another stone, now lost.

THE BAYEUX TAPESTRY.

This celebrated work is an historical document of the greatest importance, since it represents many events doubtless well known at the period of its execution, but of which no other record now exists. Tradition assigns it as the work of Matilda, the wife of William I.: the subject is his Conquest of England ; and a critic in the *Athenæum* has observed the wonderful similarity of *narration* that appears between these and the marbles recently brought from Nineveh, not only in the same battle-incidents, homage to royalty, and evident haste in executing a commission, but the varied size of the figures according to rank, the shape of the trees (some radiating in buds with fanciful stems), and the marking of the waves, and minuteness of architecture, combined with an utter defiance of perspective.

The Bayeux Tapestry lay disregarded until 1724, when it was published by Montfaucon. Napoleon I. had it conveyed from Bayeux to Paris, where it was shown to inflame the minds of the people for the invasion of England. In 1814 it was exhibited, coiled round a roller set in a frame with a winch. The name of the *Toile de St. Jean* was given to it, because it was displayed to the people on St. John's Day, when it was hung round the nave of the cathedral of Bayeux. It is now preserved under glass in the public library at Bayeux.

The Tapestry has originally formed one piece, and measures two hundred and twenty-seven feet in length, by about twenty inches in breadth. The groundwork of it is a strip of rather fine linen-cloth, which, through age, has assumed the tinge of brown holland. The stitches consist of lines of coloured worsted laid side by side, and bound down at intervals with cross-fastenings. The parts intended to represent flesh (the face, hands, or naked legs of the men) are left untouched by the needle. The lower border is supposed to represent the fables of Æsop ; under the battle of Hastings, dead bodies supply the border. Considering the age of the Tapestry, it is in a remarkably perfect state. The first portion of it is somewhat injured, and the last five yards of it are very much defaced. The colours chiefly used are dark and light blue, red, pink, yellow, buff, and dark and light green. In the words of Mr. Hudson Gurney, in the *Archæologia*, "the colours are as bright and distinct, and the letters of the superscriptions as legible, as if of yesterday."

The Tapestry contains 623 men (the Saxons wearing mustachios, the Normans none), 202 horses, 55 dogs, 505 various other animals, 37 buildings, 41 ships and boats, and 49 trees ; in all 1512 figures. Among the 1512 figures only three are females. Upon the numerous shields are no indications of the lion, fess or chevron ; the devices are confined to dragons, spots, and crosses.

Among the principal events of the Tapestry are—the Mission of Harold by Edward Rex (the Confessor); Departure of Harold ; Harold and Guy in conference; Harold's oath ; Death of Edward ;·Harold upon his throne ; News brought to William ;

Embarkation of the Normans; Landing in Pevensey Bay; and the Battle of Hastings.

FINDING OF THE REMAINS OF THE DAUGHTER OF WILLIAM THE CONQUEROR AND HER LORD.

Few archæological discoveries equal in interest the following finding of the remains of a princess of England and her husband, after a lapse of nearly eight centuries:

In October 1845, in the formation of the Brighton and Hastings railway, the workmen had to cut through the spot at Lewes the site of the principal Cluniac monastery in England, founded soon after the Norman conquest by William Earl of Warrene, and his wife Gundrad, Gundrada, or Gundfreda, the fifth daughter of William the Conqueror. At about two feet from the surface, the workmen met with an oblong leaden coffer or chest, surrounded with Caen stones; on removing which appeared legibly inscribed upon the upper end of the coffer-lid the word

GVNDRADA

Next the workmen brought to light a second coffer, slightly larger than the other, and inscribed

WilLE...

which was at once assigned to William de Warrene. The lids of the coffers were not fastened, but merely *flanged* over the edges. Both are ornamented externally with a sort of lozengy or network pattern in relievo, such as our plumbers to this day ornament coffins with. The bones of both skeletons, and the teeth, were in fine preservation. The height of the earl must have been from 6 feet 1 inch to 6 feet 2 inches, and that of the countess from 5 feet 7 inches to 5 feet 8 inches. The name upon the lid, of Gundred, is given in its Latinised form of Gundrada, and William by the usual contraction Willelmᵉ. The character before the M appears to be a compound letter, expressing both E and L, and the U S are represented by the mark so constantly used in the MM. of the middle ages. Mr. Lower, F.S.A., suggests that the letters are not of later date than the earlier part of the thirteenth century. Now the characters in the name of Gundrada tally exactly with those in the same word on her marble tomb, extant in Southover church; thus establishing two facts, viz. first, that now, after a separation of two centuries, the bones of the noble Gundreda and her tomb are again brought into juxtaposition; and secondly, the coffers, or cists, and the tomb are unquestionably coeval.

An interesting inquiry, (says Mr. Lower,) arises out of this discovery. The remains have certainly been removed from their original resting-place, and reinterred in the coffers, in conformity with a practice not unusual in early times. Gundrada died at Castle Acre, in Norfolk — *vi partûs cruciata* — on the 27th of May 1085, and was buried at Lewes Priory, as proved by the charter of De Warrene, made shortly prior to his own decease, in which he expresses his desire to be interred by her side. The church is believed to have been the place of interment. As the convent increased in affluence, a new church was commenced building in 1243, but not finished until 1268. Mr. Lower assumes, therefore, that the bodies of the founders were in this interval exhumed from the old church (which would then be dismantled), and deposited in the coffers, for reinterment in the chapter-house, upon the site of which there is reason to believe the bones were found. The two coffers were subsequently placed in a tomb, erected for their reception, in · Southover church; the original sculptured slab forming the upper portion of the memorial.

The subject is further discussed and illustrated in Mr. Lower's excellent *Handbook to Lewes*, second edition, 1854.

THE NEW FOREST, HANTS.

For the making of this Forest sixty parishes were "cleared," extending thirty miles in length between Salisbury and the sea, and which no Saxon might enter but at the peril of his life, for the Normans were the authors of the Game-laws. The forest was peculiarly fatal to the Conqueror's family. It was there in the year 1081 Richard, his eldest son, was mortally wounded. In 1100, Richard, son of Duke Robert, and nephew of William Rufus, was killed there by an arrow; and the Red King himself perished there in like manner the same year.

SAXON AND NORMAN NAMES OF PROVISIONS.

The names of provisions throw some light upon the mode of living among the higher and lower classes of our population. Bread, with the common productions of the garden, such as pease, beans, eggs, and some other articles which might be produced in the cottage-garden or yard, retain their Saxon names, and evidently formed the chief nourishment of the Saxon portion of the population. Of meat, though the word is Saxon, they ate probably little; for it is one of the most curious circumstances connected with the English language, that while the living animals are called by Anglo-Saxon names, as oxen, calves, sheep, pigs, deer, the flesh of those animals when prepared for the table is called by names which are all Anglo-Norman—beef, veal, mutton, pork, venison. The butcher who killed them is himself known by an Anglo-Norman name. Even fowls when killed receive the Norman name of poultry. This can only be explained by the circumstance that the Saxon population in general was only acquainted with the living animals, while their flesh was carried off to the castle and table of the Norman possessors of the land, who gave it names taken from their own language. Fresh meat, salted, was hoarded up in immense quantities in the Norman castles, and was distributed lavishly to the household and idle followers of the feudal possessors. Almost the only meat obtained by the peasantry, unless, if we believe old popular songs, by stealth, was *bacon*, and that also is still called by an Anglo-Norman name.—*Gentleman's Magazine.*

ASSASSINATION OF THOMAS À BECKET.

In the *Quarterly Review*, No. 186, the circumstances attending the murder of this bold priest have been carefully collated, and present some new researches. Contrary to the received notion, Becket was not killed in front of the altar of Canterbury Cathedral; he was slain in the choir confronting his pursuers, when they succeeded in arresting his flight upwards to the sacrosanct chapel of St. Blaise, in the roof of the cathedral. The assassins had challenged him, on the part of Henry, in the course of the afternoon, and a long-continued angry altercation had passed between them in the presence of the monks, who surrounded their archbishop, in his private chamber. When the murderers left to get their arms, the monks hurried Becket by the cloisters into the church, in the vain hope of sanctuary. When Tracy, one of the assassins, attacked Becket, the latter grappled with and flung him on the floor of the choir. Fitzurse then struck at the archbishop with his sword, but only wounded him slightly in the head; breaking, however, the arm of Grim, a German monk, which was raised to ward off the blow. Another sword-cut prostrated Becket; and then, as he lay, Tracy smote him with such force that he cut off the crown of his head, cleaving through brain and bone, and breaking his sword on the stone pavement. So ended the career of the archbishop. The well-known legend has it that evil befell the murderers by sea and land, and that no one of them ever after throve or prospered; and such was, indeed, the popular belief for nearly seven centuries. But the facts are totally different. Moreville, who kept back the crowd at the door of the choir while the associate assassins were doing the king's will on Becket, lived and died Chief-Justice in Eyre, north of Trent—that is to say, one of the principal judges of England. Tracy was created Grand Justiciary of Normandy by Henry within four years of the assassination. Fitzurse went to Ireland, and founded the Celto-Norman sept, known as the Mac Mahons of the county of Wexford; and Bret, the fourth murderer, died in his bed in due course, after spending a long life in the enjoyment of his estates in Devonshire: thus negativing the historical justice.

ORIGIN OF MAGNA CHARTA.

King John having exercised the power of recruiting men for repairing fortresses, bridges, and roads; of levying contributions of corn and cattle in his journeys; and of seizing beasts of burden, carts, and agricultural implements;—this touched the interests of the proprietors of the soil and the serfs, who helped to "clothe" it. The barons combined, resisted, and

extorted Magna Charta. Strange to say, this great instrument
of national freedom had no nobler origin than this! Indeed, one
article of the great Charter forbids the destruction of houses,
woods, or *men*, without the special license of the *proprietor*,
who had full power over the life of Englishmen.   It is a great
mistake to suppose that the war of the barons against John
Lackland was waged for the benefit of the subjects, or that the
treaty of Runnymede secured their liberties.   They were never
thought of by either party, except as liable to be slaughtered
like cattle in the barbarous reprisals which the belligerents
made on one another's properties.—*N. British Review*, No. 12.

Magna Charta, if not the original, a copy made when King John's
seal was affixed to it, was acquired by the British Museum with the
Cottonian Library.   It was nearly destroyed in the fire at Westminster
in 1731; the parchment is much shrivelled and mutilated, and the seal
is reduced to an almost shapeless mass of wax.   The Ms. was carefully
lined and mounted, and is now secured under glass.   It is about two feet
square, is written in Latin, and is quite illegible.   It is traditionally
stated to have been bought for fourpence, by Sir Robert Cotton, of a
tailor, who was about to cut up the parchment into measures!   But
this anecdote, if true, may refer to another copy of the Charter preserved at the British Museum, in a portfolio of royal and ecclesiastical
instruments, marked Augustus II. art. 106; and the original Charter
is believed to have been presented to Sir Robert Cotton by Sir Edward
Dering, lieutenant-governor of Dover Castle; and to be that referred
to in a letter dated May 10, 1630, extant in the Museum Library, in
the volume of Correspondence, Julius C. III. fol. 191.

"The Commissioners on the Public Records regarded the original of Magna
Charta preserved at Lincoln as of superior authority to either of those in the
British Museum, on account of several words and sentences being inserted in the
body of that Charter, which in the latter are added at the foot, with reference-
marks to the bar places where they were to be added. These notes, however,
possibly may prove that one of the Museum Charters was really the first written,
to which those important additions were made immediately previous to the
sealing on Runnymede, and therefore the actual original whence the more perfect transcripts were taken."—Richard Thomson, author of *An Historical Essay
on the Magna Charta of King John, &c.* 1829."

NO NEW ENGLISH SOVEREIGN IN MAY.

It is remarkable that among the thirty-three sovereigns
who have sat on the English throne since William the Conqueror, although each of the eleven months has witnessed the
accession of one or more, the month of May has not been so
fortunate, none having ascended the throne within its limits.

* At Lacock Abbey, about midway between Chippenham and Melksham, in
the middle chamber of the tower, reserved as a depository for writings, is preserved the Magna Charta of King Henry III., of inestimable value, being the
only perfect one in the kingdom: it is 12½ inches broad, and in length, including
the fold 20½ inches; the seal is of green wax, pendent by a skein of green silk.
This Charter seems to have been designed for the use of the knights and military tenants in Wiltshire, and to have been deposited here by Ela, Countess of
Salisbury, foundress of the abbey and first abbess, and who succeeded her husband in the office of sheriff of Wiltshire.

BIRTH OF EDWARD, FIRST PRINCE OF WALES.

In the magnificent fortress of Carnarvon is commonly said to have been born, April 25, 1284, the second son of Edward I., the first created Prince of Wales and Earl of Chester; who became heir-apparent to the crown by the death of his elder brother Alphonso. The "Eagle Tower" of the castle was long pointed out as the room in which the prince was born; but the Rev. Mr. Hartshorne has, by long and laborious research, demonstrated that little had been done towards building the castle in 1284, when Edward I. entered Carnarvon for the first time; and records show that the Eagle Tower was built by Edward II.; so that his birth must have taken place in one of the earliest-built apartments of the fortress, and could by no possibility have occurred in the Eagle Tower.

QUEEN ELEANOR'S CROSSES.

The origin of these memorials is thus described by Holinshed:

" In the nineteenth yeare of king Edward (L 1290), Queene Elianor, King Edwards wife, died upon St. Androws even at Hirdeble, or Herdelle (as some have), neere to Lincolne, the King being as then on his wale towards the borders of Scotland; but having now lost the iewell which he most esteemed, he returned towards London to accompanie the corps vnto Westminster, where it was buried in S. Edwards chapell, at the feet of King Henry the third. She was a godlie and modest princesse, full of pitie, and one that showed much fauour to the English nation, readie to releeve euerie mans greefe that susteined wrong, and to make them freends that were at discord, so far as in hir laie. In euerie towne and place where the corps rested by the waie, the King caused a crosse of cunning workmanship to be erected in remembrance of hir, and in the same was a picture of hir ingrauen. Two of the like crosses were set up at London, one at Charing, and the other in Westcheape."

Walsingham also says:

" In every place and town where the corpse rested, the king commanded a cross of admirable workmanship to be erected to the queen's memory, that prayers might be offered for her soul by all passengers; in which cross he caused the queen's image to be depicted.''

There exists, however, evidence of the crosses having been erected, not by the king's orders, but in pursuance of the queen's own will, and with funds which she left for that purpose.

From the accounts of the executors of Queen Eleanor, printed from the original Ms. in 1841, for the Roxburghe Club, by Beriah Botfield, Esq., it appears that these celebrated crosses were nine in number: viz. at Lincoln, Northampton, Stony Stratford, Woburn, Dunstable, St. Alban's, Waltham, Cheap and Charing in London. That of Geddington, often considered is one of them, is not recorded in the roll. This, with Waltham, Northampton, and Newark, alone remain, and have been restored.

Charing Cross appears to have been the most sumptuous of the whole. It was built of Caen stone, and Dorset marble steps; it was highly decorated, and had paintings, and metal figures gilt, and statuettes of Eleanor and others. It was voted down by the Long Parliament, and removed in 1647; some of the stone was subsequently made into knife-hafts.

PAY OF TROOPS IN THE THIRTEENTH CENTURY.

The pay assigned to Troops who, having contributed the stipulated service for their holdings or assessments, were required to render further assistance to the king in his wars, we discover in the Roll of Expenses of King Edward I., at Ruddlan Castle, Wales, in 1281-2. From this document we find:

The pay of	Per diem.	In modern money.
A knight	12d.	15s.
An esquire	12d.	15s.
An archer	2d.	2s. 6d.
A cross-bowman	2d.	2s. 6d.
A captain of twenty (bowmen)	4d.	5s.
A constable (of 100 bowmen)	6d.	7s. 6d.

PRICES OF AGRICULTURAL LABOUR IN THE FOURTEENTH CENTURY.

In the year 1352, the 25th of Edward III., wages paid to haymakers were but 1d. per day; a mower of meadows 3d. a-day, or 5d. an acre; reapers of corn, in the first week in August, 2d., in the second, 4d. per day, and so on until the end of the month, without meat, drink, or other allowance, finding their own tools. For threshing a quarter of wheat or rye, 2½d.; a quarter of beans, pens, barley, or oats, 1½d. By the 13th of Richard II., in the year 1389, the wages of a bailiff of husbandry was 13s. 4d. a-year, and his clothing once during that time at most; a carter, 10s.; shepherd, 10s.; ox-herd, 6s. 8d.; cow-herd, 6s. 8d.; swine-herd, 6s.; a woman-labourer, 6s.; a day-labourer, 6s.; a driver of ploughs, 7s. From this time up to the 23d of Henry IV., the price of labour was fixed by the justices by proclamation. In 1444, 23d Henry VI., the wages of a bailiff of husbandry were 23s. 4d. per annum, and clothing of the price of 5s., with meat and drink; chief hind, carter, or shepherd, 20s., and clothing, 4s.; common servant of husbandry, 15s., clothing, 3s. 4d.; woman-servant, 10s., clothing, 4s. In time of harvest, a mower, 4d. a-day — without meat and drink, 6d.; a reaper or carter, 3d. a-day — without meat and drink, 5d.; a woman-labourer, and other labourers, 2d. a-day — without meat or drink, 4½d. By the 11th Henry VII., 1496, there was a like rate of wages, only with a little advance.

THE BATTLE OF POICTIERS.

On Monday, the 19th day of September 1356, was won this most extraordinary victory that the annals of the world can produce; yet, before two centuries had passed, the spot where these mighty deeds were enacted was unknown. In an after-age, the point was eagerly investigated and contested; but at length, in 1743, the exact position of the English army seems to have been ascertained. Nevertheless, the traveller will search for that fatal field long before he finds it; but if he seek out a peasant's house called *Les Bordes*, near some tall trees, he may be led to the ground where the Black Prince was intrenched. But the vineyard mentioned by Froissart is no longer there: still the hollow way between its steep banks is to be seen; and the intrenchments of the English camp may yet be traced. The peasant declares, too, in ploughing the slopes, he frequently turns up human bones and rusty armour and heads of arrows. At a little farmhouse, also, not far from the spot, some broken lances and large bones are shown; and that is all which now remains to attest the field of Poictiers.

Man may well ask his heart, as he passes over the spot, " Is this all, indeed ?—all for which so many heroes have died—to be forgotten—to have their very burial-places scarcely known —the glorious feats and gallant actions which, even in dying, they thought would be immortal, overwhelmed beneath the lumber of history, or blotted out by fresh comments on the same bloody theme—the throne they fought for, and the lands they won, passed unto other dynasties, and all the objects of their mighty daring as unachieved as if they had not been !"— James's *History of Edward the Black Prince.*

AN HISTORIC ROAD INTO LONDON.

Kent Street, Southwark, originally "Kentish Street," a wretched and profligate part of St. George's parish, in 1633 was described as " very long and ill-built, chiefly inhabited by broom-men and mumpers;" and for ages it has been noted for its turners' shops and broom and heath yards. Yet, what long lines of conquest and devotion, of turmoil and rebellion, of victory, gorgeous pageantry, and grim death, have poured through this narrow inlet of old London ! The Roman invader came along the rich marshy ground now supporting Kent Street (says Bagford, in a letter to his brother-antiquary Hearne); thousands of pious and weary pilgrims have passed along this causeway to St. Thomas of Canterbury; here the Black Prince rode with his royal captive from Poictiers, and the victor of Agincourt was carried in kingly state to his last earthly bourne. By this route Cade advanced with his 20,000 insurgents from Blackheath to Southwark; and the ill-fated Wyat marched to discomfiture and death. And to the forma-tion of the Dover Road, in our time, Kent Street continued part of the great way from Dover and the continent into the metropolis.—*Curiosities of London.*

THE JERUSALEM CHAMBER IN WESTMINSTER ABBEY.

This celebrated apartment, situated on the left side of

Dean's Yard, has in its windows some painted glass of Richard II.'s time; and upon its south wall the curious painting of Richard II. sitting in his regal paraphernalia, in the coronation-chair. Henry IV. breathed his last in this chamber, into which he had been brought when seized with apoplexy, while worshipping at St. Edward's shrine, March 20, 1413. He was then preparing for a voyage to the Holy Land, having recently assumed the Cross in consequence of a prediction that "he should die in *Jerusalem,*" which had been made to him in the early part of his life. "He became so syke," says Fabian, "while he was makynge his prayers, to take there his leve, and so to spede hym upon his iournaye, that such as were aboute hym feryd that he wolde have dyed right there; wherefore they, for his comforte, bare hym into the Abbottes place and lodged hym in a chamber, and there, upon a paylet, leyde him before the fyre." Shortly after, on recovering his senses, the king inquired where he was; and on being told in the *Jerusalem Chamber,* he adverted to the prophecy, and soon after expired. The event is related upon this authority in Shakspeare's *King Henry IV.* part ii. act iv. sc. 4. The same story is told in Rastell's *Pastime of Pleasure,* and by Holinshed; but the latter writer adds this caution: "Whether this was true that so he spake, as one that gave too much credit to foolish prophecies and vain tales, or whether it was fained, as in such cases it commonly happeneth, we leave it to the advised reader to judge." The actors and the scenes differ in the different cases; but the equivoque arises in all upon the name "Jerusalem."

The late Dr. Vincent pointed out a remarkable coincidence in a passage of Anna Comnena relating to the death of Robert Guiscard, king of Sicily, in a place called Jerusalem, at Cephalonia. In Lodge's *Devils Conjured* is a similar story of Pope Sylvester. And Fuller, in his *Church History,* relates something of the same kind about Cardinal Wolsey, of whom it had been predicted *that he should have his end at Kingston,* which was thought to be fulfilled by his dying in the custody of Sir William Kingston.—See Cavendish's *Life of Wolsey.*

THE BATTLES OF WAKEFIELD AND TOWTON.

The first of these two bloody "Wars of the Roses" was fought at Wakefield between Richard Duke of York, and Margaret Queen of Henry VI. The latter, at the head of 18,000 men, appeared unexpectedly before Sandal Castle, and taunted the Duke of York with being afraid to meet a woman! He drew up his men on the green facing Wakefield; but was surprised by an ambuscade, in which he, and 1800 of his men, were cut to pieces. The Lord Clifford ferociously stabbed the

Earl of Rutland, a youth of sixteen or seventeen years old, and cut off the duke's head, to present to the queen :

> " Where York himself before his castle-gate,
>   Mangled with wounds, on his own earth lay dead,
> Upon whose body Clifford down him sate,
>   Stabbing the corpse, and cutting off the head,
> Crown'd it with paper, and to wreake his teene,
> Presents it so to his victorious queene."   *Drayton.*

But at Towton, the English Pharsalia, in the following year, took place the greatest battle ever fought in this country, between the Lancastrians, about 60,000 in number, and 40,000 Yorkists. The former at length gave way; but endeavouring to gain Tadcaster Bridge, so many fell into the small river Cock as quite choked its course, and the Yorkists went over their backs to pursue their brethren. The number slain was estimated at 37,776; and the blood shed amidst the snow, which at that time covered the ground, on the thaw ran down the ditches of the fields for two or three miles. Proclamations forbidding quarter were issued before the engagement. Like Leipsic, it reached over the night ; but unlike Leipsic, even the hours of darkness brought no rest. They fought from four in the afternoon, throughout the whole night, on to noon the next day. Like Waterloo, it was fought on a Sunday. And the accounts of contemporary writers state, in words very like the letters of Mont St. Jean, that for weeks afterwards the blood stood in puddles, and stagnated in gutters, and that the water of the wells was red. No inaccuracy is more frequent in ancient authors than that of numbers, and generally on the side of exaggeration. But on this occasion we can form a more correct estimate of the carnage by the concurrence of unusually respectable testimonies ; and perhaps, in these times, it will give the best idea of it to say, that the number of Englishmen slain exceeded the sum of those who fell at Vimiero, Talavera, Albuera, Salamanca, Vittoria, and Waterloo.

The long and sanguinary contests between the houses of York and Lancaster led to the extinction, by death or banishment, of many aristocratic families; others it involved in jealousies, rivalries, and hatreds, fatal to their interests as a body. In the parliament preceding the outbreak of the War of the two Roses fifty-three peers, besides bishops, took their seats in the upper chamber. In the first parliament of Henry VII. their number had fallen to twenty-five; by new creations he raised it to forty. In that thirty years' war, more than a million of men had perished ; and in this destruction of human life, the ruling class came in for more than their share.

MURDER-WOUNDS " BLEEDING AFRESH."

The popular superstition that the wounds of a murdered

body will " bleed afresh" when touched by the murderer, is thus referred to in Shakspeare's *Richard III.* act i. sc. 2:

> " Dead Henry's wounds
> Open their congealed mouths, and bleed afresh."

Drayton says, the simple proximity will produce the effect:

> " If the vile actors of the heinous deed
> Near the dead body happily be brought,
> Oft 't hath been proved the breathless corpse will bleed."

The belief is shown to have been universally established in Scotland as late as 1668, when the Crown counsel, Sir George Mackenzie, in the trial of Philip Standsfield, thus alludes to a deposition sworn by several witnesses on that trial :

> "God Almighty himself was pleased to bear a share in the testimonies which we produce. That divine power which makes the blood circulate during life has ofttimes, in all nations, opened a passage to it after death upon such occasions, but most in this case; for after the wounds had been sewed up, and the body designedly shaken up and down,—and which is most wonderful, after the body had been buried for several days, which naturally occasions the blood to congeal,—upon Philip's touching it, the blood darted and sprang out, to the great astonishment of the chirurgeons themselves, who were desired to watch this event; whereupon Philip, astonished more than they, threw down the body, crying, ' O God, O God !' and cleansing his hand, grew so faint that they were forced to give him a cordial."

LIVING IN THE REIGN OF HENRY VII.

The records of the Percy family, in the time of Henry VII., show that the permanent household numbered 166 persons, and the average of guests was fifty ; and the whole of the washing for those 216 persons was for one year 40*s.*, a sum probably equal to 40*l.* in the present day, most of which was for the chapel-linen. From Midsummer to Michaelmas was the only time they indulged in fresh meat, and the instructions say : " My lord has on his table, for breakfast, at seven in the morning, a quart of beer and wine, two pieces of salt fish, six red herrings, four white ones ; and, on flesh-days, half a chine of beef or mutton boiled." At dinner, men ranking as knights had a tablecloth, which was washed once a month ; they had no napkins, and the fingers were extensively used in feeding. Until the thirteenth century, straw was the bed of kings ; and before that date the king and his family slept in the same chamber. The first change was to throw a coverlid over the sleeper, then another was used, and the persons undressed, their linen being substituted for blankets. Beatrice says she would " as lief sleep in the woollen," which shows that such a thing was done even in Shakspeare's time.— *W. Tite, F.S.A.*

HOW WOLSEY WON HIS WAY.

Henry VII. having business of importance with the Emperor Maximilian, who was then in Flanders, sent for Wolsey, explained his wishes, and ordered him to prepare to set out. It was not long past noon when he took leave of the king at Richmond; at four o'clock he was in London, at seven at Gravesend. By travelling all night, he reached Dover just as the packet-boat was about to sail. After a passage of three hours he reached Calais, whence he travelled post, and the same evening appeared before Maximilian. Having obtained what he desired, he set off again by night, and on the next day but one reached Richmond—three days and some few hours after his departure. The king, catching sight of him just as he was going to Mass, sharply inquired why he had not set out. "Sire, I am just returned," answered Wolsey, placing the Emperor's letters in his master's hands. Henry was delighted, and Wolsey saw that his fortune was made.

Wolsey possessed little taste for learning; but, seeing the wind of public favour blow in that direction, he readily spread his sails before it. He got the reputation of a profound divine by quoting a few words of Thomas Aquinas, and the fame of a Mæcenas and Ptolemy by inviting the learned to his gorgeous entertainments. "O, happy cardinal," exclaimed Erasmus, "who can surround his table with such torches!"

THOMAS CROMWELL AND "THE JELLY-PARDONS" OF BOSTON.

When young Thomas Cromwell was a clerk in the English factory at Antwerp, two of his fellow-countrymen from Boston, in Lincolnshire, applied to him how they should appear before the Pope, "to get the renewal of the *greater and lesser pardons*" necessary for the repair of Boston harbour. Cromwell proposed to go with the applicants; and hearing that the pope, Julius, was very fond of dainties, he provided some exquisite *jelly*, prepared after the English fashion, and set out for Italy. Upon reaching there,—"Kings and princes alone eat of this preserve in England," said Cromwell to the Pope. A cardinal tasted the delicacy: "Try it," he exclaimed; and the Pope, relishing this new confectionery, immediately signed the pardons, on condition, however, that the receipt for the jelly should be left with him. "And thus were the *jelly-pardons* obtained," says the annalist. It was Cromwell's first exploit; and the man who began his busy career by presenting jars of confectionery to the Pope, was also the man who was destined to separate England from Rome.

EARLY LIFE OF SIR THOMAS MORE.

How often is the course of a great man shaped by a single event! Sir Thomas More, when young, resisted Henry VII.'s demand from the Commons for a subsidy for the marriage of

his eldest daughter; the king thereupon threw More's father,
then a judge, into the Tower, and fined him one hundred
pounds. *Had not the king died,* Sir Thomas was determined
to have gone over sea, thinking " that being in the king's
indignation, he could not live in England without great
danger." (See Roper's *Life.*) Soon after the accession of
Henry VIII. More's fortunes brightened.

SIR THOMAS MORE AT CROSBY PLACE.

More, after his marriage in 1507, resided for some years in
Bucklersbury. In what year he purchased Crosby Place, Bishops-
gate, is uncertain: but it was probably soon after his return
from his mission to Bruges, in 1514 and 1515; and as this journey forms the groundwork of the *Utopia,* there is reason to infer
this charming romance to have been written at Crosby Place,
to which the picture in the preface of Sir Thomas's domestic
habits may apply. There is little or no doubt that More wrote
his *History of Richard the Third* at Crosby Place, however it
may be with the *Utopia.* Here, too, More probably received
Henry VIII. ; for this was just the time he was in high favour
with the king, who then kept his court at Castle Baynard's
and St. Bride's.—*Curiosities of London.*

FIRST MEETING OF ERASMUS AND SIR THOMAS MORE.

Shortly after his arrival in England, happening to dine with
the lord mayor, Erasmus noticed on the other side of the table
a young man of nineteen, slender, fresh-coloured, with blue
eyes, coarse hands, and the right shoulder somewhat higher
than the other. His features indicated affability and gayety,
and pleasant jests were continually dropping from his lips. If
he could not find a joke in English, he would in French, and
even in Latin and Greek. A literary contest soon ensued between Erasmus and the English youth. The former, astonished
at meeting with any one that could hold his own against him,
exclaimed: *Aut tu es Morus aut nullus!*—"You are either
More or nobody;" and his companion, who had not learnt the
stranger's name, quickly replied: *Aut tu es Erasmus aut dia-
bolus!*—"You are either Erasmus or the devil." More flung
himself into the arms of Erasmus; and hence sprang one of
the most interesting friendships in the whole range of literary
history.

ERASMUS AND THE NEW TESTAMENT.

When Erasmus published his edition of the Greek Testament, Archbishop Lee, from being his friend, became his im-
placable adversary. "If we do not stop this leak," said he,
when he heard of the New Testament, "it will sink the ship."

Although a poor Greek scholar, Lee drew up some annotations on Erasmus's book, which the latter called "mere abuse and blasphemy." They were passed secretly from hand to hand, and extensively read, but not published. Lee was too much afraid. "Why did you not publish your work?" asked Erasmus, with cutting irony. "Who knows whether the holy father, appointing you the Aristarchus of letters, might not have sent you a birch to keep the whole world in order?" *Erasmus's Letters.*

TOURNAMENT OF THE FIELD OF CLOTH-OF-GOLD.

At Calais exists an interesting memorial of this pageant of the last days of chivalry. Such is the ancient Wool-staple, situated in the Rue de la Prison, now called the Cour de Guise, from its being given by Henry II. of France to that gallant nobleman after the capture of Calais from the English, in 1557. An edifice of wood was constructed in London from the design of the above building, and was conveyed to Calais, among other preparations for the famous interview at the Field of Cloth-of-Gold between Henry VIII. and Francis I. It was painted to represent stonework; and its front elevation, which corresponds with the building at Calais, is shown in the picture of the interview which Holbein painted by order of Henry VIII., and which is now preserved in Hampton-Court Palace.

THE ABOLISHER OF MONASTERIES.

There lived in Wolsey's household a man who was said to be the son of a blacksmith at Putney, near London. He had resided on the continent, visited Rome, had gathered wisdom from travel, and was now one of the cardinal's confidential servants. Two days before the parliament met that was to ruin his master, he said to a fellow-servant, "I intend, God willing, this afternoon, when my lord hath dined, to ride up to London, and so to the court, where I shall either make or mar, or I come again." This was Thomas Cromwell, the abolisher of monasteries. He advised Henry to become himself "head of the Church," by which means he could at once rescue his "princely authority" from "the spirituality," "accumulate to himself great riches," and get married. Thus he cleverly appealed to Henry's three dominant passions—the love of power, of money, and of Anne Boleyn. The spiritual authority, now transferred to the king's person, was delegated to this creature for a season, and Cromwell became president of the convocation as vicar-general of England. Lodge human power over the conscience where you will, it is the abomination that maketh desolate set up in the holy place; and so Britain found to her cost during all the time of the Tudors and the Stuarts.—*North British Review,* No. 9.

HOW TYNDALE'S BIBLE WAS FIRST PRINTED IN ENGLAND.

At this time printing was executed much better at Paris than in London; and, owing to a singular conjunction of circumstances, Thomas Cromwell got a license for Grafton and Whitchurch to print the Bible *there*. The work was, however, interrupted by the Inquisition; when not only the sheets, but the types and printers, were carried to England, to the great improvement of the art there. The Bible was soon finished, and ordered to be set up in every church in the kingdom; and the priests were forbidden to hinder the people from reading it there on pain of deprivation. And thus were fulfilled the words of Tyndale the martyr: "If God spare my life, ere many years, *I will cause a boy that drives the plough to know more of the Scriptures than you do.*" After the edition of 1539 there were four others of the large Bible, printed at the expense of 30,000*l.*, advanced by Antony Marler, a citizen of London, who obtained an order to have them set up in the churches. The price was fixed by authority at 7*l.* 10*s.*, and for the bound copies 9*l.* During the reign of Edward VI. Tyndale's Bible was printed more than thirty times, while of that with Cranmer's revision only half the number was called for. The first Scottish edition of the Scriptures was published at 4*l.* 13*s.* 4*d.*, and yet the Bible was in almost every house !—*North British Review*, No. 9.

THE PRINCESS ELIZABETH AT HATFIELD.

The ancient palace of Hatfield was granted, in 1550, by Edward VI. to his sister, the Princess Elizabeth; and here, upon the breaking out of Sir Thomas Wyatt's rebellion, in the reign of Queen Mary, Elizabeth was committed to the care of Sir Thomas Pope, having been removed thither from Woodstock. From various records it appears that the princess lived in splendour and affluence at Hatfield; that she was often admitted to the diversions of the court, and that her situation was by no means a state of oppression and imprisonment, as it has been represented by some historians. Here Elizabeth received the news of her sister's decease, and of her own accession to the throne, as she was seated beneath an oak in the park; and a great portion of the trunk of the tree is preserved to the present day, protected by a lead covering, and enclosed by a fence. When Queen Victoria visited Hatfield in 1843, her Majesty was much interested with this memorial, and had a small branch lopped from the trunk as a memento of her visit.

It does not appear that Queen Elizabeth often resided in or visited Hatfield during her long reign. The north end of the building, which formed the western front of the old palace, and still remains here, is traditionally said to have been that

K

in which the princess resided. It is possible these apartments may have been occupied by Elizabeth before her final settlement at Hatfield, under Sir Thomas Pope's care; but the portion of the palace subsequently tenanted by the princess has been taken down.

The Privy Garden, which adjoined these apartments, still exists on the western side of the present mansion. Like all gardens of the same period, it is very small, being only 150 feet square: it is encompassed by a stately arched hedge; a close walk, or avenue, of limes runs round the sides; in the centre of the plot is a rockwork basin; the angles of the garden are occupied by small grass-plots, having a mulberry-tree in each, reputed to have been planted by King James I.; and they are bordered with herbaceous plants and annuals. This unique garden is most carefully preserved, as a solitary memorial of the horticultural taste of the Elizabethan period, and as a connecting link in the interest which the venerable remains of the episcopal palace never fail to excite. The Great Hall, in which the Ladye Elizabeth was often entertained with plays and sumptuous pageants,—the walls hung with tapestry, and the cupboards garnished with gold and silver vessels,—is now a stable for thirty-two horses: it has a finely-constructed open timber roof, and is kept throughout in good repair.

In the library at Hatfield are preserved several memorials of Elizabeth: including an amusing pedigree of the queen, emblazoned in 1529, tracing her ancestry to Adam (1); here are many of her autograph letters; her cradle, of oak, finely carved; and five highly-finished original portraits of Elizabeth, including the large picture by Zucchero. A portion of the collection was the private property of Elizabeth, and includes portraits of her court and household, some of the finest specimens of Zucchero, De Heere, Hilliard, Mark Garrard, and other portrait-painters of Elizabeth's reign. Here also are Zucchero's well-known portrait of Lord Burghley, bearing the treasurer's staff; Holbein's picture of the entertainment given by Cardinal Wolsey to Henry VIII. to meet Anne Boleyn; Petrarch's Laura, by Raphael, &c.

The State-papers in the collection extend through the successive administrations of Lord Burghley and his son the Earl of Salisbury, and include documents which came into Lord Burghley's possession from his connection with the court. Here are no less than 13,000 letters, from the reign of Henry VIII. to that of James I. Among the earlier Mss. are copies of William of Malmesbury's and Roger Hoveden's English History; a splendid Ms. on vellum, with a beautifully-executed miniature of King Henry VII.; a translation from the French of the Pilgrimage of the Soul, with the autograph of King Henry VI., to whom it once belonged. Of the time of Henry VIII. are a Treatise on Councils, by Cranmer; and the original Depositions touching the divorce of Anne of Cleeves. Of Edward VI., here is the proclamation made on his ascending the throne, which is not noticed by historians. Of the reign of Mary, is the original Council-book. The historical Mss. of Elizabeth's reign contain memoranda in Lord Burghley's hand ; the Norfolk Book of Entries, or copies of the Duke's letters on Mary Queen of Scots ; a copious official account of the Earl of Northumberland's conspiracies, &c. Here are plans, maps, and charts, from Henry VIII. to the present reign ; the actual draft of the proclamation declaring James king of England, in the handwriting of Sir Robert Cecil ; and various Mss. illustrating Raleigh's and the Gunpowder plots.

Southward of Hatfield are two very interesting houses : Gubbins, or Gobions, near North Mims, once the seat of Sir Thomas More ; and Tyttenhanger, the former residence of the powerful abbots of St. Alban's, to which King Henry VIII. and his queen Catherine retired in the summer of 1528.

THE SPANISH ARMADA,

which set sail for the invasion of England in 1588, failed through various disasters. In all the rencontres the English proved victorious. Their ships were lighter, and their sailors more dexterous, than those of the Spaniards. The Spanish guns were planted too high, while every shot from the English proved effectual. Then came the stratagem of the fireships ; and lastly, the dreadful storm which dispersed the whole fleet. The statements at the time, apparently authorised, say : 15 ships sunk, and 4981 men ; sunk, &c. upon the coast of Ireland, 17 ships, 5394 men ; total, 32 ships and 10,165 men.

In the Royal Library in the British Museum is a rare volume, which was finished at Lisbon, May 9, 1588, while the fleet was in port there ; and which copy was then procured for Lord Burghley, who has noted in his own hand, in the margins of the different pages, particulars of the defeat, as in the following :

Galeon S. Philippe : " taken at Flushyng, 31 July." D. Francisco de Toledo : " this man escaped into Nuport." La Nao Capitana : " this ship was taken by Sir Francis Drake." El Gran Grifon Capitana : " this man's ship was drowned 17 September, in the Ile of Furemare, Scotland." Barca de Amburg : " she was drowned over against Ireland." San Pedro Mayor : " wrecked in October in Devonshire, neare Plimmouthe." La Galeaça Capitana nombrada S. Lorenço : " this was drowned afor Callys."

This work has twelve charts of the coast of England, showing the different situations of the Spanish armada and the English fleet through the whole contest. And the different actions and positions represented in these charts are minutely engraved and explained in a rare tract, 1590, in the Museum library.

Camden says : " Several moneys were coined ; some in memory of the victory, with a fleet flying with full sails, and this inscription, *Venit, vidit, fugit,*—' It came, it saw, it fled ;' others in honour of the queen, with fireships and a fleet all in confusion, inscribed *Dux fœmina facti*—that is, ‘A woman was conductor of the exploit.’ The medals and jettons struck on the occasion were entirely Dutch ; none were struck in England. The most remarkable, of considerable size, represents the Spanish fleet upon the obverse, with the words *Flavit Jehovah, et dissipati sunt*, 1588,—‘Jehovah blew, and they were scattered.’ Reverse, a church on a rock beaten by the waves, *Allidor, non lœdor.*”

The House of Lords (burnt in 1834) was hung with tapestry, representing the defeat of the Armada. It was woven by Spiering, from the designs of Henry Cornelius Vroom, at Haarlem, for Lord Howard, of Effingham, Lord High Admiral of the English fleet which engaged the Armada ; and was sold by him to James I. It consisted originally of ten compartments, with borders containing portraits of the officers of the English fleet. The hangings were engraved by Pine in 1739, with illustrations from charts, medals, &c.

In the British Museum is *The English Mercurie*, pretending to give a report of the defeat of the Spanish admiral, written by the lord-admiral, and to have been published at the time ; but the whole is a clumsy forgery copied from a confused account of the same events by Camden. The statement of this *English Mercurie* being “the earliest English newspaper is equally groundless.”

EXECUTION OF SIR WALTER RALEIGH.

Raleigh was executed on the 29th of October (old style) 1618, in Old Palace Yard, at eight in the morning of Lord Mayor’s Day ; “so that the pageants and fine shewes might draw away the people from beholding the tragedie of one of the gallantest worthies that ever England bred.” Early in the morning his keeper brought a cup of sack to him, and inquired how he was pleased with it ? “As well as he who drank of St. Giles’s bowl as he rode to Tyburn,” answered the knight, and said, it was good drink, if a man might but tarry by it. “Prithee, never fear, Ceeston,” cried he to his old friend Sir Hugh, who was repulsed from the scaffold by the sheriff, “I shall have a place !” A man bald from extreme age pressed forward “to see him,” he said, “and pray God for him.” Raleigh took a richly-embroidered cap from his own head, and placing it on that of the old man, said, “Take this, good friend, to remember me, for you have more need on it than I.” “Farewell, my lords,” was his cheerful parting to a courtly group who affectionately took their leave of him, “I have a long journey before me, and I must e’en say good by. Now I am going to God,” said that heroic spirit, as he trod the scaffold ; and, gently touching the axe, added, “this is a

sharp medicine, but it will cure all diseases." The very heads-
man shrank from beheading one so illustrious and brave, until
the unquailing soldier addressed him, "What does thou fear?
Strike, man!" In another moment the mighty soul had fled
from its mangled tenement. Cayley adds: The head, after
being shown on either side of the scaffold, was put into a
leather bag, over which Sir Walter's gown was thrown, and
the whole conveyed away in a mourning-coach by Lady Raleigh. It was preserved by her in a case during the twenty-
nine years which she survived her husband, and afterwards
with no less piety by their affectionate son Carew, with whom
it is supposed to have been buried at West Horsley, in Surrey.
The body was interred in the chancel near the altar of St.
Margaret's, Westminster.

In the Pepysian Collection at Cambridge is a ballad with
the following title: "Sir Walter Rauleigh his Lamentation,
who was beheaded in the Old Pallace of Westminster the 29th
of October 1618. To the tune of Welladay."

BERNINI'S BUST OF CHARLES I.

Vandyke having drawn the king in three different faces,—
a profile, three-quarters, and a full face,—the picture was sent
to Rome for Bernini to make a bust from it. Bernini was un-
accountably dilatory in the work; and upon this being complained of, he said that he had set about it several times, but
there was something so unfortunate in the features of the face
that he was shocked every time that he examined it, and forced
to leave off the work; and, if there was any stress to be laid
on physiognomy, he was sure the person whom the picture
represented was destined to a violent end. The bust was at
last finished, and sent to England. As soon as the ship that
brought it arrived in the river, the king, who was very impatient to see the bust, ordered it to be carried immediately to
Chelsea. It was conveyed thither, and placed upon a table in
the garden, whither the king went, with a train of nobility, to
inspect the bust. As they were viewing it, a hawk flew over
their heads with a partridge in his claws, which he had wounded
to death. Some of the partridge's blood fell upon the neck of
the bust, where it remained without being wiped off. This
bust was placed over the door of the king's closet at Whitehall,
and continued there till the palace was destroyed by fire.[*]—
Pamphlet *On the Character of Charles I.*, by Zachary Grey, LL.D.

THE CALVES'-HEAD CLUB.

In a blind alley about Moorfields met the Calves'-Head Club,

[*] Pennant states the bust to have been subsequently placed in Westminster
Hall; but this is questioned.

where an axe hung up in the club-room, and was reverenced as a principal symbol in this diabolical sacrament. Their great feast of calves' heads was held the 30th of January (the anniversary of the martyrdom of king Charles I.), the club being erected "by an impudent set of people, in derision of the day, and defiance of monarchy." Their bill of fare was a large dish of calves' heads, dressed several ways; a large pike, with a small one in his mouth, as an emblem of tyranny; and a large cod's head, to represent the person of the king (Charles I.) singly, as by the calves' heads before they had done him together with all them that suffered in his cause; and a boar's head, with an apple in its mouth, to represent the king by this as bestial, as by the others they had done foolish and tyrannical. After the repast, the *Eikon Basilike* was burnt, anthems were sung, and the oath was sworn upon Milton's *Defensio Populi Anglicani.* The company consisted of Independents and Anabaptists; Jerry White, formerly chaplain to Oliver Cromwell, said grace; and the table-cloth being removed, the Anniversary Anthem, as they impiously called it, was sung, and a calf's skull filled with wine or other liquor, and then a brimmer, went about to the pious memory of those worthy patriots that had killed the tyrant, &c.—See the *Secret History of the Calves'-Head Club*, 6th edit. 1706.

HISTORIC INNS.

The George and Blue Boar, Holborn, is associated with a great event in our history. Here was intercepted Charles I.'s letter, by which Ireton discovered it to be the king's intention to destroy him and Cromwell, which discovery brought about Charles's execution. Nearly opposite the George and Blue Boar was the Red Lion, the largest inn in Holborn; and where the bodies of Cromwell, Ireton, and Bradshawe, were carried from Westminster Abbey, and next day dragged on sledges to Tyburn—a retributive coincidence worthy of note.

GOLD MEDAL AND GEORGE OF CHARLES I.

The unfortunate monarch, shortly before his execution, presented to Bishop Juxon, his faithful attendant, a handsome gold medal, which, according to tradition, the bishop received from the king on the scaffold. It is a pattern with a mint-mark (a rose), probably for a 5l. or 6l.-piece, presented by the engraver to his majesty for approval. It is the work of Rawlins, who also engraved at Oxford the rare crown-piece struck for that city, with its representation upon it. The portrait of the king on this coin is exactly similar to that on the medal, allowing for the difference of costume. The likeness is very good. The medal weighs 1 oz. 10 dwts. 13 grains. It was devised by Bishop Juxon to Mrs. Rachael Gayters; from her it came to her granddaughter, Miss Gayters, who married the Rev. James Commeline, the father of the rector of Red Marley, Worcestershire; the latter gentleman presented it to his son, who, in 1835, sold it to Lieutenant-Colonel John Drummond. Charles is known to have presented to Bishop Juxon the identical George (the jewel of the order of the Garter) which he wore but a few moments previous to his decapitation. The George descended to Sir George Chetwynd from his maternal ancestress, the daughter of Elizabeth Juxon, a niece of the bishop, and the wife of James St. Amond, Esq., of Covent Garden.

HANDKERCHIEF OF CHARLES I.

A few years since, a silversmith of Bath had in his possession the pocket-handkerchief used by Charles I. at the time of his execution. It is of very fine white cambric, and is neatly marked with the imperial crown and the initials C. R. This handkerchief was purchased at the sale of the effects of the late Mr. W. M. Pitt, of Dorchester, accompanied by this certificate:

"This was King Charles the First's handkerchief, that he had on the scaffold when he was beheaded, January ye 30th, 1648. From my cousin, Anne Foyle, 1733. Certificate by me, July 25th 1828, W. M. Pitt. As to the authenticity of the fact, I can only state that I was informed by my father, that Mrs. Anne Foyle was a cousin of his mother, whose father was much attached to the cause of the king, was present at his death, and obtained by some means or other this handkerchief: from her father she obtained it, and she gave it to my grandmother, Lora Pitt, as is stated on the cover herein enclosed; the endorsement was written ninety years after the event took place, and my grandmother was born in the reign of Charles II. I myself know that that endorsement is in the handwriting of my grandmother, and who evidently believed the above to be true; and this I certify ninety years after the writing of that endorsement by my grandmother."

CHARLES I. AND HIS TIMES.

This grand crisis of morals, religion, and government is yet but imperfectly understood, notwithstanding so many books have been written and published in illustration of it. Coleridge attributes this labour lost to the want of genius or imagination in these works: "Not one of their authors seems to be able to throw himself back into that age: if they did, there would be less praise and less blame bestowed on both sides."

FELTON, THE ASSASSIN.

When Felton was examined, after his assassination of George Villiers, Duke of Buckingham, at Portsmouth, in August 1628, there was found sewed in the crown of his hat "a writing to show the cause why he put this cruel act into execution." Of this paper the following is a copy:

"That man is cowardly, base, and deserveth not the name of a gentleman or Souldier, that is not willing to sacrifice his life for the honor of his God, his kinge, and his countrie. Lett no man Commend me for doeing of it, but rather discommend themselves as the cause of it; for If God had not taken away or harts for or sinnes, he would not have gone so longe unpunished.   JO. FELTON."

This unique document was found among the Evelyn papers at Wotton in Surrey. Sir Edward Nicholas, secretary of state, who had the first possession of it, was one of the persons before whom Felton was examined at Portsmouth. His daughter married Sir Richard Browne, and the celebrated John Evelyn married the only daughter of Sir Richard Browne; and Lady Evelyn, the widow of his descendant, presented the writing to the late Mr. Upcott, one of the editors of Evelyn's *Diary*.

THE PATRIOT HAMPDEN.

Near to the estate in Buckinghamshire, which the family of Hampden had received from Edward the Confessor, is the field of Chalgrove, where John Hampden fell; and hard by is the church of Great Hampden, where the patriot is buried. To the late Lord Nugent "the design suggested itself of marking, by a simple memorial of a solid and enduring kind, the spot where Hampden received his mortal wound, and of e'ecting it on the anniversary of the second centenary of the fatal day at Chalgrove."* The memorial was inaugurated, amidst many thousand spectators, on the 19th of June 1843,—the actual anniversary of the fight, the 18th, falling on a Sunday. The monument bears the following inscription :

"Here, in this field of Chalgrove, John Hampden, after an able and strenuous but unsuccessful resistance in parliament, and before the judges of the land, to the measures of an arbitrary court, first took arms, assembling the levies of the associated counties of Buckingham and Oxford, in 1642; and here, within a few paces of this spot, while fighting in defence of the free monarchy, and the ancient liberties of England, he received a wound of which he died, June 18, 1643. In the two hundredth year from that day this stone was raised in reverence to his memory."

The monument also bears the names of those by whose subscriptions it was erected; and the arms of Hampden and his deathless motto : *Vestigia nulla retrorsum.*

Never did patriotism become more familiar in the mouths of the people than "the cause for which Hampden bled in the field." The very name is synonymous with patriot :

"Some village Hampden, that with dauntless breast
The little tyrant of his fields withstood."

SIR RICHARD WILLIS'S PLOT AGAINST CHARLES II.

At No. 13 Lincoln's Inn, from 1645 to 1650, lived John Thurloe, secretary to Oliver Cromwell, who one night came thither for the purpose of discussing secret and important business. They had conversed together for some time, when

* From an eloquent memoir, by Mr. John Forster, prefixed to *Some Memorials of John Hampden*, by Lord Nugent, 3d edit., 1854.

Cromwell suddenly perceived a clerk asleep at his desk. This happened to be Mr. Morland (afterwards Sir Samuel Morland), the famous mechanist, and not unknown as a statesman. Cromwell, it is affirmed, drew his dagger, and would have despatched him on the spot had not Thurloe, with some difficulty, prevented him. He assured him that his intended victim was certainly sound asleep, since, to his own knowledge, he had been sitting up the two previous nights. But Morland only feigned sleep, and overheard the conversation, which was a plot for throwing the young King Charles II., then resident at Bruges, and the Dukes of York and Gloucester, into the hands of the Protector; Sir Richard Willis having planned that on a stated day they should pass over to a certain port in Sussex, where they would be received on landing by a body of 500 men, to be augmented on the following morning by 2000 horse. Had they fallen into the snare, it seems that all three would have been shot immediately on their reaching the shore; but Morland disclosed the designs to the royal party, and thus frustrated the diabolical scheme.

FIFTH-MONARCHY MEN.

This wild sectarian movement originated in the days of the Puritans, when, in addition to the four great monarchies which have appeared in the world, some of the enthusiasts thought that Christ was to reign temporarily upon earth, and to establish *a fifth monarchy.*

JEFFREY HUDSON, THE DWARF.

The dwarf who is made to play a part in Scott's *Peveril of the Peak* is Jeffrey, or Sir Jeffrey Hudson, as he was called, after Charles I., in a frolic, had dubbed him with knighthood. He was born in 1619, and when eight years old, he was presented by the Duke of Buckingham to the Queen Henrietta Maria in a pasty! The queen appointed the little fellow to be one of her pages, and the courtiers made him their pet; but the wits made him the butt of their cheap and cruel wit. Davenant made him the hero of a mock epic called *Jeffreidos*, in which the dwarf fights a single combat with a turkey-cock:

> " Jeffrey straight was thrown, when faint and weak,
>   The cruel fowl assaults him with his beak."

Jeffrey was quick and sagacious, and was intrusted by the queen with some negotiations of consequence; but he was vain and ill-tempered, and was often squabbling with a gigantic porter at the palace; and the effigies of the two disputants are sculptured on a stone to be seen to this day upon a house-front in Newgate Street, London. At Petworth is a magnificent picture by Vandyke of the queen seated and Sir Jeffrey standing beside her; and the curious may see the dwarf's clothes preserved in the collection of Sir Hans Sloane, in the British Museum.

When the Civil War broke out, Sir Jeffrey was appointed a captain in the royal army. In 1644, he followed his royal mistress to France; and there, having been insulted by the Hon. Master Crofts, he challenged his antagonist to a duel with pistols. Crofts appeared armed with a squirt, but Sir Jeffrey was not thus to be trifled with; a real duel followed, and Crofts fell mortally wounded at the first shot. In 1682, Jeffrey was arrested on a charge of being concerned in the popish plot; and he died in his prison, aged 63.

Jeffrey Hudson wore very long moustachios, had an enormous head and large hands, but would have been accounted handsome had he been taller: at thirty years old, he was only 18 inches high; but from this age he rapidly grew to 3 ft. 9 in. In normal cases men rarely grow half-an-inch in height after thirty.

WEARING OAK ON THE TWENTY-NINTH OF MAY.

The origin of wearing this badge is commonly believed to be to commemorate the preservation of Charles II. in the oak, on May 29. Now, Charles fought the battle of Worcester on Wednesday, the 3d of September 1651; he fled from the field, attended by Lords Derby and Wilmot, and others, and arrived early next morning at Whiteladies, about three-quarters of a mile from Boscobel House. At this place Charles secreted himself in a wood, and in a tree (from the king's own account, a pollard oak), since termed "the royal oak;" and at night Boscobel House was his place of refuge. At Whiteladies he exchanged his habilaments for those of the faithful Penderell. Subsequently he embarked at Shoreham on the 15th of October, and landed next day at Fescamp in Normandy. On his return to England, Charles entered London on his birthday, the 29th of May, when the Royalists displayed the branch of oak, from that tree having been instrumental in the king's restoration: hence the custom of wearing oak on this day, and not from Charles being then concealed in the oak. It may be added, that the oak could scarcely have been in sufficient leaf in May to have concealed the king. Boscobel House is situated near Bridgnorth, Salop, 140 miles from the metropolis; and that part of it which rendered such essential service to the sovereign is still shown. The oak has long been removed; but another, presumed to have been a seedling from it, occupies its place, and is walled round for preservation.

CROMWELL'S "FORTUNATE DAY."

The 3d of September was always regarded by Cromwell as his "fortunate day." On the two successive anniversaries of that day he gained his famous victories of Dunbar and Worcester; yet subsequently, on that very day, agreeably with a strange prophecy of Colonel Lindsey, the Protector breathed his last. The Monday before, August 30th, was the most windy day that had happened for twenty years; and the following Friday, on which Oliver died, there was also a high wind, which produced these very opposite lines: Waller says Oliver died

"In storms as loud as his immortal fame;"

and Godolphin,

"In storms as loud as was his crying sin."

THE GUNPOWDER PLOT.

At Ashby St. Leger, near Daventry, remains to this day the gatehouse of the ancient manor of the Catesby family, of which was Robert Catesby, the contriver of the Gunpowder Plot, and who is stated to have inveigled, by his persuasive eloquence, several of the other twelve conspirators. They are believed to have met in a room over the gateway, called the "Plot Room." Catesby was shot with Thomas Percy, by the sheriffs' officers, in attempting to escape at Holbeach, shortly after the discovery of the treason.*

Guido, or Guy Fawkes, was a soldier of fortune in the Spanish service; he was a native of Yorkshire, and a schoolfellow of Bishop Morton, at York. In the Bodleian Library, at Oxford, are preserved the rusty and shattered remains of the lantern which Fawkes carried when taken prisoner. It is of iron, and a dark lantern; the movement for enclosing the light being precisely the same as in those in use at the present day. The top, squeezed up and broken, is preserved with it in the case, as is also the socket for the candle. The horn or glass which once filled the door is quite gone. On a brass

---

* Catesby Hall is otherwise noted than for its association with the Gunpowder Plot. The house formerly belonged to Sir Richard Catesby, one of the three favourites who ruled the kingdom under Richard III.; the others being Sir Richard Ratcliffe and Viscount Lovell, on whom the following humorous distich was made:

"The Rat, the Cat, and Lovell, our Dog,
Rule all England under the *Hog;*"

alluding to the king's adoption of a boar as one of the supporters of the royal arms. After the battle of Bosworth, this Sir William Catesby was beheaded at Leicester, and his lands escheated; but Henry VII. (1496) restored them to Catesby's son George, from whom they descended, in course of time, to Sir William Catesby, who was convicted, during the reign of Elizabeth (1581), of harbouring Jesuits here, and celebrating mass. His son and successor was the above conspirator, Robert Catesby.

plate affixed to one side of the lantern, the following Latin inscription is engraved in script hand :

" Latorna illa ipsa quâ usus est et cum quâ deprehensus Guido Faux
in cryptâ subterraneâ ubi domo Parlamenti difflande operam dabat.
Ex dono Rob. Heywood, nuper Academia procuratoris, Apr. 4°, 1641."
And the following is written on a piece of paper, and deposited in the
glass-case with the lantern, along with two or three prints and papers
relating to the Powder Plot : " The very lantern that was taken from
Guy Fawkes when he was about to blow up the Parliament House. It
was given to the University in 1641, according to the Inscription on it,
by Robert Heywood, proctor of the University."

The famous *Monitory Letter* to Lord Mounteagle, which led
to the discovery and frustration of the plot, originated in each
of the conspirators adopting his own method of giving effectual warning to those lords for whom he felt particularly interested. This letter is preserved in the Parliament Office ; and
in *Archæologia*, vol. xii. p. 200, is an engraved facsimile. There
is scarcely a doubt of its having been concerted by Tresham,
but by whom written is unknown. But at Ightham, near Seven-
oaks, in the church is a mural monument to Dame Dorothy
Selby, who died in 1641, and is traditionally said to have
written the Monitory Letter, which is thus referred to in the
inscription :

" Whose arts disclosed that plot, which, had it taken,
    Rome had triumph'd, and Britain's walls had shaken."

At the south-east corner of Old Palace Yard stood the house
through which the conspirators in the plot carried their barrels
into the vault, the kitchen beneath the great hall of the old
palace, used as the House of Lords. '

CAPTURE OF " THE UNFORTUNATE" DUKE OF MONMOUTH.

Somerset and Dorset were the closing scenes of Monmouth's
career. When the duke came within ten miles of White Lack-
ington House, one mile distant from Ilminster, he was met by
two thousand persons on horseback, whose number increased
to twenty thousand. His grace, his party, and attendants,
took refreshment under the famed sweet Spanish chestnut-tree,
now standing, which measures at three feet from the ground
upwards of twenty-six feet in circumference.

The decisive battle of Sedgemoor was fought on the 5th of
July, after which Monmouth and his friends fled across the
boundaries of Wiltshire, and at Woodyate's Inn, near Salisbury,
on the road to Blandford, turned their horses adrift ; and thence
crossed the country, nearly due south, to " the island," in the
parish of Horton, in Dorsetshire, where, in a field called to this
day " Monmouth Close," was found the would-be king. An
ash-tree, at the foot of which he was discovered crouched in a

ditch, and half-hid under the fern, was standing a few years ago, and bore the carved initials of persons who had visited it; and it was propped up for preservation.

On his capture, the duke was first taken to the house of Anthony Etterick, Esq., a magistrate, who resided at Holt, which adjoins Horton. Tradition, which records the popular feeling rather than the fact, reports that the poor woman who informed the pursuers that she had seen two strangers lurking in the island—her name was Amy Farrant—never prospered afterwards; and that Henry Parkin, the soldier who, spying the skirt of the smock-frock which the duke had assumed as a disguise, recalled the searching-party just as they were leaving the island, burst into tears, and reproached himself bitterly for his fatal discovery.—*Notes and Queries,* No. 6.

In the British Museum is the pocket-book which was taken from Monmouth when he was captured; it is certified in the handwriting of James II.

THE REVOLUTION OF 1688.

At Whittington, between Chesterfield and Dronfield, is a small public-house, where, in 1688, certain patriotic noblemen met to concert measures for overthrowing the Popish government, and securing the Protestant establishment by the personal influence of the Prince of Orange. The sign of the public-house was then the Cock and Pyot, now the Cock and Magpie. The room where the patriots met is now called the " Plotting Parlour ;" there is preserved the chair in which sat the Earl of Devonshire, the president. In 1788 the centenarial day was kept with great pomp by the nobility, gentry, and people of the neighbourhood, who visited the Revolution Parlour, and proceeded from thence in grand procession to Chesterfield. The public-house was sold in 1847 for 735*l.*

" ALL FOR THE BEST."

When Bernard Gilpin was summoned up to London to give an account of himself and his creed before Bonner, he chanced to break his leg on the way; and on some persons retorting upon him a favourite saying of his own, that " nothing happens to us but what is intended for our good," and asking him whether it was for his good that he had broken his leg, he answered, that " he made no question but it was." And so it turned out, for before he was able to travel again Queen Mary died, and he was set at liberty.

THE HORSEFERRY, WESTMINSTER.

At the time of the Usurpation, a wooden house was built for a small guard posted here. M. de Lauzun thus mentions the

ferry in his account of the escape of the queen of James II.,
December 9, 1688 : Sir Edward Hales being in attendance with
a hackney-coach, "we drove from Whitehall to Westminster,
and arrived safely at the place called the Horseferry, where I
had engaged a boat to wait for me."

The same author adds : "The king, attended by Sir Edward
Hales, who was waiting for him, descended the back stairs,
and crossing Privy Gardens, as the queen had done two nights
before, proceeded to the Horseferry, and crossed the Thames
in a little boat with a single pair of oars to Vauxhall. He
threw the Great Seal into the river by the way; but it was
afterwards recovered, in a net cast at random, by some fishermen." "Very early one morning the Duke of Marlborough,
with his hounds, desired to cross by the ferry ; one Wharton,
the waterman at hand, was subsequently rewarded by the duke
obtaining for him a grant of the ferry-house, the present
owner of which is a descendant of Wharton."—Walcott's
Westminster, p. 333.

DEATH OF JAMES II.

When James lay in his last illness at St. Germain's, he addressed the Prince of Wales, his son, with equal firmness and
piety, telling him that "however splendid a crown appeared,
the time is sure to come when it is a matter of perfect indifference; that nothing is worth loving but God, or desiring
except eternity. He exhorted him never to forget his duty to
his mother, and his attachment and gratitude to the King of
France, from whom he had received so many favours."

At James's desire, Louis XIV. went to see him, when he
requested that he might be buried in the parish church of
St. Germain, without any ceremony, like one of the poor of
the parish, and with only these words for his epitaph : "Here
lies James the Second, king of England."

But the body was kept unburied until 1793 or 1794 in the church of
the English Benedictine Monastery at Paris, where it was exhibited for
money. It was not until 1824 that the corpse, or the greater portion of
it, was conveyed to St. Germain, where it was buried with great pomp
in the parish church, most of the English then in Paris or the neighbourhood joining in the funeral procession. The intestines of the king
were given, soon after his death, to the Irish College in Paris ; where
also his body lay after the destruction of the Church of the Benedictines,
and before its final interment at St. Germain. The brain of the king
was given to the Scotch College in Paris, and the heart to the Convent
at Chaillot. In the chapel of the Scotch College in Paris is a monument,
with a long Latin inscription, erected in 1703 by James Duke of Perth,
to the memory of James II. An urn once stood over the monument,
containing the king's brain ; but this was destroyed at the period of the
Revolution. Near this is a slab covering the heart of his queen, and
another the intestines of his daughter Louisa. A monument of white
and grey marble was also erected to the king at St. Germain by order

of George IV.: it boars a Latin inscription, in which James is charac-
torised as

" Magnus in prosperis, in advorsis major."

—*Communicated by Dr. Wreford to the Athenæum,* Nov. 30, 1850.*

RECOGNITION OF JAMES III., KING OF ENGLAND AND SCOTLAND, BY LOUIS XIV.

When Louis XIV. visited James, then on his death-bed, he
told him to tranquillise his mind on the subject of the Prince
of Wales, and that he would acknowledge him king of England
and Scotland; upon which all the English who were in the
apartment fell on their knees, and cried, "God save the king!"
The death of James is thus recorded by Dangeau:

" The king of England died at St. Germain's, at three o'clock. He
has always desired, *from a sentiment of piety*, to die of a Friday.—*Friday,* 18*th September* 1701.

The king, on going abroad, went to St. Germain's to visit the new
king of England, James III.; he did not stay long with him, and then
went to visit the queen his mother.

All the foreign ministers came as usual to the king's levee, except
the English ambassador, who affects to be angry at the king's recognition of King James III. There is, however, nothing in that contrary
to the treaty of Ryswick; there are even examples of two kings of the
same country recognised at the same time: King Casimir, whom we
have seen die in Paris, was, before he was king of Poland, recognised
as king of Sweden, though there was another king on the throne, with
whom even we were in alliance.—*Thursday,* 20*th of September* 1701."

THE VESSEL IN WHICH WILLIAM III. CAME TO ENGLAND.

This celebrated craft, according to the most reliable accounts, was built on the Thames in the earlier part of the
seventeenth century, and was afterwards purchased by the
Prince of Orange, or his adherents, and was selected by the
prince to convey himself and suite to England; and he bestowed
upon her the name of *The Princess Mary*, in honour of his
illustrious consort, the daughter of James II. During the
whole of William's reign, the ship held a place of honour as
one of the royal yachts. It was next regularly used as the
pleasure-yacht of Queen Anne. The vessel came into the
possession of King George I., by whose order she ceased to
form part of the royal establishment. About the middle of
the last century she was sold by the government to the Messrs.
Walters, of London, from whom she received the name of the
Betsy Cairns, in honour, we are told, of some West Indian
lady of that name. After being long employed in the West
Indian trade, she was disposed of, and converted into a collier,
and employed between Newcastle and London. She was after-

* At Ambleteuse, a seaport town near Calais, King James II. landed, on his
flight from England, in the year 1688; and at this place Cæsar embarked his
cavalry when he passed over into Britain.

wards (*circa* 1825) again sold, and finally, on the 17th of February 1827, while pursuing her voyage from Shields to Hamburg, with a cargo of coals, she struck upon the "Black Middens," a dangerous reef of rocks north of the mouth of the Tyne, and in a few days afterwards became a total wreck. She had been regarded with an almost superstitious feeling of interest and veneration; and a "memorable prophecy" was said to be associated with her fortunes, viz. "that the Catholics would never get the better while the *Betsy Cairns* was afloat." The remnant of her original timbering was extremely fine. There was a profusion of rich and elaborate oak-carvings, the colour of the wood, from age and exposure, closely resembling that of ebony. Snuffboxes and souvenirs of various kinds were made of the wood, and brought exorbitant prices. Each of the members of the then corporation of Newcastle was presented with one of these boxes of old British oak.—Abridged from the *Durham County Advertiser.*

BOTH SIDES OF THE QUESTION.

Swift received his deanery, which he ever held as a most inadequate reward, for his services to the Marlborough and Tory faction, in the course of 1713; but he had given his great offence to the Duchess nearly three years before, or immediately after his venal quarrel with the Whigs for their not giving him church-promotion so rapidly as he wished. In the *Examiner* of November 23, 1710, he published a paper reflecting most severely on the Duke of Marlborough's insatiable avarice and enormous peculations. The Duke, he said, had had 540,000*l.* of the public money for doing work which a warrior of ancient Rome (an odd parallel) would have received only 994*l.* 11*s.* 10*d.*; and at the end of his paper there was an innuendo that the Duchess, in the execution of her office as mistress of the robes during eight years, had purloined no less than 22,000*l.* a-year. Here is the account itself from the *Examiner*, in a volume in reply to Sarah's, entitled *The Other Side of the Question*, and published in the same year:

A Bill of Roman Gratitude.

Imprim.	£	*s.*	*d.*
For frankincense, and earthen pots to burn it in	4	10	0
A bull for sacrifice	8	0	0
An embroidered garment	50	0	0
A crown of laurel	0	0	2
A statue	100	0	0
A trophy	80	0	0
1000 copper medals, value one halfpenny each	2	1	8
A triumphal arch	500	0	0
A triumphal car, valued as a modern coach	100	0	0
Casual charges at the triumph	150	0	0
	£994	**11**	**10**

A Bill of British Ingratitude.

Imprim.						£	s.	d.
Woodstock	.	.	.	.	.	40,000	0	0
Blenheim	.	.	.	.	.	200,000	0	0
Post-office grant	.	.	.	.	.	100,000	0	0
Mildenheim	.	.	.	.	.	30,000	0	0
Jewels, &c.	.	.	.	.	.	60,000	0	0
Pall-Mall grant, the Westminster rangership, &c.					10,000	0	0
Employments	.	.	.	.	.	100,000	0	0
						£540,000	0	0

The anonymous author of *The Other Side of the Question* does not name Swift, but says this account was drawn up many years ago in the *Examiner*, for the use of the Marlborough family, "by one of the greatest wits that ever did honour to human nature."

"THE PORTEOUS MOB," AT EDINBURGH.

This notorious tumult took place in Edinburgh in September 1736. Porteous was captain of the city-guard. At the examination of a criminal named Wilson, whose fate had excited an extraordinary sympathy, Porteous, dreading a rescue by the mob, who suddenly became tumultuous, ordered the guard to fire on them, when six persons were killed and eleven wounded. For this Porteous was tried, and condemned to death; but he was afterwards reprieved by Queen Caroline, then regent. Resolved, however, that he should not thus escape the fate which they conceived he merited, the mob, on the evening of the day previous to that on which he was to have been executed, broke into the jail in which he was confined; and having dragged him out, led him to the Grassmarket,—the usual place of execution at that period,—and there hanged him by torchlight on a dyer's pole.

WEARING THE PHILABEG.

Thomas Rawlinson, an iron-smelter, and an Englishman, was the person who, about or prior to A.D. 1728, introduced the philabeg, or short kilt, worn in the Highlands. This fact is established in a letter from Ewan Baillie, of Aberiachan, in the *Edinburgh Magazine*, 1785, and in the *Culloden Papers*.

The earliest dress of the Highlanders consisted of a large tartan wrapper, extending from the shoulders to about the knees, *in one piece*, when Rawlinson's workmen finding this garment inconvenient, separated the lower part from the upper, so that they might, when heated, throw off the upper, and leave the lower. which thus became the philabeg, or *short* kilt.

THE PEACE OF UTRECHT DEFERRED BY THE SLAVE-TRADE.

Peace with France might have been concluded with Great Britain on infinitely better terms two years before the Treaty of Utrecht; but the negotiations were broken off principally on account of an *assiento* made with the French Guinea Company, who were to furnish to the English 4800 negroes annually, which Great Britain most pertinaciously insisted on, and Louis XIV. most reluctantly conceded, although he gained political objects of great magnitude. Several bloody battles, and still more bloody sieges, took place, and much treasure was expended; but the English nation persisted in engrossing this now reprobated privilege, which, although nominally limited to 4800 negroes, furnished a pretext for smuggling in three times that number. On such matters, national feelings seem periodically subject to hot and cold fits.—*Notes to assist the Memory, &c.*

A RELIC OF CULLODEN.

A Perthshire gentleman, nearly related to the ducal family of Athol, possesses the plaid, or scarf, worn by the Marquis of Tullibardine at the battle of Culloden. It is of the Murray tartan, and is in capital preservation. The only rent or blemish is found at one of the corners, and it bears evident marks of having been caused by a sword-cut. This is mended very neatly, but by tartan-cloth of a different description. Several brownish spots of stain are visible, considered to be caused by drops of blood. The scarf in question is fully three yards long, exclusive of the fringes, is two feet in width, and is such as would be worn over the breast and shoulders of the gentleman of the time. Tullibardine was one of those romantic and enthusiastic spirits whose loyalty survived disaster, defeat, suffering, and the long lapse of years. We need not follow his career step by step to the cruel field of Culloden, where he was taken prisoner, and carried to London. He escaped the axe of Balmerino and Kilmarnock, it may be said, by dying in the Tower of a painful malady on the 9th July 1746.

TOMB OF QUEEN CAROLINE AND GEORGE II.

Queen Caroline was buried in Westminster Abbey; and George II., on his deathbed, twenty-three years afterwards, directed that his remains should be placed close by hers—a side of each of the coffins to be removed; in order that the cerements might be in actual contact. This story has been doubted; but a few years since, it becoming the duty of one of the Chapter (the Rev. H. H. Milman) to superintend some operation within that long-sealed vault, the royal coffins were found on the same raised slab of granite exactly in the condition described; the sides that were abstracted still leaning against the wall behind.—*Quarterly Review*, No. 164.

NELSON'S LEFT-HAND.

During the captaincy of Nelson, he became intimate with a person on board ship, who was officially engaged in writing, which he accomplished with his left hand. Captain Nelson, attentively observing him one day while thus occupied, said: "Parnell, I cannot think how you manage to write with your left hand." The result of this remark was, that Nelson was taught to perform the task which had excited his wonder; little dreaming that the disastrous loss of his arm at Teneriffe would leave him no other alternative in committing his ideas to paper than to write with the left hand.

WHAT IS JACOBINISM?

In a letter from Mr. James Workman, of the Middle Temple, to the Duke of Portland, in 1797, he defines Jacobinism to be "the system of politics adopted by the Jacobin club of Paris from the year 1793 to the time of its destruction; and acted upon in various places by Le Bon, Freron, Collot d'Herbois, Carrier, Marat, and Robespierre. By Jacobinism," he says, "I mean that system which drenched France with blood; inundated it with tears; proscribed probity, virtue, and philosophy; annihilated commerce, arts, and sciences; honoured Vandalism and robbery; corrupted moral principle; delegated the power of life and death to the most ferocious of men; erected 50,000 bastilles, and filled them with pretended conspirators; massacred age in its bed of pain; murdered infancy in the mother's womb; violated chastity in the moment of death; fatted the monsters of the ocean with human flesh; changed the Rhone and the Loire to rivers of blood,—Vaucluse to a fountain of tears,—Nantes to a sepulchre,—Paris, Arras, Bordeaux, Strasburg, to slaughter-houses,—and France to one vast theatre of horror, pillage, and murder."

WELLINGTON AT THE BATTLE OF WATERLOO.

During the first part of the action, the Duke of Wellington stood in the angle formed by the crossing of two roads, and on the right of the highway, beneath a solitary elm, afterwards known as "the Wellington Tree." After being mutilated and stripped by relic-hunters who visited the battle-field, this tree was purchased, in 1818, by Mr. Children, the eminent chemist; and among the memorials made from its wood is a chair, now in Windsor Castle, presented to George IV. by Mr. Children: it is placed in the guard chamber, near a memorial of the great

Nelson—a portion of the mast of the *Victory.* Another chair made of the wood was given by Mr. Children to the Duke of Wellington, and in this he mostly sat for his portrait ; a third chair is in the possession of the Duke of Rutland, at Belvoir Castle.   There is also in the British Museum a portion of the tree, having an iron chain inside it, which must have been wound round it when a sapling, and over which the wood had subsequently grown.   Mr. Children himself had a cabinet made of this wood to contain minerals, now in the possession of his son-in-law and daughter ; and many of his friends possess smaller articles manufactured from the tree. ·

The Duke of Wellington said that he remembered the tree perfectly, and that, during the battle, a Scotch sergeant had come to him to tell him that he had observed it was a mark for the enemy's cannon, begging him to move from it.   A lady said, "I hope you did, sir."   The hero replied, "I really forget ; but I know I thought it very good advice."

The late Lord Ward, in a letter to the Bishop of Landaff, the year after the battle of Waterloo, says : "The term ' Battle of Waterloo' must have been adopted for the sake of euphony, as no part of the battle reached that village, the struggle having taken place nearer to Brussels."   Lord Ward visited the tree near which the duke stood for so many hours with his staff, and found it pierced with at least a dozen balls, and observes, "It is quite marvellous how he escaped.   After the battle the duke joined in the pursuit, and followed for some miles.   Colonel Harvey, who was with him, advised him to desist, as the country was growing less open, and he might be fired at by a straggler from behind a hedge.   The duke shouted out : ' Let them fire away ; the battle is over, and my life is of no value now ! '"

One of the three letters written by the duke *from the field* was a brief note, which, having enumerated some who had fallen, ends thus emphatically : "*I have escaped unhurt.   The finger of Providence was on me.*"   What the impulse was which dictated these extraordinary words we leave to the opinion of those who read them. . . .   When the dreadful fight was over, the duke's feelings, so long kept at the highest tension, gave way ; and, as he rode amidst the groans of the wounded and the reeking carnage, and heard the rout of the vanquished and the shouts of the victors, fainter and fainter through the gloom of night, he wept, and soon after wrote the words above quoted from his letter.

MONEY-PANIC OF 1832.

Panics have been produced sometimes by extraordinary means.   Thus, in May 1832, a "run upon the Bank of England"

was produced by the walls of London being placarded with the
emphatic words, "To stop the duke, go for gold;" advice
which was followed, as soon as given, to a prodigious extent.
The Duke of Wellington was then very unpopular; and on
Monday, the 14th of May, it being currently believed that the
duke had formed a cabinet, the panic became universal, and
the run upon the Bank of England for coin was so incessant,
that in a few hours upwards of half a million was carried off.
Mr. Doubleday, in his *Life of Sir Robert Peel*, states it to be
well known that the above placards were "the device of four
gentlemen, two of whom were elected members of the reformed
parliament. Each put down 20*l.*; and the sum thus clubbed
was expended in printing thousands of these terrible missives,
which were eagerly circulated, and were speedily seen upon
every wall in London. The effect is hardly to be described.
It was electric."

WELLINGTON'S BED-CHAMBER.

At the north-east angle of Apsley House, Hyde Park Corner, upon the ground floor, is "the duke's bedroom," which
is narrow, shapeless, and ill-lighted; the bedstead small, provided with only a mattress and bolster, and scantily curtained
with green silk; the only ornaments of the room being an
unfinished sketch of the present Duchess of Wellington, two
cheap prints of military men, and a small portrait in oil. Yet
here slept the great duke, whose "eightieth year was by." In
the grounds and shrubbery he took daily walking exercise;
where, with the garden-engine, he was wont to enjoy exertion.[*]
* * * "In fine afternoons, the sun casts the shadow of the
duke's equestrian statue full upon Apsley House, and the sombre
image may be seen gliding spirit-like over the front."—*Quarterly Review*, No. 184.

Part of the site of Apsley House was a piece of ground given by
George II. to an old soldier, Allen, whom the king recognised as having
served in the battle of Dettingen. Upon this spot Allen built a small
tenement, in place of the apple-stall kept by his wife; and on the erection of Apsley House, in 1784, the ground was sold for a considerable
sum by Allen's successors to Apsley, Lord Bathurst. The apple-stall is
shown in a print dated 1766.

---

[*] As did the Duke's great antagonist, Napoleon. January 2, 1820. General
Bonaparte was "amusing himself with the pipe of the fire-engine, spouting
water on the trees and flowers in his favourite garden."—*Journal of Capt. Nicholls;
Captivity of Napoleon at St. Helena; Sir Hudson Lowe's Letters and Journals,* 1853.

The Seven Wonders of the World.

THIS phrase has been for ages applied to seven historical monuments of the constructive skill and magnificent art of the antique world. They are:

1. THE GREAT PYRAMID OF EGYPT,

the most gigantic of the three pyramids near the village of Giseh, about eleven miles from the banks of the Nile, forming a line to the westward of the city of Cairo. Herodotus was informed by the priests of Memphis that the great pyramid was built by Cheops, king of Egypt, about 900 B.C., or 450 years before he visited that country; that the body of Cheops was placed in a room beneath the bottom of the pyramid; and that the chamber was surrounded by a vault, to which the waters of the Nile were conveyed by a subterranean tunnel. Pliny and Diodorus Siculus agree in stating, that 360,000 men were employed twenty years in erecting this pyramid; and in contrast with this vast labour Sir John Herschel, calculating the weight of the pyramid to be 12,760 million pounds of granite,[*] at a medium height of 125 feet, adds, that it could have been raised by the effort of about 630 chaldrons of coal, a quantity consumed in some foundries in a week.

Herodotus states, that 1600 talents of silver were expended in providing the workmen with leeks, onions, and other food; and one great object of the Egyptian rulers in erecting this and other stupendous monuments was, to prevent the evils of over-populousness by accustoming the lower orders to a spare diet and severe labour. It may here be sufficient to state, that the pyramid consists of a series of platforms, each smaller than the one on which it rests, and consequently presenting the appearance of steps, which diminish in length from the bottom to the top; and of these steps there are 203. The entrance is in the north face. Within are passages leading to chambers lined with granite; in one of which, the King's Chamber, is a red granite sarcophagus, in which Cheops is supposed to have been entombed. This pyramid, the largest building in the world, has lost its apex and its casing. There is a second pyramid, retaining at its apex a portion of its casing, which is the tomb of Sensuphis. A third pyramid, the least ancient, was

---

[*] Three times that of the stone in Plymouth Breakwater.

built by Mycerinus according to Herodotus, and by Queen Nitocris according to Manetho. The date of the pyramids is, by the Newtonian chronology, between 1451 and 1153 B.C., or nearly 600 years after Abraham's visit to Egypt. "It has been supposed by some," says Wilkinson, "that, from the pyramids not being mentioned in the Bible or in Homer, they did not exist before the Exodus, or in the time of the poet. The presence of the name of Rameses the Great (who preceded the Trojan war) sufficiently answers the latter objection."

The base of the great pyramid has been often stated to equal that of the area of Lincoln's Inn Fields ; but the fact is otherwise : the base of the pyramid measures 764 feet on each side : whereas Lincoln's Inn Fields, although 821 feet on one side, is only 625 feet 6 inches on another, so that the area of the pyramid is greater by many thousand square feet.—Colonel Howard Vyse *On the Pyramids.*

2. BABYLON,

in Greek Βαβυλών, derives its name from a Hebrew word signi· fying Babel, the confusion of tongues (Gen. xi. 1-9) ; or from another expression signifying the court or city of Belus. In Dan. iv. 27 it·is termed "Babylon the great ;" and by Josephus (Antiq. viii. 6, 1), ἡ μεγάλη Βαβυλών, "the lady of the kingdoms ; the glory of the whole earth." It was the metropolis of the province of Babylon, and of the Babylonio-Chaldean empire. Its foundations were laid with those of the tower of Babel.[*]

Herodotus states that the walls of Babylon were sixty miles in circumference, built of large bricks cemented with bitumen, and raised round the city in the form of a square, protected on the outside by a ditch lined with the same material. They were 87 feet thick and 350 feet high. According to Quintus Curtius, four-horse chariots could pass each other on them. The city was entered by twenty-five gates on each side, of solid brass, and strengthened by 250 towers.[†] (See also p. 29.)

The Palace of Nebuchadnezzar was a most magnificent and stupendous work. Its outer wall embraced six miles. Within were two other embattled walls, besides a great tower. The

---

[*] Mr. Rich, in 1812, examined what were called "the Ruins of Babylon," near the modern town of Hillah, on the Euphrates. The most stupendous mass of ruins was an oblong mound, 762 yards in circumference, surmounted with a solid pile of brick, 37 feet high. This mound, *Birs Nimroud*, there is reason to believe with Niebuhr and Mr. Rich, was the Tower of Babel, or Belus, "which is pretty nearly in the same state in which Alexander saw it." Major Rennel considers the Pyramids of Egypt to be palpable imitations of the Babylonian Tower.

[†] Mr. Grote (*Hist. Greece*) institutes the following comparison with works of the kind in our time: "Though the walls of Nineveh and Babylon were much larger than those of Paris as it now stands, yet when we compare the two, not merely in size, but in respect of costliness, elaboration, and contrivance, the latter will be found to represent an infinitely greater *amount of work.*"

Hanging-Gardens are attributed by Diodorus to Cyrus, who constructed them in compliance with the wish of his queen to possess elevated groves such as she had enjoyed on the hills around her native Ecbatana; for Babylon was flat. To gratify this wish, an artificial mountain was reared, 400 feet on each side; while terraces, one above another, rose to a height that overtopped the walls of the city, 300 feet in elevation. The ascent from terrace to terrace was by flights of steps; while the terraces themselves were reared to their various stages, resting on ranges of regular piers, one over the other. Mr Rich found upon the site a hollow pier, 60 feet square, lined with fine brick laid in bitumen, and filled with earth; this corresponds with Strabo's description of the hollow brick piers which supported the Hanging-Gardens, and in which piers the large trees grew

3. THE GOLD AND IVORY STATUE OF JUPITER OLYMPIUS,

the masterpiece of Phidias, the greatest artist that ever lived; was executed by him for the people of Elis, and surpassed his celebrated statue of Minerva in the Parthenon. The Jupiter was set up in the temple of that deity at Olympia, near Elis, where the Olympic games were celebrated. Pausanias describes the statue from personal observation, which Strabo corroborates. The god was formed of gold and ivory, 58 English feet in height, seated on a throne, and almost touching the roof of the temple. Upon his head was an olive crown; in his right hand he bore a winged figure of Victory, also of gold and ivory, crowned, and holding a wreath. In the god's left hand he bore a lofty sceptre, surmounted with an eagle. His sandals and robe were of gold, the latter painted with animals and flowers, particularly lilies. The throne was formed of ivory and ebony, inlaid with gold, set with precious stones, and sculptured with graceful figures. The faces of the steps bore bas-reliefs of classic myths, and the footstool rested upon four couchant lions. In this work Phidias embodied Homer's impersonation of the god:

> " He spoke, and awful bends his sable brows,
> Shakes his ambrosial curls, and gives the nod,
> The stamp of fate, and sanction of the god;
> High Heaven with trembling the dread signal took,
> And all Olympus in the centre shook."

The heathen historians tell us that Phidias received for his skill the testimony of Jupiter himself: when the artist prayed the god would make known if he was satisfied, immediately the pavement of the temple was struck by lightning; and the spot was afterwards marked by a bronze vase. Crowds flocked to Elis to behold this wonder; and in Greece and Italy it was held as a calamity to die without seeing it. Nor was the adpiration merely the superstition of the multitude; for a Roman senator, when looking at this Jupiter of ivory and gold, had his mind moved as though the god were present. The able restoration of this figure has been learnedly commented on by M. Quatremère de Quincy.

The Doric temple in which this statue was placed was in extreme length 369 feet, breadth 182 feet, as traced by Mr. Cockerell, from the foundation: many of the blocks of marble weigh nearly nine tons each; and each of two remaining capitals is computed to weigh more than twenty-one tons. These masses were raised 70 feet, and the flutings of the columns would contain a man in their hollow as in a niche. The pediments were sculptured with the wars of the Giants and the siege of Troy; upon the entablature stood a row of Atlantes, each 25 feet high, and supporting an upper entablature at 110 feet above the floor: the chest of one of these giants, restored, measured more than 6 feet. The nave of the temple was 18 feet higher and 2 feet broader than the nave of St. Paul's Cathedral. Of this splendid edifice the basement alone remains.

4. THE TEMPLE OF DIANA OF THE EPHESIANS,

at Ephesus (the modern Natolia), the capital of the twelve Ionian cities in Asia Minor, was built around the famous image of the goddess. This edifice was burnt down on the night in which Alexander was born, by an obscure person named Eratostratus, who thus sought to transmit his name to posterity. Alexander made an offer to rebuild the temple, provided he was allowed to inscribe his name on the front; which the Ephesians refused. Aided, however, by the whole of Asia Minor, they erected a still more magnificent temple, which occupied them two hundred and twenty years. Pliny describes it as 425 feet long by 220 broad, and supported by 127 columns, each 60 feet high, and contributed by some prince; thirty of them were richly carved. Chersiphron was the architect. The altar was the work of Praxiteles. The famous sculptor, Scopas, is said to have chiselled one of the columns. Apelles contributed a splendid picture of Alexander the Great. The temple was built of cedar, cypress, and even gold; and within it were treasured offerings to the goddess, as paintings, statues, &c., the value of which almost exceeded computation. Nero is said to have despoiled the temple of much of these treasures; but it continued to exist until it was finally burnt by the Goths in the reign of Gallienus, A.D. 253-268.

Vitruvius considers this temple as the first edifice in which architecture was brought to perfection, and the first in which the Ionic order was employed. Its remains consist of walls of immense blocks of marble, in the fronts of which are small perforations wherein were sunk the shanks of the brass and silver plates with which the walls were faced. Some of the vast porphyry columns of the front portico lie prostrate upon the site; others were taken by Constantine to build his new city of Constantinople. The heathen temple was likewise despoiled to erect the Christian church of Santa Sophia, in which these columns again support an anti-Christian edifice.

"But," says the Rev. Dr. Walsh, the traveller, "the most interesting circumstance of this building to me is, the great illustration it gives to the Acts of the Apostles. Here is the place where St. Paul excited the commotion among the silver and brass smiths who worked for the temple; and over the way was the theatre, into which the people rushed, carrying with them Caius and Aristarchus, Paul's companions. Hence they had a full view of the front of the temple, which they pointed out as that 'which all Asia worshippeth;' and in their enthusiasm they cried out, 'Great is Diana of the Ephesians, to whom such a temple belonged!'"

5. THE MAUSOLEUM, OR TOMB, OF MAUSOLUS.

This king, the eldest of the three sons of Hecatomnus, the wealthiest of the Carian dynasty, died B.C. 353; when his widow and sister, Artemisia, erected to his memory, at Halicarnassus (now Budrun), a superb tomb, which, by its artistic celebrity, has given the name of mausoleum to tombs and sepulchres of stately character. The tomb of Mausolus was designed by Phiteus and Satyrus; it was nearly square in plan, 113 by 93 feet; around its base was a peristyle of 36 Doric columns, said to have been 60 feet high, while the superstructure rose in a pyramidal form to the height of 100 feet. To adorn its sides with sculpture, Artemisia employed Bryaxis, Timotheus, Leochares, Scopas, Praxiteles, and Pythis. Artemisia died before the monument was completed; when the artists are said to have finished the work for their own honour and the glory of art. Mr. Vaux, in his admirable *Handbook of Antiquities in the British Museum*, says, "Strabo in the first, Pausanias in the second, Gregory of Nazianzus in the fourth, Constantine Porphryogenitus in the tenth, and Eudosia in the eleventh centuries, respectively speak of it in terms which imply that it was still existing during those periods; while Fontanus, the historian of the siege of Rhodes, states that a German knight, named Henry Schelegelhott, constructed the citadel at Budrun out of the Mausoleum," and decorated its walls with the marbles and bas-reliefs. The existence of these marbles had long been known; when, in 1846, they were, through the exertions of Sir Stratford Canning, presented by the Turks to the British nation, and are now in the British Museum, which thus possesses fragments of two of the Seven Wonders of the World—the Mausoleum, and a fragment of the casing of one of the Pyramids of Egypt. That the bas-reliefs now in the Museum were inserted in the Budrun walls by the knights' of Rhodes, is proved by the escutcheons, Latin sentences, and date 1510, as well as by an inscription on a shield borne by one of the figures. The marbles consist of 11 slabs, 64 feet 11 inches long, sculptured with a battle between the Greeks and Amazons; Heracles, too, appearing among the combatants.* The sculptures in style considerably resemble the Choragic monument of Lysicrates at Athens. There were, between the columns, statues of Parian marble; at each angle of the basement a portico, surmounted with a colossal equestrian statue; bas-reliefs on the terraces; two octagonal towers on the second terrace, which was planted with cypresses; and from the third terrace rose the crown of the pyramid, with a colossal group in marble of Phaeton in his quadriga. When Anaxagoras saw this costly work, he exclaimed, "How much money is changed into stone!" '

The Mausoleum seems to have existed in the time of Strabo; and from its description by Pliny has been modelled the steeple of St. George's Church, Bloomsbury, London.

6. THE PHAROS OF ALEXANDRIA,

so named from the island on which it stood, was surrounded by water. It consisted of several stories and galleries of a prodigious height, with a lantern at the top continually burning. It was built by one of the Ptolemies, A.M. 3670; and the architect, as the inscription stated, was Sostratus Cnidius. How long this structure stood is not very certain; but it was so famous, that all lighthouses after it were called by the common name of Pharos.

"The modern Pharos," according to Mr. Lane, "is a poor successor of the ancient building erected by Sostratus Cnidius; though from a distance it has rather an imposing appearance. Several Arab historians mention the telescopic mirror of metal which was placed at the summit of the ancient Pharos. In this mirror, vessels might be discerned at sea at a very great distance. El Makreezee relates that part of the Pharos was thrown down by an earthquake in the year of the Flight 177 (A.D. 793-4); that Ahmad Ibn-Tooloon surmounted it with a dome of wood; and that an inscription upon a plate of lead was found upon the northern side, buried in the earth, written in ancient Greek characters, every letter of which was a cubit

* This myth may relate to the invasion of Asia Minor by some Scythian nation, among whom, as in the case of the Massagetæ in the time of Cyrus, women had the right of sovereignty.—*W. S. W. Vaux, F.S.A.*

in height and a span in breadth. This was perhaps the inscription placed by the original architect, and which, according to Strabo, was to this effect : ' Sostratus Cnidius, the son of Dexiphanes, to the protecting gods, for the sake of the mariners.' It is also related by Es-Sooyootee, that the inhabitants of Alexandria likewise made use of the mirror above mentioned to burn the vessels of their enemies, by directing it so as to reflect the concentrated rays of the sun upon them."

The ancient Pharos was 450 feet in height, or 50 feet higher than St. Paul's Cathedral; and its cost was 800 talents Attic (165,000*l.*), and in Alexandrian double that sum.

7. THE COLOSSUS OF RHODES.

In the days of its prosperity, the island of Rhodes is said to have been adorned with 3000 statues, and upwards of 100 colossal figures; of the latter, there was one distinguished as "the Colossus of Rhodes." It was erected with the spoil which Demetrius left behind him when he raised the siege which he had so long carried on against that city. This famous Colossus was consecrated to the Sun, the tutelar deity of Rhodes. It was, according to Pliny, the work of Chares of Lindus (one of the cities of Rhodes), a pupil of Lysippus; its height was 70 cubits (about 105 feet), the cost of its erection about 300 talents (about 70,000*l.*), and the time consumed in it twelve years. Fifty-six years after its completion (224 B.C.), this statue was thrown down by an earthquake; and in Pliny's time it was still lying on the ground, a wonder to behold. Few persons, he says, could embrace the thumbs, and the fingers were longer than the bodies of most statues; through the fractures were seen huge cavities in the interior, in which immense stones had been placed to balance it while standing. Vigenaire and Du Choul, two antiquaries of the sixteenth century, imaginatively describe the statue to have been placed across the harbour of Rhodes, with a stride of fifty feet from rock to rock : vessels passed under it in full sail; a lamp blazed in its right hand; an internal spiral staircase led to its summit; . and round its neck was suspended a glass, in which ships might be discerned as far off as the coast of Egypt.

After the overthrow of the Colossus, Greece and Egypt offered to contribute large sums to restore the figure; but the Rhodians declined, alleging that they were forbidden by an oracle to do so; and the fragments of the statue lay scattered on the ground until the Saracens became masters of the island —a period of nearly 900 years. In the year 655, an officer of the Caliph Othman collected the valuable materials and sold them to a Jewish merchant of Edessa, who is said to have laden nine hundred camels with the brass.

FOR WHAT PURPOSE WERE THE PYRAMIDS OF EGYPT ERECTED?

This question has been much controverted.

One opinion is, that the Pyramids were *the granaries of Joseph*, which may be confuted by the smallness of the rooms, and the time required in building.

The Arabians generally think they were built by King Saurid, before the Deluge, as a refuge for himself and the public records from the Flood.

Josephus, the Jewish historian, who wrote A.D. 71, ascribes them to his countrymen during their captivity in Egypt.

Shaw and Bryant believed them to be temples, and the stone-chest a tank for holding water for purification. Pauw, contemporary with Shaw and Bryant, considers the Great Pyramid as the tomb of Osiris.

Others suppose the Pyramids to have been associated with worship ; in conjunction with which it may be mentioned, that in the Sandwich Islands, Ellis, the missionary, saw a solid pyramidal structure, in front of which the images were kept, and the altars fixed.

But the greater number of writers, ancient and modern, believe the Great Pyramid to be the tomb of Cheops, the alleged builder : Maillet, in 1760, added, that the chambers were built for shutting up the friends of the deceased king with the dead body ; and through the holes on each side of the central chamber they were to be supplied with food, &c. ; yet more absurdly, an old Moulah, in 1799, told Buonaparte, when in Egypt, that the object was to keep the buried body undecayed, by closely sealing up all access to the outward air.

Another ingenious theory ascribes the Pyramids to the Shepherd Kings, a foreign pastoral nation which oppressed Egypt in the early times of the Pharaohs. Wilkinson says :

"I do not pretend to explain or decide the real object for which these stupendous monuments were constructed, but feel persuaded that they have served for tombs, and have also been intended for astronomical purposes. For though it is vain to look for the pole-star at the bottom of a passage descending at an angle of 27°, or to imagine that a *closed* passage, or a pyramid covered with a smooth and inaccessible casing was intended for an observatory ; yet the form of the exterior might lead to many useful calculations. They stand exactly due north and south ; and while the direction of the faces to the east and west might serve to fix the return of a certain period of the year, the shadow cast by the sun, or the time of its coinciding with their slope, might be observed for a similar purpose."

Aristotle's opinion, now generally adopted (*Pol.* v. li.), is that the Pyramids were built "to keep the people well employed and poor ;" because "It suits tyranny to reduce its subjects to poverty, that they may not be able to compose a guard ; and that being employed in procuring their daily bread, they may have no leisure to conspire against their tyrants."

Baron Dupin calculates that the combined action of the steam-engines at work in Britain, some twenty years since, could raise from the quarries, and place as they now are, all the stones of the Great Pyramid in eighteen hours !

𝔥istoric 𝔖apings and 𝔒rigins.

THE RIDDLE OF THE SPHINX.

THE Riddle which the Sphinx learned from the Muses, and the solution of which she proposed to the Thebans as a condition of her withdrawal from the state, was as follows : " What animal has one voice, at first four, then two, and at last three feet ?" The difficulty long perplexed the Thebans, and several were destroyed by the Sphinx. Ænon, son of Creon, perished in this manner ; when his father promised the crown and Jocasta to the explainer of the riddle. Œdipus applied his powerful mind to the subject ; and having discovered the meaning, told King Creon that the animal described by the Sphinx was *man*, who, in infancy, from using his hands as well as his feet in walking, may be said to have four feet (all-fours) ; in afterlife, employs but two ; and in old age, to these he adds a staff, which may be reckoned a third. For this solution Œdipus* received the promised rewards ; and the Sphinx threw herself headlong from the citadel. Hence the name of Œdipus became applied to a person who unravelled a point difficult to understand. Thus, in the *Andria* of Terence, when Simo is surprised at Davus not understanding his proposition, he replies: *Davus sum, non Œdipus.*

" VILLANOUS WORDS."

Princes do rather pardon ill-deeds than villanous words. Alexander the Great forgave many sharp swords, but never any sharp tongues ; no, though they but told him truly of his error : and certainly it belongs to those that have warrant from God to reprehend princes, and none else, especially in public. It is said that Henry IV. of France had his heart more inflamed against the Duke of Biron for his overbold and biting taunts that he used against him before Amiens than for his conspiracy with the Spaniard or Savoyan ; for he had pardoned ten thousand of such as had gone further, and drawn their swords against him. The contemptuous words that Sir John Perrot used of our late Queen Elizabeth were his ruin, and not the counterfeit letter of the Romish priest produced against him. So fared it with some other greater than he, that thereby ran the same,

---

* Œdipus was for his sins driven from the city by the Thebans after they had put out his eyes, when he cursed his sons for not protecting him from injury ; but an old writer (1582) oddly says : " Œdipus was glad to scratch out his eyes, because he could not endure to behold the vices of his children."

and a worse fortune, soon after.—Sir Walter Raleigh's *History of the World.*

THE GREEK KALENDS.

The Kalendæ, or Kalends, was the name given by the Romans to the first day of every month ; and the Greeks having no Kalends, the Romans used the phrase *Ad Kalendas Græcas* proverbially to denote a period which would never arrive. The French have adopted the Latin expression, with no variation, to convey the same idea—*Aux Calendes Grecques.*

WHY WERE THE MUSES CALLED PIERIDES ?

Pierus, a rich man of Thessaly, was the father of nine daughters. They were all musical, and so vain of their talents, that they presumed to rival the Muses in song, and challenged them to a trial of vocal skill. The contest ended in the entire defeat of the daughters of Pierus ; and their audacity was punished by the transformation of the whole nine into magpies. It was supposed that the victorious Muses afterwards assumed the name of the conquered daughters of Pierus, and commanded themselves to be styled "Pierides," on the same principle that Minerva caused herself to be called "Pallas," she having slain the giant of that name. Some, however, are of opinion that the Muses were called "Pierides," either because they were natives of Pieria in Thessaly, or that they resided on Mount Pierus.

Mr. Grote says : The narrow strip between the mouths of the Peneius and the Haliakmon was the original abode of the Pierian Thracians, who dwelt close to the foot of Olympus, and among whom the worship of the Muses seems to have been a primitive characteristic. Grecian poetry teems with local allusions and epithets which appear traceable to this early fact, though we are unable to follow it in detail.—*Hist. Greece,* vol.iv.

THE PALLADIUM.

Erichthonius, the pupil and favoured companion of Athene (Minerva or Pallas), is said to have placed in the Acropolis the original Palladium, or wooden statue of that goddess, believed to have dropped from heaven. There was likewise a Palladium in Troy, which it was declared could not be taken whilst that statue remained within the walls. Hence the term has come to denote any effectual defence, protection, or safety. Thus, we say, trial by jury is the palladium of our civil rights.

"EVERY MAN IS THE ARCHITECT OF HIS OWN FORTUNES"

was the professional figure employed by Appius Claudius the Blind, and borrowed from his occupation as an architect in former years. He is said to have introduced it in the appeal by which Rome became the mistress of the world.

"EX PEDE HERCULEM."

The following origin of this proverb is to be found quoted by Aulus Gellius, from Plutarch:

Pythagoras ingeniously calculated the great stature of Hercules by comparing the length of various stadia in Greece. All those courses were nominally 600 feet in length; but Hercules was said to have measured out the stadium at Olympia with his own feet, while the others followed a standard of later days. The philosopher argued that by how much the Olympic course exceeded all others in length, by the said proportion did the foot of Hercules exceed that of men of a subsequent age; and again, by the same proportion must the stature of Hercules have been pre-eminent.

Several proverbs of a similar meaning are collected in *Diogenian*, vol. iv.: the most common is *ex ungue leonem.*

"NE SUTOR ULTRA CREPIDAM."

This well-known saying, that a shoemaker should not go beyond his last, originated with Apelles, the celebrated Greek painter, who set a picture which he had finished in a public place, and concealed himself behind it, in order to hear the criticisms of passers-by. A shoemaker observed a defect in the shoe, and the painter forthwith corrected it. The cobbler came again the next day, and encouraged by the success of his first remark, began to extend his censure to the leg of the figure; when the angry painter thrust out his head from behind the picture, and told the shoemaker to keep to his trade.

PUBLIC DINNERS AT ATHENS.

The public dinners at the Prytaneium, of which the archons and a select few partook in common, were either first established, or perhaps only more strictly regulated, by Solon: he ordered barley-cakes for their ordinary meals, and wheaten loaves for festival-days, prescribing how often each person should dine at the table. The honour of dining at the Prytaneium was maintained throughout as a valuable reward at the disposal of the government.—*Grote's History of Greece*, vol. iii.

"THE IPHICRATIDES" LEGGINGS.

Mr. Grote describes a species of leggings which the Athenian Iphicrates devised for his soldiers; and, in his fondness for parallel, the historian observes: "The name *Iphicratides*, given to these new-fashioned leggings or boots, proves to us that Wellington and Blucher are not the first eminent generals who have lent an honourable denomination to boots and shoes."
—*History of Greece*, vol. ix.

THE SANDWICH

is believed to have been named after the Earl of Sandwich, the celebrated statesman of the reigns of George II. and George III. Grose, the antiquary, and a contemporary of the earl, notes the Sandwich as "said to have been a favourite dish of the Earl of Sandwich."

THE HELOTS AND DRUNKENNESS.

The service in the Spartan house was all performed by Helots, the treatment of whom at Sparta betokens less of cruelty than of ostentatious scorn. Such is proved by the statement that Helots were compelled to appear in a state of drunkenness, in order to excite in the Spartan youths a sentiment of repugnance against intoxication.

LOVE OF TRUTH.

Herodotus tells us of the ancient Persians, that "from the age of five years to twenty they instruct their sons in only three things: to manage the house, to make use of the bow, and *to speak truth.*"

"VENI, VIDI, VICI."

In these memorable words Cæsar announced the victory which he gained over the Pharnaces, at Zela, in Asia Minor.

An account of this victory, with all the circumstances attending it, will be found in Cæsar's Commentaries *De Bello Alexandrino*, but without any mention of the words "*Veni, vidi, vici.*" The authority for these is in Plutarch's life of Cæsar, where we read that when Cæsar celebrated his Pontic triumph, the well-known words were eagerly caught at and made a prominent figure in the spectacle—so, at least, we learn from Suetonius: *Pontico triumpho inter pompæ fercula trium verborum pratulit titulum—'Veni, vidi, vici;' non acta belli significantem, sicut cæteri, sed celeriter confecti notam.*

"STRIKE; BUT HEAR ME!"

When, in the synod of Peloponnesian chiefs, Themistocles reopened the discussion, and prematurely expressed his fears and anxiety as to the abandonment of Salamis, the Corinthian Adeimantus rebuked him by saying: "Themistocles, those who in the public festival-matches rise up before the proper signal, are scourged." "True (rejoined the Athenian); but those who lag behind the signal win no crowns." Adeimantus then lifted up his stick to strike Themistocles; upon which the latter addressed to him the well-known observation, "Strike; but hear me!"

TRUTH IN A PIT.

Cleanthes said that "truth was hid in a pit." "Yes," answers the poet; "but you Greek philosophers were the first that put her there, and then claimed so much merit to yourselves for drawing her out."

CYNOSURE.

Cynosura (from two Greek words signifying the *tail of the dog*) is a name given to the lesser bear. According to Aratus and Hyginus, Cynosure was one of the nymphs of Mount Ida, who nursed Jupiter. But it is at least probable that, before the Greeks adapted their mythology to the constellations, they had, from some oriental source, the habit of figuring ursa minor as a dog, and that the tail of the dog was the pole-star. Many persons may probably know this word only from the two lines of Milton's *Allegro* :

> "Where perhaps some beauty lies,
>   The cynosure of neighbouring eyes."

These lines have puzzled many; though the reference to the pole-star, and the property of the magnet, gives the image a degree of fitness for poetry which the etymology of the word alone would hardly suggest.—*Penny Cyclopædia.*

"HEWING BLOCKS WITH A RAZOR."

This phrase is as old as Livy, who relates that king Priscus, defying the power of an augur, desired him to cut a whetstone in two with a razor as a proof of his magic, which he did. Hence, in Goldsmith's *Retaliation:*

> "To eat mutton cold, and *cut blocks with a razor.*"

"NO ROYAL ROAD TO GEOMETRY."

Euclid, who opened a school of mathematics at Alexandria, in the reign of the first Ptolemy, was once asked by that sovereign whether he could not explain his art to him in a more compendious way; to which Euclid made the celebrated answer, that there was no royal road to geometry. Upon this Dr. Johnson has observed; "Other things may be seized by might, or purchased with money; but knowledge is to be gained only by study, and study to be prosecuted only in retirement."

BREAKING PRISCIAN'S HEAD.

Priscian was a great grammarian, about the year 528; and when any one spoke false grammar, he was said to *break Priscian's head.* Dr. Nash, in his *Notes to Hudibras,* thinks Butler humorously supposes Priscian, who received so many blows upon the head, to have been much averse to taking off his hat, and therefore calls him the founder of Quakerism.—See *Hudibras*, part ii. canto 2.

PASQUIN AND PASQUINADE.

Pasquin is the name given to a mutilated fragment of an ancient statue, found in Rome in the sixteenth century, and considered to represent Menelaus supporting the dead body of Patroclus. It was named Pasquin from Pasquino, a tailor, who lived hard by where the statue was found, "many years since," says Parisio, in his *Antiquities of Rome*, published 1660. Pasquin's shop was the resort of the gossips of Rome; and he was a wag, and his witticisms were styled *pasquinate*, which hence became applied to epigrams and lampoons,—a kind of composition for which the modern Romans are noted. We subjoin a few specimens.

When Mezzofanti was made a cardinal, Pasquin declared that it was a very proper appointment; for there could be no doubt that the Tower of Babel, *il Torre di Babel*, required an interpreter. On the visit of the Emperor Francis to Rome, the following appeared: *Gaudium urbis, Flatus provinciarum, Risus mundi*. On the election of Pope Leo X. in 1440, the following satirical acrostic appeared, to mark the date MCCCCXL: *Multi cæci cardinales creaverunt cæcum decimum (X.) Leonem*. During a bad harvest, in the time of Pius XI., when the loaf of two bajocchi had decreased considerably in size, the passion of the Pope for the inscription which records his munificence on two-thirds of the statues in the Vatican was satirised by the exhibition of one of these little rolls, with the inscription: *Munificentiâ Pii Sexti*. Pasquin's distich on the appointment of Holstenius and his two successors as librarians of the Vatican is historically interesting. Holstenius had abjured Protestantism, and was succeeded in his office by Leo Allatius, a Chian, who was in turn succeeded by a Syrian, Evode Assemani, on which Pasquin said:

> "Præfuit hereticus. Post hunc, schismaticus. At nunc
> Turca præest. Petri bibliotheca, vale!"

When Urban VIII. published his celebrated decree excommunicating all persons who took snuff in the churches of Seville, Pasquin quoted from Job: "Wilt thou break a loaf driven to and fro? and wilt thou pursue the dry stubble?"— Selected and abridged from the *Handbook for Central Italy*.

THE BUSKIN AND SOCK.

The word Buskin is the translation of the Greek and Latin word *Cothurnus*, which signifies a high-heeled shoe or boot used by the Greek and Roman tragic actors, to give an appearance of elevation to their stature, in conjunction with the mask and other stage-properties. *Cothurnus* in Latin is used in contra-distinction to *Soccus*, the flat-soled shoe worn by comedians.

Hence, in English authors, the words *buskin* and *sock* are often used for the tragic and comic drama. So Dryden :

> " Great Fletcher never treads in buskins here,
> Nor greater Jonson dares in socks appear."

ROSCIUS, THE ROMAN ACTOR,

was the son of a man of fortune, who was killed in the proscription of Sylla, when his estates were confiscated. Roscius's singular merit in his art recommended him to the friendship of the greatest men in Rome. The excellence of his acting surpassed all that the Romans had ever seen; so that when a man excelled in any other profession, it grew into a proverb to call him "a Roscius."[*] To him Horace alludes, in his Epistle to Augustus, calling him *doctus*, to mark his perfect knowledge of his art. The graces of his action, the melody of his voice, and his conception of character, were perfect ; but a disagreeable squint impaired his countenance, and, from the expression of Tacitus, probably affected both eyes : yet the Romans would not allow him to wear a mask, because by it they would lose some of the finest tones of his voice. Roscius's daily pay for acting is said to have been about thirty pounds sterling. Pliny computes his yearly receipts at 4000*l.* ; Cicero, at 5000*l.* He was generous, benevolent, and a contemner of money ; and after he had gained an ample fortune from the stage, he played for some years gratuitously. Cicero was his great friend, and, in an action brought against him respecting a slave, the Roman orator defended his friend in an eloquent oration, of which the greater part is still extant.

CANARD, OR HOAX.

M. Quetelet, in the *Annuaire de l'Académie Française*, attributes the first application of this term, as above, to Norbert Cornelissen, who, to give a sly hit at the ridiculous pieces of intelligence in the public journals, stated an interesting experiment had just been made calculated to prove the extraordinary voracity of ducks. Twenty were placed together : and one of them having been killed and cut up into the smallest possible pieces, feathers and all, was thrown to the other nineteen, and most gluttonously gobbled up. Another was then taken from the nineteen, and, being chopped small like its predecessor, was served up to the eighteen, and at once devoured like the other ; and so on to the last, who thus was placed in the position of having eaten his nineteen companions. This story, most pleasantly narrated, ran the round of all the journals of

---

[*] Garrick was popularly styled " the British Roscius." Churchill wrote a severe satire upon theatrical managers and performers, entitled the *Rosciad.* The term " Young Roscius" has been applied to several precocious children.

Europe. It then became almost forgotten for about a score of years, when it came back from America with amplifications; but the word remained in its novel signification.

THE CYNICS

were a sect of Greek philosophers of the school of Socrates, and are said to have been named from the Greek for dog-like, from their snarling disposition; though others derive it from the gymnasium called Cynosarges, in which Antisthenes, the founder of this school, used to lecture. The Cynics held that virtue was the only object at which men ought to aim, and that most of the sciences and arts, as they do not tend to make men virtuous, but sometimes, on the contrary, interfere with the attainment of it, are unprofitable and pernicious. The true philosopher, they considered, was he who could discard all the comforts and charities of life, and triumph over his bodily wants, so as to be able to live only for virtue. The result of these principles was great strictness of morals, and voluntary penances; and some members of the sect, as Antisthenes and Diogenes, deserved and obtained great celebrity.

Diogenes was the son of a money-changer of Sinope, whence they were both expelled on a charge of "adulterating the coinage;" which has given rise to the remark: "Who would imagine that Diogenes, who in his younger days was a falsifier of money, should in the after-course of his life be so great a contemner of metal?" Diogenes escaped to Athens, where he is said to have lived in a tub in the temple of Cybele; but Sir Thomas Browne questions whether the home of Diogenes were a tub framed of wood, and after the manner of ours, or rather made of earth, as learned men conceive, and so more clearly make out the expression of Juvenal,

"Della magni, non ardent Cynici," &c.

The great merit of the Cynic philosophy was that it paved the way for the establishment of Stoicism, which succeeded and superseded it, just as the philosophy of Epicurus supplanted that of Aristippus.

THE STOICS AND THE EPICUREANS.

These were two of the sects which chiefly engrossed the philosophical part of Rome in the time of Cicero, and are thus characterised by Middleton, in his life of that illustrious man:

"The *Stoics* were the bigots or enthusiasts in philosophy, who held none to be truly wise or good but themselves; placed perfect happiness in virtue, though stripped of every other good; affirmed all sins to be equal; all deviations from right equally wicked; to kill a dunghill cock without reason, the same crime as to kill a parent; that a wise man could never forgive; never be moved by anger, favour, or pity; never be deceived; never repent; never change his mind. (*Pro Muren.* 29.)

But as the Stoics exalted human nature too high, so the Epicureans depressed it too low; as those raised it to the heroic, these debased it to the brutal state. They held pleasure to be the chief good of man, death the extinction of his being; and placed their happiness consequently in the secure enjoyment of a pleasurable life; esteeming virtue on no other account than as it was a handmaid to pleasure, and helped to insure the possession of it by preserving health and conciliating friends. Their wise man had therefore no other duty but to provide for his own ease, to decline all struggles, to retire from public affairs, and to imitate the life of their gods, by passing his days in a calm, contemplative, undisturbed repose, in the midst of rural shades and pleasant gardens."

Thomas Taylor, the Platonist, writes: "The doctrine of the Stoics, Peripatetics, and Platonists, holds that *the true man is intellect*, or the most excellent part of man; that the body is nothing more than the instrument of the rational soul; and that external possessions are indeed the good of the body, but are totally foreign to the exalted good of the mind. This doctrine, while it adds vigour to the efforts of the virtuous, attacks with irresistible force that ignoble opinion of the Epicurean vulgar, that the body is a part of man."

The corrupt part of the sect of Epicurus (says Swift) only borrowed his name, as the monkey did the cat's claw to draw the chestnut out of the fire.

WHO WERE THE FIRST SYCOPHANTS?

Sycophant (*sycophanta*)—a tale-bearer, a false accuser, a deceiver, parasite, smell-feast. The name arose upon this occasion: There was an act in Athens that none should transport figs out of the territory of Attica; such as gave information of those that, contrary to this law, conveyed figs into other parts were termed *Sycophants*, from *Sycos*, which is in Greek a fig.—Blount's *Glossography*.

THE SYMPOSIACS.

These were table entertainments of the ancients, and were part of the education of the times, their discourses being commonly the canvassing and solution of some question, either philosophical or philological, always instructive, and usually pleasant; for the cups went round with the debate, and men were merry and wise together, according to the proverb. Plutarch says, that one Lamprias, a man eminent for his learning, and a philosopher, disputed best, and unravelled the difficulties of philosophy with most success, when he was at supper, and well warmed with wine.—*Dryden.*

THE PERIPATETICS.

When Aristotle, the most eminent of Plato's scholars, retired with his followers to a gymnasium, called the Lyceum, from a custom which they observed, of teaching and disputing as they walked in the porticoes of the place, they obtained the name of Peripatetics, or the walking philosophers.—Middleton's *Life of Cicero.*

The term Peripatetic is ludicrously applied to one who is obliged to walk, or cannot afford to ride.—*Tatler.*

CRETAN PHILOSOPHY.

Epimenides has said that all the Cretans are liars; but, being a Cretan himself, he lied—he lied when he said so. Then the Cretans are not all liars; then Epimenides has not lied; then the Cretans are liars, &c.

EXAMPLE OF A SORITES.*

Themistocles used the following argument to prove that his little son, under ten years of age, governed the whole world: My son governs his mother; his mother governs me; I, the Athenians; the Athenians, the Greeks; Greece commands Europe; Europe, the whole world: therefore my son governs the whole world.—*Notes to assist the Memory, &c.*

HORSE-CHESTNUT AND A CHESTNUT-HORSE.

Wideness of difference between things nominally the same.— In one of Queen Anne's parliaments there were two members named Montague Matthieu and Matthew Montague. Some one having attributed opinions to the first gentleman which ought to have been ascribed to the second, the latter, in repudiating the charge, stated that, notwithstanding the similarity of name, there was as much difference between them as between a horse-chestnut and a chestnut-horse.

The illustration has been treated with much humour by George Colman in his *Broad Grins.*

THE PHILIPPICS.

This invective declamation is named from the orations of Demosthenes against Philip of Macedon, to rouse the Athenians against his crafty policy. They are the masterpieces of that great orator. Leland has translated them; but to express the simplicity, perspicuity, and force of the original, would require the translator to possess powers the same in kind as those which Demosthenes himself possessed, and near them in degree.

Cicero's orations against Marc Antony were also called Philippics from their being rivals of the invectives of Demosthenes. They cost Cicero his life; and Antony, having procured his murder, had his head and hands fixed on the rostra in the Forum, wherein the orator had delivered the Philippics.

* 'Sorites' is an accumulative syllogism, or one heaped on another.

"A ROLAND FOR AN OLIVER."

" Froissard, a countryman of ours, records,
England all Olivers and Rowlands bred
During the time Edward the Third did reign."
Shakspeare's King Henry VI. part L act L sc. 2.

Oliver and Roland were two of the most famous in the list of Charlemagne's twelve peers ; and their exploits are the theme of the old romances. From the equally doughty and unheard-of exploits of these champions arose the saying of, *Giving a Roland for an Oliver*, for giving a person as good as he brings.

"ALL IS LOST, SAVE HONOUR."

It was on the day of the fatal battle of Pavia that Francis I. wrote his mother a letter containing the oft-quoted words, "All is lost, madam, save honour." But Francis spoilt his letter by its conclusion, " *et ma personne, qui est sauvé:*" The selfish tyrant has got much credit by this omission, which, however, should not now be persevered in.

CATCHING A TARTAR.

The Tartars, it is said, had much rather die in battle than take quarter. Hence the proverb, "Thou hast caught a Tartar." A man catches a Tartar when he falls into his own trap ; or having a design upon another, is caught himself. "Help, help," cries one ; "I have caught a Tartar !" "Bring him along," answers his comrade. "He will not come," says he. "Then come without him," quoth the other. "But he will not let me," says the Tartar-catcher.

Peck, in his *Life of Milton*, relates : Bajazet was taken prisoner by Tamerlane, who, when he first saw him, generously asked, "Now, sir, if you had taken me prisoner, as I have you, tell me, I pray, what you would have done with me ?" "If I had taken you prisoner," said the foolish Turk, "I would have thrust you under the table when I did eat, to gather up the crumbs with the dogs ; when I rode out I would have made your neck a horsing-block ; and when I travelled, you also should have been carried along with me in an iron cage, for every fool to hoot and shout at." "I thought to have used you better," said the gallant Tamerlane : "but since you intended to have served me thus, you have (*caught a Tartar*, for hence I reckon came that proverb) justly pronounced your doom."

ORIGIN OF "HURRAH !"

The word is pure Slavonian, and is commonly heard, from the coasts of Dalmatia to Behring's Straits, when any of the population living within these limits are called on to give proof of courage and valour. The origin of this word belongs to the primitive idea that every man that dies heroically for his country goes straight to heaven—*Hu-raj* ("to paradise") ; and it is so

that in the shock and ardour of battle the combatants utter
that cry, as the Turks do that of "Allah!" each animating
himself by the certitude of immediate recompense to forget
earth, and to contemn death.

"GONE TO JERICHO."

In the Patent Rolls of the manor of Blackmore, near Col-
chester, occurs (18th February, 20 Hen. VIII., 1528-9) an entry
of a tenement called *Jericho*, reported to have been one of the
king's pleasure-houses. Hence, when the luxurious monarch
was missing, the cant phrase among the courtiers was that
"he was gone to Jericho."—See *Camden Miscellany*, vol. iii.

STOCKS, BARNACLES, AND BILBOES.

Barnacles, or Bernicles, appear to be first mentioned by
Joinville, the chronicler of St. Louis:

"And the Saracens, seeing that the king would not comply with
their demands, threatened to put him in the *bernicles*, which is the
most grievous torture they can put any one to. And these are two
great beams of wood, which are fastened to a head; and when they put
any one in them, they lay him on his side between the two beams, and
pass his legs across great pins; then shut down the piece of wood that
is uppermost, and make a man sit down on the beams, from whence it
comes that there remains not half a foot of bones in the body that are
not crushed and broken; and still worse to make the matter, at the end
of three days they put the legs, which are all swollen, back again into
these bernicles, and break them anew, which is a most cruel thing, as
well you may believe; and with bullock's sinews they tie down his head
for fear he should move himself therein."

The two holes for the feet must have suggested the name
of 'barnacles' for a pair of spectacles, used as a low conven-
tional jest-word.

THAT STORKS WILL ONLY LIVE IN REPUBLICS AND FREE STATES.

Sir T. Browne shows this to be "a petty conceit to advance
the opinion of popular policies, and from antipathies in nature to disparage monarchical government." Pliny states, that
among the Thessalians, who were governed by kings, and had
abundance of serpents, it was no less than capital to kill a stork;
that the Egyptians honoured them, where government was
from all times monarchical; that Bellonius affirmeth men
make them nests in France; and that relations make them
common in Persia, and the dominion of the Great Turk.

"BEGIN AT THE BEGINNING."

Very few quotations are used oftener than "*commence par
le commencement*," the originator of which was the gay and

witty Count Anthony Hamilton, the accomplished courtier of
James II.   In one of his tales, written in ridicule of the
Arabian Nights, and called "the Ram," the principal character
is the Ram, the attendant on a giant, whose spirits to compose,
he tells a tale, thus abruptly beginning: " Since the wounds
of the white fox the queen failed not to visit him."   " Friend
Ram," said the giant, " I understand nothing of all that.   If
you could *begin at the beginning*, you would please me more ;
for all those tales that begin in the middle only muddle the
imagination."

LEVIATHAN.

Gesenius very justly remarks, that this word, which denotes
any twisted animal, is especially applicable to every great ten-
ant of the waters, such as the great marine serpents and crocodiles ; and, it may be added, the colossal serpents and great
manitors of the desert.   In general, it points to the crocodile ;
and Job xii. is unequivocally descriptive of that saurian.   Some
misstatements and much irrelevant learning have been bestowed
upon the leviathan.   Viewed as the crocodile of the Thebaid,
it is not clear that it symbolised the Pharaoh, or was a type of
Egypt, any more than of several Roman colonies (even where
it was not indigenous, as at Nismes in Gaul, on the ancient
coins of which the figure of one chained occurs), and of cities
in Phœnicia, Egypt, and other parts of the coast of Africa.
But in the Prophets and Psalms, there are passages where Pharaoh is evidently apostrophised under the name of leviathan ;
though other texts more naturally apply to the whale, notwithstanding the objections that have been made to that interpreta-
tion of the term.—Kitto's *Cyclopædia of Biblical Literature.*

ORIGIN OF " THE CONJURING-CAP."

In the dark ages, when magic was publicly professed in
universities, we read of a sovereign who entered boldly into
the cheat.   Erricus, king of Sweden, had his enchanted cap,
and pretended, by the additional assistance of some magical
jargon, to be able to command spirits to trouble the air, and to
turn the winds themselves ; so that when a great storm arose,
his ignorant subjects believed that the king had got his conjuring cap on : and from this fact originated the custom of our
mountebanks and legerdemain-men playing their tricks in a
conjuring-cap.

"A FEATHER IN HIS CAP."

In the British Museum are two Mss. (Harleian Collection,
No. 7314, and Lansdowne, No. 775), descriptive of Hungary in
1598, in which the writer says of the inhabitants: " It hath

been an auncient custome amongst them, that none should
weare a fether but he who had killed a Turk, to whome onlie
yt was lawfull to shew the number of his slaine enemyes by the
number of fethers in his cappe." Does not this passage explain
the phrase, "That will be a feather in his cap"?

"BLACK BOOKS."

To be in the Black Books implies out of favour; a phrase
said to be borrowed from the black book of the English monasteries, which was a detail of the scandalous enormities practised
in religious houses. It was compiled by order of the visitors
under Henry VIII., to blacken them, and thus hasten their
dissolution. Books which relate to necromancy are also called
black books; but of much earlier date is the black book of the
exchequer, said to have been composed in the year 1175, by
Gervase of Tilbury, nephew of Henry II.

THE ACADEMY DELLA CRUSCA.

Crusca is an Italian term, signifying *bran;* hence the
Academy *della Crusca,* or the *Bran* Academy, which was established in 1582, at Florence, for purifying and perfecting the
Tuscan language. Its device is a sieve, and its motto, *Il piu
bel fior ne coglie;* that is, it gathers the finest flour thereof.
In the hall where the academy meets every thing bears allusion to the name and device: the seats are in the form of a
baker's basket, their backs being like a shovel for moving corn;
the cushions, of grey satin, are in the form of sacks, or wallets;
and the branches for lights resemble sacks.

ORIGIN OF THE PICNIC.

It is hard to say when this species of entertainment became
fashionable; but we have an account of a very distinguished
picnic that took place more than two centuries and a quarter
ago, on the birthday of Charles Prince of Wales, afterwards
Charles I. Mainwaring, in a letter to the luxurious earl of
Arundel, dated November 22, 1618, says: "The prince his
birthday has been solemnised here by the few marquises and
lords which found themselves here; and (to supply the want
of lords) knights and squires were admitted to a consultation,
wherein it was resolved that such a number should meet at
Gamiges, *and bring every man his dish of meat.* It was left to
their own choice what to bring; some chose to be substantial,
some curious, some extravagant. Sir George Young's invention bore away the bell; and that was four huge brawny pigs,
piping hot, bitted and harnessed with ropes of sarsiges, all tied
to a monstrous bag pudding."[*]

* The picnic, under the name of ἔρανος, was known to the Greeks.

WORTH OF HISTORY.

When, after the victory of Aumale, in which Henry IV. was wounded, he called his generals round his bed, to give him an account of what had occurred subsequently to his leaving the field, no two could agree on the course of the very events in which they had been actors; and the king, struck with the difficulty of ascertaining facts so evident and recent, exclaimed, " *Voilà ce que c'est l'histoire!*"—" What then is history!"

" Give me my liar," was the phrase in which Charles V. was used to call for a volume of history; and certainly no man can attentively examine any important period of our annals without remarking that almost every incident admits of two handles, almost every character of two interpretations; and that by a judicious packing of facts the historian may make his picture assume nearly what form he pleases without any direct violation of truth.—*Quarterly Review*, 1832.

MACHIAVELISM.*

The doctrine which Machiavel taught unto Cæsar Borgia, to employ time in mischievous actions, and afterwards to destroy them when they have performed the mischief, was not of his own invention. All ages have given us examples of this goodly policy; the latter having been apt scholars in this lesson to the more ancient, as the reign of Henry VIII. here in England can bear witness; and therein especially the Lord Cromwell, who perished by the same unjust law that himself had devised for the taking away of another man's life.—Sir Walter Raleigh's *History of the World*.

SPARE MOMENTS.

The great French Chancellor D'Aguesseau employed *all* his time. Observing that Madame D'Aguesseau always delayed ten or twelve minutes before she came down to dinner, he composed a work entirely in this time, in order not to lose an instant. The result was, at the end of fifteen years, a work in three large volumes quarto, which went through several editions.

" BROAD DEVONSHIRE."

We read much of Sir Walter Raleigh's pronunciation captivating Queen Elizabeth, and winning the Earl of Essex; according to Aubrey, Raleigh retained the accent of his native province. " I have," says Aubrey, " heard old Sir Thomas

---

* It has been well said of Machiavelli, that he had the credit or discredit of having been the first to erect into a science, and reduce to theory, the art of obtaining absolute power by deception and cruelty, and of maintaining it afterwards by the simulation of leniency and virtue.

Mallet, who knew Sir Walter, say that he spoke *broad Devonshire* to his dying day."

JOHN LILBURN.

It was said of John Lilburn, while living, by Judge Jenkins, "that if the world was emptied of all but himself, Lilburn would quarrel with John, and John with Lilburn;" which part of his character gave occasion for the following lines at his death :

> " Is John departed, and is Lilburn gone ?
> Farewell to both, to Lilburn and to John.
> Yet being dead, take this advice from me,
> Let them not both in one grave bury'd be ;
> Lay John here, and Lilburn thereabout,
> For if they should meet they would fall out."
>
>   *Notes to Butler's Hudibras.*

THE VICAR OF BRAY.

The village of Bray, about one mile from Maidenhead, in Berkshire, is noted for the versatility of principle manifested by one of its incumbents; whence "the Vicar of Dray" has become a proverbial expression for a man who can shift his principles with the times. The well-known song of "the Vicar of Bray" represents this personage as living in the time of Charles II. and his successors, down to George I. ; but Fuller, in his *Worthies of England,* gives the following account : "The vivacious vicar hereof, living under King Henry VIII., King Edward VI., Queen Mary, and Queen Elizabeth, was first a Papist, then a Protestant, then a Papist, then a Protestant again. He had seen some martyrs burnt (two miles off) at Windsor, and found this fire too hot for his tender temper. This vicar being taxed by one for being a turncoat and an unconstant changeling, ' Not so,' said he, 'for I always kept my principle, which is, to live and die the Vicar of Bray.'" (vol. i. p. 29, Nicholl's ed. 1811).

Mr. Rawlins, in a letter to Mr. Brome, dated June 14, 1735, says : "I have had a long chase after the Vicar of Bray, on whom the proverb. Mr. Hearne, though born in that neighbourhood, and should have mentioned it (Leland, *Itinerary,* vol. v. p. 114), knew not where he was, but in his *last letter* desired me if I found him out to let him know it. I am informed it is Simon Alleyn or Allen, who was Vicar of Bray about 1540, and died 1588, so was Vicar of Bray near fifty years. You now partake of the sport that has cost me much pains to take" (*Letters from the Bodleian,* vol. ii. part i. p. 100). In a note in Nichols's *Select Poems,* 1782, vol. viii. p. 234, the song of the Vicar of Bray "is said to have been written by an

officer in Col. Fuller's regiment, in the reign of King George I."
(Notes to Mackay's *Book of English Songs.*)

" WILLIE WASTLE."

When Oliver Cromwell was at Haddington, he sent a summons to the governor of Hume Castle, ordering him to surrender. The governor replied :

" That he, Willie Wastle, stood firm in his castle,
   That all the dogs of his town should not drive Willie Wastle down."

This gave rise to the game of Willie Wastle among children.

REGALITY OF GENIUS.

Gibbon, speaking of his own genealogy, refers to the fact of Fielding being of the same family as the Earl of Denbigh, who, in common with the imperial family of Austria, is descended from the celebrated Rodolph of Hapsburgh. " While the one branch," he says, " have contented themselves with being sheriffs of Leicestershire and justices of the peace, the others have been emperors of Germany and kings of Spain ; but the magnificent romance of *Tom Jones* will be read with pleasure when the palace of the Escurial is in ruins, and the imperial eagle of Austria is rolling in the dust."

MRS. PARTINGTON AND HER MOP.

This " labour in vain" will be found in the Rev. Sydney Smith's speech at Taunton on the Lords' rejection of the Reform Bill, October 1831, in the following passage :

" The attempt of the Lords to stop the progress of reform reminds me very forcibly of the great storm off Sidmouth, and of the conduct of the excellent Mrs. Partington on that occasion. In the winter of 1824, there set in a great flood upon that town : the tide rose to an incredible height, the waves rushed in upon the houses, and every thing was threatened with destruction. In the midst of this sublime and terrible storm, Dame Partington, who lived upon the beach, was seen at the door of her house with mop and pattens, trundling her mop, squeezing out the sea-water, and vigorously pushing away the Atlantic Ocean. The Atlantic was roused ; Mrs. Partington's spirit was up ; but I need not tell you that the contest was unequal. The Atlantic beat Mrs. Partington. She was excellent at a slop or a puddle ; but she should not have meddled with a tempest."

" THE PILOT THAT WEATHERED THE STORM."

This phrase was applied by Canning to Pitt, the darling Minister.

Middleton, in his *Life of Cicero*, quoting the Familiar Letters, says : " He oft compares the statesman to the pilot, whose art consists in managing every turn of the winds, and applying even the most perverse to the progress of his voyage ; so as by changing his course, and enlarging his circuit of sailing, to arrive with safety, though later, at his destined port."

IMPERIAL COMPLIMENTS.

Alexander I., emperor of Russia, was affable, and could unbend without any sacrifice of dignity. Gracious in speech, he knew the art of paying delicate compliments. After the capitulation of Paris, he said to the Parisians, "If I arrive late, accuse only French valour ;" and when Madame de Staël complimented the Czar by saying that " his people, without a constitution, were blessed with such a sovereign," he made this happy answer, "I am but a fortunate accident."

PARALLEL OF PITT AND PERICLES.

Sir Nathaniel Wraxall has remarked some very strong points of resemblance between Pericles and Pitt. Both were many years the ministers of a free people. Both long enjoyed extraordinary popularity and corresponding power. The same fascinating power of persuasion was common to both. Disinterestedness and superiority to all personal acquisition alike distinguished them. Pericles had, indeed, the advantage of inheriting a larger paternal fortune than the English minister ; but he no more increased it at the national expense than did Pitt. Both survived, if not the public favour, yet the public prosperity ; and beheld their friends accused or sacrificed to public clamour. The fate of Phidias, Pericles' friend, charged with converting to his own use a part of the gold confided to him for ornamenting the statue of Minerva, bears a striking analogy to Lord Melville's impeachment, founded on his supposed appropriation or alienation of the public money. But the Scottish minister ultimately escaped, while the great antiquity perished in prison. Pitt, like Pericles, engaged in a long and disastrous conflict with foreign enemies ; the latter when he commenced the Peloponnesian war, the former with revolutionary France. Neither of them survived to witness its termination. The Athenian, after sustaining the severest afflictions and privations in his family, sank under the attacks of a pestilential malady, in the third year of hostilities. The English statesman closed his memorable career precisely at the same period of the renewed struggle against the French Republic, or rather, against the military despotism of its foreign ruler.—*Posthumous Memoirs of his own Times*, by Sir N. Wraxall.

THE SEVEN AGES OF MAN.

Shakspeare's charming creation of " the Seven Ages of Man" (see *As you like it*) is a conception of a subject which has been treated by various writers through a period of two thousand years.

The Ages of Man have been discussed by heathens, by Jews, and by Christians; but the division has not always been into *seven*. The septennary periods are suspected to have been derived from the speculations of cabalistic philosophers upon the secret powers of numbers, and upon the climacterical year. The earliest instance which Mr. John Winter Jones could find of the division of human life into stages occurs in the Greek verses attributed to Solon, who flourished about 600 years before Christ, and which are introduced by Philo-Judæus into his *Liber de mundi opificio;* wherein also occurs, "Hippocrates says that there are *seven ages*;" and we find this division in the Midrash or Ecclesiastes, written about the ninth century, where, in six stages, man is compared to some animal.

In a beautiful Hebrew poem of the twelfth century, we find man's life divided into *ten* stages. The windows and sculptures of several cathedrals show the Ages of Man to have been pictorially illustrated at a still earlier period. In the Arundel Mss., No. 83, is a beautifully illuminated example, executed early in the fourteenth century; and a Byzantine Ms., fourteenth or fifteenth century, contains a morality called "The foolish Life of the deceitful World," arranged in three concentric circles, and of which the Seven Ages of Man form a part.* (See Didron, *Iconographie Chrétienne*, p. 409)

In Germany, the subject has passed into a rhyming proverb, which, in a small book, printed at Augsburg, 1518, is illustrated in *ten ages*, each with a woodcut, representing the man the particular beast he is supposed to resemble at each in question, and the hermit. In a Dutch work, printed at Antwerp in 1520, is illustrated man's course through the world, in ten ages (10 to 100); and at each ten years man changes, and acquires the nature and peculiarities of some beast, as here represented in woodcuts and verse. Sir Thomas More, when a boy, about the end of the fifteenth century, "devysed in hys father's house in London a goodly hangyng of fyne payntod clothe, with nyne pageauntes, and verses over." In the British Museum is a coarse but spirited woodcut,† of about the middle of the fifteenth century, and roughly coloured, in which, around "the wheel of life, which is called fortune," are the figures of man in his seven stages: this curious piece is engraved in *Archæologia*, vol. xxxv., illustrating Mr. Winter Jones's learned paper.

The subject has long occupied the thoughts of the physician, the moralist, the speculative philosopher, and the poet. Instances may be found in the literature and art of all countries, and from the earliest periods. In Rosellini's *Monumenti dell' Egitto e della Nubia*, a very curious instance occurs of a date far anterior to any previously mentioned; the mode of treatment is quite peculiar.

The progress of the soul, from man's heels to his head, as described by Prior in his *Alma*, is but another version of the "Seven Ages." A

---

* Lady Calcott found in the cathedral of Sienna, in one of the side chapels, seven figures, each in a compartment, inlaid in the pavement, representing the Seven Ages of Man, supposed to have been executed by Antonio Frederighi, in 1476.

† This woodcut was found pasted inside what had been the covers of an old edition or manuscript of the *Moralia super Biblica* of N. de Lyra. The practice of pasting on the inside of the covers of books prints upon moral or religious subjects, has been the means of preserving many specimens of engraving of the fifteenth century, which would otherwise have been irretrievably lost. We are more indebted to this practice of our forefathers than is generally known.

poem, dated 1653, describes the life of man in twelve ages, each corresponding with a month.

Mr. Martin, the librarian at Woburn Abbey, published, in 1848, a very interesting little volume on Shakspeare's Seven Ages.

GASCONADES.

The inhabitants of the province of Gascony, in France, have long been celebrated for their lively sallies, called *Gasconades* (in French *Gasconnades*), the point of which consists in immoderate boasting of wit, wealth, or valour. The Dictionary of the French Academy, as an illustration, gives : He says he would fight ten men. But, wit and piquancy should be intermixed with self-exaltation, as in the following : A Gascon, in proof of his nobility, asserted that in his father's castle they used no other firewood but the batons of the different marshals of France of his family.

ZOILUS, THE CRITIC.

The name of Zoilus has been for ages applied to the incarnation of spiteful criticism : he was a literary Thersites, shrewd, witty, and hateful ; and his carpings raised him to the bad eminence of being called the Homeromastix, or scourge of Homer. Here is a fragment of Zoilus. When the companions of Ulysses were transformed into swine by Circe, in the Tenth Book of the *Odyssey*, they had the head and voice and body and bristles of swine, but retained human consciousness, and cried as they went along to their sties. This passage was censured as childish by Longinus, who tells us that Zoilus called these transformed companions χοιρίδια κλαιοντα — " weeping porkers !" The pen of a fierce critic is " the sword of Zoilus."

ARCHIMEDES AND THE LEVER.

The apothegm of Archimedes—" Give me a lever long enough and a prop strong enough, and I will move the world"— arose from his knowledge of the possible effects of machinery ; and, however it might astonish a Greek of his day, would not be readily admitted to be as theoretically possible as it is practically impossible ; for, in the words of Dr. Arnott, Archimedes " would have required to move with the velocity of a cannonball for millions of years to alter the position of the earth by a small part of an inch. This feat of Archimedes is, in mathematical truth, performed by every man who leaps from the ground, for he kicks the world away from him whenever he rises, and attracts it again when he falls."

XANTHIPPE, THE SCOLD.

Xanthippe, the wife of Socrates, was so peevish, fretful, and

N

discontented, as to bequeath to posterity her name as a common appellation for a scold.

FRIAR BACON'S BRAZEN HEAD.

Friar Bacon was the popular name of Roger Bacon, the learned monk, born near Ilchester in 1214. The legend of his Brazen Head will be found in a rare tract, 1652, wherein it is pretended that he discovered, "after great study," that if he could succeed in making a head of brass which should speak, and hear it when it spoke, he might be able to surround all England with a wall of brass. By the assistance of Friar Bungay, and a devil, likewise called into the consultation, he accomplished his object, but with this drawback—the head when finished was warranted to speak in the course of one month, but it was quite uncertain when; and if they heard it not before it had done speaking, all their labour would be lost. After watching for three weeks, fatigue got the mastery over them, and Bacon set his man Miles to watch, with strict injunctions to awake them if the head should speak. The fellow heard the head at the end of one half-hour say, "Time is;" at the end of another, "Time was;" and at the end of another half-hour, "Time's past;" when down it fell with a tremendous crash; but the blockhead of a servant thought that his master would be angry if he disturbed him for such trifles!

Still, the origin of the Brazen Head has been much disputed. Gower imputes it to Grossa Testa, bishop of Lincoln; others to Albertus Magnus; but some believe the story to be nothing more than a moral fable. Bacon's Brazen Head is said to have been set up in a field at Bothwell, near Leeds.

TENDO-ACHILLIS

is the name by which anatomists designate the strong sinew which is continued from the fleshy part of the back of the leg to the bone of the heel. It is so called from the fabulous story of Thetis, the mother of Achilles, having dipped him while an infant in the Styx, which rendered him invulnerable, except in the heel by which she held him; and he was killed at last by a wound in the heel.

BŒOTIA.

Bœotia, a country of Greece, possessed a thick and heavy atmosphere—

"Incrasso acre Bœotûm" (*Horace*)—

which was supposed to render the inhabitants dull and stupid. They paid, said Cornelius Nepos, more attention to the improvement of bodily strength than to the cultivation of the mental faculties. Yet this country produced Epaminondas,

Pelopidas, Plutarch, Hesiod, and Pindar. Again, strangers were treated with less respect in Bœotia than elsewhere in Greece : hence came the epithet Bœotian, discourteous, stupid, dull, and thick-headed.

ANTIQUITY OF FALSE EYES.

M. Payen, in 1856, exhibited to the Academy of Sciences of Paris some Artificial Eyes from mummies, found in a mound near Arica, in Peru, and which most likely belong to the time of the Incas. They resemble eyes in the faces painted on the coffins of the mummies of the ancient Egyptians, from whom the art of making them may have been derived by the Peruvians. The mound in which they were found is indicated by Peruvian historians as one of those in which it was the custom to inter such persons as desired to be buried alive, on the death of a king or a great noble. Now, it is thought that the eyes may have been put into the corpses for purposes of priestly imposture ; the Peruvians, in the time of the Incas, having a veneration for bright eyes, and even adoring the animals which possessed them.

COMEDY AND TRAGEDY.

The first comedy was acted at Athens, on a scaffold, by Saffrarian and Dolon, 562 B.C. ; and tragedy was first acted at Athens, in a waggon or cart, 535 B.C., by Thespis.

> " At first, the tragedy was void of art ;
> A song, where each man danc'd and sang his part ;
> And of god Bacchus roaring out the praise,
> Sought a good vintage for their jolly days :
> Then wine and joy were seen in each man's eyes,
> And a fat goat was the best singer's prize.
> *Thespis*, at first, who, all besmear'd with lee
> Began this pleasure for posterity ;
> And with his carted actors and a song,
> Amus'd the people as he pass'd along.
> Next Æschylus the different persons plac'd,
> And with a better mark his players grac'd ;
> Upon a theatre his verse express'd,
> And show'd his hero with a buskin dress'd.
> Then *Sophocles*, the genius of his age,
> Increas'd the pomp and beauty of the stage,
> Engag'd the chorus-song in every part,
> And polish'd rugged vice by rules of art."　　*Dryden.*

Melpomene is the president muse of tragedy : she is represented as a splendidly attired young woman, with a serious countenance ; she wears a buskin, and holds a dagger in one hand, and in the other a sceptre and crowns.

Thalia is the muse of comedy : she leans on a column, holds a mask in her right hand, and carries a shepherd's crook.

HALCYON DAYS.

This figure for quiet and peaceful stillness came from the coast of Sicily; where the halcyon, or king's fisher bird, is stated to breed in the sea, and there is said to be always a calm during her incubation, about fourteen days:

> " Amidst our arms as quiet you shall be
> As halcyon brooding on a winter's sea."   *Dryden.*

" THE GOLDEN ASS"

is the best-known work of Apuleius, the Platonic philosopher, who was accused of being a magician, and winning his wife by sorcery. *The Golden Ass* is a running satire on the absurdities of magic, the crimes of the priesthood, and the systematic outrages of thieves and robbers. The hunters after the philosopher's stone affected to find in this work authority for their vagaries. The episodes are the most valuable portion of the book, especially that of Psyche. Many persons have taken all that is related in it for true history : St. Augustine could not make up his mind as to its worth ; some of the ancients have spoken contemptuously of it ; and Macrobius makes it over to nurses and gossips.

SIN AND SHAVING THE BEARD.

Luther was one day being shaved and having his hair cut in the presence of Dr. Jonas. He said to the latter, "Original sin is in us like the beard. We are shaved to-day, and look clean, and have a smooth chin; to-morrow our beard has grown again, nor does it cease growing while we remain on earth. In like manner, original sin cannot be extirpated from us ; it springs up in us as long as we exist. Nevertheless we are bound to resist it to the utmost of our strength, and to cut it down unceasingly."

"THE WISE MEN OF GOTHAM."

At a last holden at Westham, October 3d, 24th Henry VIII., for the purpose of preventing unauthorised persons from setting "nettes, pottes, and innoyances, or anywise taking fish, within the privilege of the march of Pevensey, the king's commission was directed to John prior of Lewes, Richard abbot of Begeham, John prior of Myehillym, Thomas Lord Dacre, and others." Upon the proceedings of this meeting, which was held at Gotham, near Pevensey, the facetious Andrew Borde, a native of that town, founded his *Merrie Tales of the Wise Men of Gotham.*

THE STORY OF THE FISH AND THE RING.

About 532 B.C. Polykrates, the despot of Samos, threw into

the sea a favourite ring of matchless price and beauty. In a few days the ring reappeared in the belly of a fine fish, which a fisherman had sent to him as a present.

Peter Damian relates, that Arnulphus, king of Lotharingia, in a fit of repentance for his depravity, threw a costly ring into a stream, saying, "If you are brought back to me, then, but not till then, shall I be assured that all my sins have been pardoned and cancelled." Thereupon the king led a very penitent life; when a fish served at dinner on a meagre day was found by the cook in possession of a fine gold ring—of course that which Arnulphus had thrown into the stream; when the king became assured of the Divine acceptance of his contrition. St. Augustine relates, that a needy cobbler of Hippo prayed to the shrine of the Thirty Martyrs for a certain article of clothing, when, in passing along the sea-shore, he took a large fish which had been thrown upon the beach, which he sold to a rich man's cook, and with the money purchased wool enough for his wife to spin into the necessary garment. Next, the cook discovered inside the fish a gold ring, and knowing at whose shrine the cobbler had prayed, he gave him back the trinket, saying, "Thus do the Thirty Martyrs find thee clothing according to thy suit."

There are other versions of this story in the *Arabian Nights Entertainments*, and elsewhere. It is also the great event of the old popular ballad of "The cruel Knight, or fortunate Farmer's Daughter;" in which the ring, which had been thrown into the sea, is restored by means of a cod-fish. The traditional heroine of this ballad is Dame Rebecca Berry, buried at Stepney, Middlesex, where, in her arms, sculptured upon her tomb, a fish and annulet are regarded as proofs of the veracity of the tale.

THE SCIENCE OF GOVERNMENT.

When Peter the Great visited Paris, he was conducted to the church of the Sorbonne, and there shown the magnificent tomb and statue erected to Cardinal Richelieu. Peter embraced the figure with great emotion, crying, "Great man, if thou wert still alive I would give thee without regret one-half of my kingdom, in order to learn of thee how to govern the other half."

"THE KING NEVER DIES."

Upon the death or demise of the king, his heir is that moment invested with the kingly office and royal power, and commences his reign the same day his ancestor dies; hence it is held a maxim that the king never dies.—Lord Bacon's *Abridgment.*

COLUMBUS AND THE EGG.

This oft-applied anecdote is thus related by Washington Irving, in his *Life of Columbus* :

"Pedro Gonzalez de Mendoza, the grand cardinal of Spain, invited Columbus to a banquet, where he assigned him the most honourable place at table, and had him served with ceremonies which in those punctilious times were observed towards sovereigns.

At this repast is said to have occurred the well-known incident of the egg. A shallow courtier present, impatient of the honours paid to Columbus, and meanly jealous of him as a foreigner, abruptly asked him whether he thought that, in case he had not discovered the Indies, there were not other men who would have been capable of the enterprise. To this Columbus made no immediate answer ; but, taking an egg, invited the company to make it stand upon one end. Every one attempted it, but in vain ; whereupon he struck it upon the table so as to break the end, and left it standing on the broken part ; illustrating in this simple manner, that when he had once shown the way to the New World nothing was easier than to follow it. This anecdote rests on the authority of the Italian historian Benzoni."

FROGS—WHY FRENCHMEN WERE SO CALLED.

"*Qu'en disent les grenouilles?*" was the common flippant phrase at Versailles (about 1791) when any new absurdity was planned, meaning, "What will the frogs say to this?" The French court, in allusion to the quaggy state of Paris formerly, when known by the name of "Lutetia," called its inhabitants "frogs."—*Piozzi's Retrospections.*

"MANNERS MAKYTH MAN."

William of Wykeham, when his growing honours required that he should adopt a coat-of-arms, with a humility not less amiable than wise in a *novus homo*, he sealed with the chevron ; the chevron being, as the learned herald, Nicholas Upton, has it, one of those bearings which *per carpentarias et domorum factores olim portabantur*. To this seal he added the celebrated motto : "Manners makyth man."

DANGER OF TAKING THINGS FOR GRANTED.

It was objected to the system of Copernicus, when first brought forward, that if the earth turned on its axis, as he represented, a stone dropped from the summit of a tower would not fall at the foot of it, but a great distance to the west, in the same manner as a stone dropped from the mast-head of a ship in full sail does not fall at the foot of the mast, but at the stern of the ship. To this it was answered : that a stone, being part of the earth, obeys the same laws and moves with it ; whereas it is no part of the ship, of which consequently its motion is independent. The solution was admitted by some, but opposed by others, and the controversy went on with spirit ; nor was it till one hundred years after the death of Copernicus that, the experiment being tried, it was ascertained that the stone thus dropped from the head of the mast does fall at the foot of it.—*Archbishop Whately.*

" REVENONS À NOS MOUTONS,"

is a proverb taken from the old French play of *Patelin*, where a woollen-draper is brought in, who, pleading against his shepherd concerning some sheep the shepherd had stolen from him, would ever and anon digress from the point to speak of a piece of cloth which his antagonist's attorney had likewise robbed him of, which made the judge call out to the draper, " *Revenons à nos moutons.*" This proverb may also be traced to that of *alia Menecles, alia Porcellus loquitur ;* and see Erasmus's explanation thereof.—*Notes to Rabelais' Works,* vol. i., 1807.

FREE TRADE.

One of the earliest uses of this phrase occurred on the opening of the Irish Parliament in 1777, when Hussey Burgh moved the address to the king, in which was the following sentence : " It is not by temporary expedients, but by an extension of trade, that Ireland can be ameliorated." Flood, who was seated in the vice-treasurer's place, said audibly : " *Why not a free trade ?*" The amendment electrified the House ; the words were adopted, and the motion was carried unanimously.

ILLUSTRIOUS GENERALS UNCROWNED.

Sir William Temple names seven generals as having deserved without having worn a crown. They are Belisarius, Ætius, Huniades, Gonsalo of Cordova, Scanderbeg, Alexander Duke of Parma, and the great Prince of Orange.

ANTIQUITY OF TARRING AND FEATHERING.

Tarring and feathering, it seems, is a European invention. One of Richard Cœur-de-Lion's ordinances for seamen was, " that if any man were taken with theft or pickery, and thereof convicted, he should have his head polled, and hot pitch poured upon his pate, and upon that the feathers of some pillow or cushion shaken aloft, that he might thereby be known for a thief, and at the next arrival of the ships to any land, be put forth of the company to seek his adventures without all hope of return unto his fellows."—*Holinshed.*

ANTIQUITY OF TIGHT-LACING.

The injurious practice of tight-lacing we have discovered in existence during the reign of Rufus or Henry I.; and in a Ms. copy of the "Lay of Syr Launfal," written about the year 1300, we have two damsels described as,

> "Their kirtles were of Inde sandel,
> T— laced, jolyf, and well."

The second line in the French original is still stronger; they are said to have been *Lacies moult estreitement,* "very straitly or tightly laced."—*Planché on Costume.*

SHAVING THE BEARD.

Bulwer, in his *Artificial Changeling,* says: "Shaving the chin is justly to be accounted a note of effeminacy, as appears by eunuchs, who produce not a beard, the sign of virility. Alexander and his officers did not shave their beards till they were effeminated by Persian luxury. It was late before barbers were in request at Rome; Varro tells us they were introduced by Ticisinus Mena. Scipio Africanus was the first who shaved his face every day; the Emperor Augustus used this practice. Diogenes, seeing one with a smooth-shaved chin, said to him, "Hast thou whereof to accuse nature for making thee a man and not a woman?" The Rhodians and Byzantines, contrary to the practice of modern Russians, persisted against their laws and edicts in shaving and the use of the razor.—Dr. Nash's *Notes to Hudibras.*

The beaux in the reign of James I. and Charles I. spent as much time in dressing their beards as modern beaux do in dressing their hair. It is well known what great difficulty the Czar Peter of Russia had in obliging his subjects to cut off their beards.

ORIGIN OF QUAKERISM.

In the year 1643, "a rude, gaunt, illiterate lad of nineteen, a shoemaker by trade, affected with the religious fervour of the age, being at a country fair in his native Leicestershire, met with his cousin and another friend there, and the three youths agreed to have a stoup of ale together. They accordingly adjourned to a tavern in the neighbourhood, and called for drink. When the first supply was exhausted, the cousin and his friend called for more, began to drink healths, and said that he who would not drink should pay the entire ale-score. The young shoemaker was alarmed at this proposal; and, as he explained the circumstances afterwards, he put his hand into his pocket, took out a groat, laid it down on the table, and said 'If it be so, I will leave you;' and so he went home. This village alehouse incident was an important

event in the history of the Anglo-Saxon race ; for through it
were to come Quakerism, the writings and teachings of Penn
and Barclay, the colony and constitution of Pennsylvania, the
republics of the West, and in no very remote degree the vast
movement of liberal ideas in Great Britain and America in
more modern times. The illiterate and upright shoemaker
who would drink no more was George Fox. 'I went away,'
he afterwards wrote in his journal ; ' and when I had done my
business, returned home. But I did not go to bed that night,
nor did I sleep, but sometimes walked up and down, and sometimes prayed, and called to the Lord.'" (Dixon's *Life of Penn.*)
During the night, the boy Fox thought he heard a voice from
heaven calling upon him to forsake such vanity. He got out ;
and, without purse or scrip, wandered to London. He soon
returned to his home at Drayton ; but was again unable to
resist the workings of the spirit, which continued for several
years.

"EVERY MAN HAS HIS PRICE."

Sir Robert Walpole, the Grand Corrupter, as he was called
in the libels of his time, is said to have thought all mankind
rogues, and to have remarked that every one had his price.
Pope refers to this :

> " Would he oblige me, let me only find
> He does not think me what he thinks mankind."

Or as he at first printed it :

> " He thinks one poet of no venal kind."

That Walpole said something very much like the saying attributed to him is what even his son does not deny ; but there
is reason to believe that he said it with a qualification—"all
those men have their price," not "all men have their price."

The saying as recorded by Richardson, the painter, who
had ample means of being well-informed, was in these words :
" There was not one, how patriot soever he might seem, of
whom he did not know the price." (*Richardsoniana*, 8vo.,
1776, p. 178.) Dr. King, whose means of information were as
good as Richardson's, records a remark made during a debate
in parliament by Walpole to Mr. W. Leveson, the brother of
the Jacobite Lord Gower. " You see," said Sir Robert, " with
what zeal and vehemence these gentlemen oppose ; and yet I
know the price of every man in this house except three, and
your brother is one of them." Dr. King adds, that Sir Robert
lived long enough to know that my Lord Gower had his price
as well as the rest. (*King's Anecdotes*, p. 44 ; see also p. 28 of
the same volume.) His son modifies the saying : " Some are
corrupt," Sir Robert Walpole said ; " but I will tell you of
one who is not ; Shippen is not." (*Walpoliana*, i. 38.) And

at another time, Horace, speaking of his father, observed to
Pinkerton : " Sir Robert Walpole used to say, that it was fortunate so few men could be prime ministers, as it was best
that few should thoroughly know the shocking wickedness of
mankind. I never heard him say that all men had their prices ;
and I believe no such expression ever came from his mouth."
(*Walpoliana*, i. 90.)

ORIGIN OF "TRUE BLUE."

In England this partisan colour was first assumed by the
Covenanters in opposition to the scarlet badge of Charles I. ;
and hence it was taken by the troops of Lesley and Montrose
in 1639. The adoption of the colour was one of those religious
pedantries in which the Covenanters affected a pharisaical ob-
servance of the Scriptural letter, and the usages of the He-
brews ; and thus, as they named their children Habakkuk and
Zerubbabel, and their chapels Zion and Ebenezer, they decorated their persons with blue ribbons, because the following
precept was given in the law of Moses : "Speak to the children of Israel, and tell them to make to themselves fringes on
the borders of their garments, putting in them *ribbons of
blue*" (Numb. xv. 38).

The colour was also a party distinction in Rome. In the
factions of the Circus of the Lower Empire, the Emperor Anas-
tasius secretly favoured the *Greens*, Justinian openly protected
the *Blues;* the latter, therefore, became the emblem of loyalty,
the former of disaffection. For some less evident reason the
Blues were looked upon as the party of the established and
orthodox Church ; and the convenient imputation of heresy
thrown forth against the others served as a pretext for every
act of rapine or oppression.

Bentley, in his *Dissertation on Phalaris*, p. 258, mentions
blue as the costume of his guards ; and quotes Cicero's *Tusculan Questions*, lib. v. for his authority.

Edinburgh has a banner which was granted to the city by
James III. : it is still esteemed a sort of palladium, and is
called, from its colour, *Blue Blanket.*

THE BLUE-STOCKING.

This term, applied to a lady of some literary taste, has been
traced by Mr. Mills, in his *History of Chivalry*, to the Society
de la Calza, formed at Venice in 1400, "when, consistently
with the singular custom of the Italians, of marking acade-
mies and other intellectual associations by some external signs
of folly, the members, when they met in literary discussion,
were distinguished by the colours of their stockings. The
colours were sometimes fantastically blended, and at other

times one colour, particularly *blue*, prevailed." The Society de la Calza lasted till 1590, when the foppery of Italian literature took some other symbol. The rejected title then crossed the Alps, and found a congenial soil in Parisian society, and particularly branded female pedantry. It then diverted from France to England, and for a while marked the vanity of the small advances in literature in female coteries.

But the *Blue-stocking* of the last century is of home-growth; for Boswell, in his *Life of Johnson*, date 1781, records of the origin of Blue-stocking Clubs:

One of the most eminent members of these societies, when they first commenced, was Mr. Stillingfleet (grandson of the Bishop), whose dress was remarkably grave; and in particular it was observed that he wore blue stockings. Such was the excellence of his conversation, that his absence was felt so great a loss that it used to be said 'We can do nothing without the *blue stockings;*' and thus by degrees the title was established. Miss Hannah More has admirably described a *Blue-stocking Club,* in her *Bas-Bleu.* The last of this club was "the lively Miss Monckton (now Countess of Cork),* who used to have the finest *bit of blue* at the house of her mother, Lady Galway."

The earliest specimen on record of a Blue-stocking, or *Bas-bleu,* however, occurs in the Greek comedy entitled *The Banquet of Plutarch.*

"GREAT EVENTS FROM LITTLE CAUSES SPRING."

"If the nose of Cleopatra had been shorter," said Páscal, in his epigrammatic and brilliant manner, "the condition of the world would have been different." The Mahomedans have a tradition, that when their prophet concealed himself in Mount Shar, his pursuers were deceived by a spider's web, which covered the mouth of the cave. Luther might have been a lawyer, had his friend and companion escaped the thunder-storm at Erfurt. Scotland had wanted her stern reformer, if the appeal of the preacher had not startled him in the chapel of St. Andrew's Castle. And if Mr. Grenville had not carried, in 1764, his memorable resolution as to the expediency of charging "certain Stamp-Duties" on the plantations in America, the western world might still have bowed to the British sceptre. Cowley might never have been a poet, if he had not found the "Faëry Queen" in his mother's parlour. Opie might have perished in mute obscurity, if he had not looked over the shoulder of his young companion, Mark Otes, while he was drawing a butterfly. Giotto, one of the early Florentine painters, might have continued a rude shepherd-boy, if a sheep drawn by him upon a stone had not attracted the notice of Cimabue as he went that way.

Cromwell was near being strangled in his cradle by a monkey: here was this wretched ape wielding in his paws the destinies of nations. Charles Wesley refuses to go with his wealthy namesake to Ireland; and the inheritance which would have been his, goes to build up the fortunes of a Wellesley instead of a Wesley; and to this decision of a schoolboy (as Mr. Southey observes) Methodism may owe its existence, and England its military—and we trust we may now add, its civil and political—glory.—*Quarterly Review.*

* The Countess of Cork died at upwards of ninety years of age, in 1840.

Ensigns, Laws, and Government.

ORIGIN OF THE DIADEM.

THE Diadem originated in a ribbon, or fillet, woven of silk,
thread, or wool. It was tied round the temples and forehead;
the two ends being knotted behind, and let fall on the neck.
It was usually white, and quite plain, though sometimes embroidered with gold and set with pearls and precious stones.
According to Pliny, the diadem was invented by Bacchus;
Athenæus assures us that topers first made use of it to protect
themselves from the fumes of wine, by tying it tightly round
their heads; and that it long afterwards came to be a royal ornament.   Swift ascribes it to the cobblers:

> " All the cobblers' temples ties,
>   To keep the pain out of their eyes ;
>   From whence 'tis plain the diadem
>   That princes wear derives from them."

ROMAN CROWNS OF TRIUMPH.

The Civic Crown, though made only of oaken leaves, was
esteemed the most reputable badge of martial virtue, and never
bestowed but for saving the life of a citizen, and killing at the
same time an enemy.

The Laurel Crown was the proper ornament of triumph, as
myrtle was of the ovation. Tiberius wore a laurel crown, in
the belief that it would protect him from lightning and thunder.

The Obsidional Crown, though made only of the common
grass that happened to be found upon the scene of action, was
esteemed the noblest reward of military glory, and never bestowed but for the deliverance of an army when reduced to the
last distress.

The Mural Crown, an embattled circlet, was given to him
who first scaled the walls of a besieged city, and there planted
a standard.

The Naval Crown was given to him who first boarded an
enemy's ship : it was a circle of gold, surmounted by nautical
emblems, including the beaks of ships : hence it was called
rostra.

THE ROLL OF BATTEL ABBEY.

This document bore the names of all persons of any consideration who fought under Duke William at the battle of

Hastings; and it is therefore considered to be invaluable as a list of the names introduced into this country by the Norman conquest. The original Roll, compiled by the monks of Battel, was hung up in their monastery, beneath some Latin verses, of which the following English version was formerly inscribed on a tablet in the parish-church of Battel :

> " This place of war is Battel called, because in battle here,
> Quite conquered and overthrown the English nation were ;
> This slaughter happened to them upon St. Celict's day,
> The year thereof (1066) this number doth array."

Of the history of the Roll subsequently to the dissolution of the monastery nothing certain is known. Three months after the surrender of the abbey, the site and lands were given by Henry VIII. to Sir Anthony Browne, ancestor of the Viscounts Montague. This family sold the mansion, with its appurtenances, to Sir Thomas Webster, Bart. (whose descendants still possess it), and resided afterwards at their other seat, Cowdray House, near Midhurst; and thither this famous document was probably carried. Cowdray was destroyed by fire in 1793, when the Roll is presumed to have perished, with every thing else of value which that lordly edifice contained.—*M. A. Lower, F.S.A.*

THE COLLAR OF SS, OR ESSES.

This decoration appeared in the reign of Henry IV., and was worn by the distinguished of both sexes; but its origin is differently accounted for. Camden says it was composed of a repetition of that letter which was the initial of Sanctus, Simo, Simplicius, an eminent Roman lawyer, and that it was particularly worn by persons of that profession. Other writers contend that it was an additional compliment of Edward III. to the Countess of Salisbury; but its non-appearance till the reign of Henry IV. is a sufficient answer to that supposition. Sir Samuel Meyrick, with much greater probability, suggests that we should consider it the initial letter of Henry's motto, *Souverain*, which he had borne while Earl of Derby, and which, as he afterwards became sovereign, appeared auspicious. The initial of a common motto of the middle ages—*Souveniez-vous de moy (Souvenez-vous de moi)*—has also been mentioned as a derivation, and supported by the remark, that a *fleur-de-souvenance*, the " forget-me-not," occasionally linked the double SS together.

THE WHITE HART OF RICHARD II.

The Badge of the White Hart was assumed by Richard II., and worn by all his courtiers and adherents, both male and female, either embroidered on their dresses or suspended by chains or collars round their necks. This device seems to have been derived by Richard from his mother, whose cognisance was a white hind. Rymer mentions that in the ninth year of his reign Richard pawned certain jewels, *à la guyse de cerfs blancs;* and in the wardrobe-accounts of his twenty-second year is an entry of a belt and sheath of a sword, of red velvet, embroidered with white harts and crowned with rosemary-branches :

"Amongst the few men that attended this unfortunate prince, after his capture by the Earl of Northumberland, was Jenico Dartois, a Gascoine, that still wore the cognisance, or device, of his master, King Richard,—that is to saye, a white hart,—and would not put it from him neither for persuasion nor threats ; by reason whereof, when the Duke of Hereford understood it, he caused him to be committed to prison within the castle of Chester. This man was the last which bare that device, and showed well thereby his constant heart towards his master."
—Ancient author, quoted by Holinshed sub anno 1399.

Richard's White Hart still remains, painted of a colossal size, on the wall over the door leading to the east cloister of Westminster Abbey. It is generally represented crowned, collared, and chained, and couchant under a tree.

HOUSEHOLD BADGES AND TAVERN SIGNS.

The cognisances of many illustrious persons connected with the middle ages are still preserved in the signs attached to our taverns and inns. Thus the "White Hart" with the golden chain was the badge of King Richard II.; the "Antelope" was that of King Henry IV.; the "Beacon" was assumed by Henry V.; the "Feathers" was the cognisance of Henry VI.; and the "White Swan" was the device of Edward of Lancaster, his ill-fated heir slain at the battle of Tewkesbúry.[*]

The name of Plantagenet is derived from the cognisance of the progenitor of the family, a sprig of the *Planta genista* (the yellow broom), adopted by him as a symbol of humility when performing a pilgrimage to the Holy Land. (Buck's *Richard III.*) King Edward IV. bore his White Rose and the Fetterlock as the particular device of the House of York ; and after the battle of Mortimer Cross he adopted the White Rose *en soleil* as his *especial* cognisance, from the parhelion that preceded that important battle, "in which three suns were seen immediately conjoyning in one." The cognisance of Richard Duke of Gloucester was a Rose, supported on the dexter side by a Bull, a badge of the house of Clare, and on the sinister side by a Boar, which boar he had found among the badges of the house of York. The latter device was the one he selected as his own personal badge, the cognisance of his retainers and household : it was sculptured under his own direction at Barnard Castle ; and this badge is scattered all over the town in houses built of the stones obtained from the ruins of the castle.

Before the Great Fire of London, in 1666, almost all the liveries of the great feudal lords were preserved at these houses of public resort. Many of their heraldic signs were then unfor-

* The badge was sewn, or fastened, to the shoulders, breast, sleeve, or other portion of the dress, as is the badge of the Watermen to their sleeves in the present day, or the Tudor badge upon the tunics of the Yeomen of the Guard.

tunately lost : but the "Bear and Ragged Staff," the ensign
of the famed Warwick, still exists as a sign in Smithfield :—
while the "Star" of the Lords of Oxford, the brilliancy of
which decided the fate of the battle of Barnet ; the "Lion"
of Norfolk, which shone so conspicuously on Bosworth field ;
the "Sun" of the ill-omened house of York, together with the
Red and White Rose, either simply or conjointly, carry the
historian and antiquary back to a distant period, although now
disguised in the gaudy colouring of a freshly-painted sign-
board.—Camden's *Remains.*

The White Horse was the standard of the Saxons before
and after their coming into England. It was a proper emblem
of victory and triumph, as we read in Ovid and elsewhere. The
position of the horse is not rampant, or prancing, as represented
in the arms of Savoy, whose princes are descended from those
of Saxony, but current, or galloping, as described in the arms of
the House of Brunswick to this day. The Saxon standard may
be seen upon Uffington Hill, where it was formed by removing
the thin layer of turf, and exposing the underlying surface of
the chalk. This White Horse is believed to have been cut after
the battle of Æcesdune, *i. e.* Ash-tree Hill, or Ash Down, in
which the West Saxons under Ethelred and Alfred, in the year
87, defeated the Danes with great slaughter upon this spot.
This rude ensign is about 374 feet in length, and as the down
is 893 feet above the sea-level, the figure may be seen at twelve
miles distance, and it has given to the beautiful country beneath the name of the Vale of the White Horse.*

The White Horse is to this day the ensign of the county of
Kent, as we see upon hop pockets and bags ; and throughout
the county it is a favourite inn-sign. The White Horse of
Hanover dates from the House of Hanover succeeding to the
throne of these realms the White Horse being the badge of
that house.

" THE SARACEN'S HEAD" INN SIGN

originated in the age of the Crusades. By some it is thought
to have been adopted in memory of the father of St. Thomas à
Becket, who was a Saracen. Selden thus explains it : "Do
not undervalue an enemy by whom you have been worsted.
When our countrymen came home from fighting with the Saracens, and were beaten by them, they pictured them with
huge, big, terrible faces (as you still see the sign of the Sara-

---

* Mr. Wise, who wrote two pamphlets upon this standard in 1738-42, says:
"If any dispute should arise among heralds about the different bearings of the
horse (above mentioned), as likewise whether he ought to be current for the
dexter part, or sinister, which, I believe, is a point not entirely settled, I think
till some other more ancient record shall be produced, they may be fairly denominated from this authentic one of 867 years' standing."

cen's head is), when in truth they were like other men. But this they did to save their own credit." (*Table-Talk.*)

But still more direct is the explanation in the feat of Richard the Crusader, who caused *a Saracen's head* to be served up to the ambassadors of Saladin. May it not also have reference to the Saracen's head of the Quintain, a military exercise antecedent to jousts and tournaments?

THE LION IN THE ARMS OF ENGLAND.

The Lion, popularly "king of beasts," and the emblem of majesty and might, is the symbol of the British nation, and is borne in the royal arms, of which it forms one of the supporters, and which it surmounts as the crest. But the maneless feline beast which occurs in the older armorial bearings is thought to have been intended to represent *a lion leoparded.* This term is still used by the heralds of France. If the full face is shown, the animal, whether maned or maneless, is in their language a leopard; if the side face alone is seen, it is a lion. Hence, with them, the lions passant and gardant of the arms of the kings of England would be either lions leoparded or lions maned. The omission of the mane, in rude tricking, would reduce them to leopards, which they were originally considered. The emperor Frederick, in choosing his presents to our Henry III., was actuated, according to Matthew Paris, by the bearing in the royal shield of England, *In quo tres leopardi transeuntes figurantur.—Capt. Smee: Zool. Trans.*

THE CAP OF LIBERTY.

After the death of Cæsar, we are told, in the *Life of Cicero,* that the conspirators marched out in a body, with a Cap, as the ensign of Liberty, carried before them on a spear. There was a medal struck on the occasion, with the same device which is still extant. The thought, however, was not new; for Saturninus, in his sedition, in 263, when he had possessed himself of the Capitol, exalted a cap also on the top of a spear, as a token of liberty to all slaves who would join with him; and Marius used the same expedient to incite the slaves to take arms with him against Sylla. For slaves to wear the cap was a prize.

ORIGIN OF "BRITANNIA."

At Lethington Castle, in East Lothian, is a full-length portrait, by Lely, of Frances Theresa Stuart, Duchess of Lennox, the most admired beauty of the court of Charles II. It is stated by Grammont that the king caused this lady to be represented as the emblematical figure *Britannia* on the coin of the realm. The portrait represents a tall woman, with that voluptuous fulness of feature and person which seems, perhaps from the taste of the painter, to characterise the beauties of this reign. She leans upon the base of a pillar, and has an aspect of the utmost sweetness. Her luxuriant hair falls upon her fair white shoulders and her half-seen bosom. She is magnificently attired in purple, and a profuse robe of green, falling away from her shoulders, comes round her limbs, and draws the purple garment nearer to her figure. Such is the reputed origin of our " Britannia ;" but a figure not unlike that on our copper-money is to be met with in the large brass coins of Hadrian and Antoninus Pius.

THE DAGGER IN THE CITY OF LONDON ARMS, AND SIR W. WALWORTH'S DAGGER.

Upon the staircase of Fishmongers' Hall, London Bridge, is a statue, carved in wood by E. Pierce, of Sir William Walworth, a fishmonger, who carries a poniard. In his hand was formerly a dagger, said to be the identical weapon with which he stabbed Wat Tyler; though in 1731 a publican of Islington pretended to possess the actual poniard. Beneath the statue is the inscription :

> " Brave Walworth, knight, lord-mayor, yᵗ slew
> Rebellious Tyler in his alarmes ;
> The king, therefore, did give in liew
> The dagger to the City armes.
> In the 4th year of Richard II. anno Domini 1381."

The reputed dagger of Walworth, which has lost its guard, is preserved by the Company : the workmanship is of Walworth's period. The weapon now in the hand of the statue (which is somewhat picturesque, and in our recollection was coloured *en costume*) is modern.

A common but erroneous belief was thus propagated; for the dagger was in the City arms long before the time of Sir William Walworth, and was intended to represent the sword of St. Paul, the patron saint of the corporation. Among other proofs are the bosses in the eastern crypt of the Guildhall, which bear the arms of London with the dagger ; which part of the crypt was built antecedent to the reign of Richard II., or probably formed part of the ancient Guildhall, erected, as some suppose, in 1119.

ST. ANDREW'S CROSS.

The cross of St. Andrew is always represented in the shape of the letter X : but that this is an error ecclesiastical historians argue, by appealing to the cross itself on which he suffered, which St. Stephen of Burgundy gave to the convent of St. Victor, near Marseilles, and which, like the common cross, is rect-angular. The cause of the error is thus explained : when the apostle suffered, the cross, instead of being fixed upright, rested on its foot and arm, and in this posture he was fastened to it: his hands to one arm and the head, his feet to the other arm and the foot, and his head in the air.—*Yepes*, t. 6, ff. 297.

WHY IS THE IRIS CALLED THE FLEUR-DE-LYS?

Because the upper part of one leaf of the three-petaled iris,* when fully expanded, and the two contiguous leaves, seen in profile, have a faint likeness to the top of the *Flower-de-Luce*, which often appears on the crowns and sceptres in the monuments of the first and second race of the kings of France, and which was probably a composition of these three leaves. Lewis VII., engaged in the second crusade, distinguished himself, as was customary in those times, by a particular blazon, and took this figure for his coat-of-arms; and as the common people generally contracted the name of Louis into Luce, it is natural to imagine that this flower was, by corruption, distinguished in process of time by the name of Flower-de-Luce. (*La Pluche.*) But some antiquaries are of opinion that the original arms of the Franks being three toads, became odious, and were gradually changed, so as to have no positive resemblance to any natural objects, and named Fleur-de-Lys.

Cowley thus quaintly relates the birth of the lily: Jupiter, in order to make Hercules immortal, clapped him to Juno's breasts while she was asleep. The lusty little rogue sucked so hard, that, too great a gush of milk coming forth, some spilt upon the sky, which made the galaxy, or Milky Way; and out of some which fell upon the earth arose the lily.

THE POPE'S BULL.

The word *Bulla*, or Bull, appears for a considerable time to have meant only a gold trinket-ring worn round the necks of children. Later, however, the *bulla* was synonymous with *annulus*, or ring; and the words *bullare* and *sigillare* meant the same thing—to seal. The pontifical *Bullæ*, or bulls, like every thing else connected with the Pope's perquisites—as his rings, his crowns, his keys—were three in number: the *annuli* consisting, imprimis, of that called *piscatory*, in virtue of which he backs his pretensions to supremacy against all the world of heretics; secondly, the large leaden seal, or bull proper; and lastly, the *signum*, for consistorial bulls.

As soon as a pope dies, the Apostolic Chamber sends for the pontifical plumber, who, in the presence of that body, cuts off the portion of the double seal, or Bulla, which bears the name of his defunct holiness, thereby rendering the other and larger moiety (impressed with the leaden images of St. Peter and St.

* The three-petaled iris still waves on the old walls of Florence.

Paul) incapable of sending out excommunications till the consecration of a new pope adds a new name, and again gives validity to the instrument.

THE TWO-HEADED EAGLE.

The origin of the device of the Eagle on national and royal banners may be traced to very early times. It was the ensign of the ancient kings of Persia and Babylon. The Romans adopted many other figures on their camp-standards; but Marius, B.C. 102, made the eagle alone the ensign of the legions, and confined the other figures to the cohorts. From the Romans, the French under the empire adopted the eagle. The emperors of the Western Roman Empire used a black eagle, those of the East a golden one. The sign of the golden eagle, met with in taverns, is in allusion to the emperors of the East. Since the time of the Romans almost every state that has assumed the designation of an empire has taken the eagle for its ensign: Austria, Prussia, Russia, Poland, and France, all took the eagle. The two-headed eagle signifies a double empire. The emperors of Austria, who claim to be considered the successors of the Cæsars of Rome, use the double-headed eagle, which is the eagle of the eastern emperors with that of the western, typifying the " Holy Roman Empire," of which the emperors of Germany (now merged in the House of Austria) consider themselves as the representatives. Charlemagne was the first to use it; for when he became master of the whole of the German Empire, he added the second head to the eagle, A.D. 802, to denote that the empires of Rome and Germany were united in him. As it is among birds the king, and being the emblem of a noble nature from its strength of wing and eye and courage, and also of conscious strength and innate power, the eagle has been universally preferred as the continental emblem of sovereignty. Of the different eagles of heraldry, the black eagle is considered the most noble, especially when blazoned on a golden shield.—*Notes and Queries.*

WHAT IS PEGASUS?

Pegasus was, strictly speaking, Bellerophon's horse; but in the *Destruction of Troy,* 4to., 1617, we read, " of the blood that issued out (from Medusa's head) there engendered Pegasus, or the *flying-horse.* By the flying-horse that was engendered of the blood issued from her head, is understood that of her riches issuing of that realme he (Perseus) founded, and made a ship named Pegase, and *this ship was likened unto an horse flying,*" &c. In another place we are told that this ship, which the writer always calls Perseus' flying-horse, " flew on the sea like unto a bird."

THE TURKISH CRESCENT.

A Correspondent of *Notes and Queries* considers that, from various authorities which he quotes, we are warranted by Turkish history and tradition in inferring—1. That the Crescent has been for several centuries a public symbol of the religion and authority of the Othman (or Ottoman) empire. 2. That it was in use as part of the standard of the Janisaries nearly a century before the taking of Constantinople by Mahomed II. 3. That it was given by the founder of Mohammedanism as a symbol to his followers, in commemoration of some unusual natural phenomenon which had more the appearance of miracle than any other event to which he could appeal in confirmation of his prophetic mission.

Again, it is related of the Sultan Othman, that he saw in a vision a half-moon. which kept increasing enormously, till its rays extended from the east to the west ; and that this led him to adopt the crescent upon his standards, with this motto, *Donec repleat orbem.*

THE LION OF ST. MARK AT VENICE.

This popular symbol of Venice, which is placed upon one of the two granite columns at the southern extremity of the Piazetta, suffered during the republican rule of the French. From the book which the lion holds, the words of the Gospel were effaced, and *Droits de l'homme et du citoyen* substituted in their stead. The lion was afterwards removed to the Invalides at Paris, but was restored after the fall of Paris.

PENN'S TREE IN PENNSYLVANIA.

The tree under which Penn signed the great treaty with the Indians of Pennsylvania, near the site of Philadelphia, was a venerable elm, " which," says Mr. Dixon, in his excellent *Life of Penn,* " served to mark the spot until the storm of 1810 threw it to the ground. It measured 24 feet in girth, and was found to be then 283 years old. A piece of it was sent home to the Penn family, by whom it was mounted on a pedestal and decorated with appropriate inscriptions ; and the remainder was manufactured into vases, work-stands, and other relics, now held sacred by their possessors. A plain granite monument has since been erected on the spot, inscribed on each face with four short and simple sentences commemorative of the great treaty." The exact date of this memorable assembly has not been specified.

THE PARLIAMENT OAK IN SHERWOOD FOREST.

In a leafy nook by the roadside from Mansfield to Edwinstown, stands this venerable oak. Tradition says that Edward I. and his retinue were chasing the deer through this once royal chase, when a messenger arrived, bearing intelligence that his majesty's new subjects in Wales were in open revolt. The monarch instantly called his knights around him, and under the branches of this oak held an urgent council. The knights, with brief resolve, cried out for prompt suppression and extirminating war. The tree is supposed to be above one thousand years old; it is now 20 feet high, and varying from 27 feet to 32½ feet in circumference. It stands within the ancient limits of Clipstone Park, the property of the Duke of Portland, whose regard for the venerable oak has caused it to be braced and supported by poles.

THE CHARTER OAK OF CONNECTICUT.

The old "Charter Oak" of Connecticut, which stood near the city of Hartford, U. S., was blown down on August 24, 1856, by a gale of wind, to the great regret of the inhabitants. When, in 1686, James II. dissolved the government of the colony, and demanded the surrender of the original charter granted by Charles II. in 1662, the governor and council refused, even resisting the terrors of three several writs of *quo warranto*. Whitehall was a long way off in those days. On the 31st October 1687, Sir Edmund Andross, and a guard of sixty soldiers, entered Hartford to seize the charter by force, if necessary. The sitting of the Assembly was judiciously protracted till evening; when the governor and council appeared about to yield the precious document, it was brought in and laid on the table. Suddenly the lights were put out, and all was darkness and silence; when the candles were again lighted, the charter had vanished. The council had not refused to give it up, but it was gone. The governor was deposed nevertheless, and the royal orders carried out; the charter had in the mean time been concealed in a gigantic oak. On James's abdication the instrument was reproduced, the old governor re-elected under it, and it remained the organic law of the colony till 1818. From this incident sprang the veneration of the people for the "Charter Oak." It is supposed to have been a very old tree when America was discovered. The day after the tree was blown down the city-band played solemn music over its trunk for two hours, and the city-bells tolled at sunset in token of the public sorrow.

THE LAWS OF SOLON.

In the third year of the 46th Olympiad, Solon being archon, the landowners and citizens, debtors and creditors, were in open feud. Solon was then called upon to legislate. His first step was to arrange matters between debtor and creditor, which he accomplished by altering the standard and lowering the rate of interest. He then deprived the nobility of a portion of their former power, by dividing all the people into four classes, regulated by property; thus, while he introduced a democracy, founding a new aristocracy. The nobility, as possessors of the largest properties, as the sole members of the court of Areopagus, as possessed of the priesthoods, and as directors of religious ceremonies, still retained an ample degree of influence. By the establishment of the Council of Four Hundred, an annually rotating college, he at once gave so many families an interest in the new order of things that there remained no chance of its being totally subverted. He finally compelled all the people to swear not to make any alteration during the next ten years, deeming that period sufficiently long for habituating them to the new constitution.

Herodotus says, that Solon exacted from the Athenians solemn oaths that *they* would not rescind any of his laws for ten years; and Plutarch informs us, that he gave to his laws force for a century absolute. The wooden rollers of Solon, like the tables of the Roman decemvirs, were doubtless intended as a permanent *fons omnis publici privatique juris.* Yet Cratinus, in one of his comedies, says: " I swear by Solon and Draco, whose wooden tablets (of laws) are now employed by people to roast their barley."*

THE OSTRACISM OF THE GREEKS.

By the Ostracism, a citizen was banished without special accusation, trial, or defence, from his native city to some other Greek city. As to reputation, the ostracism was a compliment rather than otherwise. The process was carried into effect by writing on a shell† (or potsherd) the name of the person whom a citizen thought it prudent for a time to banish; a day was named; the agora was railed round, with ten entrances left for the citizens of each tribe, and ten separate casks or vessels for depositing the suffrages, shells or potsherds. If at the end of the day the number of votes against any one person was 6000, that person was ostracised; if not, the ceremony ended in nothing. Ten days were allowed to him for settling his affairs; he was then required to depart from Attica for ten years, but retained his property, and suffered no other penalty.

There was at Syracuse a similar institution, called the *Petalism*, because in taking the votes the name of the citizen intended to be banished was written upon a leaf of olive instead of a shell or potsherd.

PUNISHMENT OF TREASON BY THE ATHENIAN LAW.

When Antiphon and Archeptolemus, two of the Four Hundred oligarchs, were found guilty by the Dikastery, and condemned to the penalties of treason, they were handed over to the Eleven (the chiefs of executive justice at Athens) to be

---

* Just as the wooden tallies were employed to light fires in our old Houses of Parliament.
† The shell of an oyster (*ostrea*), whence the name of *Ostracism*.

put to death by the customary draught of hemlock. Their
properties were confiscated; their houses were directed to be
razed, and the vacant sites to be marked by columns, with
the inscription, "The residence of Antiphon the traitor—of
Archeptolemus the traitor." They were not permitted to be
buried either in Attica or in any territory subject to the Athenian dominion; and their children were deprived of the citizen-
ship. Such was the sentence of the Athenian law of treason.
It was engraved on the same brazen column as the decree of
honour to the slayers of Phrynicus; from that column it was
transcribed, and has thus passed into history.—*Grote's History
of Greece*, vol. vii.

LACEDÆMONIAN LAW AGAINST COWARDS.

The punishment of such as fled from battle, whom they
called at Sparta *trepidantes*, was this: they could bear no office in the commonwealth; it was a shame and reproach to
give them any wives, and also to marry any of theirs; who-
soever met them might lawfully strike them, and they must
abide it, not giving them any word again; they were compelled to wear poor tattered cloth gowns, patched with cloth
of divers colours; and, worst of all, to shave one side of their
beards, and the other not.

DRACO AND HIS LAWS.

When the Athenian lawgiver Draco, B.C. 624, put in writing these ordinances, so that they might be "shown publicly"
and "known beforehand," he did not meddle with the political
constitution; and in these ordinances Aristotle finds little
worthy of remark, except the extreme severity of the punishments awarded;[*] petty thefts, or even proved idleness of life,
being visited with death or disfranchisement. Yet Mr. Grote
does not consider Draco to have been more rigorous than the
sentiment of the age. "Indeed, the few fragments of the Dra-
conian tables which have reached us, far from exhibiting indis-
criminate cruelty, introduce for the first time into the Athenian
law mitigating distinctions in regard to homicide founded on
the variety of concomitant circumstances." These ordinances
of Draco are all that have come down to us; the rest of his
ordinances are said to have been repealed by Solon on account
of their intolerable severity; so they appeared to the Athenians
of a later day, and even to Solon, who had to calm the wrath
of a suffering people in actual mutiny. He repealed the punishment of death for theft, which Draco had annexed to that

---

[*] Demades remarked of Draco's laws, that they were written with blood
and not with ink.

crime, and enacted as a penalty compensation to an amount
double the value of the property stolen.

THE PANDECTS OF JUSTINIAN.

The Pandects (*pandectæ*, "embracing all") are a digest of
Roman law, made by order of Justinian from the writings of
Roman jurists. The earliest Ms. is preserved in the Laurentian
Library at Florence, and was captured by the Pisans when they
stormed Amalfi in 1135. It was formerly generally believed,
but on insufficient evidence, that, in consequence of their discovery, the study of the civil law was revived, and its jurisprudence ultimately adopted throughout the greater part of
Europe. This Ms. was preserved at Pisa with as much veneration as if it had been the palladium of the republic; and
when, after the fall of Pisa in 1406, it was removed to Florence,
equal veneration long continued to be paid to it. Tapers were
lighted, monks and magistrates stood bareheaded as before
holy relics, and the books were opened beneath a silken pall.
The work is written in a bold and beautiful character, "is composed of two quarto volumes, with large margin, on a thin
parchment, and the Latin characters betray the hand of a Greek
scribe." (*Gibbon*.) Copies of the Florentine edition of the Pandects of 1553 will be found in the British Museum, and in the
Bodleian Library at Oxford.

THE INSTITUTES OF JUSTINIAN.

In the Biblioteca Capitolare at Verona many of the manuscripts are palimpsests, and one of them furnished the "Institutes
of Caius," compiled in the reign of Caracalla. It was known
that this treatise was the foundation of the "Institutes of Justinian," but not a fragment of it could be found. Gibbon says:

> A rumour devoid of credence has been propagated by the enemies of
> Justinian, that the jurisprudence of ancient Rome was reduced to ashes
> by the author of the Pandects, from the vain persuasion that it was now
> either false or superfluous. Without usurping an office so invidious, the
> emperor might safely commit to ignorance and time the accomplish-
> ment of this destructive wish. Before the invention of printing and
> paper, the labour and the materials of writing could be purchased only
> by the rich; and it may reasonably be computed that the price of books
> was a hundredfold their present value. Copies were slowly multiplied,
> and cautiously renewed; the hopes of profit tempted sacrilegious scribes
> to erase the characters of antiquity; and Sophocles or Tacitus was
> compelled to resign the parchment to missals, homilies, and the golden
> legend. If such was the fate of the most beautiful compositions of
> genius, what stability could be expected from the dull and barren works
> of an obsolete science ?

Years after the death of Gibbon, this sagacity was verified
by the zeal of Niebuhr, who, on his way to Rome in 1816, examined the capitular library at Verona. Two small fragments,

relating to jurisprudence, not palimpsests, had been published by Maffei ; but he had not ascertained their author. Niebuhr suspected that they were parts of the " Institutes of Caius ;" and upon further examination he discovered the whole remainder, or nearly so, of this ancient text-book of the Roman law, palimpsested, beneath the homilies of St. Jerome, literally verifying Gibbon's words ; and subsequently the "Institutes" were published.

The veracity of Justinian, in his Institutes, has been impeached ; for, says Lord Mahon, "we find him boasting of the warlike fatigues he had borne, and we can hardly suppress a smile on recollecting that this prince, so weary with laborious campaigns, had never quitted his palace at Constantinople, unless for the villas in its neighbourhood."

AGRARIAN LAWS.

The term *Agrarian* signifies "relating to lands"—*agrarius, ager* (Lat.), land ; and the Agrarian Laws of Rome were substantially a question similar to that of the Crown lands in our colonies. The rich became squatters upon them, and obtained a possessory title. An Agrarian Law, or the sending out of a colony, was a measure for dividing the public land among the poorer citizens without payment. If the Romans had adopted the plan of selling the public land at a moderate price, they would probably have prevented the fierce party-conflicts which their Agrarian Laws provoked.—*Edinburgh Review*, No. 200.

THE BED OF JUSTICE.

This expression (*lit de justice*) literally denoted the seat or throne upon which the king of France was accustomed to sit when personally present in parliaments ; and from this original meaning the expression came in course of time to signify the parliament itself. Under the ancient monarchy of France a bed of justice denoted a solemn session of the king in parliament. According to the principle of the old French constitution, the authority of the parliament, being derived entirely from the crown, ceased when the king was present ; consequently, all ordinances enrolled at a bed of justice were acts of the royal will, and of more authenticity and effect than decisions of parliament.

The last Bed of Justice was assembled by Louis XVI. at Versailles, on the 6th of August 1788, at the commencement of the French Revolution, and was intended to enforce upon the parliament of Paris the adoption of the obnoxious taxes which had been previously proposed by Calonne at the Assembly of Notables. The resistance to this measure led to the assembly of the States-general, and to the Revolution.

THE CODE NAPOLEON.

When Napoleon I. was forming the Code Napoleon, he astonished the Council of State by the readiness with which he illustrated any point in discussion by quoting whole passages, extempore, from the Roman civil law ; a subject thought entirely foreign to him, as his whole life had been passed in the camp. On being asked by Treilhard how he had acquired so familiar a knowledge of law, he replied : " When I was a lieutenant, I was once unjustly put under arrest. . The small room assigned for my prison contained no furniture but an old chair and a cupboard : in the latter was a ponderous volume, which proved to be a digest of the Roman law. As I had neither paper, pens, ink, nor pencil, you may easily imagine this book to have been a valuable prize to me. It was so bulky, and the leaves were so covered by marginal notes in manuscript, that had I been confined a hundred years, I need never have been idle. I was only ten days deprived of my liberty ; but on recovering it, I was saturated with Justinian and the decisions of the Roman legislators. It was thus I acquired my knowledge of the civil law."

ORIGIN OF THE CENSORSHIP OF THE PRESS.

Mayence was the cradle as well of the art of printing as of the efforts made by its enemies to fetter the spread of knowledge. Towards the close of the fifteenth century—that memorable epoch in the annals of religious and civil liberty— Berthold, archbishop and elector of Mayence, was the first to take alarm at the dangers which impended over the dominion of darkness. He enjoys the unenviable distinction of having been the author of the first edict which established a censorship of books. It is dated on the 4th of January 1486, and is extant in Galenus' *Cod. Diplom.*, lib. iv. 469. It prohibits any individual within the archbishop's domains, whether ecclesiastic or layman, from translating into the vernacular German any book whatever, be it in Greek, Latin, or any living foreign tongue ; or from buying, selling, and bartering it, or re-bartering, or in any way circulating it, unless he shall have previously sought and obtained license to print or circulate it from a board appointed for that purpose. This board was composed of the professors of the four faculties of the then existing university of Mayence, Drs. Bertram, Dietrich, Von Meschede, and Eler. · It was their duty to examine all manuscripts, &c., and pronounce whether they should be allowed to be printed or not. And they showed much zeal, as well as tact, in preventing any outcry from being raised in the execution of this duty. The penalties inflicted on offenders against the

e-lict were very severe for that time of day : the publication
was confiscated, the author was excommunicated, and he was
mulcted in the sum of one hundred golden gilders for behoof
of the archiepiscopal chest.   A regular code of instructions
was also drawn up for the guidance of the censors.

OLD ENGLISH LAW AGAINST BEGGARS.

Mr. Froude, in his valuable *History of England*, says :

For an able-bodied man to be caught a third time bogging was held
a crime deserving death, and the sentence was intended on fit occasions
to be executed. The poor man's advantages, which I have estimated
at so high a rate, were not purchased without drawbacks. He might
not change his master at his will, or wander from place to place. He
might not keep his children at home unless he could answer for their
time. If out of employment, preferring to be idle, he might be demanded
for work by any master of the "craft" to which he belonged, and compelled to work whether he would or no. If caught begging once, being
neither aged nor infirm, he was whipped at the cart's tail. If caught
a second time, his ear was slit, or bored through with a hot iron. If
caught a third time, being thereby proved to be of no use upon this
earth, but to live upon it only to his own hurt and to that of others, he
suffered death as a felon. So the law of England remained for sixty
years. First drawn by Henry, it continued unrepealed through the
reigns of Edward and of Mary, subsisting, therefore, with the deliberate
approval of both the great parties between whom the country was divided. Re-considered under Elizabeth, the same law was again formally
passed ; and it was therefore the expressed conviction of the English
nation that it was better for a man not to live at all than to live a profitless and worthless life. The vagabond was a sore spot upon the commonwealth, to be healed by wholesome discipline, if the gangrene was
not incurable ; to be cut away with the knife, if the milder treatment of
the cart-whip failed to be of profit.

CAGES AND STOCKS IN LONDON.

Cages and stocks were ordered to be set up in every ward
of the city, by Sir William Capell, draper and lord mayor, in
1503. We have an instance of their use in 1555, when, upon
the death of Pope Julius III., Stephen Gardiner, Bishop of
Winchester and lord chancellor, wrote to Bonner, Bishop of
London, to command him, in Queen Mary's name, to order
those prayers to be used throughout his diocese which the
Roman Church has appointed during a vacancy in the papal
see. " Vpon this commandment," says John Fox, in his *Acts
and Monuments of Martyrs*, 1610, " there were hearses set vp,
and diriges sung for the said Julius in diuers places. At which
time it chanced a woman to come into Saint Magnus Church,
at the bridge-foot in London, and there seeing an hearse and
other preparation, asked what it meant : and other that stood
by said it was for the Pope, and that she must pray for him.
'Nay,' quoth she, 'that I will not ; for he needeth not my

prayer : and seeing he could forgiue vs all our sins, I am sure he is cleane himselfe ; therefore I neede not pray for him.' She was hearde speake these words of certaine that stood by ; which by and by carried her vnto the cage at London Bridge, and bade her coole herselfe there." In some of the editions of Fox there is an eugraving of this circumstance, which shows that the stocks and cage stood by one of the archways on the bridge, and in one of the vacant spaces which looked on the water. The last stocks remembered in London were those of St. Clement Danes parish, Strand, on the south side of Portugal Street, and not removed until 1820-26.

ARCHERY TENURES.

The provision of an equipped archer to attend the king in his wars is the frequent sergeantry for lands at this time. Thus, the service for the manor of Faintree, in Shropshire, in 1211, is " a foot soldier for a bow and arrows, for the king's army in Wales." In 1274 the soldier is bound to stay with the host only " till he has shot away his arrows." In 1284 the archer has "to attend the king in his Welsh wars, with a bow, three arrows, and a terpolus;" the latter, probably, an "archer's stake," not the mere small iron *caltrop*, of which the provision of one only by each archer would be of little use in impeding a charge of cavalry. The duty of the bowman who had only to stay in the field till he had shot away three arrows was sufficiently easy ; but on other occasions the archer did not escape so lightly. The manor of Chetton, in Shropshire, supplies in 1283 an archer for the king's host in Wales, who is to take with him a flitch of bacon, and to remain with the army till he has eaten it all up.—*Blount's Ancient Tenures, and Eyton's Antiquities of Shropshire.*

BURNING ALIVE.

Little more than seventy-five years have elapsed since a girl, just turned fourteen, was condemned to be burnt alive, having been found guilty of treason as an accomplice with her master in coining, because, at his command, she had concealed some whitewashed counters behind her stays. The master was hanged. The fagots were placed in readiness for her execution ; and it was averred in the House of Commons, by Sir William Meredith, at the time, that "the girl would have been burnt alive on the same day had it not been for the humane but casual interference of Lord Weymouth. Mere accident saved the nation from this crime and this national disgrace. But so torpid was public feeling in those days, that the law remained unaltered till the year 1790 ; till which time the sheriff who did not execute a sentence of this kind was liable to prosecution ; though it may well be believed no sheriff was then inhuman enough to adhere to the letter of such a law.— *Quarterly Review*, No. 87.

PUNISHMENT OF AN INFIDEL.

In 1689 Casimir Lyszynski, a gentleman of Poland, who was convicted of denying the existence of a God, was executed at Warsaw. The manner of his punishment was very particular. As soon as his body was burnt, his ashes were put into a cannon, and shot into the air towards Tartary.—*Spectator*, No. 389.

WITCHCRAFT-LAWS IN ENGLAND.

Before the enactment of any penal statute for the imaginary offence of Witchcraft, the trials and convictions were numerous. Witness the case of Bolingbroke and Margery Jenkins, whose incantations Shakspeare has rendered familiar to us in the second part of *King Henry VI.* Witness the successive statutes of Henry VIII., of Elizabeth, and James I.; the last only repealed in 1736, and passed while Coke was attorney-general, and Bacon a member of the Commons! Witness the exploits of Hopkins, the witch-finder-general, against the wretched creatures in Lancashire ;

> " Some only for not being drowned,
> And some for sitting above ground
> Whole nights and days upon their breeches,
> And feeling pain, were hanged for witches."
>
> *Hudibras*, part ii. canto ii.

Zachary Grey, the editor of *Hudibras*, says he himself perused a list of 3000 victims executed during the dynasty of the Long Parliament alone! What absurdities exceed those sworn to in the case of the luckless Lancashire witches,[*] sacrificed, as afterwards appeared, to the villany of the impostor Robinson, whose story was dramatised by Heywood and Shadwell! How melancholy is the spectacle of a man like Hale condemning Amy Duny and Rose Cullender, in 1664, on evidence, though corroborated by the opinion of Sir Thomas Browne, a child would now be disposed to laugh at! A better order of things, it is true, commences with the chief-justiceship of Holt. The evidence against Mother Munnings, in 1694, would, with a man of weaker intellect, have sealed the fate of the unfortunate old woman ; but Holt charged the jury with such firmness and good sense, that a verdict of not guilty, almost the first then on record in a trial for witchcraft, was found. In about ten

[*] The name of this celebrated case, " the Lancashire Witches," will be long remembered, partly from Shadwell's play, but more from the ingenious and well-merited compliment to the beauty of the females of that province, which it was held to contain.

other trials before Holt, from 1694 to 1701, the result was the same. Wenham's case, which followed in 1711, sufficiently evinced the change which had taken place in the feelings of the judges; but when Chief-Justice Powell asked the jury on their giving in the verdict, "whether they found her guilty upon the indictment for conversing with the devil in the shape of a cat," the foreman answered, "We find her guilty of that." It is almost needless to add that a pardon was procured for her. And yet, frightful to think, after all this, in 1716, Mrs. Hicks and her daughter, aged nine, were hanged at Huntingdon for selling their souls to the devil, and raising a storm by pulling off their stockings and making a lather of soap!

With this crowning atrocity the catalogue of murders in England closes; the penal statutes against witchcraft being repealed in 1736, and the pretended exercise of such arts being punished in future by imprisonment and pillory. Barrington, in his observations on the statute 20 Henry VI., does not hesitate to estimate the numbers of those put to death in England on this charge at 30,000! Yet the case of Rex *v.* Weldon, in 1809, and the still later case of Barker *v.* Ray, in Chancery (August 2, 1827), prove that the popular belief in such practices lasted to our days.

It is supposed that there were no executions for witchcraft in England subsequently to the year 1682, when three unhappy women were hanged at Exeter on their own confession; but the statute of James I., c. 12, so minute in all its enactments against witches, was not repealed till the 9th Geo. II., c. 5.

THE EARLIEST-COINED MONEY.

Throughout the early parts of Scripture, as well as through the poems of Homer, not a single passage occurs from which we can infer either the use or the existence of stamped money. It is now agreed that the Egyptians had no coined money. Herodotus states the Lydians to have been the first people who coined gold and silver. The Parian Chronicle, however, ascribes the first coinage of copper and silver money to Pheidon, king of Argos, 895 B.C., in Ægina, which Ælian corroborates; and our best numismatic antiquaries agree in considering the coins of Ægina, from their archaic form and appearance, as the most ancient known. They are of silver, and bear on the upper side the figure of a turtle, and on the under an indented mark.

Pheidon also first established a scale of weights and measures, which M. Boeckh considers to have been borrowed immediately from the Phœnicians, and by them originally from the Babylonians, the common origin being the Chaldæan priesthood.

Coins are among the most certain evidences of history. In the later part of the Greek series they illustrate the chronology of reigns. In the Roman series, they fix the dates and succession of events. Gibbon observes, that if all our historians were lost, medals, inscriptions, and other monuments, would be sufficient to record the travels of Hadrian. The reign of Probus might be written from his coins.

WHAT WAS A POUND IN A.D. 1000 ?

In Alsace, at the end of the tenth century, the common money for current purposes was the pfennig. It was of copper, and sixty of them weighed exactly one marc, or half a pound avoirdupois, or 120 of them were a pound weight. The price of a sheffel, or bushel of wheat, weighing sixty pounds, or the same nearly as our English bushel, was seven of these pfennigs. Copper probably bore a higher value in proportion to silver than it does in the present day; or the bushel of wheat was sold for less than a penny-farthing. About two hundred and fifty years later, in the same country, the same measure of wheat was sold at twenty-four pfennigs, or about threepence-farthing. It appears by the accounts preserved in the cathedral of Strasburg that the wages paid to the masons employed in the erection of that edifice were from one and a half to two of these pfennigs. At the building of the great bridge of Dresden, in the thirteenth century, the labourers were paid two pfennigs daily; and, according to some fragments of mining accounts of Tillot and Château Lambert, the operative miners received no more than two pfennigs.—*Jacob on the Precious Metals.*

RENT OF AN ISLAND.

The island of Bombay is held by a tenure totally different from that by which we hold any other part of our Indian dominions. It was part of the dowry of Queen Catherine, the neglected Portuguese consort of Charles II. His majesty got it in the year 1661; and after eight years' possession, finding that he gained nothing by the poor place, he granted it to the East India Company, to be holden "of us and our heirs, as of the manor of East Greenwich, in free and common socage, at a rent of ten pounds in gold, payable yearly." This spot, rented at 10*l.* a-year, in perpetuity, 217 years ago, now contains a town with a population of 400,000 souls, has a trade valued in exports and imports at 14,000,000*l.*, and is the seat of a subordinate government, extending over 10,000,000 of people. — *Edinburgh Review,* No. 200.

SLAVE-TRADE IN ENGLAND.

In England it was common, even after the Conquest, to export slaves to Ireland; till, in the reign of Henry II., the Irish came to a non-importation agreement, which put a stop to the practice. William of Malmesbury accuses the Anglo-Saxon nobility of selling their female servants as slaves to foreigners. In the canons of a council at London, in 1102, we read :- "Let no one from henceforth presume to carry on that wicked traffic, by which men of England have hitherto been sold like brute animals." And Giraldus Cambrensis says, that the English before the Conquest were accustomed to sell their children and other relations to be slaves in Ireland, without having even the pretext of distress or famine, till the Irish, in a national synod, agreed to emancipate all the English slaves in the kingdom.

THE PRIVILEGE OF SANCTUARY.

By this very ancient and curious Saxon law, if a person accused of any crime,—excepting treason and sacrilege, in which the Crown and the Church were too nearly concerned,—had fled to any church or churchyard, and within forty days after went before the coroner, made a full confession of his crime, and took the oath provided in that case, that he would quit the realm, and never return again without leave of the king, his life should be safe. At the taking of this oath he was brought to the church-door, where being branded with an A., signifying "abjured," upon the brawn of the thumb of his right-hand, a port was then assigned to him from which he was to leave the realm, and to which he was to make all speed, holding a cross in his hand, and not turning out of the highway either to the right hand or the left. At this port he was diligently to seek for passage, waiting there but one ebb and flood, if he could immediately procure it ; and if not, he was to go every day into the sea up to his knees, essaying to pass over. If this could not be accomplished within forty days, he was again to put himself into sanctuary. These privileges of sanctuary and abjuration were taken away in 1621 by the statute of 21st James I. Sanctuary was also a sacred asylum.*

* To sanctuary Richard of Gloucester removed the Lady Anne, when, says the chronicler of Croyland, he "discovered the maiden in the attire of a kitchen-girl in London," in which degrading garb Clarence had concealed her; and Gloucester "caused her to be placed in the Sanctuary of St. Martin," while he openly and honourably sought from the king his assent to their marriage. The Lady Anne had been the playmate of Gloucester's childhood, and the object of his youthful affections. Before either had passed the age of minority, she had drunk deeply of the cup of adversity; from being the affianced bride of the heir-apparent to the throne, and receiving homage at the French court as Princess of Wales, she was degraded to assume the disguise of a kitchen-girl in London, reduced to utter poverty by the attainder of herself and parents. Such was the condition of Warwick's proud but destitute child, the ill-fated co-heiress of the Nevilles, the Beauchamps, the Despencers, and in whose veins flowed the blood of the highest and noblest in the land. The Croyland historian exonerates Richard from the unfounded charge of seeking the affection of "young Edward's bride" before the tears of "widowhood" had ceased to flow ; and equally so of his outraging a custom most religiously and strictly observed in the fifteenth century, which rendered it an offence against the Church and society at large for " a widow" to espouse a second time before the first year of mourning had expired.—Halsted's *Richard III.*

CABINET COUNCILS.

It is remarkable how a change of very great importance in our system of government was brought about by pure accident. The custom of a king being present in a Cabinet Council of his ministers, which was the obvious, and had always been the usual, state of things, was put an end to when the Hanoverian princes came to the throne, from their ignorance of the English language. The advantage thence resulting of ministers laying before the sovereign the result of their full and free deliberations—an advantage not at all originally contemplated—caused the custom to be continued, and so established, that it is most unlikely it should ever be changed.—*Dr. Whately.*

It has not been the practice in modern times for the sovereign to consult the members of the Privy Council on political matters ; indeed, the number of members of that body, amounting to nearly 200, would make such a reference to their advice impossible. Her Majesty has an undoubted right to command the services of any and every Privy Councillor ; but none have a right to obtrude their advice except those members of the Council who are nominated by her Majesty as a committee of the whole body, and which is commonly known as the Cabinet.— *Letter from the Earl of Derby, 1856.*

THE STYLE OF "YOUR MAJESTY."

Up to the time of the Emperor Charles V., when a king of France, England, or Spain, was addressed, he was styled "Your Grace ;" but Charles, wishing to place himself in a higher rank than other monarchs, demanded the title of "Majesty ;" a distinction which did not long continue, for the other sovereigns of Europe quickly followed his example ; and in our day all kings, whether rulers of small or great states, are equally styled "Your Majesty."

THE DAUPHIN OF FRANCE

was the title given to the eldest son of the king of France under the Valois and Bourbon dynasties. The Counts of Albon and Grenoble assumed the title of Counts of Vienna, of whom Guy VIII. is said to have been surnamed Le Dauphin, because he wore a dolphin as an emblem on his helmet or shield. The surname remained to his descendants, who were styled Dauphins, and the country which they governed was called Dauphiné. Humbert II., de la Tour de Pisa, the last of the Dauphin dynasty, gave up his sovereignty by treaty to King Philippe de Valois in 1349. (*Moreri, &c.*). From that time the eldest son of the King of France has been styled Dauphin, in the same manner as the eldest son of the Queen of England is styled Prince of Wales. Since the dethronement of the elder branch of the Bourbons in 1830, the title of Dauphin has been disused. The last who bore it was the Duke of Angoulême, son of Charles X.

P

THE CITY OF LONDON AND THE PEERAGE.

Sir Geoffrey Bullen, Lord Mayor in 1453, was grandfather to Thomas Earl of Wiltshire, father to Anne Bullen, and grandfather to Queen Elizabeth—the highest genealogical honour the City can boast of.

"The ennobled families of Cornwallis, Capel, Coventry, Legge, Cowper, Thynne, Ward, Craven, Marsham, Pulteney, Hill, Holles, Osborne, Cavendish, Bennet, and others, have sprung either directly or collaterally from those who have been either mayors, sheriffs, or aldermen of London; and a very large portion of the peerage of the United Kingdom is related, either by descent or intermarriage, to the citizens of the metropolis."—*Thomas Moule.*

Mr. Sims, of the British Museum, in his *Manual for the Genealogist,* says: "At present there are few English families who pretend to higher antiquity than the Norman invasion; and it is probable that not many of these can authenticate their pretensions. On making an abstract of the English *printed* peerage, it appears that out of 249 noblemen, the number of thirty-five laid claim to having traced their descent beyond the Conquest; forty-nine, prior to the year 1100; twenty-nine, prior to the year 1200; thirty-two, prior to the year 1300; twenty-six, prior to the year 1400; seventeen, prior to the year 1500; twenty-six, prior to the year 1600; and thirty, but little prior to the year 1700. The number of peers entered in that peerage is 294, exclusive of the Royal Family; but of that list no satisfactory conclusion could be drawn as to the commencement of the pedigrees of forty-five noblemen."

RECORDS.—" LENGTH OF THE LAW."

Some faint idea of the bulk of our English records may be obtained from the fact, that a single statute, the Land Tax Commissioners' Act, passed in the first year of the reign of George IV., measures, when unrolled, upwards of *nine hundred feet,* or nearly twice the length of St. Paul's Cathedral within the walls; and if ever it should become necessary to consult the fearful volume, an able-bodied man would be employed during three hours in coiling and unrolling the monstrous folds.—*Quarterly Review.*

IRELAND ASSIGNED BY A RING.

Pope Hadrian assigned to our King Henry II. the territorial possession of Ireland, and invested him with full powers over the country by a gold ring set with magnificent emeralds; inasmuch as all islands are said by ancient right to belong to the Roman Church, being presents to her from Constantine.

THE CLAIM OF THE KINGS OF ENGLAND TO THE CROWN OF FRANCE.

The claim of the kings of England to the crown of France dates back to the time of Edward III., who claimed through his mother Isabel, daughter of Philip IV., surnamed *Le Bel*. But the title was, it must be acknowledged, defective in this, that it was incompatible with the Salic law, which ruled in that country. Nevertheless, the claim was supported by force of arms, and for a time successfully, our Henry VI. having been crowned king at Rheims. The war of the Roses distracted the attention of our monarchs from these pretensions, and they gradually fell into neglect. At length, A.D. 1527, Henry VIII., in a treaty, called the *Tractatus Aureus*, because the seal put to it was of gold, entered into an arrangement in this matter with Francis I., to the following effect, viz. "That, notwithstanding his claim and style of France, he and his successors should suffer the most Christian king and his successors quietly to enjoy all dominions then in his possession as precisely as if the king of England could make no claim to them;" on the other hand, the king of France, for himself and his successors, covenanted to pay 50,000 crowns yearly to the kings of England, and to deliver yearly 50,000 crowns' worth of salt of Bruage, without demanding any payment for it, and agreed to leave the king of England in unmolested enjoyment of those territories which he then held in France. The tribute of crowns and salt was soon discontinued,[*] and thus in strictness the surrender of title on the part of the king of England was invalidated.

Rousset, in his work on *Les Intérêts Présens des Puissances de l'Europe*, published in 1733, states: "Nevertheless the kings of England continue to assume titles and arms of the kings of France, being resolved not to abandon their pretensions. They even boldly use this title in the treaties which they have made with that crown. There was even a custom introduced, and practised up to the time of the two last kings, of a ceremony performed in London on New-Year's Day, the object of which was to preserve their right entire. The king, the princes, and the peers and ambassadors, assembled on that day in the church of St. Paul, when a herald cried out with a loud voice the name of the reigning sovereign, adding, 'by the grace of God king of Great Britain and of France;' and at the same time threw a glove down at the entrance of the church, which the French ambassador took up, saying: *Salvo jure, et sine præjudicio Christianissimi Galliarum regis*, that is to say, 'Saving

---

[*] See Sir George Carew's "Relation of the State of France under King Henry IV., on his Return from his Embassy in 1609, and addressed to King James I."

the right, and without prejudice to the most Christian king of France.' A minute of this protestation was then drawn up, which was registered, and the French ambassador sent the glove to Paris. The two last kings have not thought proper to follow up this custom, either with a view not to disoblige France, or as being an act hardly necessary to preserve their pretensions."

In Dangeau's *Mémoires de Louis XIV.*, we find at the death of William III. the following corroborative entry : "The kings of France mourn in violet, the king of England also mourns in violet, *because he still claims to be king of France.* It startles us thus to see two kings of France."

THE CORONATION-STONE IN WESTMINSTER ABBEY—THE REGALIA OF SCOTLAND.

This famous stone was brought in 1297 by King Edward I. from the abbey of Scone, with the sceptre and gold crown of the Scottish sovereigns. It is called the Prophetic or Fatal Stone, from the ancient belief of the Scots, that whenever it should be lost, the power of the nation would decline. It was also superstitiously called "Jacob's pillow." It is of reddish-gray sandstone, 26 by 16¾ inches, and 10½ inches thick.

Mr. Joseph Hunter, F.S.A., in a communication to the Archæological Institute, in 1856, stated, it appeared, from a document which had recently been found among the records of England, that King Edward had treated the relic with all the veneration due to it. With the intention of employing it for the same august purpose in England as it had been used for in Scotland, he proposed to make it a part of a throne or royal chair, and gave orders to his goldsmith to have a copper chair made for it. After the work had been proceeded with, he changed his mind, and ordered instead a chair of wood to be made for it ; and it is in connection with this wooden chair that it now exists. To show the estimation in which he held the stone, he had it placed in the most sacred situation in all England—near the altar and shrine of St. Edward—where it still remains, with the chair of wood which he ordered to be constructed. Mr. Cosmo Innes said he found, from the chronicles of the period, that King Edward had intended to return the stone to Scotland, and had made arrangements to that effect with reference to a treaty on the subject, when the citizens of London, who had come to feel a great interest in the preservation of the stone amongst them, remonstrated against its restoration, and King Edward did not follow out his intention. This is not the only instance of a stone being used as a coronation-seat in this country. There is another on which Saxon kings had been crowned, almost similar to the Scone stone. Mr. Robert Chambers considers there to be good reason to believe that the kings did not sit upon the stone, but that they stood upon it, when they were crowned. There is one in Sweden, on which it is ascertained that the kings stood during the ceremony of coronation.

Mr. Joseph Robertson, referring to a query of Mr Hunter, as to what became of the ancient Regalia of Scotland carried off by King Edward, said that on the flight of Baliol from the court of Edward and his capture at Dover, the crown was found amongst his baggage, and it was then deposited at St. Thomas à Becket's shrine at Canterbury ;

and it was probable that, with other things, it was carried away and destroyed at the Reformation. The supposition that the crown in the Tower is the ancient crown of Scotland is a modern tradition without any foundation.

"THE CHAMPION AT THE CORONATION."

This chivalrous and dignified office is conferred by the feudal manor of Scrivelsby, Lincoln, inherited successively by the Marmyons, the Ludlows, and the Dymokes. In *Domesday Book* it is holden by Robert de Spencer; it was shortly after conferred, with the castle of Tamworth, on Robert de Marmyon, Lord of Fontney, whose ancestors were, it is said, hereditary champions to the Dukes of Normandy previously to the invasion of England. Scrivelsby was, by the terms of the grant, to be held by grand sergeantry, "to perform the office of champion at the king's coronation." From the Marmyons it passed to the Ludlows; when Margaret de Ludlow, the lady of Scrivelsby, wedding Sir John Dymock, a knight of ancient Gloucestershire family, invested him with the championship, which high office he executed at the coronation of Richard II. Having chosen the best charger save one in the king's stables, and the best suit of harness save one in the royal armoury, he rode in armed to the teeth, and challenged, as the king's champion, all opposers of the young monarch's title to the crown: whence to this time the Dymokes have enjoyed the estate, and performed the duties its tenure enjoins. The present male representative, Sir Henry Dymoke, Bart., succeeded to the estates and championship, on the decease of his father, the Rev. John Dymoke, in 1828; having previously performed the duties as deputy for that gentleman at the coronation of king George IV.

Haydon, the historical painter, thus describes this ancient feudal ceremony (*Autobiography*, vol. ii.), which he witnessed in Westminster Hall: "The hall-doors were opened, and the flower-girls entered, strewing flowers. The distant trumpets and shouts of the people, the slow march, and at last the appearance of the king, crowned and under a golden canopy, and the universal burst of the assembly at seeing him, affected everybody. . . . . After the banquet was over, came the most imposing scene of all, the championship. Wellington, in his coronet, walked down the hall, cheered by the officers of the Guards. He shortly returned, mounted, with Lords Anglesey and Howard. They rode gracefully to the foot of the throne, and then backed out. The hall-doors opened again; and outside, in twilight, a man in dark-shadowed armour appeared against the shining sky. He then moved, passed into darkness under the arch, and suddenly Wellington, Howard, and the champion stood in full view, with doors closed behind them. This was certainly the finest sight of the day. The herald then read the challenge; the glove was thrown down. They all then proceeded to the throne."

Historic Doubts.

ERRORS IN PRINT.

"Shall be deposed by those have seen't,
Or, what's as good, produced in print."—*Hudibras.*

The vulgar imagine that every thing they see in print must be true; and sometimes their betters fall into this mistake. When Mr. Martin was thrown into the prison of the Inquisition for neglecting to pay due respect to a religious procession at Malaga, one of the father inquisitors took much pains to convert him. Among other abuses which he cast on the reformed religion and its professors, he affirmed that King William was an atheist, and never received the sacrament. Mr. Martin assured him this was false to his own knowledge; when the reverend father replied: "I read, I read; never tell me so. I have read it in a French book."

WHO BUILT BALBEC?

Lamartine has the following speculation in reply to this question: "It is alleged that not far from Balbec, in a valley of the Anti-Libanus, human bones of immense magnitude have been found. Oriental traditions, and the monument erected on what is called the Tomb of Noah, mark this spot as the dwelling-place of the patriarch. The first generation of his descendants probably long retained the gigantic stature and the strength assigned to man before the total or partial submersion of the globe. These monuments may be their work. Even supposing that the human race had never exceeded its present proportions, it is possible that the properties of human intelligence may have undergone a change. Who can say but that primitive intelligence might have invented mechanical powers capable of moving, like grains of dust, masses which an army of 100,000 men could now scarcely shake? Be this as it may, it is certain that some of the stones at Balbec, which are 62 feet long, 20 broad, and 15 thick, are the most prodigious masses which have ever been moved by human power. The largest stones in the Pyramids of Egypt do not exceed 18 feet; and these are only exceptional blocks, placed for the sake of peculiar solidity in some parts of the edifice."

EPIC POETRY OF EARLY GREECE.

Of the many epic poems which existed in Greece during the

eighth century before the Christian era, none have been preserved except the Iliad and Odyssey. The Æthiopis of Arctinus, the Ilias Minor of Lesches, the Cyprian Verses, the Capture of Œchalia, the Return of the Heroes from Troy, the Thebaïs, and the Epigoni,—several of them passing in antiquity under the name of Homer,—have all been lost, besides others, to the number of about thirty.

Homer is essentially the poet of the broad highway and the marketplace; touching the common sympathies and satisfying the mental appetencies of his countrymen with unrivalled effect, but exempt from ulterior views, either selfish or didactic, and immersed in the same medium of practical life and experience, religiously construed, as his auditors. No nation has ever yet had so perfect and touching an exposition of its early social mind as the Iliad and Odyssey exhibit. (*Grote's Hist. Greece,* vol. ii.)

Mr. Grote, after an examination of the various conflicting opinions, places the date of the Iliad and Odyssey at some periods between 850 B.C. and 760 B.C.

BIRTHPLACE OF HOMER.

Seven different cities laid claim to the birth of Homer, Smyrna and Chios being the most prominent. Most of these cities had legends to tell of his romantic parentage, his alleged blindness, and his life of an itinerant bard acquainted with poverty and sorrow; whilst of the eight different epochs assigned to Homer's existence, the oldest differs from the most recent by 460 years.

The blindness of Homer is mentioned in the Homeric Hymn to the Delian Apollo, cited by Thucydides as unquestionably authentic. The Delphian Oracle reported Homer to be a native of Ithaca, the son of Telemachus and Epickaste; and his genealogy has been traced up to Orpheus.

IS THE SIEGE OF TROY A LEGEND?

We select and abridge these details from the *History of Greece*, by Mr. Grote, who observes: "that the genuine Trojan war, although literally believed, reverentially cherished, and numbered among the gigantic phenomena of the past by the Grecian public, is in the eyes of modern inquiry essentially a legend, and nothing more." And in reply to the inquiry whether this be not a legend, embodying portions of historical matter, whether there was not really some historical Trojan war, Mr. Grote remarks: "that as the possibility of it cannot be denied, so neither can the reality of it be affirmed." "Yet," says the historian elsewhere, "the Trojan horse, with its accompaniments, Sinon and Laocoon, is one of the capital and indispensable events in the epic: Homer, Arctinus, Lesches,

Virgil, and Quintus Smyrnæus, all dwell upon it emphatically as the proximate cause of the capture."*

THEBES OF "THE HUNDRED GATES."

Homer speaks of the fame of this ancient Egyptian city for opulence and warlike strength :

> "Thebes, where through each her hundred portals wide
> Two hundred charioteers their coursers guide."

The "hundred gates" here mentioned were a stumbling-block to the commentators in the day of Diodorus. The city is not known to have been surrounded with a rampart; "there are no signs of walls round it, nor were walled towns common in Egypt." But there are remains of such wide gates about their temples, which, as Diodorus observes, agree with the poet. Others think the gates to mean palaces of princes, or great men of the city, each of whom could send out so many chariots to the war. Yet the general opinion of the moderns is, that "the city had not a hundred gates, but many propylæa to the temples, *i.e.* many-gated, extended by poetic license to hundred-gated (*hecatompylon*)." Again, the hundred gates are thought to have been the outlets of the great rectangular enclosure still to be seen in Western Thebes.

THE ASSASSINS.

From the fanatical crimes of this sect, the word Assassin has found a place in European languages. These Assassins had in the twelfth century the possession of many hill-forts in Syria; and from their colony of Mount Libanus went forth the secret ministers of the revenge or the avarice of their sheik; to whom his followers vowed a blind obedience, believing that his commands were those of a divinity, and that if they fell in the discharge of the duties assigned them, all the joys of paradise would be their reward. In every variety of disguise these missionaries of the dagger found their way to the courts of princes in the East and in the West; and Christian and Mussulman equally dreaded the danger against which no vigilance could guard.

There are few words the etymology of which has more baffled the ingenuity of the learned than Assassins. Perhaps the following may not be very remote from the truth. Throughout all the East a preparation of hemp, which we call *bang*, is universally used "to exhilarate the feelings by a luxurious species of intoxication." This is known to the Orientals by

---

* Mr. Maclaurin, in the *Transactions of the Royal Society of Edinburgh*, attempts to prove that Troy was really not taken by the Greeks. This whim is as old as Dio Chrysostom, who wrote an elaborate tract, still extant, to demonstrate his paradox.

the name of *Haschish;* and those who are addicted to it are
called *Haschischin* and *Haschaschin*, " two expressions," says
De Sacy, " which explain why the Ismaelians have been called
by the historians of the Crusades, at one time *Assisini*, and
at another *Assassini;* so that instead of a " secret murderer,"
" assassin" implies, in point of fact, " an habitual drunkard."—
Quarterly Review, No. 48.

WHO WAS APOLLONIUS OF TYANA ?

He lived in the time of Domitian, embraced the doctrines
of Pythagoras, travelled far, both east and west, and greatly
sought to reform pagan worship.   Philostratus and others
relate of him many improbable wonders,—that he raised the
dead, rendered himself invisible, was seen at Rome and Puteoli
on the same day, and proclaimed at Ephesus the murder of
Domitian at the very instant of its perpetration at Rome. Dion
Cassius, the consular historian, vehemently asserts the last statement to be true ; but elsewhere he denounces Apollonius as a
cheat and impostor.

" WAS MAHOMET INSPIRED WITH A DOVE ?"

Shakspeare's King Henry VI. part i. act i. sc. 2.

Mahomet had a dove " which he used to feed with wheat
out of his ear, which dove when it was hungry lighted on
Mahomet's shoulder, and thrust its bill in to find its breakfast ;
Mahomet persuading the rude and simple Arabians that it was
the Holy Ghost."—*Raleigh's Hist. of the World*, part i. c. vi.

WHO WROTE " DE IMITATIONE CHRISTI ?"

The following reply is a condensed note from Brunet's
Manuel du Libraire, vol. ii. :

Who is the true author of the *Imitatio?* Two centuries of dispute
on this subject have not been able to inform us ; and more than one
hundred and twenty works, written to throw light on the question, have
only served to render the solution more difficult.

The more ancient testimonies appear favourable to Jean Gerson,
chancellor of the Church of Paris ; but, on the other hand, Thomas à
Kempis counts numerous partisans.   The defenders of these two competitors have triumphantly refuted those persons who have wished to
bring forward Jean Gerson, Abbé of Vercail, who lived in the thirteenth
century, as the author of the *Imitatio;* and after that, we cannot admit
this last candidate.

Such is moreover the opinion of Mr. Gence, an industrious scholar,
who has made a particular study of every thing which relates to this
subject, and who has published *Considerations on the Question relative
to the Author of the ' Imitation*,' at the end of the learned dissertation
of Mr. Barbier on the *Sixty French Translations of the Imitation.* Paris,
1812.

WAS BELISARIUS DEPRIVED OF HIS EYES, AND REDUCED TO BEG ITS BREAD?

In 563. a conspiracy was formed for the murder of Justinian. The conspirators were detected, torture was used to wring from them the names of their accomplices; and some domestics of Belisarius accused their master. He was ignominiously deprived of his guards and domestics; his fortunes were sequestered, and he was detained a close prisoner in his palace. The accused were tried in the following year, when sentence of death was executed on the greater number. The past services of Belisarius served to mitigate his fate; and, according to a frequent practice at the Byzantine court with eminent state prisoners, the decree of death was relaxed into one of blindness, and his eyes were accordingly put out. It was then that, restored to liberty, but deprived of all means of subsistence by the preceding confiscation of his property, Belisarius was reduced to beg his bread before the gates of the convent of Laurus. The platter of wood or earthenware which he held out for charity, and his exclamation, "Give a penny to Belisarius the general," remained for many years impressed on the people.

He was brought back, most probably, as a prisoner, to his former palace; a portion of his treasures was allotted for his use; and these circumstances may have given some colour for the assertion two or three centuries afterwards, of his having been restored to honours and to freedom.

Such is the statement of Lord Mahon, in his *Life of Belisarius*, wherein he has patiently investigated the various obscure and contradictory accounts, and thus stands the case. The mendicity of Belisarius is contradicted by one original writer of the ninth century, and asserted by two of the eleventh or twelfth. One of the latter was Tzetzes, the earliest writer extant who attested the mendicity and loss of sight of Belisarius; to which the researches of Lord Mahon have added the evidence of a writer in Banduri's *Imperium Orientale*, dedicated to the emperor Alexius Comnenus; this evidence is anonymous, but its testimony on other points is indisputable. Many eminent scholars concur in their belief of the blindness of Belisarius. Gibbon dissents, as does Alciat; but almost the only argument of the latter is,—Agathias and Procopius are silent upon the subject, whereas their histories conclude some years before the disgrace of Belisarius.

Various modern writers, such as Marmontel, in his romance of *Belisaire*, have given the story of the blindness a popular character, as have the works of Gerard, and other painters. In the Louvre is a statue from the Prince Borghese's collection at Rome; it clearly represents the act of begging, and till the middle of the last century was unanimously considered as Belisarius. But, by the aid of a passage in Suetonius, Winkleman supposes the figure to represent Augustus propitiating Nemesis. The statue has since been attributed to Chrisippus, and is at present inscribed Posidonius. Its attitude accords with Belisarius; but its skilful sculpture is not of his period.

MYSTERIOUS ROYAL DEATHS.

The mysterious deaths of Richard II. and Edward V. are remarkable instances of the difficulties of correctly writing medieval history. In the case of Richard II. we are certain of nothing, except that he is not alive now. On the 6th of October 1399, he was seen openly of men; on the 12th of March 1400, a corpse purporting to be his was shown at St. Paul's; but the countenance was displayed only, from the eyebrows to the chin; and the impression of the multitude was, that it was not their sovereign. We may think the motives and the agents of this deed so obvious as to set the matter at rest, but the people did not; and it is an instance of the state of public feeling at the time that they could not unhesitatingly believe in such an every-day occurrence as a murder. Edward V. and his brother disappear in a similar manner, with this additional mystery, that they are not only never seen, or supposed to be seen, dead, but that they, or persons supposed to be them, reappear alive. A circumstance very characteristic of these times is, that we have the most minute circumstances of these events, of which we know nothing at all. King Richard is carried to Pomfret Castle, where, as he held out a long while against starvation, Sir Piers Exton and seven assistants are sent to despatch him. The king defends himself bravely for twenty minutes, and destroys two of his assailants; but Sir Piers gets behind him on a step, and beats out his brains with a double-handed battle-axe. When the tomb of this "Stuart of the Plantagenets" was opened some time back, the skull was actually examined for a trace of the fatal wound, but in vain.

By some writers Richard is stated to have died of a broken heart; but this is a cause commonly attributed to mysterious deaths: the unfortunate captive is sure to expire from sorrow and despair at his miserable circumstances.

Now in the case of Richard and Edward, the latest edition of the latest history contains excursive arguments on each of these two questions, and will still be considered by many to leave the matter as it found it. But it was discovered that the excessive secrecy of villany defeated its own objects, and that a murder was profitless if the victim was believed to be still alive. Accordingly, in the case of Henry VI., we are relieved from this doubt; for his corpse was so exposed that no person could possibly deny his death. He was killed in the Tower by the duke of Gloucester, who crossed the Thames for that purpose in a small boat at two in the afternoon of Tuesday the 21st of May 1471. The weapon was a knife, and the wound was in the ribs. The exposure of the body appears to be the only reliable evidence of the death.

Thus the common law of England most reasonably declares that there can be no coroner's inquest on a murder without the production of the body, or its fragmentary representative; and the jury, to be quite sure that they have a real, and not an imaginary subject of investigation, proceed in a body to view the corpse. But no such equitable grace is accorded to the writer of medieval history.—*English Review*, No. 2.

WHO WAS ROBIN HOOD?

Great and long has been the discussion about Robin Hood, whether he was a myth or a real personage. A correspondent of *Notes and Queries*, No. 165, thus briefly sums up what, he shows, there are good grounds for inferring:

"1. The name of Robin Hood was no patronymic, but a purely descriptive name. 2. It was the name of the ideal personification of a class—the outlaws of former times. 3. Robin's fame had extended throughout England, Scotland, and France; and, so far as can at present be seen, it seems to have pertained equally to those three countries. 4. Though men of the name of Robin Hood have existed in England, that of itself would afford no ground for inferring that one of them was the Robin Hood of romantic tradition; but any pretence for such a supposition is taken away by the strong evidence, both Scotch and French, now adduced in support of the opposite view."

"A TALE OF A TUB."

During Sir Thomas More's chancellorship an attorney in his court, named Tubb, gave an account of a cause in which he was concerned, which the chancellor (who, with all his gentleness, loved a joke) thought so rambling and incoherent, that he said at the end of Tubb's speech, "'Tis a tale of a tub;" plainly showing that the phrase was then familiarly known. It is thought to have originated from some comparison of a rambling story to the practice of throwing "a tub to the whale."

In Sebastian Munster's *Cosmography* is a woodcut of a ship, to which a whale is coming too close for her safety, and the sailors are throwing "a tub to the whale," evidently to play with. The practice of throwing a tub or barrel to a large fish, to divert the huge animals from gambols dangerous to a vessel, is also mentioned in an old prose translation of the *Ship of Fools;* and this scene is one of the illustrations in the early editions of Swift's *Tale of a Tub.*

JOAN OF ARC.

Two French writers, MM. Renzie and Delepierre, have published ancient documents to prove that Joan of Arc, the Maid of Orleans, was living long after the period when she is said to have been burned by the English at Rouen. The martyrdom is a myth. According to history and poetry she was burned in 1431; but on the 1st of August 1439, the council of the city of

Rouen made her a gift of 210 livres, "for services rendered by her at the siege of the said city."

POPULAR ERRORS RESPECTING RICHARD III.

No other of the sovereigns in English history has been so vilified as Richard III. Walpole describes them as childish improbabilities, that place Richard's reign on a level with the story of "Jack the Giant-killer."

No record of Richard's time or reign affords any foundation for the mistakes, discrepancies, and falsifications, related of him, except John Rous, the recluse of Warwick, whose history, in Latin, of the kings of England was dedicated to Henry VII. Now, Rous was an avowed Lancastrian, and a bitter enemy of the line of York; and he simply alleges that Gloucester was "small of stature, having a short face, and uneven shoulders," which have been exaggerated into a crooked back.

Stow declared "that he could find no such deformity in King Richard III. as historians commonly relate;" and Stow, who was born forty years after Richard's death, had been told by some ancient men who had seen the king, that he was "of bodily shape comely enough, only of low stature."

"For the hump-backed and crooked form there is no adequate authority," says Sharon Turner.

Sir Thomas More is the acknowledged origin of the preparatory tales refuted by Stow, but revived and exaggerated by the Tudor chroniclers, and copied by Shakspeare, who has merely versified the language of those early historians who based their authority on More, who resided with Bishop Morton, the inveterate enemy of Gloucester.

Shakspeare follows Holinshed; so also does Hume; and Holinshed copies Hall, and Hall follows Polydore Vergil, who was not only a staunch Lancastrian, but was employed by Henry VII. to compile the history of his period.

Surtees has observed, that "the magic powers of Shakspeare have struck more terror to the soul of Richard than fifty Mores or Bacons armed in proof." "In the reign of King James I. the middling classes were familiarly acquainted with Shakspeare's plays, and referred to them for English history," says Coleridge; and the Great Duke of Marlborough, Lord Chatham, and Southey the poet laureate, acknowledged their principal acquaintance with English history to have been derived from Shakspeare's historical dramas.

Thus has the last monarch of the chivalrous Plantagenets been depicted unfaithfully to historical records; and "the Lancastrian partialities of Shakspeare, and a certain knack at embodying them, have turned history upside-down, or rather inside-out." (Sir W. Scott's *Rob Roy.*)

Sir George Buck was the first historian who attempted to defend Richard; and he has been followed by Horace Walpole, Lord Orford, in his *Historic Doubts.*

Granger says: "Mr. Walpole has brought various presumptive proofs, unknown to Buck, that Richard was neither that deformed person, nor that monster of cruelty and impiety, which he has been represented by our historians." (*Hist. England*, vol. I.)

Sir George Buck agrees with Philip de Comines, and with the Rolls of Parliament; and research of late years into our ancient records, state-papers, and parliamentary history, places Buck's history in a more credible light than could have been allowed to it some years since, and fixes both him and Lord Orford as higher authorities than those who wrote professedly to please the Tudor dynasty

Yet the prejudiced pen of Lord Bacon describes Richard as "a prince in military virtue approved, jealous of the honour of the English nation, and likewise a good law-maker for the ease and solace of the common people." His just and equitable laws (*Bacon*), his wise and useful statutes, his provident edicts, and bold enactments, have indeed been eulogised by the soundest lawyers (*Sharon Turner*), and called forth the admiration of the most profound politicians (*Buck*). "In no king's reign," said Sir Richard Baker, "were better laws made than in the reign of this man." And so sensible appears Lord Bacon to have been of the injustice done to Richard, that he says : " Even his virtues themselves were conceived to be feigned."

The Chronicles of Fleetwood, a Yorkist, and Warkworth, a Lancastrian, both within about the same period, exculpate Gloucester from the charge of the murder of Edward of Lancaster. "All the other narratives," says Mr. Bruce, in his introduction to *Fleetwood's Chronicle*, "either emanated from partisans of the adverse faction, or were written after the subsequent triumph of the House of Lancaster."

Proof, presumptive or circumstantial, has been adduced to fix the murder of Henry VI., or of his young heir, on the Duke of Gloucester.

The other heavy and fearful charges and dark deeds which have rendered the name of Richard so odious, are laboriously investigated in Halsted's *Richard III.*, 2 vols. 8vo., 1844.

WAS THE DUKE OF CLARENCE DROWNED IN MALMSEY ?

Foremost among the "childish improbabilities" of the time of Richard of Gloucester may be placed the popular report in Fabyan and Hall, that Clarence was drowned by Gloucester in a butt of malmsey wine, in the Tower of London, 18th February 1478. First, Sir Thomas More insinuates that Gloucester's efforts to save Clarence were fable; next Lord Bacon accuses him of contriving his brother's death ; and Shakspeare characterises him as the associate of the murderers ; while Sandford makes him the actual murderer. But no contemporary record exists of the drowning, or of Gloucester's participation in the execution. It is conjectured that Clarence was sentenced to be poisoned, and that the fatal drug may have been conveyed to him in "malvoesie," or malmsey, then a favourite wine. All that is positively known is simply that he was put to death "secretly within the Tower." (*Chronicle of Croyland.*)

Dr. Lingard says : " The manner of his death has never been ascertained ; but a silly report was circulated that he had been drowned in a butt of malmsey wine ;" which tale Bayley (*Hist. Tower*) thinks owes its origin to the duke's great partiality for that liquor. Hence

"Maudlin Clarence in a malmsey-butt."—*Lord Byron.*

THE BALLAD OF "THE BABES IN THE WOOD."

That the popular legend of "The Babes in the Wood,"— " one of the darling songs of the common people, and the delight of most English men in some part of their age" (*Addison*),—was a disguised recital of the reported murder of his young nephews by Richard III. can scarcely be doubted from the general resemblance of the ballad to Sir Thomas More's and Shakspeare's account of the dark deed. Throughout the tale there is a marked resemblance to several leading facts connected with Richard III. and his brother's children, as well as a singular coincidence between many expressions in the poetical legend and the historical details of the time. Among other evidence adduced in the Appendix to Halsted's *Life of Richard III.* is that of a rude representation of a stag surmounting the black-letter copy of the ballad at Cambridge; a *hind*, or female stag, being the badge of the unfortunate Edward V. Again, the tale corresponds essentially with the chroniclers; and its moral altogether closely resembles the reflections with which Fabyan, Grafton, Hall, and Holinshed terminate their relation of the event.

JANE SHORE, HER TRUE HISTORY.

Neither of our writers gives the name of this memorable woman's parents. Sir Thomas More says: " what her father's name was, or where she was born, is not certainly known." But both Sir Thomas More and Stow tell us that she was born in London. She was married, "somewhat too soon," to William Shore, goldsmith and banker, of Lombard Street, it is thought at the age of sixteen or seventeen years. She lived with Shore seven years; and about 1470 she became concubine to king Edward IV., "the most beautiful man of his time." In his resplendent court she delighted all by her beauty, pleasant behaviour, and proper wit; for she could "read well and write," which few of the highest ladies then could. Edward died in 1482; and within two months Jane was accused by Gloucester, the usurper, of sorcery and witchcraft, who caused her to be deprived of the whole of her property, about 3000 marks, a sum now equal to about 20,000*l.*; she was then committed to the Tower, but was acquitted for want of proof of sorcery. She was next committed by the sheriffs to Ludgate prison, charged with having been the concubine of Hastings; for which she walked in penance from the cathedral to St. Paul's Cross, with a taper in her hand, wearing only her kirtle, or petticoat, in London streets; and then again committed to Ludgate, where she was kept close prisoner. Meanwhile, Lynom, the king's solicitor, would have married Jane but for the interference of king Richard. After his death at Bosworth, Jane was liberated from Ludgate. She never married again, nor was her property restored to her. There is a tradition that she strewed flowers at the funeral of Henry VII. Calamitous was the rest of her life, and she died in 1533 or 1534, when more than fourscore years old; and no stone tells where her remains were deposited. Sir Thomas More says of her penury and good deeds: "At this day she beggeth of many at this day living, that at this day had begged if she had not been." For almost half a century Jane Shore was a living monitress to avoid illicit love, however fascinating; and the biographer, poet, and historian, made her so for nearly three centuries after her death.

Thomas Churchyard, who died in 1604, wrote a poem showing "How Shore's wife, King Edward the Fourth's concubine, was by King Richard despoyled of all her goods, and forced to doe open penance." Dr. Percy, in his *Reliques*, prints a ballad from a black-letter copy in the Pepys Collection. It is entitled "The Woefull Lamentation of Jane Shore, a goldsmith's wife in London, some time King Edward IV. his Concubine. To the tune of 'Live with me,' &c." Here the poet makes Jane die of hunger after doing her penance, and a man be hanged for relieving her; both of which are fictions, that led to the popular error of Jane's dying of hunger in a ditch, and thus giving its name to Shoreditch, now proved to have been named after Sir John Shoreditch, lord of a manor called Shoreditch, long before Jane was born.

THE RED AND WHITE ROSES.

The precise period at which the Red and White Roses were adopted as hostile emblems in the divided house of Plantagenet has never been satisfactorily ascertained; but a contemporaneous Ms. in the Bodleian Library at Oxford proves that the white rose was an hereditary cognisance of the house of York, and borne as such by the duke when he inherited the title. Camden states that the Lancastrians derived the badge of the red rose from their ancestor, Edmund, first earl of Lancaster, "on whose person," says Sanford, "was originally founded the great contention betwixt the two royal houses of Lancaster and York." Again, Camden, in his *Remains*, asserts that "Edmund Crouch-backe, second son of Henry III., used a red rose, wherewith his tomb at Westminster is adorned." Also that "John of Gaunt, fifth duke of Lancaster, took a red rose to his device, as it were, by right of his first wife, the heiress of Lancaster, grandchild to the above-named Edmund Crouch-backe;" and that "Edmund of Langley, duke of York, his younger

brother, adopted as his emblem the white rose."*—Note to
Halsted's *Richard III.*

OTWAY'S "VENICE PRESERVED."

The Spanish conspiracy of Ossuma, Bedmar, and Toledo,
against Venice, in 1618, is amongst the most interesting of
such events: first, as furnishing, through the elegant work
of St. Real, the materials for the best of Otway's dramas,
Venice Preserved; and, secondly, as presenting some historical
problems on which the learning and ingenuity of modern
writers have been abundantly exercised, and in regard to
which the disputants have arrived at the most opposite con-
clusions. Two learned and ingenious authors,—the Prussian
diplomatist, Chambrier, a member of the Academy of Berlin,
in his Essay *Sur les Problémes Historiques;* and Count Daru, in
his *History of Venice,*—have actually denied entirely the existence of any Spanish conspiracy against Venice; while the latter
even represents Venice as truly the conspirator against Spain.—
Quarterly Review, 1837.

"WHITTINGTON AND HIS CAT."

The fable of the Cat is probably borrowed from the East.
Sir William Gore Ouseley, in his *Travels,* relates, on the authority of a Persian Ms., that, in the tenth century, one Keis,
the son of a poor widow in Siráf, embarked for India, with his
sole property, a cat.

"There he fortunately arrived at a time when the palace was so infested by mice or rats that they invaded the king's food, and persons
were employed to drive them from the royal banquet. Keis produced
his cat; the noxious animals soon disappeared; and magnificent rewards were bestowed on the adventurer of Siráf, who returned to that
city, and afterwards, with his mother and brothers, settled in the
island; which, from him, has been denominated A'sis, or, according to
the Persian, *Keish.*"†

WAS WOLSEY A BUTCHER'S SON?

The rumour formerly ran undisturbed, that Wolsey was the
son of a butcher; but his faithful biographer, Cavendish, says
nothing of Wolsey's father being in trade. He tells us that
he was "an honest poor man." A rare tract, entitled *Who was*

---

* Among the Harleian Mss. is an original document containing the names
of the slain in the desperate battles between the Houses of York and Lancaster
in fifty-four years, numbering 8 kings, 12 dukes, 1 marquis, 17 earls, 1 viscount,
and 24 barons.
† The "Cat" is believed to have been a ship formerly known as the *catta,* or
the collier, which is to this day called a cat; and Whittington, there is reason
to credit, amassed much of his wealth by bringing coal into the Thames, by
privilege, in face of the prohibitory statute. Still this does not explain that
part of Whittington's story of which Sir Gore Ouseley relates the above parallel.
—See the Reviewer's observations upon "Catts," in the *Athenæum,* No. 1528.

Cardinal Wolsey? (in the collection of the Duke of Devonshire) states that Wolsey was born at Long Melford, *near Ipswich*, (not at Ipswich, as generally stated), at which place his father was a butcher.

Steevens considers the term "keech" has a peculiar application to Wolsey as the son of a butcher:

> "I wonder
> That such a *keech* can with his very bulk
> Take up the rays o' the beneficial sun."
>
> *King Henry VIII.*, act i. so. 1.

But, Falstaff, in *Henry IV.* (part i.) is called by Prince Henry "a greasy tallow keech." A "keech" is a lump of fat; and it appears to us that Buckingham, in the first-quoted passage, denounces Wolsey, not as a butcher's son, but as an overgrown bloated favourite, that

> "Can with his very *bulk*
> Take up the rays o' the beneficial sun."

WHAT BECAME OF THE HEADS OF BISHOP FISHER AND SIR THOMAS MORE.

Fisher, Bishop of Rochester, and Sir Thomas More, were two of the most eminent persons who were executed for not acknowledging King Henry VIII. as supreme head of the Church of England. Bishop Fisher was executed on St. Alban's Day, the 22d of June 1535, about ten in the morning; and his head was to have been erected upon Traitors' Gate, London Bridge, the same night: but that it was delayed, to be exhibited to Queen Anne Boleyn. We gather these particulars from a curious duodecimo, written by Hall, but attributed to Dr. Thomas Baily, 1665, who further relates:

"'The next day after his burying, the head, being parboyled, was pricked upon a pole, and set on high upon London Bridge, among the rest of the holy Carthusians' heads that suffered death lately before him. And here I cannot omit to declare unto you the miraculous sight of this head, which, after it had stood up the space of fourteen dayes upon the bridge, could not be perceived to wast nor consume: neither for the weather, which was then very hot, neither for the parboyling in hot water, but grew dayly fresher and fresher, so that in his lifetime he never looked so well; for his cheeks being beautified with a comely red, the face looked as though it had beholden the people passing by, and would have spoken to them; which many took for a miracle that Almighty God was pleased to shew above the course of nature in thus preserving the fresh and lively colour in his face, surpassing the colour he had being alive, whereby was noted to the world the innocence and holiness of this blessed father that thus innocently was content to lose his head in defence of his Mother the Holy Catholique Church of Christ. Wherefore the people coming daily to see this strange sight, the passage over the Bridge was so stopped with their going and coming, that almost neither cart nor horse could passe; and therefore at the end of fourteen dales the executioner was commanded to throw downe the head, in the night-time, into the River of Thames; and in the place thereof was set the head of the most blessed and constant martyr Sir Thomas More, his companion and fellow in all his troubles, who suffered his passion" on Tuesday "the 6th of July next following, about nine o'clock in the morning."

The bodies of Fisher and More were buried in the chapel of St. Peter in the Tower; the head of More, says his greatgrandson, in his Life of him, printed in 1726,

"Was pott upon London Bridge, where as trayters' heads are sett vpon poles; and haning remained some moneths there, being to be cast into the Thames, because roome should be made for diuerse others, who in plentiful sorte suffered martyrdome for the same supremacie, shortly after it was bought by his daughter Margarett, least,—as she stoutly affirmed before the councell, being called before them for the same matter,—it should be foode for fishes; which she buried where she thought fittest. It was very well to be knowen, as well by the lluelle fauour of him, which was not all this while in anie thing almost diminished, as also by reason of one tooth which he wanted whilst he liued: heroin it was to be admired, that the hayres of his head being almost gray before his martyrdome, they seemed now, as it were, readish or yellow."

The chancellor's pious daughter is said to have preserved this relic in a leaden case, and to have ordered its interment, with her own body, in the Roper vault, under a chapel adjoining St. Dunstan's, Canterbury, where it was seen in the year 1715, and again subsequently.

THE TRUE ROMANCE OF "KENILWORTH."

The unfortunate Anne Dudley (for so she subscribes herself in the Harleian Ms., 4712), the first wife of Lord Robert Dudley, Queen Elizabeth's favourite, and, after Anne's death, Earl of Leicester, was daughter of Sir John Robsart. Her marriage took place June 4, 1550, the day following that on which her lord's eldest brother had been united to a daughter of the Duke of Somerset; and the event is thus recorded by King Edward, in his Diary: "4. S. Robert dudeley, third sonne to th' erle of warwic, married S. John Robsartes daughter; after which mariage ther were certain gentlemen that did strive who should first take away a gose's heade wich was hanged alive on tow cross postes." Soon after the accession of Elizabeth, when Dudley's ambitious views of a royal alliance had opened upon him, his countess mysteriously died at the retired mansion of Cumnor, near Abingdon, Sept. 8, 1560; and although the mode of her death is imperfectly ascertained (her body was thrown downstairs as a blind), there appears far greater foundation for supposing the earl guilty of her murder than usually belongs to such rumours; all her other attendants being absent at Abingdon fair, except Sir Richard Verney and his man. The circumstances, distorted by gross anachronisms, have been woven by Sir Walter Scott into his delightful romance of *Kenilworth.*

Of the gose and poste, this explanation has been suggested : the gose was intended for poor Amy, and the cross-poste for the Protector Somerset and his rival, Dudley Duke of Northumberland, both of whom were bred to the wicked trade of ambition. It is plain that the people had a very suspicious opinion of Leicester. His general mode of murder was by poison ; and it is said that he so perished himself.

THE RING SENT BY QUEEN ELIZABETH TO THE EARL OF ESSEX.

The story of the Ring said to have been sent by Lord Essex to Queen Elizabeth through the Countess of Nottingham, has been much discussed by historical writers.

There are two versions of the anecdote. The principal facts are the same in each—that the queen had given a ring to Essex, which was to serve him in time of need ; that he employed the Countess of Nottingham to transmit it to the queen ; that she consulted her husband, who forbade her to do so ; and that on her deathbed she made a full confession to the queen of all the facts, alleging her husband's prohibition as her excuse. The whole of the evidence in support of the above is the mention of it in Osborn's *Memoirs of Queen Elizabeth,* published fifty-five years after her death ; the subsequent narration of it in M. de Maurier's Memoirs ; Lord Clarendon's authority to confirm the fact that "such a loose report had crept into discourse ;" and the narrative of Lady Elizabeth Spelman, the great granddaughter of the Earl of Monmouth, and the great-great niece of the Countess of Nottingham. On the other hand, there is no contemporaneous account of the kind in either of the three detailed accounts of the queen's last illness ; and that by the Earl of Monmouth, an eye-witness, shows that so far from any thing having occurred to disturb the queen's friendly relations with Lord Nottingham, he was actually sent for as the only person whose influence would be sufficiently powerful to induce her to obey her physicians.

Now, whatever might be the supposed indignation of Elizabeth against her dying cousin, Lady Nottingham, it is clear that as the real offender was Lord Nottingham, he would naturally have more than shared in her displeasure ; and it is very improbable that a fortnight after the queen had shaken the helpless wife on her deathbed, the husband, by whose authority the offence was committed, should have continued in undiminished favour. The existence of the ring would do but little to establish the truth of the story, even if but one had been preserved and cherished as the identical ring ; but as there are two, if not three, which lay claim to that distinction, they invalidate each other's claims. One is preserved at Hawnes in Bedfordshire, the seat of the Rev. Lord John Thynne ; another is the property of C. W. Warren, Esq. ; and we believe the third is deposited for safety at Messrs. Drummonds' bank. The ring at Hawnes is said to have descended in unbroken succession from Lady Frances Devereux (afterwards Duchess of Somerset) to the present owner. The stone in this ring is a sardonyx, on which is cut in relief a head of Elizabeth, the execution of which is of a high order. That the ring has descended from Lady Frances Devereux affords the strongest presumptive evidence that it was not *the* ring. According to the tradition, it had passed from her father into Lady Nottingham's hands. According to Lady Elizabeth Spelman, Lord Nottingham insisted upon her keeping it. In her interview with tho queen, the countess might be supposed to have presented to her the token she had so fatally withheld; or it might have remained in her family, or have been destroyed; but the most improbable circumstance would have been its restoration to the widow or daughter of the much-injured Essex by the offending Earl of Nottingham. The Duchess of Somerset left a "long, curious, and minute will, and in it there is no mention of any such ring." If there is good evidence for believing that the curious ring at Hawnes was ever in the possession of the Earl of Essex, one might be tempted to suppose that it was the likeness of the queen, to which he alludes in his letters as his "fair angel," written from Portland Road, and at the time of his disgrace, after the proceedings in the Star-Chamber, and when still under restraint at Essex House.

Had Essex at this time possessed any ring or token which by presenting would have entitled him to a restoration to favour, it seems most improbable that he should have kept it back, and yet attended to this likeness of the queen, whose gracious eyes encouraged him to be a petitioner for himself. The whole tone of the letter is, in fact, almost conclusive against the possibility of his having in his possession any gift of hers endowed with such rights as that of the ring which the Countess of Nottingham is supposed to have withheld.—*Abridged from the Edinburgh Review*, No. 200.

LILLY THE ASTROLOGER

is the Sidrophel of *Hudibras.* He was consulted by the Royalists, with the king's privity, whether the king should escape from Hampton Court, whether he should sign the propositions of Parliament, &c.; and had twenty pounds for his opinion. Till Charles's affairs declined, he was a cavalier; but after 1645 he engaged body and soul in the cause of the Parliament. Late in life he practised medicine at Hersham, in the parish of Walton-upon-Thames; but probably the most profitable trade of Dee, Kelly, and Lilly, and others of that class, was that of spies, which they were for any country or party that employed them.

LILLY FORETELS THE GREAT PLAGUE AND FIRE OF LONDON.

While this impudent cheat is ridiculed for his absurdities, let him have credit for as lucky a guess as ever blessed the pages even of "Francis Moore, physician." In his "Astrological Predictions for 1648" occurs the following passage, in which we must needs allow that he attained to something like prophetic strain, when we call to mind that the Great Plague of London occurred in 1665, and the Great Fire in the year following:

"In the year 1656 the aphelium of Mars, who is the generall signification of England, will be in Virgo, which is assuredly the ascendant of the English monarchy, but Aries of the kingdom. When this absis, therefore, of Mars shall appear in Virgo, who shall expect less than a strange *catastrophe* of human affairs in the commonwealth, monarchy, and kingdom of England ! There will then, either in or about these times, or near that year, *or within ten years more or less of that time*, appear in this kingdom so strange a revolution of fate, *so grand a catastrophe* and great mutation unto this monarchy and government, as never yet appeared ; of which, as the times now stand, I have no liberty or encouragement to deliver my opinion,—only, *it will be ominous to London, unto her merchants at sea, to her traffique at land, to her poor, to her rich, to all sorts of people inhabiting in her or her liberties,* BY REASON OF SUNDRY FIRES AND A CONSUMING PLAGUE."

This is the prediction which, in 1666, led to Lilly's being examined by a committee of the House of Commons, not, as has been supposed, that he might " discover by the stars who were the authors of the Fire of London," but because the precision with which he was thought to have foretold the event gave birth to a suspicion that he was already acquainted with them, and privy to the (supposed) machinations which had brought about the catastrophe. Curran says there are two kinds of prophets—those who are really inspired, and those who prophesy events which they intend themselves to bring about. Upon this occasion Lilly had the ill luck to be deemed one of the latter class.

THE POISONING OF SIR THOMAS OVERBURY.

In the rare book, *Truth brought to Light by Time,* we read that Overbury was poisoned with aquafortis, white arsenic, mercury, powder of diamonds, lapis cortilus, great spiders, and cantharides,—whatever was, or was believed to be, most deadly, " to be sure to hit his complexion." The murder was perpetrated with fiendish perseverance. It appeared upon the trials that arsenic was always mixed with his salt. Once he desired pig for dinner, and Mrs. Turner put into it lapis cortilus; at another time he had two partridges sent him from the court, and water and onions being the sauce, Mrs. Turner put in cantharides instead of pepper; so that whatever he took was poisoned.

Overbury made his brags that he had won for Somerset the love of his lady by his letters and industry. . . . " To speak plainly," says Bacon, in arraigning Somerset, "Overbury had little that was solid for religion or moral virtue, but was wholly possest with ambition and vain-glory. . . . He was naught and corrupt ; . . a man of unbounded and impudent spirit."

Mrs. Turner's execution affected the fashions. Her sentence was, *to be hang'd at Tiburn in her yellow Tiffiny Ruff and Cuff, being she was the first inventer and wearer of that horrid garb;* never since which was ever any seen to wear the like.

" Sir Jervas Yelvis also was executed in full dress, hee being arrayed in a black suit, and black jerkin with hanging sleeves (aptly worn on the occasion), having on his head a crimson sattin cap, laced from the top downward and round about; under that a white linnen nightcap with a border, and over that a black hat with a broad rybon and ruffe-band, thick

couched with a lace, and a pair of skie-coloured silk stockings,
and a pair of three-soaled shoes."

WHO WAS THE MAN IN THE IRON MASK?

In the reign of Louis XIV. an unknown prisoner, of noble
mien, was sent in profound secrecy to an island on the coast
of Provence. The captive wore while travelling a mask said
to have been of iron; a strict order having been given that if
he disclosed his features, he should instantly be put to death.
The king's minister, Louvois, visited him, spoke to him while
standing, treating him with the greatest respect. From Pigno-
rol he was removed to other prisons, the same governor accom-
panying him; ultimately to the Bastille in Paris. Here he
was treated with the same consideration; and the governor
seldom sat down in his presence. He played the guitar, and
dressed sumptuously. The same secrecy was preserved; even
the physician who attended him never saw his face. No com-
plaint ever escaped him, nor did he attempt to make himself
known. He died in 1703, after twenty-four years' imprisonment, and was buried at night. The war-minister who succeeded Louvois was entreated, even on his death-bed, by his
son-in-law to explain the mystery of "the Man in the Iron
Mask;" but he replied, it was a solemn secret of state which
he had sworn never to reveal.

Various surmises have arisen respecting the name and station of the
masked prisoner. At one time he was Fouquet, the disgraced minister
of finance; at another, an Armenian patriarch. Some persons were sure
it was Louis Comte de Vermandois, son of Louis XIV. and Mdlle. de la
Vallière, though he was said to have died and been buried in 1683.
Others declared the person to be the Duc de Beaufort, who, however,
had to all appearance been slain and beheaded by the Turks, at the
siege of Candia. Next, he was imagined to be the Duke of Monmouth,
whom the Londoners, if their eyes had not deceived them, saw executed
on Tower Hill in 1685. But the opinion for some time generally received
was, that he was a son of Anne, mother of Louis XIV.; and it was at
one time boldly asserted that he was a twin-brother of that monarch.

Amidst these various notions, the following existed, but until 1825
obtained little credit: that "the Man in the Iron Mask" was Count
Ercole Antonio Matthioli, a senator of Mantua, a private agent of
Ferdinand Charles Duke of Mantua, and that he suffered this long and
strange imprisonment for having deceived and disappointed Louis XIV.
in a secret treaty for the purchase of the fortress of Casal, the key of
Italy; the agents of Spain and Austria having offered him a higher
bribe. Yet their infamous scheme could not have been brought to light
without exposing the shame of all the principals concerned.

The truth of this latter statement was proved beyond any
reasonable doubt in 1826, by the publication of "The True
History of the State Prisoner commonly called the Iron Mask,
extracted from documents in the French Archives, by the
Hon. George Agar Ellis." In this work it is established that

immediately after Louis perceived that he had been duped, Matthioli was arrested by the king's order. Though armed, he offered no resistance, but was carried that night to Pignerol; the leader of the party alone knowing the prisoner, whom, for better concealment, he named L'Estang. During his confinement at Pignerol his mind began to wander; when he was placed in the same room with an insane Jacobin monk. In 1681 the count and his companion were removed in a litter, and under military escort, to Exiles, a few leagues from Pignerol. Here the monk died; and in 1687 St. Mars, the custodian, who had removed with his charge to the Isle of St. Marguerite, reported of *one prisoner only*, whom we are warranted in concluding was Matthioli, *the man in the iron mask*. During his removal hither, he is thought to have been first compelled to wear a mask to hide his features, *not, as has been erroneously stated, a mask made of iron*, which could not have been borne upon the face for any long continuance of time, but one of black velvet, strengthened with whalebone and fastened behind the head with a padlock, and further secured by a seal, which did not prevent the prisoner from eating and drinking, or impede his respiration. At St. Marguerite he passed eleven years, and was described by Voltaire as richly dressed, supplied with laces from Paris, served at table with silver-plate, wearing a mask of iron, and plucking out the hairs of his beard with steel pincers,—all which were gross exaggerations. In 1698 St. Mars removed with his prisoner to the Bastille. Matthioli travelled in a litter; and when St. Mars halted near his own estate of Pulteau, the unknown was seen in a black mask,—a circumstance talked of in the neighbourhood until our time. The peasants observed that his teeth and lips were seen, that he was tall, and had gray hair. His imprisonment extended to twenty-four and a half years, according to the horrible order issued by Louis, "that he should have nothing which could make life agreeable." He died in November 1703, being then sixty-three years of age; although the register of his burial states him as "*Marchiali, aged about forty-five years*." But persons who died in the Bastille were frequently interred under false names and ages; and Louis and the Duke of Mantua were still alive. On the decease of the prisoner, his keepers scraped and whitewashed his prison-walls; the doors and window-frames were burnt; and all the metal vessels, whether of copper, pewter, or silver, which had been used in his service were melted down. When the records of the Bastille were made public in 1789, the register was searched in vain for any thing that would throw light on this affair: the leaf of the register which contained it had been carefully removed. Such is the true story of the Iron Mask.

The lovers of romance who still wish to know more of the magnificent conjectures of former days are referred to Voltaire, Dutens, St. Fois, La Grange Chancel, Gibbon, the Père Griffet, the Chevalier de Taulès, and Mr. Quintin Craufurd. Of these accounts perhaps Voltaire's is the least curious,* and Mr. Craufurd's the most so; because the first did not seek for truth, but only wished to invent a moving tale; while the latter was most anxious to arrive at the truth, and had all the advantages of his researches of the former writers upon the same subject.—*O. Agar Ellis.*

WHEN WAS THE POTATO INTRODUCED INTO IRELAND?

History dates the introduction of the Potato into the British Isles at about 1586; and Youghal, in the south of Ireland, the residence of its introducer, Sir Walter Raleigh, is named as the spot whereon it was first cultivated, about or prior to the year 1602; from which locality it subsequently spread over the country. As the estates of Raleigh passed to the Boyle family in 1602, the potato must have been planted before that period. Clusius, the botanist of Leyden, who wrote in 1586, says the potato was cultivated in Italy prior to that date; and Cuvier denied that Europe derived the potato from Virginia. The researches of Banks also favour this conclusion; and he states that Coccius, in his *Chronicle*, printed in 1553, mentions potatoes under the term *papas.* Herriott, who accompanied Raleigh's expedition to Virginia, described them under the name of *openawk.* In Irish, they are still variously called *potatos, praten,* or *phottie,* mere Hibernicisms of the English word potato. Sir Robert Southwell, President of the Royal Society, stated, at one of its meetings in 1693, that potatoes had been introduced into Ireland by his grandfather, who first had them of Sir Walter Raleigh.

But at what time the potato became a staple article of the food of the Irish people is neither clear. It was first grown in gardens as a rarity, used at table as a delicacy, and described by herbalists as an introduced exotic (Gerard mentions it in 1597); but it is not believed to have been cultivated by the people as a general article of food until the end of the 17th or the beginning of the 18th century. In 1662 it was proposed to the Royal Society to prevent "famine by dispersing potatoes throughout all parts of England," which proposition is

* Voltaire strove to heighten the mystery by stating that no person of consequence had disappeared unaccounted for during the period above named.— Among the attempts made to revive the mystery, is the statement of Desodoard, in his *History of the French Revolution,* that among the documents found in the Bastille was a card numbered 64 389,000, and bearing these words, "Foucquet, from the Isle of St. Marguerite, with a *Mask of Iron;*" then "XXX," and underneath "Kernadurin." Desodoard had seen this card in the hands of those who had found it: there is evidence that Foucquet was confined at l'Ignerni, whence he escaped; and it is by Desodoard thought that he may have been retaken, and then imprisoned at St. Marguerite; he was brought to the Bastille in 1691. At the close of 1850 fresh evidence was stated to be in the possession of a person in the subalpine town of Pinerolo.

noticed in Evelyn's *Sylva*. In 1663, Mr. Boyle read to the Royal Society a letter from his gardener at Youghal (the cradle of the potato), in which he describes this esculent as "very good to pickle for winter salads, and also to preserve;" but this paper shows that the potato had not then become an article of common food amongst the Irish, even around the locality where it was first cultivated. Yet, Sir W. Petty, in 1672, speaks of it as their food; D'Urfey, in his *Irish Hudibras*, in 1689; and after the arrival of William III., the natives are said to have been prevented enjoying their "beniclabber (thick milk) and pottadoes." John Dunton, in his *Conversation in Ireland*, 1699, describes the Irish cabin, with ground behind it "full of their dearly-beloved potatoes;" and a dish of potatoes boiled in their general entertainment; while, in the Keens of that day, allusion is made to the "pigs and potato-garden." The potato was introduced from Ireland into Lancashire about 1633, and that was the first district in which it was extensively cultivated.—Abridged from the *Census of Ireland*, 1851.

JOHN O' GROAT'S HOUSE.

The only visible remains of the celebrated John o' Groat's house are the still-reputed foundations of a cottage, erroneously supposed to have been the most northerly dwelling on the mainland of Scotland. "John Groat" still appears inscribed on the fishing-boats: a corruption of John de Groot, the name of a Dutchman who, it is said, settled here about the reign of James I., and immortalised himself by settling a dispute among his nine sons respecting the point of precedence, by opening as many doors in his house, assigning one to each, by which means they passed in and out without mutual molestation. His name has been bequeathed to the cowries, called John o' Groat's buckies, which cover the beach.

PAPYRUS.

Pliny is in error in saying that papyrus was not used for paper before the time of Alexander the Great; for papyri of the most remote Pharaonic period are found with the same mode of writing as that of the age of Cheops. (*Wilkinson*, vol. iii. p. 50.) A papyrus now in Europe, of the date of Cheops, establishes the early use of written documents, and the antiquity of paper made of the byblus long before the time of Abraham. As papyrus was expensive, few documents of that material are found, and these are generally rituals, sales of estates, and official papers. Papyrus was used until about the seventh century of our era. A soldier's leave of absence has been discovered written upon a piece of broken earthenware.— *Dr. Kitto's Cyclopædia of Biblical Literature.*

Miscellanea.

ORIGIN OF THE NAME JESUIT.

WHEN the little band of the first followers of Don Ignatius de Loyola, the founder of "the Great Order," were deliberating what answer they should return to those who were continually questioning them as to their calling and their institute, Ignatius (says Orlandinus), afraid that, in imitation of the Dominicans, the Benedictines, the Franciscans, and many other religious societies thus attacked, his devoted companions would adopt their founder's name as their designation, begged them to leave in his hands the decision of the point. They complied, unaware, perhaps, of the humility which dictated the request; and Ignatius, ever full of military ideas, said: "As our general is no other than Jesus Christ; as His cross is our standard; His law, even in its counsels, our rule; His name our chief consolation and our only hope,—let us tell men the simple truth—that we are the little battalion of Jesus Christ." Such is the origin of the title, "Society of Jesus," which has been vulgarised into the shorter and more *portable* name of Jesuits.

Few men are aware what a proportion of the illustrious characters of the last three hundred years have been the pupils of the Jesuits. Buffon, Bossuet, Condé, Massillon, represent distinct classes of great men, and stand almost at the head of those classes. They were pupils of the Jesuits. Voltaire was a pupil of the Jesuits. His irreligion he certainly did *not* get among them, and his talents came from God; but the most remarkable feature of his literary character bears the impress of the Jesuit education, which that too celebrated man enjoyed and abused, and turned at once against the Jesuits and against his Maker.— Miles Gerald Keon, in the *Oxford and Cambridge Review.*

THE PROPAGANDA COLLEGE AT ROME,

which dates from the beginning of the seventeenth century, is founded upon the most comprehensive plan ever yet devised for any purpose, in any age or country. Its object is to educate young men of every complexion, natives of every habitable part of the globe, for the service of the altar, and the propagation of the Roman Catholic faith in their own language and amongst their own countrymen. Accordingly, professors direct the studies of these youths through the medium, not only of Latin, the common language of the college, but also of the native tongue of each: and hence the extraordinary circumstance of upwards of forty different languages spoken within its walls;

amongst which are the Hebrew, the ancient and modern Chaldean, the Samaritan, Syriac, Arabic, modern and ancient Armenian, Persian, Turkish, Kourdish, ancient and modern Greek, Latin, Italian, Maltese, Coptic, Ethiopian, various African dialects, three different dialects of Chinese, other dialects of Asia and India, comprising Hindustani, Pegu, Georgian, &c.; and the various languages of Europe, such as the Irish and other branches of the Celtic tongue, the German, Dutch, English, French, Spanish, Portuguese, Polish, Bulgarian, &c.

ANCIENT USE OF RINGS.

The various uses of Rings in early ages are associated with many interesting incidents.

Both the Pagan and Christian world seem to have used the *House-keeper's Sigillum*, or Seal-ring, for securing the household stuff and other property. Xenophon, in his *Economics*, states that Greek matrons had this power of sealing up, or placing the seal upon, the house-goods; and, at Rome, Cicero's mother—a model housekeeper, as her two sons attest—was accustomed to enhance to consumers the merits of some poor thin wine, *vile Sabinum*, by affixing to each amphora her official signet. Again, the stingy masters of some Roman households not only sealed up pantry, safe, and cellar, but all the broken victuals of the house. Now, with the Roman slaves, had only valuables been under the custody of the seal, households might have lived in peace; but when all food was thus put out of reach, the consequences were such as might have been expected. Slaves watched their opportunity, and helped themselves. "Seal as we will," says Pliny, "it shall be of no avail; so easy is it to pluck rings from the masters' fingers when drunk, oppressed with sleep, or dying;" and this misdemeanour the famished slaves made no scruple of committing whenever an opportunity presented itself.

Contract-rings were used for sealing covenants; and *Pronubal*, or *Pledge-rings*, passed between the contracting parties in marriages. When the marriage settlement had been properly sealed, rings bearing the names of the newly-married couple were handed round to the guests. Plutarch thus alludes to this custom: "When Cinna was overtaken in his flight by a petty officer, who fell upon him sword in hand, he flung himself upon his knees, and drawing off a costly ring, presented it to the enemy, praying for life; but his pursuer, haughtily telling him that his business there was not to seal a marriage settlement, but to put an execrable tyrant to death, despatched him on the spot."

Among the relics in the cathedral of Perugia is one affirmed to be the very ring of espousals which St. Joseph gave to the Virgin Mary. The Talmud having announced that such a fiancial pledge had passed between them, the Church of Rome asserted this to be the ring. It is made of one whole stone, green jaspor or a plasma, hollowed out, and itself forming both hoop and bezil, unalloyed with any metal. The device intaglioed on it is supposed to be flowers bursting from the bud.

The Christian pledge-ring was, if possible, held in still greater veneration than its pagan predecessor; and before the Council of Trent matrimonial alliances might be legally contracted without sacerdotal assistance, from the benediction bestowed on it by the priest.

Rings were presented on birthdays; and Photius relates, that a man having become tired of his wife presented her with a ring of divorce.

Lot-rings were the means of settling priority among soldiers in Homer's day. Plutarch relates, that when Timoleon's were about to rush across the river Damyrina, in Sicily, the general, seeing the danger, bade the soldiers to throw their rings into a helmet, and draw lots for the precedence; when the first ring drawn bore an intaglioed military trophy; which so excited the troops that they, in a body, forded the river, routed the enemy, and took many stands of arms, and slew a thousand of them.

The ring was sometimes placed on the lips of a chatterbox, as an intimation to hold his tongue. Thus, when Hephæstion had peeped into a "private and confidential" note from Olympias to her son, Alexander, fearing lest he should divulge the contents, drew off his signet, and placing it on Hephæstion's lips, enjoined on him to hold his tongue.

Rings were often indicative of station, craft, or calling. Magistrates adopted an official ring. Physicians wore them from the time of Hippocrates. Lawyers would not undertake a brief without a sardonyx on finger. Ancient musicians wore countless costly rings on both hands; and conjurors had their ring, through which, amongst other feats, they drew an egg, prepared for the purpose by long maceration in vinegar.

A ring may vaticinate future events. Æsop was present at a public assembly of the Samians, when an eagle, which had been some time hovering in the sky, making a sudden swoop, pounced upon the "great seal," and bearing it aloft, let it drop into the bosom of a slave; when Æsop, turning soothsayer, exclaimed: "Learn, O Samians, that since the eagle, who is the king of birds, has carried off the royal signet, and deposited it in the mantle of a slave, you may certainly infer that there are some here among you who will, if they can, abolish your existing laws, and reduce your king to slavery."

The possession of certain rings has been the cause of a war. Cæpio and Drusus fell out (says Pliny) in bidding for a costly ring sold by auction; and when it was knocked down to one, each hated the other from that day; and this trifling feud at length involved the state in the miseries of a civil war. Another ring, in more modern days, set two Indian potentates fighting; and for twenty years deluged the kingdoms of Aracan and Pegu in blood. Verres is charged by Cicero with stripping off people's rings when he took a fancy to them. Marc Antony outlawed Nonius in the hope of getting possession of a hazel-sized opal ring valued at 20,000 sesterces; but Nonius carried it with him into exile, and would not part with it. And Sylla and Marius quarrelled about wearing a ring intaglioed with the betrayal of Jugurtha, in which both had participated.

Winckelmann, the antiquary, was murdered by a servant for a very precious ring which he wore. Conrad, a Neapolitan prince, flying from Charles king of Naples, was discovered to a sailor by his ring, and was put to death. Richard Cœur-de-Lion, having made a three-months' truce with Saladin, had reached Vienna on his return home, when, fearing to fall into the hands of Leopold, the Austrian archduke, whom he had affronted, he took a cook's place in a gentleman's family, but was recognised by his rings, arrested, and thrown into prison.

Pliny traces the origin of the public taste for rings at Rome to Pompey's display of the Mithridatic jewels through the streets. Martial wrote two spiteful epigrams against one Zoilus, charging him with swamping a fine sardonyx in a pound of gold; and in the second, twitting him with carrying as much gold in rings on his hands as whilom he had worn of iron-rings about his ankles in slavery. As at Rome, so at Athens : Lucian speaks of a Greek who bound sixteen rings round his fingers ; and Aristophanes describes persons " ringed-from-the-roots-to-the-very-tips-of-the-fingers." And finally, on the lids of Egyptian sarcophagi may be seen lay-figures displaying hands laden with rings, in emulation of any Greek or Roman exquisite.—Selected and abridged from Papers in *Fraser's Magazine*, 1856.

A COSTLY ROBE.

When Dionysius captured Kroton, the largest city of Magna Græcia, B.C. 387, he plundered the temple of Here, near Cape Likimium, of its splendid treasures, among which was a robe skilfully wrought and sumptuously decorated, the votive offering of a Sybarite named Alkimenes. Dionysius sold this robe to the Carthaginians for the prodigious price of 120 talents, or about 27,000l. sterling. This may appear an incredible sum ; but the robe was probably dedicated to the recently introduced Hellenic deities, whom the Carthaginians were peculiarly anxious to propitiate, in the hope of averting or alleviating the frightful pestilences wherewith they had been so often smitten ; and the honour done to the new gods would be mainly estimated according to the magnitude of the sum laid out.—Abridged from *Grote's History of Greece*, vol. xi.

ORIGIN OF A METRE.

After Haroun-al-Raschid had put to death his great vizier, Jafar, of whose power, popularity, and magnificence, he had become so jealous, the poets were forbidden to write his elegy. In order to evade this prohibition, one of his female slaves, an ingenious person, invented a metre before unknown, and thus touched the hearts of all Bagdad. This metre is called to this day the *fenn mowal*.

" MODERN ATHENS."

The resemblance between Athens and Edinburgh, which has been remarked by most travellers who have visited both capitals, has conferred upon the Scotch metropolis the title of " Modern Athens." Stuart, author of the *Antiquities of Athens*, was the first to draw attention to this resemblance ; and his opinion has been confirmed by the testimony of many later writers. Dr. Clarke remarks that the neighbourhood of Athens is just like the Highlands of Scotland enriched with the splendid remains of art ; and Mr. H. W. Williams observes that the distant view of Athens from the Ægean Sea is extremely like that of Edinburgh from the Firth of Forth, though certainly the latter is considerably superior.

THE BED OF PROCRUSTES.

Procrustes, called by Pausanias Polypæmon, was, in mythology, a robber of ancient Greece, who placed on an iron bed the travellers who fell into his hands, which their statue was made to fit by cutting off the projecting limbs, or by stretching them to suit its dimensions : whence the metaphorical expression of *the Bed of Procrustes.*

UTOPIAN SCHEMES.

Sir Thomas More, in his curious philosophical work, *Utopia*, has delineated his ideas of a perfect commonwealth, which he places in the imaginary isle of Utopia, where the society is constructed on the principle that no one in the state shall have a right to separate property, since separate property is said to involve the unequalled distribution of property, and thus occasion great suffering to those who are obliged to labour, and mental depravation to those who live on the labours of others. In this imaginary island all are contented with the necessaries of life ; all are employed in useful labour ; no man desires in clothing any other quality besides durability. Since wants are few, and every individual engages in labour, there is no need for working more than six hours a-day. Neither laziness nor avarice find a place in this happy region ; for why should the people be indolent when they have so little toil, or greedy when they know that there is abundance for each ? It is, however, difficult to determine whether the opinions expressed in the *Utopia* are to be considered as More's real sentiments. But the work has added a word to the English language : schemes of national improvement founded on theoretical or visionary views being since then termed *Utopian.*

Sir Thomas More's *Utopia* is written in very good Latin, and was first published at Louvain, 1516. It has been translated into English by Robinson, by Bishop Burnet, and by A. Cayley.

"TENTERDEN STEEPLE THE CAUSE OF GOODWIN SANDS."

"Here, by the way, I will tell you a merry toy," said Latimer one day in the pulpit. "Master More was once sent in commission into Kent to help to try out, if it might be, what was the cause of Goodwin Sands and the shelf that stopped up Sandwich Haven. He calleth the country afore him, such as were thought to be men of experience ; and among others came in an old man with a white head, and one that was thought to be little less than one hundred years old. So Master More called the old aged man unto him, and said : 'Father, tell me, if you can, what is the cause of this great arising of the sands and shelves hereabout that stop up Sandwich Haven ?' 'Forsooth, sir' (quoth he), 'I am an old man, for I am well-nigh an hundred ; and I think that Tenterden Steeple is the cause of the Goodwin Sands. For I am an old man, sir, and I may remember the building of Tenterden Steeple, and before that steeple was in building there was no manner of flats or sands.'"—*Latimer's Sermons*, vol. i. p. 251.

ERASMUS, HIS EARLY LOVE OF PEARS.

When, in 1480, the youthful Erasmus made his profession at Gouda, in the convent-garden grew a pear-tree, which the prior had reserved for his own proper use; but Erasmus had taken a private survey of the forbidden fruit. The consequence was, that the pears began to vanish, and the moment a jargonelle had reached the melting point, it was sure to evaporate overnight. The prior was in despair; and, unable to put trust in any brother, he resolved himself to be the watchman from a window which looked into the orchard. Towards morning, he thought he saw something in his favourite tree, and was delighted at having caught the depredator. But just then, perhaps it was the cold of morning which made his reverence sneeze; thus scaring the thief, who dropped from among the branches, and limped off to his cell, imitating to the life the gait of a lame brother. That morning, after matins, and when all the inmates were assembled in the refectory, the prior called up the cripple-monk, and charged him with the theft. The poor fellow was thunderstruck, and protested his innocence; but all his asseverations only made the prior furious, and added penitential psalms to the next week's bread and water. At last suspicion turned towards the right quarter; and it was not long before the cunning novice found it expedient to quit the convent.

EARLY ROMAN ART.

In the middle of the fifth century A.U.O. the arts began to flourish in Rome; and the celebrated group still extant of the she-wolf nurturing the twin-founders of the city was set up in the Capitol. "Let no one," says Niebuhr, "suppose that the Romans before they adopted the civilisation of the Greeks were barbarous. That people which under its kings constructed such gigantic sewers, and which at this time possessed a painter like Fabius Pictor, and a sculptor able to produce a work like the Capitoline she-wolf, cannot have been without some kind of literature." To this era belongs the sarcophagus of Lucius Cornelius Scipio, the oldest sepulchral monument yet discovered in Rome,—an existing proof of the excellence of sculpture in the fifth century of the Roman age.

INDEX.

AARON's Breastplate, 2.
Actæon, Story of, 67.
Adonis, Story of, 62.
Adonis's Gardens, 63.
Æsculapius, 64.
Agesilaus, How disabled from the Fight, 18.
Agrarian Laws, 201.
Agricultural Labour in 14th Century, 121.
Alexander and Diogenes, 26.
Alexander at the Granicus, 26.
Alexandria, Pharos of, 155.
Alfred and the Neatherd's Wife, 110.
"All for the best," 141.
"All is lost, save Honour," 168.
American War with Great Britain, 108.
Amphion and his Lyre, 18.
Andrew's, St., Cross, 193.
Angels, the Seven Holy, 3.
Anne, the Lady, in Sanctuary, 208.
Ants, Colossal, producing Gold, 76.
Apis, the Sacred Bull of Egypt, 2.
Apollo, Temple of, at Delphi, 60.
Apollonius of Tyana, Who was he? 217.
Appeal, Reasonable, 25.
Apsley House and Wellington, 149.
Ararat, Traditions of, 2.
Arch of Titus, at Rome, 44.
Archery Tenures, Curious, 204.
Archimedes at the Siege of Syracuse, 54.
Archimedes and the Lever, 177.
Argonauts, Voyage of the, 72.
Argosie, the Term, 77.
Argus and his Hundred Eyes, 57.
Armada, the Spanish, 131.
Army terrified by an Eclipse, 29.
Arthur, King, 112.
"As rich as Crœsus," 23.
Assassins, Origin of the, 216.

Atlantis, the Isle, 72.
Atlas supporting the Heavens, 66.
Augean Stable, the, 65.
Aurungzebe, 93.

BALBEC, who built? 214.
"Babes in the Wood," Ballad of the, 223.
Babylon, 151.
Babylon, How it fell, 29.
Bacon, Friar, his Brazen Head, 176.
Badges, Household, and Tavern Signs, 190.
Bail, First, in Rome, 37.
Bajazet and Tamerlane, 168.
Battel Abbey Roll, 188.
Bavarian Bravery, 96.
Bayeux Tapestry, the, 115.
Becket, Thomas, Assassination of, 118.
Bed of Justice, the, 201.
Beelzebub, 7.
Beetles, Egyptian Worship of, 8.
Beggars, Old English Law against, 203.
"Begin at the Beginning," 169.
Belisarius, Blindness and Beggary of, 218.
Belisarius, Escapes of, 81.
"Belly and the Members," the, 36.
"Black Books," 171.
Blue-Stocking, the, 186.
Bœotia, Country of, 179.
Both Sides of the Question, 144.
Bray, the Vicar of, 173.
Brazen Bull of Phalaris, 53.
Brescia, the Orphan of, 91.
Brian Borolhme's Harp, 114.
Briareus and his Hundred Hands, 67.
Britannia, Origin of, 192.
British Museum, Magna Charta in, 119.
"Broad Devonshire," 172.

Bruce's Travels, 78.
Brutus and his Mother, 42.
Buccaneers, Who were they? 178,
Burning Alive, 204.
Buskin and Sock, 163.

"'Cabala with the Stars," 62.
Cabinet Councils, 202.
Cadmus and the Dragon, 57.
Caligula and his Horse, 42.
Canard, or Hoax, 164.
Capitol, the, How saved by Geese, 37.
Cæsar and the Bird of Omen, 42.
Cæsar passing the Rubicon, 40.
Cæsar's Triumphs, 41.
Cages and Stocks in London, 203.
Calves'-Head Club, the, 133.
Camillus and Wellington, 43.
Candlestick, the Seven-branched, 44.
Carolina and George II., Tomb of, 146.
Carthage, Founding of, 49.
Carthage and Great Britain compared, 51.
Carthage, Lamartine on, 51.
Catesby Hall, 139.
Cats, Egyptian Worship of, 8.
"Cave of Trophonius," 61.
Censorship of the Press, Origin of, 202.
Centaurs, Origin of the, 56, 67.
Cerberus and Geryon, 66.
Champion, the, at the Coronation of English Sovereigns, 213.
Charlemagne, Birthplace and Burial-place of, 83.
Charles I., Bernini's Bust of, 133.
Charles I., Gold Medal and George of, 134.
Charles I., Handkerchief of, 135.
Charles I. and his Times, 135.
Charles II., Willis's Plot against, 136.
Charles V. and History, 172.
Charles XII., Escape of, 95.
Charles Martel, 82.
Charon, Fable of, 67.
Charter Oak of Connecticut, 197.
Chimæra, the Monster, 67.
Christ, the Person of, 4.
Church, First Christian, in Britain, 112.
"Cimmerian Gloom," 58.
Circus, Roman, Sports of the, 38.

City of London and the Peerage, 210.
Clarence, Was he drowned in Malmsey? 222.
Classic Charms, 58.
Cloaca Maxima of Rome, 46.
Coals and Window-glass, Roman, in Britain, 113.
Cock, Omen of the, 23.
Code Napoleon, the, 202.
Colossus of Rhodes, the, 156.
Columbus and the Egg, 182.
Column of Trajan at Rome, 45.
Combat in the Ice, 84.
Comedy and Tragedy, 179.
Conjuring Cap, Origin of, 170.
Coriolanus, 34.
Corioli, Site of, 34.
Cowards, Lacedæmonian Law against, 192.
Coronation Stone in Westminster Abbey, 212.
Coronation of George IV., 213.
Coroner's Law, 220.
Crescent of the Turks, 195.
Cretan Philosophy, 157.
Crete, Labyrinth of, 61.
Crocodiles, Egyptian Worship of, 8.
Crœsus, Rich as, 28.
Cromwell's Fortunate Day, 139.
Cromwell, Thomas, and "Jelly-Pardons" of Boston, 126.
Cross, Holy, History of, 5.
Crown, Iron, of Lombardy, 86.
Crown, Luke's Iron, 87.
Crowns of Triumph, Roman, 133.
Crusade of Children, 84.
Culloden, Relic of, 146.
Curtius and the Gulf, 34.
Cyclopean Architecture, 29.
Cynics, the, 165.
Cynosure, 161.

Dædalus, Exploits of, 67.
Dagger in the City of London Arms, 192.
Damien's Bed of Steel, 87.
Damocles, the Sword of, 54.
Damon and Pythias, Story of, 53.
Darius, How he won the Crown of Persia, 24.
Dauphin of France, 209.
"De Imitatione Christi," Who wrote, 217.
Deaths, Mysterious Royal, 219.
Della Crusca Academy, 171.

Deucalional Deluge, the, 68.
Diana of the Ephesians, Temple of, 153.
Diadem, Origin of the, 188.
Dido, Story of, 50.
Dinners, Public, at Athens, 160.
Draco and his Laws, 199.
Dreams, Fortunate, 36.
Dionysius's Ear, 54.

Eagle, the, a Bird of Omen, 34.
Eagle, the, Two-headed, 195.
Edward, First Prince of Wales born, 120.
Edward V., Death of, 219.
Egypt, Great Pyramid of, 150.
Egypt, Pyramids, What built for, 157.
Eleanor's, Queen, Crosses, 120.
Elephant and Castle, the, 112.
Elephant, the First seen in England, 111.
Eleusinian Mysteries, the, 66.
Elizabeth, Princess, at Hatfield, 129.
Embalming, Egyptian, 10.
Emperors of the East, State of, 72.
Emperor and the Merchant, 41.
Endymion, Sleep of, 63.
England, Kings of, their Claim to the Crown of France, 21.
Enoch and Early Death, 1.
Enoch's Pillars, 1.
Epic Poetry of Early Greece, 214.
Epicurus, Sect of, 166.
Erasmus, his Early Love of Pears, 240.
Erasmus and the New Testament, 127.
Errors in Print, 214.
Etruscan Architecture, 29.
Etruscans, Who were they? 81.
"Every Man has his Price," 185.
"Every Man is the Architect," &c., 159.
"Ex Pede Herculem," 160.
Eyes, False, Antiquity of, 172.

Fabulous Localities of Classic History, 74.
Factions, Curious, 87.
Famine, Horrors of, 80.
"Feather in his Cap," Origin of, 170.
Felton, the Assassin, 135.
Field of Cloth-of-Gold Memorial, 128.

Fifth-Monarchy Men, 137.
Fights, Naval, Chances of, 48.
Fish and Ring, Story of, 180.
Fisher, Bishop, and Sir T. More, What became of their Heads, 226.
Flaying Alive, 90.
Forest, the New, Hants, 117.
Forum, the, of Rome, 12.
France, Succession to the Throne of, 108.
Frederick the Great and Arnold the Miller, 102.
Free Trade, Origin of, 183.
Frenchmen, Why called Frogs, 182.
Friday, Is it an Unlucky Day? 109.

Gasconades, 177.
Gaza, Siege of, 27.
Generals, Illustrious, Uncrowned, 183.
Genius, Regality of, 174.
Geometry, No Royal Road to, 161.
Gethsemane, the Garden of, 7.
Gigantology disproved by Science, 67.
Glaucus, How saved from Drowning in Honey, 24.
Gog and Magog, 110.
"Golden Ass," the, 180.
Golden Fleece, the, 72.
Gordian Knot cut by Alexander, 26.
Gotham, the Wise Men of, 180.
Government, Science of, 181.
"Great Events from Little Causes spring," 187.
Greece and Egypt, 12.
Greece, Localities of, 12.
Greece, the Seven Wise Men of, 14.
Greek Fire, What is it? 20.
Greek Kalends, the, 162.
Greeks, Ancient and Modern, 13.
Grotius, Escape of, 92.
Gundrada, Remains of, 116.
Gunpowder Plot, the, 132.
Gustavus Adolphus and Wallenstein, 100.
Gustavus III., Secret Chests of, opened, 107.
Guy Fawkes's Lantern, 132.
Gyges and his Ring, 57.

Halcyon Days, 180.
Hampden the Patriot, 126.
Hannibal, How he eat through the Alps with Vinegar, 51.

Hatfield, Elizabethan and other
　Memorials at, 130.
Heads of Bishop Fisher and Sir
　T. More, 226.
Helots and Drunkenness, 161.
"Hewing Blocks with a Razor,"
　162.
Historic Inns, 134.
Historic Road into London, 122.
History, worth of, 172.
Holy Cross, History of, 5.
Homer, Birthplace of, 215.
Homer, Did he compose the Iliad
　and Odyssey ? 13.
Honey of the Hymettus, 24.
Horatii and Curatii, the, 33.
Horse, Wooden, at the Siege of
　Troy, 15.
Horse-chestnut and Chestnut-
　horse, 167.
Horseferry, Westminster, 141.
Hudson, Jeffrey, the Dwarf, 157.
Hugonot or Huguenot, 89.
"Hurrah," Origin of, 103.
Hymen, the God, Origin of, 66.

Imperial Compliments, 125.
"Incredibilia" of the Ancients, 66.
Infidel, Punishment of, 205.
Iphicratides' Leggings, 150.
Ireland assigned by a Ring, 210.
Iris, Why called the Fleur-de-lis,
　194.
Iron Mask, Man in the, 231.

Jacobinism, What is it ? 147.
James II., Death of, 142.
James III. recognised by Louis
　XIV., 143.
Jane Shore, her True History,
　223.
Jericho, Gone to, 162.
Jericho, Holy Rose of, 4.
Jerusalem, Chamber in Westmin-
　ster Abbey, 122.
Jesuit, Origin of the Name, 235.
Joan of Arc, 220.
Job, War-horse of, 3.
John o' Groat's House, 234.
Jupiter Olympius, Statue of, 152.
Justinian, Institutes of, 200.
Justinian, Pandects of, 200.

Kenilworth, True Romance of,
　227.
King, the, never Dies, 131.

Lacock Abbey, Charter at, 119.
Lamps, Everlasting, 43.
Leonidas and his Band, 21.
Leviathan Explained, 170.
Leyden, John of, 82.
Liberty, Cap of, 192.
Lilburn, John, 173.
Lilly, the Astrologer, 229.
Lilly foretels the Great Plague
　and Fire of London, 229.
Lion in the Arms of England, 102.
Lion of St. Mark at Venice, 196.
Living temp. Henry VII., 125.
Lombardy, Iron Crown of, 86.
London, Great Plague and Fire of,
　229.
Louis XIV. and his Wig, 96.
Luke's Iron Crown, 87.
Lutzen and Salamanca, Battles of,
　compared, 101.

Machiavelism, 172.
Magna Charta, Origin of, 118.
Mahomet, Was he Inspired with
　a Dove? 217.
Man in the Iron Mask, Who was
　he? 231.
Man, Seven Ages of, 176.
"Manners makyth Man," 182.
Marat, the French Revolutionist,
　103.
Marathon, Memorials of, 21.
Marco Polo, Veracity of, 74.
Marius on the Ruins of Carthage,
　52.
Marlborough, Victories of, 144.
Martin's "Fall of Babylon," 30.
Mausoleum of King Mausolus, 154.
May, no New English Sovereign
　in, 119.
Medea, the Sorceress, 66.
Metre, Origin of, 238.
Milo of Crotona, Strength of, 17.
"Modern Athens," 238.
Monarchy, the Smallest in the
　World, 103.
Monasteries, the Abolisher of, 129.
Money, the Earliest Coined, 206.
Money Panic of 1832, 148.
Monmouth, James Duke of, cap-
　tured, 140.
Moon, Is it Inhabited? 18.
More, Sir Thomas, his Residence
　at Crosby Place, 127.
More, Sir Thomas, and Erasmus,
　First Meeting of, 127.

Moro, Sir Thomas, Early Life of, 126.
Mummies, the Latest, 11.
Mummies, Use of, 11.
"Mummy Wheat," 9.
Murder Wounds "Bleeding a-fresh," 124.
Muses, Why called Pierides, 152.

Napoleon I., Character of, 100.
Napoleon I., Portrait of, 106.
Napoleon I., Surrender of, 105.
Napoleon's Threatened Invasion of England, 104.
"Ne Sutor ultra Crepidam," 160.
Nelson's Left Hand, 147.
Nemi, the Great Ship of, 90.
Nero's Golden House, 41.
Nestor, Exploits of, 15.
Nineveh, the Story of, 28.
Niobe, Fate of, 63, 67.

Oak, Charter, of Connecticut, 197.
Oak, Parliament, in Sherwood Forest, 196.
Oak worn on May 29, 132.
Œdipus, How he won a Kingdom, 23.
Œdipus and the Sphinx, 158.
Offor, a Fair one, 95.
Orpheus, Story of, 66, 67.
Ostracism of the Greeks, 198.
Otway's "Venice Preserved," 225.
Overbury, Sir Thomas, Poisoning of, 230.
Owl, the, a Bird of Omen, 68.

Padua, the Founder of, 85.
Palladium, the, 159.
Papyrus, 234.
Parliament Oak in Sherwood Forest, 196.
Partington, Mrs. and her Mop, 174.
Pasquin and Pasquinade, 163.
Paying the Debts of an Army, 27.
Pecunia—Money, 35.
Peerage, the British, 210.
Pegasus, What is? 195.
Pelasgic Architecture, 29.
Penn's Tree in Pennsylvania, 196.
Peripatetics, the, 166.
Perseus, Exploits of, 64.
Pet Animals, 104.
Peter the Great in England, 97.
Peter the Great, Memorials of, 96.

Pharos of Alexandria, 155.
Philabeg, Wearing the, 145.
Philip and Alexander, 25.
Philip, How Assassinated, 26.
Philippics, the, 157.
Philomela, the Nightingale, 57.
Picnic, Origin of the, 171.
"Pillars of Hercules," 73.
"Pilot that Weathered the Storm," the, 174.
Pitt and Pericles, a Parallel, 175.
Plantagenet, Badge of, 190.
Poictiers, Battle of, 121.
Poisoning of Sir Thomas Overbury, 230.
Poland, First Partition of, 102.
Pope Joan, 82.
Pope's Bull, the, 191.
"Porteous Mob," Edinburgh, 145.
Porus on his Elephant, 25.
Potato, When Introduced into Ireland, 233.
"Potter's Field," the, 7.
Pound, What was it in 1000? 207.
Prester John, Who was he? 80.
Prague, Defenestration of, 99.
Pré-aux-Clercs at Paris, 92.
Prediction Fatally Verified, 62.
Prediction Fulfilled, 95.
Presage, Effect of, 98.
Priscian's Head, Breaking, 162.
Procrustes, Bed of, 239.
Prometheus and Promethean Fire, 68.
Propaganda College at Rome, 235.
Provisions at Rome in the 11th Century, 35.
Provisions, Saxon and Norman Names of, 117.
Pyramids of Egypt, 150, 157.
Pythagoras and Beans, 58.
Pythagorean Abstinence, 60.
Pythagorean Metempsychosis, 59.
Python, the, 60.

Quakerism, Origin of, 184.

Raleigh, Sir Walter, Execution of, 132.
Raleigh, Sir Walter, and the Potato, 233.
Records, "Length of the Law," 210.
Regulus and the Great Serpent, 52.
Rent of an Island, 207.
"Revenons à nos Moutons," 163.

Revolution of 1688, 141.
Richard II., Death of, 219.
Richard II., White Hart of, 189.
Richard III., Cognisance and Badge of, 190.
Richard III., Popular Errors respecting, 221.
Richelieu, Cardinal, and Peter the Great, 181.
Rienzi, the Story of, 83.
Right-handed and Left-handed, 58.
Rings, Ancient Use of, 216.
Ring sent by Queen Elizabeth to the Earl of Essex, 228.
Rivers, Crossing, on Inflated Skins, 20.
Robe, Costly, 238.
Robin Hood, Who was he? 220.
"Roland for an Oliver," 168.
Romart Art, Early, 240.
Roman Circus, Sports of the, 38.
Roman Forum, the, 42.
Romans, Degenerate, 82.
Rome, Earliest Record of, 37.
Rome founded on a Volcano, 32.
Rome, Final Overthrow of, 44.
Rome, Seven Hills of, 32.
Rome, Walls of, 45.
Romulus and Remus, Story of, 31.
Roscius, the Roman Actor, 164.
Roses, the Red and White, 224.
Rubicon, Cæsar passing the, 40.

SAILOR'S, English, Stratagem, 86.
Sanctuary, Privilege of, 208.
Sandwich, Origin of, 161.
San Marino, Saving of, 103.
"Saracen's Head" Inn, Sign, 191.
Saragossa, Women at the Siege of, 105.
Sardis, How taken by the Persians, 22.
Saturnalia, the, 37.
Scipio Africanus, Silver Shield of, 53.
Scylla, 67.
Seneca on Alexander the Great, 27.
Seven Ages of Man, 175.
Seven Hills of Rome, 32.
Sforza, Duke of Milan, 83.
Shaving the Beard, 184.
Sibylline Books, the, 65.
Sin and Shaving the Beard, 180.
Singing Swans, 57.
Sisyphus, Stratagems of, 69.
Slave-Trade in England, 207.

Slavery in Rome, 85.
Solon, Laws of, 197.
Sorites, Example of, 167.
Spare Moments, 172.
Sphinx, Riddle of the, 158.
SS., Collar of, 189.
Stocks, Barnacles, and Bilboes, 169.
Stoics and Epicureans, 166.
Storks in Republics and Free States, 169.
"Strike, but hear me!" 161.
Stumbling, Omen of, 81.
Swede Stone, the, 101.
Sybarites, Who were the? 55.
Sycophants, the First, 166.
Symposiacs, the, 166.
Syracuse, Great Siege of, 54.

TABERNACLE, the Jewish, 2.
Taking for Granted, Danger of, 182.
"Tale of a Tub," the, 220.
Tamerlane's Iron Cage, 85.
Tantalus, Story of, 70.
Tarring and Feathering, Antiquity of, 183.
Tartar, Catching a, 168.
"Tearless Battle," the, 47.
Telemachus, Adventures of, 73.
Tendo-Achillis, 178.
"Tenterden Steeple the Cause of Goodwin Sands," 239.
Thebes of "the Hundred Gates," 216.
Thermopylæ, Memorials of, 21.
Thirty Years' War, 99.
Thong, Artifice of, in founding Cities, 49.
Tight-Lacing, Antiquity of, 184.
Titus, Arch of, at Rome, 44.
Totila, the End of, 81.
Tower of Oblivion, the, 62.
Towton, Battle of, 124.
Tragedy, a Real one, 91.
Transmigration of Souls, 59.
Treason punished by the Athenian Law, 198.
Troops' Pay in 13th Century, 121.
Trophonius, Cave of, 61.
Troy, the Plains of, 16.
Troy, Siege of, 15.
Troy, Siege of, Is it a Legend? 215.
"True Blue," Origin of, 166.
Truth, Love of, 161.
Truth in a Pit, 162.
Turkish Crescent, the, 195.

Turnus, Drowning of, 46.
Tusculum, Celebrity of, 47.
Tyndale's Bible first printed in England, 128.

ULTIMA Thule, 77.
Ulysses, Wanderings of, 74.
Utopian Schemes, 239.
Utrecht, Peace of, and the Slave-Trade, 146.

VENERABLE Bede, 113.
" Veni, Vidi, Vici," 161.
" Venice Preserved," by Otway, 224.
Vicar of Bray, the, 173.
Victory, Exaggerated, 81.
Vienna, Close of the Battle of, 94.
" Villanous Words," 158.
Virgil's Rural Economy, 48.
Voyage, Remarkable, 72.

WAKEFIELD, Battle of, 123.
Wandering Jew, the, 77.
Wallenstein and his Astrologer, 99.
Wobbe, Edward, the Traveller, 75.
Wollington at the Battle of Water-loo, 147.
Wellington's Bedchamber, 149.

Wellington, Generosity of, 108.
" Wheat, Mummy," 9.
Wheat, the Seven-eared, 9.
Where did Cain slay Abel? 1.
White Horse, Standard of, 191.
" Whittington and his Cat," 225.
William III., Vowel in which he came to England, 143.
" Willie Wastle," 174.
Witchcraft Laws in England, 205.
Wolsey, Was he a Butcher's Son? 225.
Wolsey, How he won his Way, 125.
Wonders of the World, the Seven, 150-157.
Wooden Wall at Athens, 18.

XANTHIPPE the Scold, 177.
Xenophon and the 10,000 Greeks, their Passage and Retreat, 19.
Xerxes, Retreat of, 22.
Xerxes scourgeth the Hellespont, 22.

YOUNG Genius, by Disraeli, 79.
" Your Majesty," Style of, 202.

ZAARDAM, Peter the Great at, 97.
Zoilus, the Critic, 177.

NOTES.

"THE PLAIN OF TROY," p. 16; "THE SIEGE OF TROY," p. 215.—Dr. William Robertson, who resided for fifteen months, in 1855 and 1856, within a few miles of the Plain of Troy, and made excursions over it at all seasons, in a paper communicated to the Royal Society of Edinburgh, in 1857, states his belief that Homer's Troy must have stood, like the Novum Ilium of Strabo, on the hill now called Hissarlik; that the mouth of the Scamander was formerly two miles to the east of its present main channel; and that the In-Topeh-Osmak and Kali-fatli-Osmak may be regarded as its terminations in the times of Homer and Strabo. He shows that these, and the other Osmaks in the valley of the Mendere, are at present merely winter channels of the river, and that in summer they would be dry nullahs but for the drainings from the extensive marshes left by the winter inundations of the plain. He believes that the bay between Koum-Kaleh and In-Tepeh was deeper in the days of Homer; and that its eastern extremity in particular has, during the last 2000 years, been materially encroached upon by deposits of mud and sand from the rivers and sea. He remarks that Homer makes no mention of a river Thymbrius, and that the Thymbra which is alluded to in the Iliad very probably stood in the valley of the Simois, to which

It has ultimately transferred its name. The Thymbra and Thymbrius of Strabo are certainly situated near the modern farm of Ak-tchai-kioi on the Kimair.

THE STANDARD OF THE WHITE HORSE, p. 191.—The historic evidence as to the White Horse being cut out on the Berkshire hill by direction of Alfred himself is very pleasantly discussed in *The Scouring of the White Horse; or the Long-Vacation Ramble of a London Clerk*, by the Author of *Tom Brown's School-Days*, 1859.

"THE TRUE ROMANCE OF 'KENILWORTH,'" pp. 227, 229.—The explanation suggested in the latter page, of the "gose and poste," is thought to be a fanciful one; since the barbarous sport of striking off the head of a live goose hung between two posts is to this day common at festivals in the Low Countries. An obliging Correspondent, Mr. W. H. Fisk, witnessed this cruel sport at a fête at Bruges, in August 1848; and he suggests that it was a common amusement in England in the sixteenth century, and that the "gose and poste," in the above instance, has no special allusion to poor Amy's fate at Kenilworth.

"WHO WAS THE MAN IN THE IRON MASK?" pp. 231-233.—Miss Brewster, in her charming *Letters from Cannes*, relates the following as one of the many fables which cluster around the "Iron Mask," which, if one only dared, one would certainly believe. "In the early days of that dreary captivity,—those days in which the prisoner (whether from fancy or memory) was described 'as of handsome face, middle height, brown skin, clear complexion, and beautiful voice,'—there was a lovely young lady in the fortress of Ste. Marguerite; she was the daughter of one of the officials, and her name was Julia de Bonpart. The mysterious prisoner fell in love with this bright sunbeam, whom he had seen from his window; and what feminine heart could resist a persecuted, royal, and masked prisoner? The father gave his consent, they were married at an altar erected in the dungeon, and the devoted wife cheered the gloom of the weary lifetime. Two little infant sons could not, however, be retained near the unfortunate parents, and were sent secretly to Corsica, under their maternal name of Bonpart. From them sprang the Buonapartes, who are therefore Bourbons. In the course of a conversation at St. Helena, it was mentioned to Napoleon by a gentleman present that a person had come to him to tell the above story, and to demonstrate from thence that Napoleon was a lineal descendant of the Iron Mask, and thus the legitimate heir of Louis XIII. The gentleman had laughed at the whole story, which made the narrator very angry; he maintained that the marriage could easily be verified by the registers of a parish of Marseilles, which he named. The Emperor said that he had heard the same story; and that such was the love of the marvellous, that it would have been easy to have substantiated something of the kind for the credulous multitude."

THE END.

JOHN TIMBS'S POPULAR WORKS.

'*Any one who reads and remembers Mr. Timbs's encyclopædic varieties should ever after be a good table talker, an excellent companion for children, a "well-read person," and a proficient lecturer.*'—ATHENÆUM.

Things Not Generally Known. By JOHN TIMBS, F.S.A. Editor of ' The Year Book of Facts,' &c. In Six Volumes, fcp. cloth, 15s.; or, the Six Volumes bound in Three, cloth gilt, or half-bound, 15s.; cloth, gilt edges, 16s. 6d. Contents:—General Information, 2 Vols,—Curiosities of Science, 2 Vols.—Curiosities of History, 1 Vol.—Popular Errors Explained, 1 Vol.

** The Volumes sold separately, as follows:—

Things Not Generally Known Familiarly Explained.
(General Information). 2 Vols. 2s. 6d. each, or in 1 Vol. 5s. cloth.

' A remarkably pleasant and instructive little book; a book as full of information as a pomegranate is full of seed.'—PUNCH.
' A very amusing miscellany.'—GENTLEMAN'S MAGAZINE.
' And as instructive as it is amusing.'—NOTES AND QUERIES.

Curiosities of Science, Past and Present. 2 Vols.
2s. 6d. each, or in 1 Vol. 5s. cloth.

' " Curiosities of Science " contains as much information as could otherwise be gleaned from reading elaborate treatises on physical phenomena, acoustics, optics, astronomy, geology, and palæontology, meteorology, nautical geography, magnetism, the electric telegraph, &c.'—MINING JOURNAL.

Curiosities of History. Fcp. 2s. 6d. cloth ; or, with
' Popular Errors,' in 1 Vol. 5s. cloth.

' We can conceive no more amusing book for the drawing-room, or one more useful for the school-room.'—ART JOURNAL.

Popular Errors Explained and Illustrated. Fcp.
2s. 6d. cloth; or, with ' Curiosities of History,' in 1 Vol. 5s. cloth.

' We know of few better books for young persons; it is instructive, entertaining, and reliable.'—BUILDER.
' A work which ninety-nine persons out of every hundred would take up whenever it came in their way, and would always learn something from.'
ENGLISH CHURCHMAN.

Knowledge for the Time: a Manual of Reading,
Reference, and Conversation on Subjects of Living Interest. Contents :—Historico-Political Information—Progress of Civilization—Dignities and Distinctions—Changes in Laws—Measure and Value—Progress of Science—Life and Health—Religious Thought. Illustrated from the best and latest Authorities. By JOHN TIMBS, F.S.A. Small 8vo. with Frontispiece, 6s. cloth.

' It is impossible to open the volume without coming upon some matter of interest upon which light is thrown.'—MORNING POST.
' We welcome this attempt to preserve the bright bits and the hidden treasures of contemporary history. It is with keen pleasure we bear in mind that this learned collector's eye watches our journalism and the daily utterance of scholars, determined that no truth shall be lost.'—LLOYD'S NEWS.

Stories of Inventors and Discoverers in Science and
Useful Arts. By JOHN TIMBS, F.S.A. Second Edition. With numerous Illustrations. Fcap. 5s. cloth.

' Another interesting and well-collected book, ranging from Archimedes and Roger Bacon to the Stephensons.'—ATHENÆUM.
' These stories by Mr. Timbs are as marvellous as the *Arabian Nights' Entertainments*, and are wrought into a volume of great interest and worth.'—ATLAS.

JOHN TIMBS'S **POPULAR WORKS**—*continued.*

Walks and Talks About London. By JOHN TIMBS,

F.S.A., Author of 'Curiosities of London,' 'Things not Generally Known,' &c. Contents:—About Old Lyons Inn—Last Days of Downing Street—Walks and Talks in Vauxhall Gardens—Last of the Old Bridewell—The Fair of May Fair—From Hicks's Hall to Campden House—Talk about the Temple—Recollections of Sir Richard Phillips—Curiosities of Fishmongers' Hall—A Morning in Sir John Soane's Museum—A Site of Speculation—Changes in Covent Garden—Last of the Fleet Prison—Forty Years in Fleet Street—Changes at Charing Cross—Railway London—Blackfriars Bridge—Raising of Holborn Valley—An Old Tavern in St. James's. With Frontispiece, post 8vo. cloth gilt, 8s 6d.

'The London of the last generation is, day by day, being rent away from the sight of the present, and it is well that Mr. Timbs is inclined to walk and talk about it ere it vanishes altogether, and leaves the next generation at a loss to understand the past history of the metropolis so far as it has a local colouring, as so very much of it has. Much of this has now gone for ever, but our author has watched the destructive course of the "improver," and thanks to his industry, many a memory that we would not willingly let die, is consigned to the keeping of the printed page, which in this instance, as in so many others, will doubtless prove a more lasting record than brass or marble.'—GENTLEMAN'S MAGAZINE.

Things to be Remembered in Daily Life. With

Personal Experiences and Recollections. By JOHN TIMBS. F.S.A., Author of 'Things not Generally Known,' &c. &c. With Frontispiece. Fcp. 3s. 6d. cloth.

'While Mr. Timbs claims for this volume the merit of being more reflective than its predecessors, those who read it will add to that merit—that it is equally instructive.'—NOTES AND QUERIES.

'No portion of this book is without value, and several biographical sketches which it contains are of great interest. . . . . "Things to be Remembered in Daily Life" is a valuable and memorable book, and represents great research, and considerable and arduous labour.'—MORNING POST.

'Mr. Timbs's personal experiences and recollections are peculiarly valuable, as embodying the observations of an acute, intelligent, and cultivated mind. "Things to be Remembered" carries with it an air of vitality which augurs well for perpetuation.'—OBSERVER.

School-days of Eminent Men. Containing Sketches

of the Progress of Education in England, from the Reign of King Alfred to that of Queen Victoria; and School and College Lives of the most celebrated British Authors, Poets, and Philosophers; Inventors and Discoverers; Divines, Heroes, Statesmen, and Legislators. By JOHN TIMBS, F.S.A. Second Edition, entirely revised and partly re-written. With a Frontispiece by John Gilbert, 13 Views of Public Schools, and 26 Portraits by Harvey. Fcap. 5s. handsomely bound in cloth.

Extensively used, and specially adapted for a Prize-Book at Schools.

'The idea is a happy one, and its execution equally so. It is a book to interest all boys, but more especially those of Westminster, Eton, Harrow, Rugby, and Winchester; for of these, as of many other schools of high repute, the accounts are full and interesting.'—NOTES AND QUERIES.

Something for Everybody; and a Garland for the

Year. By JOHN TIMBS, F.S.A., Author of 'Things Not Generally Known,' &c. With a Coloured Title, post 8vo. 5s. cloth.

'This volume abounds with diverting and suggestive extracts. It seems to us particularly well adapted for parochial lending libraries.'—SATURDAY REVIEW.

'Full of odd, quaint, out-of-the-way bits of information upon all imaginable subjects is this amusing volume, wherein Mr. Timbs discourses upon domestic, rural, metropolitan, and social life; interesting nooks of English localities; time-honoured customs and old-world observances, and, we need hardly add, Mr. Timbs discourses well and pleasantly upon all.'—NOTES AND QUERIES, July 28, 1861.

A SERIES OF ELEGANT GIFT-BOOKS.

Truths Illustrated by Great Authors; A Dictionary

of nearly Four Thousand Aids to Reflection, Quotations of Maxims, Metaphors, Counsels, Cautions, Proverbs, Aphorisms, &c. &c. In Prose and Verse. Compiled from the Great Writers of all Ages and Countries. Eleventh Edition, fcap. 8vo. cloth, gilt edges, 568 pp. 6s.

'The quotations are perfect gems; their selection evince sound judgment and an excellent taste.'—DISPATCH.
'We accept the treasure with profound gratitude—it should find its way to every home.'—ERA.
'We know of no better book of its kind.'—EXAMINER.

The Philosophy of William Shakespeare; delineating,

in Seven Hundred and Fifty Passages selected from his Plays, the Multiform Phases of the Human Mind. With Index and References. Collated, Elucidated, and Alphabetically arranged, by the Editors of 'Truths Illustrated by Great Authors.' Second Edition, fcap. 8vo. cloth, gilt edges, nearly 700 pages, with beautiful Vignette Title, price 6s.

☞ A glance at this volume will at once show its superiority to Dodd's 'Beauties,' or any other volume of Shakesperian selections.

Songs of the Soul during its Pilgrimage Heaven-

ward; being a New Collection of Poetry, illustrative of the Power of the Christian Faith; selected from the Works of the most eminent British, Foreign, and American Writers, Ancient and Modern, Original and Translated. By the Editors of 'Truths Illustrated by Great Authors,' &c. Second Edition, fcap. 8vo. cloth, gilt edges, 638 pages, with beautiful Frontispiece and Title, price 6s.

☞ This elegant volume will be appreciated by the admirers of 'The Christian Year.'

The Beauty of Holiness; or, The Practical Christian's

Daily Companion; being a Collection of upwards of Two Thousand Reflective and Spiritual Passages, remarkable for their Sublimity, Beauty, and Practicability; selected from the Sacred Writings, and arranged in Eighty-two Sections, each comprising a different theme for meditation. By the Editors of 'Truths Illustrated by Great Authors.' Third Edition, fcap. 8vo. cloth, gilt edges, 536 pp., 6s.

'Every part of the Sacred Writings deserves our deepest attention and research, but all, perhaps, may not be equally adapted to the purposes of meditation and reflection. Those, therefore, who are in the constant habit of consulting the Bible will not object to a selection of some of its most sublime and impressive passages, arranged and classed ready at once to meet the eye.'—EXTRACT FROM PREFACE.

Events to be Remembered in the History of England.

Forming a Series of Interesting Narratives, extracted from the Pages of Contemporary Chronicles or Modern Historians, of the most Remarkable Occurrences in each Reign; with Reviews of the Manners, Domestic Habits, Amusements, Costumes, &c. &c., of the People, Chronological Table, &c. By CHARLES SELBY. Twenty-fifth Edition, 12mo. fine paper, with Nine Beautiful Illustrations by Anelay, price 3s. 6d. cloth, elegant, gilt edges.

N.B.—A SCHOOL EDITION, without the Illustrations, 2s. 6d. cloth.

☞ Great care has been taken to render this book unobjectionable to the most fastidious, by excluding everything that could not be read aloud in schools and families, and by abstinence from all party spirit, alike in politics as in religion.

BOOKS FOR NURSERY OR MATERNAL TUITION.

The First or Mother's Dictionary. By Mrs. JAMESON (formerly Mrs. MURPHY). Tenth Edition. 18mo. 2s. 6d. cloth.

a,e Common expletives, the names of familiar objects, technical terms and words, the knowledge of which would be useless to children, or which could not well be explained in a manner adapted to the infant capacity, have been entirely omitted. Most of the definitions are short enough to be committed to memory ; or they may be read over, a page or two at a time, till the whole are sufficiently impressed on the mind. It will be found of advantage if the little pupils be taught to look out for themselves any word they may meet with, the meaning of which they do not distinctly comprehend.

School-Room Lyrics. Compiled and Edited by ANNE KNIGHT. New Edition. 18mo. 1s. cloth.

La Bagatelle ; intended to introduce Children of five or six years old to some knowledge of the French Language. Revised by Madame N. L. New Edition, with entirely New Cuts. 18mo. 2s. 6d. bound.

This little work has undergone a most careful revision. The orthography has been modernized, and entirely new woodcuts substituted for the old ones. It is now offered to parents and others engaged in the education of young children, as well adapted for familiarizing their pupils with the construction and sounds of the French language, conveying at the same time excellent moral lessons.

' A very nice book to be placed in the hands of children ; likely to command their attention by its beautiful embellishments.'—PAPERS FOR THE SCHOOLMASTER.

' A well-known little book, revised, improved, and adorned with some very pretty new pictures. It is, indeed, French made very easy for very little children.'
THE SCHOOL AND THE TEACHER.

Chickseed without Chickweed: being very Easy and Entertaining Lessons for Little Children. In Three Parts. Part I. in words of three letters. Part II. in words of four letters. Part III. in words of five or more letters. New Edition, with beautiful Frontispiece by Anelay, 12mo. 1s. cloth.

A book for every mother.

Peter Parley's Book of Poetry. With numerous Engravings. New Edition, revised, with Additions, 16mo. 1s. 6d. cloth.

This little volume consists, in part, of extracts from various publications, and in part of original articles written for it. It is designed to embrace a variety of pieces, some grave, and some gay ; some calculated to amuse, and some to instruct ; some designed to store the youthful imagination with gentle and pleasing images ; some to enrich the mind with useful knowledge ; some to impress the heart with sentiments of love, meekness, truth, gentleness, and kindness.

Cobwebs to Catch Flies ; or Dialogues in short sentences. Adapted for Children from the age of three to eight years. In Two Parts. Part I. Easy Lessons in words of three, four, five, and six letters, suited to children from three to five years of age. Part II. Short Stories for Children from five to eight years of age. 12mo. 2s. cloth gilt.

⁎ The Parts are sold separately, price 1s. each.

DELAMOTTE'S WORKS
ON ILLUMINATION, ALPHABETS, &c.

A Primer of the Art of Illumination, for the use of Beginners, with a Rudimentary Treatise on the Art, Practical Directions for its Exercise, and numerous Examples taken from Illuminated MSS., and beautifully printed in gold and colours. By F. DELAMOTTE. Small 4to, price 9s, cloth antique.

'A handy book, beautifully illustrated; the text of which is well written, and calculated to be useful......The examples of ancient MSS. recommended to the student, which, with much good sense, the author chooses from collections accessible to all, are selected with judgment and knowledge, as well as taste.'—ATHENÆUM.

'Modestly called a Primer, this little book has a good title to be esteemed a manual and guide-book in the study and practice of the different styles of lettering used by the artistic transcribers of past centuries....An amateur may with this silent preceptor learn the whole art and mystery of illumination.'—SPECTATOR.

'The volume is very beautifully got up, and we can heartily recommend it to the notice of those who wish to become proficient in the art.'—ENGLISH CHURCHMAN.

'We are able to recommend Mr. Delamotte's treatise. The letterpress is modestly but judiciously written; and the illustrations, which are numerous and well chosen, are beautifully printed in gold and colours.'—ECCLESIOLOGIST.

The Book of Ornamental Alphabets, Ancient and Mediæval, from the Eighth Century, with Numerals. Including Gothic, Church-Text, large and small; German, Italian, Arabesque. Initials for Illumination, Monograms, Crosses, &c., &c., for the use of Architectural and Engineering Draughtsmen, Missal Painters, Masons, Decorative Painters, Lithographers, Engravers, Carvers, &c. &c. Collected and Engraved by F. DELAMOTTE, and printed in Colours. Sixth Edition, royal 8vo. oblong, price 4s. cloth.

'A well-known engraver and draughtsman has enrolled in this useful book the result of many years' study and research. For those who insert enamelled sentences round gilded chalices, who blazon shop legends over shop-doors, who letter church walls with pithy sentences from the Decalogue, this book will be useful. Mr. Delamotte's book was wanted.'—ATHENÆUM.

Examples of Modern Alphabets, Plain and Ornamental. Including German, Old English, Saxon, Italic, Perspective, Greek, Hebrew, Court Hand, Engrossing, Tuscan, Riband, Gothic, Rustic, and Arabesque, with several original Designs, and Numerals. Collected and Engraved by F. DELAMOTTE, and printed in Colours. Royal 8vo. oblong, price 4s. cloth.

'To artists of all classes, but more especially to architects and engravers, this very handsome book will be invaluable. There is comprised in it every possible shape into which the letters of the alphabet and numerals can be formed, and the talent which has been expended in the conception of the various plain and ornamental letters is wonderful.'—STANDARD.

Mediæval Alphabet and Initials for Illuminators.
By F. G. DELAMOTTE. Containing 21 Plates, and Illuminated Title, printed in Gold and Colours. With an Introduction by J. WILLIS BROOKS. Small 4to. 6s. cloth gilt.

'A volume in which the letters of the alphabet come forth glorified in gilding and all the colours of the prism interwoven and intertwined and intermingled, sometimes with a sort of rainbow arabesque. A poem emblazoned in these characters would be only comparable to one of those delicious love letters symbolised in a bunch of flowers well selected and cleverly arranged.'—SUN.

The Embroiderer's Book of Design, containing Initials, Emblems, Cyphers, Monograms, Ornamental Borders, Ecclesiastical Devices, Mediæval and Modern Alphabets and National Emblems. By F. DELAMOTTE. Printed in Colours. Oblong royal 8vo. 2s. 6d. in ornamental boards.

The Fables of Babrius. Translated into English Verse from the Text of Sir G. Cornewall Lewis. By the Rev. JAMES DAVIES, of Lincoln Coll. Oxford. Fcp. 6s. cloth antique.

'"Who was Babrius?" The reply may not improbably startle the reader. Babrius was the real, original Æsop. Nothing is so fabulous about the fables of our childhood as their reputed authorship.'—DAILY NEWS.

'A fable-book which is admirably adapted to take the place of the imperfect collections of Æsopian wisdom which have hitherto held the first place in our juvenile libraries.'—HEREFORD TIMES.

NEW ANECDOTE LIBRARY.

Good Things for Railway Readers. 1000 Anecdotes, Original and Selected. By the Editor of 'The Railway Anecdote-book.' Large type, crown 8vo. with Frontispiece, 2s. 6d.

'A capital collection, and will certainly become a favourite with all railway readers.'—READER.

'Just the thing for railway readers.'—LONDON REVIEW.

'Fresh, racy, and original.'—JOHN BULL.

'An almost interminable source of amusement, and a ready means of rendering tedious journeys short.'—MINING JOURNAL.

'Invaluable to the diner-out.'—ILLUSTRATED TIMES.

Sidney Grey: a Tale of School Life. By the Author of 'Mia and Charlie.' Second Edition, with six beautiful Illustrations. Fcp. 4s. 6d. cloth.

The Innkeeper's Legal Guide: What he Must do, What he May Do, and What he May Not Do. A Handy-Book to the Liabilities, limited and unlimited, of Inn-Keepers, Alehouse-Keepers, Refreshment-House Keepers, &c. With verbatim copies of the Innkeeper's Limited Liability Act, the General Licensing Act, and Forms. By RICHARD T. TIDSWELL, Esq., of the Inner Temple, Barrister-at-Law. Fcp. 1s. 6d. cloth.

'Every licensed victualler in the land should have this exceedingly clear and well arranged manual.'—SUNDAY TIMES.

The Instant Reckoner. Showing the Value of any Quantity of Goods, including Fractional Parts of a Pound Weight, at any price from One Farthing to Twenty Shillings; with an Introduction, embracing Copious Notes of Coins, Weights, Measures, and other Commercial and Useful Information: and an Appendix, containing Tables of Interest, Salaries, Commissions, &c. 24mo. 1s. 6d. cloth, or 2s. strongly bound in leather.

☞ Indispensable to every housekeeper.

Science Elucidative of Scripture, and not antago-nistic to it. Being a Series of Essays on—1. Alleged Discrepancies; 2. The Theories of the Geologists and Figure of the Earth; 3. The Mosaic Cosmogony; 4. Miracles in general—Views of Hume and Powell; 5. The Miracle of Joshua—Views of Dr. Colenso: The Supernaturally Impossible; 6. The Age of the Fixed Stars—their Distances and Masses. By Professor J. R. YOUNG, Author of 'A Course of Elementary Mathematics,' &c. &c. Fcp. 8vo. price 5s. cloth lettered.

'Professor Young's examination of the early verses of Genesis, in connection with modern scientific hypotheses, is excellent.'—ENGLISH CHURCHMAN.

'Distinguished by the true spirit of scientific inquiry, by great knowledge, by keen logical ability, and by a style peculiarly clear, easy, and energetic.'
NONCONFORMIST.

'No one can rise from its perusal without being impressed with a sense of the singular weakness of modern scepticism.'—BAPTIST MAGAZINE.

Mysteries of Life, Death, and Futurity. Illustrated

from the best and latest Authorities. Contents:—Life and Time; Nature of the Soul; Spiritual Life; Mental Operations; Belief and Scepticism; Premature Interment; Phenomena of Death; Sin and Punishment; The Crucifixion of Our Lord; The End of the World; Man after Death; The Intermediate State; The Great Resurrection; Recognition of the Blessed; The Day of Judgment; The Future States, &c. By HORACE WELBY. With an Emblematic Frontispiece, fcp. 5s. cloth.

' This book is the result of extensive reading, and careful noting; it is such a common-place book as some thoughtful divine or physician might have compiled, gathering together a vast variety of opinions and speculations, bearing on physiology, the phenomena of life, and the nature and future existence of the soul. We know of no work that so strongly compels reflection, and so well assists it.' — LONDON REVIEW.

' A pleasant, dreamy, charming, startling little volume; every page of which sparkles like a gem in an antique setting.' — WEEKLY DISPATCH.

' The scoffer might read these pages to his profit, and the pious believer will be charmed with them. Burton's "Anatomy of Melancholy" is a fine suggestive book, and full of learning; and of the volume before us we are inclined to speak in the same terms.' — ERA.

Predictions Realized in Modern Times. Now first

Collected. Contents:—Days and Numbers; Prophesying Almanacs; Omens; Historical Predictions; Predictions of the French Revolution; The Bonaparte Family; Discoveries and Inventions anticipated; Scriptural Prophecies, &c. By HORACE WELBY. With a Frontispiece, fcp. 5s. cloth.

' This is an odd but attractive volume, compiled from various and often little-known sources, and is full of amusing reading.' — CRITIC.

' A volume containing a variety of curious and startling narratives on many points of supernaturalism, well calculated to gratify that love of the marvellous which is more or less inherent in us all.' — NOTES AND QUERIES.

Tales from Shakespeare. By CHARLES and Miss

LAMB. Fourteenth Edition. With 20 Engravings, printed on toned paper, from designs by Harvey, and Portrait, fcp. 5s. 6d. cloth elegant.

The Tongue of Time; or, The Language of a Church

Clock. By WILLIAM HARRISON, A.M., Domestic Chaplain to H.R.H. the Duke of Cambridge; Rector of Birch, Essex. Sixth Edition. with beautiful Frontispiece fcp. 3s. cloth, gilt edges.

Hours of Sadness; or, Instruction and Comfort for

the Mourner: Consisting of a Selection of Devotional Meditations, Instructive and Consolatory Reflections, Letters, Prayers, Poetry, &c., from various Authors, suitable for the bereaved Christian. Second Edition, fcp. 4s. 6d. cloth.

The Pocket English Classics. 32mo. neatly printed,

bound in cloth, lettered, price Sixpence each :—

THE VICAR OF WAKEFIELD.	SCOTT'S LADY OF THE LAKE.
GOLDSMITH'S POETICAL WORKS.	SCOTT'S LAY.
FALCONER'S SHIPWRECK.	WALTON'S ANGLER, 2 PARTS, 1s.
RASSELAS.	ELIZABETH; OR, THE EXILES.
STERNE'S SENTIMENTAL JOURNEY.	COWPER'S TASK.
LOCKE ON THE UNDERSTANDING.	POPE'S ESSAY AND BLAIR'S GRAVE.
THOMSON'S SEASONS.	GRAY AND COLLINS.
INCHBALD'S NATURE AND ART.	GAY'S FABLES.
BLOOMFIELD'S FARMER'S BOY.	PAUL AND VIRGINIA.

WORKS BY THE AUTHOR OF 'A TRAP. TO CATCH A SUNBEAM.'

'In telling a simple story, and in the management of dialogue, the Author is excelled by few writers of the present day.'—LITERARY GAZETTE.

A Trap to Catch a Sunbeam. Thirty-fifth Edition, price 1s.

'Aide toi, et le ciel t'aidera, is the moral of this pleasant and interesting story, to which we assign in this Gazette a place immediately after Charles Dickens, as its due, for many passages not unworthy of him, and for a general scheme quite in unison with his best feelings towards the lowly and depressed.'—LITERARY GAZETTE.

⁂ *A Cheap Edition of the above popular story has been prepared for distribution. Sold only in packets price 1s. 6d. containing 12 copies.*

Also, by the same Author,

'COMING HOME;' a New Tale for all Readers, price 1s.
OLD JOLLIFFE; not a Goblin Story. 1s.
The SEQUEL to OLD JOLLIFFE. 1s.
The HOUSE on the ROCK. 1s.
'ONLY;' a Tale for Young and Old. 1s.
The CLOUD with the SILVER LINING. 1s.
The STAR in the DESERT. 1s.
AMY'S KITCHEN, a VILLAGE ROMANCE: a New Story. 1s.
'A MERRY CHRISTMAS.' 1s.
SIBERT'S WOLD. Third Edition, 2s. cloth, limp.
The DREAM CHINTZ. With Illustrations by James Godwin. 2s. 6d. with a beautiful fancy cover.

Sunbeam Stories. A Selection of the Tales by the Author of 'A Trap to Catch a Sunbeam,' &c. Illustrated by Absolon and Anelay. FIRST SERIES. Contents:—A Trap to Catch a Sunbeam—Old Jolliffe—The Sequel to Old Jolliffe—The Star in the Desert—'Only'—'A Merry Christmas.' Fcap. 3s. 6d. cloth, elegant, or 4s. gilt edges.

Sunbeam Stories. SECOND SERIES. Illustrated by Absolon and Anelay. Contents:—The Cloud with the Silver Lining—Coming Home—Amy's Kitchen—The House on the Rock. Fcap. 3s. 6d. cloth elegant; 4s. gilt edges.

Minnie's Love: a Novel. By the Author of 'A Trap to Catch a Sunbeam.' In 1 vol. post 8vo. 6s. cloth.

'An extremely pleasant, sunshiny volume.'—CRITIC.
'We were first surprised, then pleased, next delighted, and finally enthralled by the story.'—MORNING HERALD.

Little Sunshine: a Tale to be Read to very Young Children. By the Author of 'A Trap to Catch a Sunbeam.' In square 16mo, coloured borders, engraved Frontispiece and Vignette, fancy boards, price 2s.

'Just the thing to rivet the attention of children.'—STAMFORD MERCURY.
'Printed in the sumptuous manner that children like best.'—BRADFORD OBSERVER.
'As pleasing a child's book as we recollect seeing.'—PLYMOUTH HERALD.

THE FRENCH LANGUAGE—*continued.*

Le Brethon's French Grammar: A Guide to the
French Language. By J. J. P. LE BRETHON. Revised and Corrected by L. SANDIER, Professor of Languages. Fourteenth Edition, 8vo. 432 pages, 7s. 6d. cloth.—Key to ditto, 7s.

VOCABULAIRE SYMBOLIQUE ANGLO-FRANCAIS.
Pour les Élèves de tout Age et de tout Degré; dans lequel les Mots les plus utiles sont enseignés par des Illustrations. Par L. C. RAGONOT, Professeur de la Langue Française.

A Symbolic French and English Vocabulary. For
Students of every Age, in all Classes; in which the most Useful and Common Words are taught by Illustrations. By L. C. RAGONOT, Professor of the French Language. The Illustrations comprise, embodied in the text, accurate representations of upwards of 850 different objects, besides nine whole-page copper-plates, beautifully executed, each conveying, through the eye, a large amount of instruction in the French Language. Eighth Edition, considerably improved, with new plates substituted, 4to. 5s. cloth.

☞ This work in the Anglo-French form having been extensively adopted, not only in Great Britain and on the Continent, but also in America, the publishers have determined to adopt it to other languages in a more portable form. The following is now ready:—

Symbolisches Englisch-Deutsches Wörterbuch: the
Symbolic Anglo-German Vocabulary; adapted from RAGONOT'S 'Vocabulaire Symbolique Anglo-Français.' Edited and Revised by FALCK LEBAHN, Ph. Dr., Author of 'German in One Volume,' 'The German Self-Instructor,' &c. With 850 woodcuts, and eight full-page lithographic plates. 8vo. 6s. red cloth, lettered.

New Book by one of the Contributors to 'The Reason Why' Series, and Assistant Editor of 'The Dictionary of Daily Wants.'

Now ready, Second and Cheaper Edition, 1 vol. crown 8vo. pp. 384, 2s. 6d. cloth.

The Historical Finger-Post: A Handy Book of
Terms, Phrases, Epithets, Cognomens, Allusions, &c., in connexion with Universal History. By EDWARD SHELTON, Assistant Editor of 'The Dictionary of Daily Wants,' &c. &c.

'A handy little volume, which will supply the place of "Haydn's Dictionary of Dates" to many persons who cannot afford that work. Moreover, it contains some things that Haydn's book does not.'—BOOKSELLER.

'It is to the historical student and antiquarian what "Enquire Within" is to the practical house wife—not dispensing with stores of hard-acquired and well-digested knowledge, but giving that little aid which, in moments of hurry and business, is the true economiser of time.'—VOLUNTEER SERVICE GAZETTE.

'The idlest reader would find it convenient to have it within reach.'
PUBLISHERS' CIRCULAR.

'Really a very useful work; and, at the present day, when everybody is expected to be up in everything, as good a handy-book for cramming on the current subjects of conversation as any that we know. About 5000 subjects have all their place in this extraordinary collection, and although termly given, the account of each is sufficient for ordinary purposes.'—ERA.

'A very desirable companion, as containing a variety of information, much of which could only be got by diligent inquiry and research. . . . Deserves a place as a book of reference on the shelves of the study or library.'
NAVAL AND MILITARY GAZETTE.

'This most useful and admirably arranged handy-book will in most cases greatly lighten the labour of investigation, and obviate a long and tedious search through voluminous publications.'—WEEKLY TIMES.

THE GERMAN LANGUAGE.

Dr. Falck Lebahn's Popular Series of German School-books.

'As an educational writer in the German tongue, Dr. Lebahn stands alone; some other has made even a distant approach to him.'—BRITISH STANDARD.

Lebahn's First German Course. Third Edition.

Crown 8vo. 2s. 6d. cloth.

'It is hardly possible to have a simpler or better book for beginners in German.'
ATHENÆUM.

'It is really what it professes to be—a simple, clear, and concise introduction to the German Language.'—CRITIC.

Lebahn's German Language in One Volume. Seventh

Edition, containing—I. A Practical Grammar, with Exercises to every Rule. II. Undine; a Tale; by DE LA MOTTE FOUQUÉ, with Explanatory Notes of all difficult words and phrases. III. A Vocabulary of 4,500 Words, synonymous in English and German. Crown 8vo. 8s. cloth. With Key, 10s. 6d. Key separate, 2s. 6d.

'The best German Grammar that has yet been published.'—MORNING POST.

'Had we to recommence the study of German, of all the German grammars which we have examined—and they are now a few—we should unhesitatingly say, Falck Lebahn's is the book for us.'—EDUCATIONAL TIMES.

Lebahn's Edition of Schmid's Henry Von Eichen-

fels. With Vocabulary and Familiar Dialogues. Seventh Edition. Crown 8vo. 3s. 6d. cloth.

'Equally with Mr. Lebahn's previous publications, excellently adapted to assist self-exercise in the German language.'—SPECTATOR.

Lebahn's First German Reader. Fifth Edition. Cr.

8vo. 3s. 6d. cloth.

'Like all Lebahn's works, most thoroughly practical.'—BRITANNIA.

'An admirable book for beginners, which indeed may be used without a master.'
I.MARSH.

Lebahn's German Classics; with Notes and Complete

Vocabularies. Crown 8vo. price 3s. 6d. each, cloth.

PETER SCHLEMIHL, the Shadowless Man. By CHAMISSO.
EGMONT. A Tragedy, in Five Acts, by GOETHE.
WILHELM TELL. A Drama, in Five Acts, by SCHILLER.
GOETZ VON BERLICHINGEN. A Drama. By GOETHE.
PAGENSTREICHE, a Page's Frolics. A Comedy, by KOTZEBUE.
EMILIA GALOTTI. A Tragedy, in Five Acts, by LESSING.
UNDINE. A Tale, by FOUQUÉ.
SELECTIONS from the GERMAN POETS.

'With such aids, a student will find no difficulty in these masterpieces.'
ATHENÆUM.

Lebahn's German Copy-Book : being a Series of Exer-

cises in German Penmanship, beautifully engraved on Steel. 4to. 2s. 6d. sewed.

Lebahn's Exercises in German. Cr. 8vo. 3s. 6d. cloth.

'A volume of "Exercises in German," including in itself all the vocabularies they require. The book is well planned ; the selections for translation from German into English, or from English into German, being sometimes curiously well suited to the purpose for which they are taken.'—EXAMINER.

Lebahn's Self-Instructor in German. Crown 8vo.

3s. 6d. cloth.

'One of the most amusing elementary reading-books that ever passed under our hands.'—JOHN BULL.

'The student could have no guide superior to Mr. Lebahn.'
LITERARY GAZETTE.

Just published, in a closely-printed Volume, in a clear and legible type, post 8vo. 6s. cloth.

The Domestic Service Guide to Housekeeping;

Practical Cookery; Pickling and Preserving; Household Work; Dairy Management; the Table and Dessert; Cellarage of Wines; Home-Brewing and Wine-Making; the Boudoir and Dressing-room; Invalid Diet; Travelling; Stable Economy; Gardening, &c. A Manual of all that pertains to Household Management: from the best and latest authorities, and the communications of Heads of Families; with several hundred new recipes.

'A really useful Guide on the important subjects of which it treats.'—SPECTATOR.

'The best cookery-book published for many years.'—BELL'S MESSENGER.

'This "Domestic Service Guide" will become, what it deserves to be, very popular.'—READER.

'This book is characterised by a kindly feeling towards the classes it designs to benefit, and by a respectful regard to religion.'—RECORD.

'We find here directions to be discovered in no other book, tending to save expense to the pocket, as well as labour to the head. It is truly an astonishing book.'—JOHN BULL.

'This book is quite an encyclopædia of domestic matters. We have been greatly pleased with the good sense and good feeling of what may be called the moral directions, and the neatness and lucidity of the explanatory details.'—COURT CIRCULAR.

Just published, with Photographic Portrait and Autograph, and Vignette of Birthplace, fcp. cloth. price 3s. 6d.; Cheap Edition, without Portrait, 2s. boards.

Richard Cobden, the Apostle of Free Trade: a

Biography. By JOHN McGILCHRIST, Author of 'The Life of Lord Dundonald,' &c.

'The narrative is so condensed, and the style at once so clear and vigorous, that the volume is eminently entitled to a popular circulation. . . . We trust it will find its way to the book-shelves of thousands of working men.'—MORNING STAR.

'The mind of Cobden, as it gradually developed itself, is unfolded before us, and the volume brings to a focus many most interesting expressions of the deceased statesman's views.'—LONDON REVIEW.

'Those who wish to know something of Richard Cobden will find instruction and interest in the book.'—READER.

The Robinson Crusoe of the Nineteenth Century.

Just published, handsomely printed, post 8vo. with Portrait and Sketch Map, 8s.

Cast Away on the Auckland Isles: a Narrative of

the Wreck of the 'Grafton,' and of the Escape of the Crew, after Twenty Months' Suffering. From the Private Journals of Captain THOMAS MUSGRAVE. Together with some Account of the Auckland Islands. Also, an Account of the Sea Lion (originally written in seal's blood, as were most of Captain Musgrave's Journals). Edited by JOHN J. SHILLINGLAW, F.R.G.S.

The TIMES Correspondent (December 19, 1865) says that Captain Musgrave's Diary 'is almost as interesting as Daniel Defoe, besides being, as the children say, "all true."'

'It is seldom, indeed, that we come upon a sea narrative now-a-days as interesting as this.'—LLOYD'S NEWSPAPER.

'Does anyone want to measure the real gulf which divides truth from fiction, let him compare Captain Musgrave's narrative with "Enoch Arden."'—READER.

'Truth is here stranger than any fiction.'—NEWS OF THE WORLD.

'A more interesting book of travels and privation has not appeared since "Robinson Crusoe;" and it has this advantage over the work of fiction, that it is a fact.'—OBSERVER.

'Since the days of Alexander Selkirk, few more interesting narratives have seen the light.'—MELBOURNE SPECTATOR.

'A stern realization of Defoe's imaginative history, with greater difficulties and severer hardships.'—COURT CIRCULAR.

WORKS IN ENGINEERING, &c.—*continued.*

A MANUAL on EARTHWORK. By ALEX. J. S. GRAHAM,
C.E., Resident Engineer, Forest of Dean Central Railway. With Diagrams.
18mo, 2s. 6d. cloth.

THE OPERATIVE MECHANIC'S WORKSHOP COM-
PANION; comprising a great variety of the most useful Rules in Mechanical
Science, with numerous Tables of Practical Data and Calculated Results. By W.
Templeton, Author of 'The Engineer's Common-Place Book,' &c. Seventh Edition,
with 11 Plates. 12mo, price 5s. bound and lettered.

THEORY of COMPOUND INTEREST and ANNUITIES,
with TABLES of LOGARITHMS for the more difficult computations of Interest, Discount, Annuities, &c., in all their Applications and Uses for Mercantile and
State Purposes. By F. Thoman, of the Société Crédit Mobilier. 12mo, 5s. cloth.

THE ENGINEER'S, ARCHITECT'S, and CONTRAC-
TOR'S POCKET BOOK (Lockwood and Co.'s, formerly Weale's), published
Annually. With Diary of Events and Data connected with Engineering, Architecture, and the kindred Sciences. The present year's Volume is much improved by
the addition of various useful articles. With 10 plates, and numerous Woodcuts, in roan tuck, gilt edges, 6s.

THE BUILDER'S and CONTRACTOR'S PRICE BOOK
(Lockwood and Co.'s, formerly Weale's), published Annually. Containing the
latest prices for work in all branches of the Building Trade, with items numbered for
easy reference. 12mo, cloth boards, 4s.

THE TIMBER MERCHANT'S and BUILDER'S COM-
PANION. Containing new and copious TABLES, &c. By William Dowsing,
Timber Merchant, Hull. Second Edition, revised. Crown 8vo, 3s. cloth.

A SYNOPSIS of PRACTICAL PHILOSOPHY. Alpha-
betically Arranged. Designed as a Manual for Travellers, Architects,
Surveyors, Engineers, Students, Naval Officers, and other Scientific Men. By the
Rev. John Carr, M.A., of Trin. Coll. Camb. Second Edition, 18mo, cloth, 5s.

THE CARPENTER'S NEW GUIDE; or, Book of Lines
for Carpenters, founded on the late Peter Nicholson's standard work. A New
Edition, revised by Arthur Ashpitel, Arch. F.S.A.; together with Practical Rules
on Drawing, by George Pyne, Artist. With 71 Plates, 4to, price £1 1s. cloth.

TREATISE on the STRENGTH of TIMBER, CAST
IRON, MALLEABLE IRON, and other Materials. By Peter Barlow, F.R.S.
V.S., Hon. Mem. Inst. C.E., &c. A New Edition, by J. F. Heather, M.A., of the Royal
Military Academy, Woolwich, with Additions by Prof. Willis, of Cambridge. With
Nine Illustrations. 8vo, 18s. cloth.

MATHEMATICS for PRACTICAL MEN; being a Com-
monplace Book of Pure and Mixed Mathematics, for the Use of Civil Engineers,
Architects, and Surveyors. By Olinthus Gregory, LL.D. Enlarged by Henry
Law. Fourth edition, revised, by J. R. Young, Author of 'A Course of Mathematics,' &c. With 13 Plates, 8vo, £1 1s. cloth.

THE LAND VALUER'S BEST ASSISTANT, being
Tables on a very much improved Plan, for Calculating the Value of Estates. By
R. Hudson, Civil Engineer. New Edition, with Additions and Corrections. 4s. bound.

A MANUAL of ELECTRICITY. Including Galvanism,
Magnetism, Dia-Magnetism, Electro-Dynamics, Magno-Electricity, and the
Electric Telegraph. By Henry M. Noad, Ph.D., F.C.S., Lecturer on Chemistry at
St. George's Hospital. Fourth Edition, entirely re-written. Illustrated by 500 Wood-
cuts, 8vo, £1 4s. cloth. Sold also in Two Parts: Part I. Electricity and Galvanism, 8vo,
16s. cloth. Part II. Magnetism and the Electric Telegraph, 8vo, 10s. 6d. cloth.

DESIGNS and EXAMPLES of COTTAGES, VILLAS,
and COUNTRY HOUSES. Being the Studies of Eminent Architects and
Builders, consisting of Plans, Elevations, and Perspective Views; with approximate
Estimates of the cost of each. 4to, 67 Plates, £1 1s. cloth.

THE APPRAISER, AUCTIONEER, and HOUSE-
AGENT'S POCKET ASSISTANT. By John Wheeler, Valuer. Second
Edition, 12mo, cloth boards, 5s. 6d.

PRACTICAL RULES on DRAWING, for the Operative
Builder, and Young Student in Architecture. By George Pyne, Author of
'A Rudimentary Treatise on Perspective.' With 14 Plates, 4to, 7s. 6d. boards.

THE BOOK FOR EVERY FARMER.

New Edition of Youatt's Grazier, enlarged by R. Scott Burn.

The Complete Grazier, and Farmer's and Cattle Breeder's Assistant. A Compendium of Husbandry, especially in the departments connected with the Breeding, Rearing, Feeding and General Management of Stock, the Management of the Dairy, &c.; with Directions for the Culture and Management of Grass Land, of Grain and Root Crops, the Arrangement of Farm Offices, the Use of Implements and Machines; and on Draining, Irrigation, Warping, &c., and the Application and Relative Value of Manures. By WILLIAM YOUATT, Esq. V.S. Member of the Royal Agricultural Society of England, Author of 'The Horse,' 'Cattle,' &c. Eleventh Edition, enlarged, and brought down to the present requirements of Agricultural Practice by ROBERT SCOTT BURN, one of the Authors of 'The Book of Farm Implements and Machines,' and of 'The Book of Farm Buildings,' Author of 'The Lessons of My Farm,' and Editor of 'The Year-Book of Agricultural Facts.' In one large 8vo. volume, pp. 784, with 215 Illustrations, price £1 1s. strongly half-bound.

'The standard, and text-book, with the farmer and grazier.'

FARMER'S MAGAZINE.

'A valuable repertory of intelligence for all who make agriculture a pursuit, and especially for those who aim at keeping pace with the improvements of the age. . . . The new matter is of so valuable a nature that the volume is now almost entitled to be considered as a distinct work.'—BELL'S MESSENGER.

'The public are indebted to Mr. Scott Burn for undertaking the task, which he has accomplished with his usual ability, making such alterations, additions, and improvements as the changes effected in husbandry have rendered necessary.'

SPORTING MAGAZINE.

'A treatise which will remain a standard work on the subject as long as British agriculture endures.'—MARK LANE EXPRESS.

'The additions are so numerous and extensive as almost to give it the character of a new work on general husbandry, embracing all that modern science and experiment have effected in the management of land and the homestead.'

SPORTING REVIEW.

'It is, in fact, a compendium of modern husbandry, embracing a concise amount of all the leading improvements of the day.'—NEW SPORTING MAGAZINE.

The Lessons of My Farm: A Book for Amateur Agriculturists; being an Introduction to Farm Practice in the Culture of Crops, the Feeding of Cattle, Management of the Dairy, Poultry, Pigs, and in the Keeping of Farm-work Records. By ROBERT SCOTT BURN, Editor of 'The Year-Book of Agricultural Facts,' and one of the Authors of 'Book of Farm Implements and Machines,' and 'Book of Farm Buildings.' With numerous Illustrations, fcp. 8s. cloth.

'A very useful little book, written in the lively style which will attract the amateur class to whom it is dedicated, and contains much sound advice and accurate description.'

ATHENÆUM.

'We are sure the book will meet with a ready sale, and the more that there are many hints in it which even old farmers need not be ashamed to accept.'

MORNING HERALD.

'A most complete introduction to the whole round of farming practice. We believe there are many among us whose love of farming will make them welcome such a companion as this little book in which the author gives us his own experience, which are worth a great deal.'—JOHN BULL.

'Never did book exercise a more salutary effect than "My Farm of Four Acres." Mr. Burn has followed suit in a very practical and pleasant little work.'

ILLUSTRATED LONDON NEWS.

SPOTTISWOODE AND CO., PRINTERS NEW-STREET SQUARE, LONDON.